VANISHED

By Fletcher Knebel

VANISHED

THE ZINZIN ROAD

NIGHT OF CAMP DAVID

By Fletcher Knebel and Charles W. Bailey II

CONVENTION

SEVEN DAYS IN MAY

NO HIGH GROUND

VANISHED

Fletcher Knebel

DOUBLEDAY & COMPANY, INC., GARDEN CITY, NEW YORK

To Laura

VANISHED

1

He was restless, curiously remote. He glanced at his wrist watch during the small formalities of greeting. Occasionally he brushed his fingers along the side of his head where the sandy hair was thinning. He gave an impression of a man already late for a plane. He was courteous, as always, but, to me, his impatience was especially marked, for Steve's normal pace under pressure was so unhurried that his friends in Washington often commented enviously on the trait.

We were three for lunch in the long, cool room, Stephen Greer, Miguel Loomis, and I. Greer motioned me to the oak chair on his left. That put Miguel on Greer's right at the heavy oak table, an unobtrusive bit of protocol that appeared to elude young Miguel.

Although I had known Stephen Greer fairly well for some years, this was the first time that I had been invited to lunch in the law firm's private dining room in the Ring Building. The conditioned air provided a haven from Washington's late August heat, which stewed on the sidewalks and soft macadam of Connecticut Avenue seven stories below.

The dining room of Greer, Hilstratter, Tomlin & DeLuca was decorated to the masculine taste, the furniture plain, dark oak with a waxed finish, the walls papered with an olive fabric on which hung a line of old prints. Wildlife scenes predominated, mallards beating spray in startled ascent from a reedy inlet, a moose standing imperiously between two tall pines, a tarpon thrashing on its tail as it sought to throw the hook. Clients could know that the firm's partners were patient, solid men who understood the link between man and nature and who sensed the rhythm of violence beneath the deceptive tranquillity of forest, lake, meadow, and sea.

The table's place settings on green mats included old English silver and china by a Danish designer. A steward in white coat busied himself in the adjoining galley as we dipped spoons into the jellied consommé.

"It's too bland," protested Greer. He showered pepper and salt over the shivering red mound.

"About right for me," I said.

Miguel ate with few comments as if in deference to his elders. He was a lean, young man with straight, black hair and skin of that mahogany color found on old, weathered bronze. His mother, a Mexican from the state of Oaxaca, had married Barney Loomis in the days when Loomis was a raw, roistering salesman of no particular means. Now Loomis headed the huge Educational Micro complex. Miguel could expect to inherit a fortune.

"All right, Mike, let's get into it," said Greer, pushing back his soup bowl. "This is one of those days around here, and I know Gene's busy too."

Greer's glance at his wrist watch became an exclamation point. He was measuring time by the minute hand. His gray eyes questioned Miguel.

"I don't like to bother you," said Miguel, "but I think it's important."

"Glad to help," said Greer, obviously anxious to jettison further amenities. "All we want to know is what and why."

I already knew part of the why. Only the intricate web of politics could bring the White House press secretary and Stephen Greer, a prominent attorney and close friend of President Paul Roudebush, to this table to listen to a young physicist who had just passed his twenty-fifth birthday. Greer and I had canceled other luncheon appointments to meet here. That was a fascinating aspect of politics, simple enough if one knew the pattern, incomprehensible if one did not. I had been hooked early by the involuted maneuvers of men in quest of power—in a word, politics—and unlike the thrashing tarpon in the wall print, I was hooked for life.

The key at this lunch was Miguel's father, Bernard Loomis. He was a blunt, flinty character, a phenomenal fund-raiser for our party in California and thus a man who could expect any reasonable favor from the administration in Washington. In addition, Loomis's Educational Micro, the Los Angeles company that supplied most of the new, cheap microfiche printing to the nation's classrooms, retained Steve Greer for Washington legal services.

Miguel, who had a master's degree in physics, was spending a year in Washington on a fellowship at the Atomic Energy Commission as part of his work toward a doctorate. He had been here since early June.

Barney Loomis had called both Greer and me and asked us to smooth Miguel's introduction to Washington social life. The reason for soliciting Greer's aid was apparent. In my case, Barney thought of me because, prior to joining Paul Roudebush's presidential campaign staff, I had done a number of chores for Educational Micro and for Barney personally through my Los Angeles public relations firm, Eugene R. Culligan and Associates. I liked Barney. His bluster was worse than his bite. Besides, he used to pay well in my pre-White House days.

So Miguel Loomis had dined out occasionally at Greer's Kenwood home and had been taken to lunch at the Metropolitan Club by Steve. I had introduced Miguel to a number of Washington restaurants, friends, and girls. I was a temporary—I suppose that's the word—bachelor since my divorce two years earlier. (Mary blamed it on my affinity for night-time politics, and I cannot deny it.) So several nights I arranged double dates, and Miguel and I had a few swinging times in such spots as the Jockey Club, the Bayou and the Dialogue in Georgetown. Thanks to Greer and me, Miguel by late August knew Washington far better than most of the young people who swarmed to the capital for summer interne jobs in the cradle of bureaucracy. We both liked Mike Loomis. He was sharp, perceptive, unspoiled, and, for a young man, rather courtly at times. He had a quick temper, but it flared without leaving smoldering coals. And he had a vein of idealism

that forced questioning cracks in the layer of juiceless cynicism
under which so many men operated in Washington.

"Of course, it's confidential," said Miguel. He inclined his head
toward the steward, who was just entering with a tray of club
steaks.

"That'll be fine," Greer told the steward. "Just leave the des-
serts on the table and we'll help ourselves when we're ready."

"Certainly, Mr. Greer." The steward had the air of a man accustomed to being banished from his place of work. "I'll come
back at three and tidy up." He brought the apple cobbler des-
serts, hung his white coat in the galley, and a moment later we
heard the rear door close.

"Okay, Mike." Greer looked expectantly at Loomis over a fork-
ful of pink-sided steak.

"Well," said Miguel, "you know I came here in June after getting my master's at Caltech. At the AEC, they put me in the administrative section for the first four months or so. I don't care
for it because it's routine office work without much connection
with physics. There are five other men on fellowships in my section, all working on Ph.D.'s as I am. The idea is to familiarize us
with how the Atomic Energy Commission works. Then this fall we
go into theoretical phases of atomic physics. We'll spend time at
places like Brookhaven and Los Alamos. Anyway, I was surprised
to learn that two of the fellowship men not only get paid by the
AEC, as I am, but also by another organization called . . ."

"Whoa!" Greer held up a hand. Miguel was speeding like a jet
on a runway. "Back up a minute. Who's paid by whom?"

"I'm sorry." Miguel's grin in his mahogany face was one of
apology. "Well, these six fellowships are AEC grants, paid directly
by the commission. But two of the six of us also get extra money—
a good deal of it, $7500 a year—from the Spruance Foundation."

"What foundation?" asked Greer.

"Spruance," said Miguel.

"I never heard of it," I said.

"That's part of what I'm going to tell you," said Miguel. The
deep black of his eyes lent him an impassioned quality, a Latin intensity also revealed in the rapid diction. "You see, I was assigned

for a couple of weeks to the accounts section. There I found that two of the fellows had a notation after their names on the pay list which said, 'Spr.'—'S P R period.' When I asked the payroll chief what that stood for, he said, 'extra compensation, Spruance.' But when I asked him what Spruance was and why these two got extra money, he became very vague, intentionally so, I thought. He said it was some special function that he didn't know much about. At any rate, he said, the system was being changed and the notation henceforth would be omitted from the pay list. Naturally, I became curious. You both know I don't have to worry about money. Still, I'm trying to make it on my own and it bugged me that two fellowship men would receive money that the rest of us didn't. It seemed unfair."

Miguel broke off for a brief attack on his steak, then resumed at full tilt. "Of course, I went to both of the men and asked them about it. One guy was very surprised I'd learned of the arrangement. He said that 'Spruance' meant 'Spruance Foundation,' an outfit that wanted to attract more bright, young fellows into physics by offering larger rewards. He said that's all he knew about it, except that he got $7500 a year, paid regularly every two weeks. The other guy was more helpful. He said the Spruance connection involved a little extra work. If I was interested, he said, he'd send one of the Spruance representatives around to talk to me. I said sure, I was interested."

"Who runs this Spruance outfit?" I cut in.

"I'm coming to that, Gene," he replied. "A couple of weeks later, a man of about 45 or 50, a good-looking guy, obviously well educated, called on me one night at the apartment. After some sparring around, he said he was from Spruance and he had a proposition that might appeal to me. He said he knew I didn't need money, but that I might be interested for what he called 'patriotic motives.' I corrected him right there. I said I wanted to make my own career without relying on Dad's money. Of course, I said, I was patriotic, too. In that case, he said, Spruance would be prepared to pay me $7500 a year indefinitely, not just while I was working on my doctorate, but as long as I remained in the field

of physics or any collateral science. I asked him what I was supposed to do in return."

"Slower, Mike, please," I said.

Miguel grinned. "Okay. The man said all I really had to do was
to listen and remember what I heard. Spruance was interested in
international developments and international ties of physicists. If
I heard of some new line of work in Italy, or Israel or Russia, I
was to report it. The more international conferences I attended
the better. Ditto for friendships with scientists of other countries.
Also Spruance wanted the names of American physicists who
worked with foreign scientists, visited them socially, or traveled
a lot. I said it all sounded pretty fuzzy. Well, he said, this was only
our first meeting, and if I was really interested, we could talk
later in more detail. I thanked him, said I'd think it over, and
get back to him. Where should I call him? Never mind that, he
said, just tell Joe—that's one of the two men on the Spruance
payroll—and he, my visitor, would get in touch with me again."

"Did he give a name?" asked Greer.

"Yes," said Miguel. "Smith. But it might as well have been Jones
or Thomas. After he left, I got to thinking about the visit. It
seemed kind of fishy. He talked a lot without saying much. Also,
I didn't like the fact that he refused to give me his phone number or business address.

"Anyway, the next day I went up to the Library of Congress and
looked up Spruance in the directory of tax-exempt foundations. It
isn't listed and never has been." After a moment at slow pace,
he was speeding up again. "Then I looked up 'Spruance Foundation' in the Washington phone book. No listing. On a hunch, I
tried the New York directory, and saw a listing for 'Spruance
Foundation' at an East Thirty-eighth Street address in New York
City. So this Monday I went up there. There's this run-down
building with a nest of old offices and a creaky elevator. Spruance
was on the third floor. It turned out the 'foundation' was just one
room, dirty windows, a filing cabinet and a girl at a typewriter
who didn't seem to have much to do. When I asked her who the
officers were, she said there was only one, a Mr. Maury Rimmel of
Washington."

"Maury Rimmel," repeated Greer. "I know Maury. He's a lobby-ist around town. Plays golf out at Burning Tree. Do you know him, Gene?"

"Just to say hello," I said. But I could see Rimmel. He had a curious habit of speaking into a man's ear as if in fear of being overheard by a third person. His face was a full moon laced with tiny purple veins like a network of canals. The few times I had seen Rimmel socially, I had the impression that he kept himself pleasantly irrigated.

"Did you talk to Rimmel?" asked Greer.

Miguel nodded. "Yes, but he was vague. He said Spruance was a group of public-spirited businessmen. He said Spruance gave liberally to the sciences and sometimes supplemented salaries of young physicists, chemists, and other scientists in an effort to build a large reserve pool of American competence in the sciences. When I asked him who the donors were, he bugged out. He said they preferred to remain anonymous. When I asked if he con-tributed, he said no money, just his time, 'as it were,' whatever that means.

"When I mentioned this to Joe, one of the men getting money from Spruance, he said, in effect, so what? He said Spruance was making a tremendous contribution to science and where the money came from was irrelevant. Anyway, to cut it short, after thinking it over for a night, I called you gentlemen."

"Why?" asked Greer. He had been fidgeting for several minutes. "I don't see why this concerns us, Mike."

"Because, Mr. Greer," said Miguel, "I think a lot of young physicists are being secretly subsidized by the CIA, and I think that's a hell of a sorry business and I think President Roudebush ought to knock it off."

Miguel Loomis was certainly geared for direct action. If he thought steps should be taken in Washington, he began at the top with the President. Not for him the customary route through a congressman or senator. And he did not write the Presi-dent a letter. He called on two men who he knew had the Presi-dent's ear. Barney Loomis had taught his son a thing or two.

"What makes you think it's the Agency?" asked Greer. Despite his impatience, he was intrigued.

"It squares with the way the CIA has been known to operate," said Miguel. "Scientists are a lot more internationalist than most people. They circulate at international meetings, exchange information around the world in Communist and non-Communist countries alike. So the CIA hires some young scientists—they wouldn't dare approach the older men with big reputations—and gets them to report whatever they pick up and inform the CIA of the conversations, beliefs, and friendships of the Americans who are pretty thick with scientists abroad.

"None of that is very specific, Mike," objected Greer. He was the defense lawyer probing a witness for the prosecution.

"Maybe so, but it has the smell," said Miguel. "How about my caller, Mr. Smith or whatever? If he wasn't trying to enlist me for some secret operation, why not give me his phone number and address? And then Spruance itself. Not listed among the foundations. Very, very vague about what it does, or where the dough comes from."

"Assuming what you say is correct," asked Greer, "what's wrong with Central Intelligence subsidizing young physicists?"

Greer had a way of challenging a man with a concentrated stare when he asked a question. In repose, his face could have been that of any bland bureaucrat. It was when he seized on a new line of thought that he tensed and became utterly absorbed. I had seen him in a number of conferences, had watched him probing and weighing, and I knew why the President relied on his judgment.

"What's wrong?" retorted Miguel. "Jesus, Mr. Greer, if you have to ask a question like that, there's no sense in explaining. We wouldn't understand each other."

"Now, Mike," admonished Greer quietly. "You're a master of physics, not a college boy. Let's both try to articulate, shall we? We certainly won't understand each other, if we don't try to explain what we mean."

"I'm a physicist, damn it," said Miguel. His dark face flushed.

"We're trained to follow the truth wherever it leads, in a laboratory at Caltech or in Moscow or Bucharest. We have to trust one another, no matter what nationality. How would you feel, if you were a leading physicist, if you found out that your young assistant on an experiment was really there to spy on you?"

"It might depend on how good a scientist he was and whether the experiment panned out," said Greer. "I know you regard that as cynical, but there's truth to it. You'll grant that over-all this Spruance operation helps build a larger body of trained physicists in this country. So, if you're correct about the CIA, what great harm is done if some vital information is collected along with the training of scientists? Mind you, intelligence must be gathered under some guise, or 'cover' as they call it. A man just can't show up in Jakarta, make appointments with high officials, and introduce himself as the new American intelligence agent."

"I said we wouldn't understand each other," said Miguel with thinly veiled despair. "The whole idea is offensive to me. American physics is being tainted and corrupted by this CIA connection." Miguel shifted in his chair. He had the look of a man who wished it were polite to leave.

"But if Spruance is really Agency money, the purpose must be in the national interest," said Greer. He said it dispassionately, but one could feel the prod. Whatever the issue or whatever his own belief, Steve Greer seldom failed to play the devil's advocate.

"Just because it's the government, it's in the national interest?" asked Miguel. His voice rose in pitch and he was speeding up again. "I don't buy that worn-out establishment line, Mr. Greer. What business does the CIA have infiltrating the ranks of science? It turned a couple of fine young physicists on our program into spies this year, and how many more around the country, I don't know. I thought that kind of thing all ended when Lyndon Johnson ordered the CIA to quit subsidizing American student and educational outfits. But it sure hasn't . . . Suppose this got out? Why, every American scientist at international conferences would be suspect. I think the CIA has been bribing men in my profession, and I despise it."

"'Bribe' is a tough word with an exact legal definition," said Greer.

"Well that's damn near what it is," said Miguel. He put down his knife and fork with a clatter and glared at Greer. "You can defend that kind of spook business if you want to, but I think it stinks. And any administration that permits it ought to be thrown out at the next election."

Greer smiled and raised a hand. "Easy, Mike. I'm not defending the Agency. I just wanted to see how strongly you felt about it."

"Plenty," said Miguel. "If something isn't done, I have a good mind to nail down the facts, then hold a press conference of my own and blow the whistle on the CIA."

"And wreck the reputations of American scientists around the world? . . . Let's think that over for a minute while we polish off the cobbler."

Greer gathered in our steak plates and passed the dessert around. I ate mine, but Miguel, obviously boiling inside, did little more than taste the cobbler. Greer ate slowly for several minutes, then pushed his chair back from the table.

"Mike," he said, "if what you surmise is true, I'd be inclined to agree with you. Right off, I see no earthly reason why the Agency should be using young physicists as a front for one of the Agency's 'black' operations. Gene? What do you think?"

"Ditto," I said. Ever since my days in newspaper city rooms, I had taken a dim view of the CIA. I suppose newspapermen instinctively distrust all secret operations. If nothing else, they impede the flow of legitimate news. Then the CIA's infiltration of student groups and university faculties some years ago left a bad taste in my mouth. Now the Agency was a colossus, and some of the things I had learned about it since arriving at the White House more than three years ago increased my misgivings.

"Just what do you want us to do?" Greer asked Miguel.

"I hoped," said Miguel, "that you could persuade the President to order the CIA to drop the Spruance subsidy of physicists—or any other scientists it may have recruited. For the sake of American scientists abroad, I'd rather see it done without publicity."

"You don't really want to sound off in public?" asked Greer.

"Only as a last resort," said Miguel, his truculence ebbing now. "The main thing is to knock it off."

Greer tucked his napkin into a silver ring. "It seems to me, we have two problems here," he said. "First, are your charges true? I suppose the only way to find out is for Gene or me to ask the President. Second, if the charges are true, is there some justifiable reason unknown to any of us?"

"I don't see what it could be," protested Miguel.

"No," said Greer, "but there may be. I tell you . . ." He was silent a moment. "No, let's see now . . ."

So we talked for perhaps fifteen minutes about Spruance and about Miguel's private investigation. Greer made several notes on a pad.

"I think we've got all the facts, Mike," Greer said at last. "Why don't you let Gene and me huddle over this and figure out the best way to approach the President. Then we'll . . . Gene will get back to you in a couple of days. In the meantime, you just go ahead with your work at the AEC. Okay?"

"Okay, Mr. Greer." Miguel arose at his place, and I noted again how much poise and dignity he had. "I'll just wait to hear from you . . . and thanks."

The good-bys said, Greer escorted Miguel a short distance down the corridor which passed the offices of the firm's junior lawyers.

When he returned, Greer asked me abruptly: "Gene, do you know whether the Agency's financing this Spruance thing?"

I shook my head. "I have no idea, Steve. How about you?"

"Never heard of it," he said. "What do you make of Mike's story?"

"I'm not sure," I said. "It seems like a chancy thing for the Agency to be doing when you consider the independence of many scientists and their antipathy for any kind of government control. On the other hand, I'm sure Mike's telling the truth as he sees it. The guy's on the level."

Greer nodded. "We all know how arrogant the Agency has been in its covert use of a lot of professional people, but this is the first time I'd heard that young scientists had been enlisted on any wide scale. . . . That name, 'Spruance,' bothers me. I've heard it around town somewhere, but just where . . . You have any objection to taking this to the President?"

"No, I think we should. Of course, if it is the Agency, maybe there's some logical explanation."

"Maybe," said Greer, "maybe not. Arthur's a devious operator. The way he's fixed on the Hill, he's not the most accountable of men."

"Arthur" was Arthur Victor Ingram, director of the Central Intelligence Agency. No other government executive had solidified himself so remarkably with Congress.

"Look, Gene," said Greer. He was standing behind his chair and running his fingers along the smoothly waxed wood. Again I had the impression of restlessness. "I'm pressed for time. Business. Why can't you take this up with Paul? Tell him you're speaking for both of us, and that we're disturbed by young Mike's charges. Also, it goes without saying, we think in view of Barney Loomis's position in the party, his son deserves a candid answer. Paul will understand that as well as we do."

"Sure," I said. "I'll see him at three-thirty for the regular check before my afternoon press conference. I'll take it up with him then."

"Fine. Then you carry through with Mike, will you?"

"No sweat. I'll check back with you by phone."

"Yes." Greer seemed uncertain. "Or rather, no. Let me call you when I get unsnarled on this business. . . . But I am interested in the outcome. I like Mike Loomis and, frankly, I don't blame him for being riled."

I thanked Steve for the lunch. We talked some more as he walked me to the elevator at a brisk pace. He had seen the President two nights ago, on Tuesday, Steve said, and it was unfortunate he had not known then about Miguel's problem because he could have broached the subject offhandedly in a social context.

I had come to the Ring Building without a White House car—my proud little sacrifice for government economy—and since there were no cabs available now, I walked the seven blocks to the White House. The humidity was deadening, and I soon shucked my coat and carried it over my arm. My shirt was limp by the time I entered the west wing lobby and exchanged a few words with the newspapermen sitting on the green leather lounges.

When I draped my coat on the back of my office swivel chair, I saw that Jill's hair as usual was enfolding the telephone, the signal lights at the phone's base were winking like darting sun beams, and she was whispering into the mouthpiece. She waved to me without looking up.

How to explain Jill Nichols? She had been whispering into that same phone for more than three years, the fey little girl's voice abrim with wonder as if each newspaperman or commentator who called was the British prime minister. Once we counted the calls for a week and found she murmured, "Mr. Culligan's office," or more simply, "Press," an average of ninety-three times a day. Her desk was chaotic, a snowstorm of slips which she ripped from a pad and on which she scribbled names and requests before shoving the sheets aside to prepare for another call. She was about as orderly as a surfers' beach party, yet she always managed to fish out the correct piece of paper when I needed it. And to Jill's further credit, she was under special pressure now because my assistant press secretary had quit two weeks ago for a fat job with the drug industry and I was undecided about a successor.

Jill's hair-do was ridiculous. Her hair was blond, trimmed in severe bangs across the forehead and hung wall-straight to her shoulders. She was twenty-four years old, but she resembled one of those teen-age girls who wear black boots and white stockings and talk obscurely about being unable to "relate" to anyone. She came to the press office right out of Swarthmore. At the outset I could not fire her because she seemed so helpless and, more important, she was the daughter of some friend of Ellen Roudebush, the President's wife.

Now I could not fire her because she was tormentingly efficient, somewhat like a clock that strikes regularly on the wrong hour, and, more important, I was in love with her. I say "in love" because I was not sure whether I loved her. I was thirty-eight, or fourteen years older than Jill, and had no hankering to become known as the poor man's William O. Douglas. Also, those fourteen years could have been three generations between us. I was a political p.r. man with about as many outside interests as the average politician, which is to say nil. Jill's world teemed with art shows, introspective novels by Yugoslavs and Chileans, classic Spanish guitar, vacations at unknown islands, and off-beat friends who spent their time groping for identity. As an idea of the chasm between us—or the generation and gender gap, as we would probably say in Washington—my best friend was a fat Buffalo pol named Hymie Klopstein. Jill's best friend was her roommate, Butter Nygaard. In her spare time, Butter twisted iron into pornographic shapes and smoked pot.

I didn't understand Jill, but she fascinated me. I saw her as many nights as I could, and sometimes, when Butter was making the scene somewhere, I spent the night at Jill's apartment in Georgetown. Jill said she loved me, but I thought I knew better. She was attracted by my status as an "insider," by the supposed glamour of my White House job and, maybe, because I never complained that my former wife, Mary, had not understood me. On the contrary, I said she probably understood me perfectly, a mistake that Jill would be ill-advised to repeat. I felt guilty at times for monopolizing Jill and keeping her off the marriage market, but she said that was her worry. When she felt like becoming "permanent," she would either marry me or move on. She meant it, too. Beneath her artless, child-like mannerisms and her feathery interests, she was self-sufficient, resilient, and, in her curious fashion, sage.

In short, I was in a box, satin-lined perhaps, but a box nevertheless. I often wondered what some of my predecessors on this frantic job would have thought of my predicament.

"How's Miguel?" asked Jill. "Butter would like to see more of him. She calls him the Aztec Apollo. Butter says he has the most beautiful body she ever saw."

"I didn't know she saw that much of it," I said. "I doubt that Mike would return the compliment." When I thought of Butter, I thought of the words "lank" and "bleak." She was no earth mother.

I told Jill about the meeting with Greer and Loomis. I always briefed Jill unless the President himself enjoined me to confidence. What Jill heard, she did not repeat.

"I think Miguel's right," she said. "The idea is perfectly revolting. . . ." But two lights blinking simultaneously on her five-eyed monster drew her back to the world of rushing deadlines. "Press," she said softly, and the hair caressed the mouthpiece again.

I had my own backed-up calls to return and I worked until three-thirty, when the President informed me on the green phone that he was ready for me.

The thought that invariably struck me when I entered the oval office overlooking the rose garden was that Paul Roudebush looked like a President. He was tall and big-framed, yet with little excess poundage and no paunch. His thick hair, once black, was now almost all gray. He had an innate reserve, not unlike Eisenhower's, that people equated with the dignity they believed the office deserved. Yet his first grin upon meeting was one of the most unaffectedly radiant I had ever seen. Unless a man were a patent heel, Paul Roudebush usually liked him at the outset with, I'm sure, a hope that time would not erode the initial reaction. There was no counterfeit to his grin. Even his political enemies warmed when it was bestowed on them. Women liked his face. They saw strength and dependability in its topography —a firm jaw, heavy eyebrows, and several comfortable furrows in the cheeks.

Paul Roudebush was a plain man at core. His mental processes were uncomplicated with few of the self-doubts that infected the intellectuals he gathered about him to help run the world's largest and most complex enterprise. He became angry, openly, but he seldom brooded. He reached decisions with reasonable speed and he wasted little time bewailing his errors. He made his mistakes, some of them beauties, but none eroded his self-confidence. "The worst error an executive can make," he used to say, "is to think that he has to be right all the time. Sixty per cent is far above average for humans, and I'll settle for that." He made only one exception to this—a presidential decision to use the big bomb.

When it came to nuclear weapons, any nuke of whatever size, Roudebush said, "there is no margin for error. I have to be a hundred per cent right."

There was, at the same time, a naïve quality about Paul that I am sure the voters sensed and found appealing. Despite his age, fifty-eight, and three decades of rubbing shoulders with some of the most hardened men in politics, he retained an almost boyish conviction that he could influence the world for the better if he just tried enough and ventured along enough new trails. He was far more of an optimist than I was. He believed in progress, in man's ability to improve his own nature, and in a bundle of allied concepts from the American ethic heritage that I had long since soured on. This attitude was at once his genius and his vulnerability.

The outlook reflected itself in odd ways that I found amusing. For instance, he was quite vain about his hair. Like Samson, he traced much of his own strength to the thick stand, and I suspect he secretly believed that a balding man, like his friend, Stephen Greer, had relinquished a hold on virility, the old saw about bald-headed men notwithstanding. Roudebush tended his hair as if it were a garden of prize blooms. He brushed it vigorously three or four times a day.

This day, a Thursday, when I entered his office, he reacted as usual. He put down a paper he was reading, and pushed his spectacles up on the luxurious gray thatch where they stared at the ceiling like a wondering owl. The warming grin lighted his face. He arose and came to the front of his desk and perched on a corner beside the only desk ornament, a pen set fashioned into a golden donkey with the pens spiking upward absurdly like antenna ears.

"How's our whispering Jill?" he asked. The man knew everything that went on around the White House.

"Now she's taken to rereading Dylan Thomas," I said. "She says his imagery is 'choreographic,' whatever she means by that."

"You behaving yourself with her?"

"Not any more than I can help."

The President's personal life was properly conventional, even humdrum, but he loved gossip and I am certain he shared vicariously in the affairs and transient loves of Washington. But here I must confess prejudice. Ellen Roudebush was not my type. She was one of those indefinite women who are so acutely conscious of what "people think" that they never manage to form and defend a personality of their own. I suspected, although I had no proof, that Paul and Ellen Roudebush lived most of their lives under an elaborate treaty in which intimacy had its own protocol like stamped visas on a passport.

"Well, what are the boys worrying about today?" Roudebush asked.

I ticked off a half-dozen items, all abreast of the news, on which I anticipated questions. I gave him my tentative answers and he agreed on all except one, which he revamped to his taste. Actually, there were no crises, for a change. August had been placid for the Roudebush administration, the minority party making most of the headlines with its Houston convention and the nomination of Governor Stanley Wolcott of Illinois as the candidate to oppose Roudebush at the November election. We both thought Wolcott would be a pushover. The opinion polls showed it. Our only real foe was overconfidence.

We finished my list in five minutes, then the President said: "I got a phone call from Steve. He told me about Miguel Loomis's problem and said you'd supply the details."

I told him about the luncheon meeting in Steve Greer's office and Miguel Loomis's suspicions. The President moved back to his chair while I talked. He sat listening to me with chin resting on chapel-like fingers.

"So it's sticky, Mr. President," I said in conclusion. "Because of Barney, we ought to give young Mike some kind of an answer."

I put the onus on Barney Loomis because I never asked about the CIA, the National Security Agency, or any other operation under wraps. That was the President's business.

"Spruance," he said, testing the word.

"Yes," I said. "I have no right to question you on this, and I hope you understand that I'm merely relaying what Miguel—"

"Don't worry about that," he cut in. "Physicists." He frowned. "Spruance Foundation? Is that name familiar to you, Gene?" "No, sir. As I told Mike, I never heard of it before."

He sat quietly, thinking, for a moment. "Gene, if this is a CIA operation, I know nothing about it. I just can't believe that it is. Arthur is inclined to run the Agency with a free hand, but something of this sort, involving young scientists . . . No, he would be sure to clear it with me. There must be some other explanation."

"I suppose so," I said. "After all, Mike is no trained investigator. Young men leap before they look."

"Yes," he said. More silence. "Still, I want to hear what Arthur has to say about this."

He flipped the key on his intercom box that connected with Grace Lalley, his secretary. "Grace, please call Arthur Ingram and set up an appointment here for three tomorrow. . . . Oh? Well, all right. Make it 4:30 then. Thanks."

The President settled back in his chair. "I want you in here at 4:30 tomorrow," he said. "You just give Arthur the highlights and then we'll see."

"Will Steve be here too?"

He frowned. "No, I don't think that will be necessary. . . . I wonder. Ingram has been riding high, wide and handsome recently. We've never hit it off, as you know, Gene. If it weren't for the campaign and his hold on Congress . . ."

The remainder of the remark went unspoken, but I knew the background as well as he did. Roudebush had inherited Arthur Victor Ingram from the previous administration. He would have preferred his own man, but he bowed to political reality. By the time of Roudebush's election, Ingram's following was so strong and influential that to dismiss him would be to provoke instant battle.

Private dining rooms in the CIA's secluded fortress in wooded Langley, Virginia, were the scenes of weekly dinners where congressmen were served deftly filtered secrets of the intelligence agency along with the prime ribs and strawberry mousse. Ingram's command suites and those of his deputy director occupied most of the top floor on the front side of the building which stretched as long as an aircraft carrier. Unlike the barren neutrality of most government offices, the CIA's executive eyrie was as tastefully decorated as an exclusive men's club. There was the hush of deep carpeting and the richness of old wood. For small groups of four or six men, Ingram used the director's own dining room with its high-backed chairs, upholstered in blue velveteen, its roughly woven grass paper of blue and gray on the walls, and its view of the forested hill which obscured the Potomac River, dividing Virginia and Maryland. For larger groups, Ingram entertained in the executive dining room across the corridor. This had a soft golden motif and thick brown carpeting. Both rooms were served from the galley by muted waiters who had survived penetrating security investigations. Ingram insisted on faultless service and imaginative dishes. His chef could boast the finest cuisine in government.

In the dinner conversation, no Capitol Hill leader was denied the most arcane fare, while even freshmen senators and congressmen could savor a few espionage morsels that catered to the latent spy in every man. Ingram was impressive at these gatherings, a charming, urbane host during the dinner hour and, later, with smoke from his thin cigar forming wreaths of subtle camouflage, he would unveil the intelligence operations in a single country.

This was usually a small nation, remote from the clamor of east-west diplomatic strife. Ingram fascinated his audience with a meticulous description of the ideology, venality, habits, mistresses, and idiosyncrasies of the country's chieftains. Ingram occasionally would even name a minor employee of the foreign government who served on the CIA payroll and casually drop his operational code name or number. This intricate picture of politics, pelf, and sometimes pederasty advanced several aims. It revealed the depth and exactitude of CIA methods without belaboring the point. It titillated the egos of those who yearned to know the inside story, which usually was every man in the room. Most important, it etched Arthur Ingram's regard for the American system, his supposedly implicit trust in the integrity and discretion of congressmen, and his desire to spread his cards candidly on the table for inspection by the legislative branch of government.

Ingram customarily ended with a humorous anecdote that cemented a personal bond between the nation's No. 1 agent and his legislative advisory sleuths. At a recent dinner, for example, Ingram told how an alert CIA operative literally "flushed" the hidden half of a Guinea legislator who was functioning as a double agent. The man had left a message in a metal capsule for a Russian KGB officer, hiding it beneath the flushing apparatus of a toilet bowl at the French embassy in Conakry during a reception. The American agent, under his cover as a soft drink salesman, slipped into the lavatory, locked the door and finally found the capsule by searching the cabinet after flushing the toilet. This feat climaxed a thorough search of the entire bathroom, for the American had cause to suspect this hour and this room as the time and place for the message drop. The note was unimportant, but it did reveal the Guinean's dual role. Ingram's congressional dinner ended on a wave of laughter.

In a word, congressmen were flattered by Ingram. He was usually available on the telephone within a few minutes for any friendly senator or House member who needed special favors abroad: information about a foreign country, a dictator, a resource, a trend. He was always helpful, considerate, and courteous. Similar treatment was accorded influential columnists and commentators. Many had scored sensational beats on Ingram's discreet tips.

By the advent of President Roudebush, Ingram had built the castle which adorns the dreams of every ambitious Washington bureau chief—a secure, independent power base. Ingram's influence and popularity on Capitol Hill and with the press were the most formidable since the peak days of the FBI's J. Edgar Hoover. The President who sought to fire Ingram was playing with TNT.

"Let's just say that Arthur is a problem," said the President. More than a hint of the relationship between Roudebush and Ingram could be found in the way the President stressed the name, "Arthur." He let it fall like a heavy stone. And it was never "Art."

"Well, we'll see what he has to say tomorrow," he added.

The compartment door swung shut on Ingram. I arose to leave and the President said: "Gene, I hope you won't mind staying late tonight. I'd like you to sit in on the first draft of my Labor Day opener. I'm not satisfied with the initial suggestions."

"Neither am I," I said. "Sure. I'll be glad to stay. I'd like to put my oar in."

I meant it. The speech writers, a couple of former professors, tended toward the elegant phrase and the abstruse thought. They had to be watched.

And so it was that I was working late that night on the second floor of the west wing when I received the puzzling telephone call from Mrs. Susannah Greer, Steve's wife.

2

She returned to the old brick house on Brookside Drive in Kenwood about six o'clock that evening. She parked her car in the garage and walked around the side of the house, noting with approval that the grass had been clipped between the flagstones.

There was no need to hurry. It was Thursday, his day for after-work golf. Susannah Greer halted before the brick steps and looked about her. The evening was cooling pleasantly now after the oppressive August day, and she could feel wavelets of contentment lapping at her mind. The big house invariably summoned this mood, a mingling of reassurance and comfort, a relief from the small vexations of the day. The house had never been a gloomy place, and now a fresh coat of white paint brightened the bricks.

The Greer home rambled over three levels as though part of it had been an afterthought, which it had. Like an extended telescope, it protruded unfashionably toward a high hedge, and the bay window of Steve's study blinked in the late sun coursing through an oak tree.

Behind Susannah, along the curb, stretched a line of cherry trees. Brookside Drive was divided by a grassy island in which a stream meandered through another stand of cherry trees. In the spring Brookside wore its pink and fragile purple blossoms like a procession of bridesmaids. But now the foliage was seared and the lawns freckled with brown patches. The only splashes of color were the zinnias and marigolds, Susannah's planned blooms of late August, beside the brick steps.

In many ways, she thought, the house resembled Steve: more comfortable than handsome, cluttered, never in style. In truth, Steve could be a bit tedious at times, but just when she began to feel bored or irritated with him, he would uncork some bizarre fantasy or hurl himself into a new venture totally divorced from his steady life as a Washington lawyer. There was the time, for instance, when he seized on Gretchen's new math and did the household accounts in "base eight," whatever that was. Or the phase when he became intrigued with Victor Borge's "inflation language" and went about dropping such idiocies as "three-getherness." Once he abandoned his early law practice for a year, uprooted the family and moved to Cambridge, where he studied Oriental art at Harvard. Then there was his Walt Whitman summer, when he followed Sue about the house, declaiming sonorously, a drink in one hand and *Leaves of Grass* in the other.

But, like the house, Steve's rambling was deceptive. At base, he too was conservative, solid, and somewhat colorless, especially when immersed in one of those incomprehensible legal briefs. He could scarcely be called handsome. The gray eyes and the thinning sandy hair gave him a faded, bookkeeperish look. But he was—what was the word?—yes, reassuring. She was sure she still loved him after twenty-six years of marriage, but what was love? A dependence, a distaste for solitude, a sharing of trouble and trivia, or something deeper and unknowable?

Susannah Greer sighed, glanced again at the house and mounted the steps. Even before she turned the key in the lock, the feeling of contentment shaded into one of anticipation, an anticipation tinged with nostalgia, perhaps because she knew that, like all moods, it too would pass.

She kicked off her shoes in the dark hallway, padded to the upstairs bedroom and removed her girdle. She always wriggled out of it with relief before taking off her dress. She hung the dress, unfastened her brassiere, then stood nude and cool for a moment, staring at the rack of clothes. She selected the dark green silk lounging slacks and a matching blouse. She put them on with a sensuous awareness of the sleek fabric against her body.

In the three years since Gretchen left home, the Greers had woven a Thursday-night ritual of their own. Thursday was the maid's day off. The evening began for Susannah with the tingle of sensuality as she stood in the bedroom, and it ended hours later when she and Stephen lay together on the low, king-sized bed and bantered over which one should reach down and pull the sheet over them.

The way stations to the aftermath of love had their signposts. When Steve arrived about seven-thirty after his short evening of golf at Burning Tree, he often eyed her appreciatively, praised the swell of her breasts or flattered her with a phrase: "Cubby, on you that outfit is a smash." Then they would have drinks in the snug library, with its old brick fireplace and its bookshelves from floor to ceiling. Martinis in the winter, daiquiris in the summer. They would exchange the gossip of the day. Steve's was usually more diverting because of his friendship with President Roudebush and leading politicians, but Sue knew most of the wives in Washington's ponderous political society and she sometimes came up with a bit that fractured Steve.

Frequently he would leave his chair and come over to kiss her. They always said they shouldn't have a third drink, but they usually did, and sometimes a fourth. Some evenings he apologized for coming home late the night before from the Wednesday-night secret sessions of the Potomac Study Club, a group of administration officials. If a fourth drink had aroused her dormant antipathy for his Wednesday-night absences, she might accuse him of fabricating the study club as an alibi for a night on the town. There was sometimes a bite to these remarks. It was not so much his Wednesday nights she resented as his adamant refusal to tell anything about the meetings, be it place, names, or topic of discussion.

Then dinner, cognac in the library and more talk until Steve propelled her toward the stairs, walking behind her and patting her rump. The whole business was slightly ridiculous for two middle-aged people—my God, Steve was forty-nine and she only three years younger—and she knew that Gretchen, for all her superior talk of "sexual experiences," would consider her father's and mother's behavior ludicrous. Still, if there were a better scenario for married love, she and Steve were not aware of it, and she had to admit that she felt superbly alive on Thursday nights.

She looked at her wrist watch. Six forty-five. And now for her own game. She would sit by the window in the deep easy chair, the one with the flowered chintz cover, and try to pretend that she was merely content and not brushed by anticipation. She put on her reading glasses, picked up a copy of *Holiday* and began to read the essay. The idea was to dampen any tingle of exhilaration, wasn't it? No, be honest, Sue. The real idea was to savor the feeling, to stretch it like taffy, to make each moment into three. She tried to concentrate on the article, but her mind refused to stay fastened. Instead, her thoughts fixed on those unexplained Wednesday nights of Steve. A secret study club of high officials, he said, but where did they meet, who were they, and what did they gas about until one and two in the morning? It was all a bit weird, she thought, and tonight she would insist that he tell her, or else. Or else what? She smiled. Or else nothing. Thursday night was too special to mar with bickering. The fact was that Steve relished his secret, and he would tell her in his own good time, no doubt with a great flourish. She went back to the magazine and this time she became engrossed in it.

And so it was more than an hour later when she realized that daylight was fading and reached up automatically to turn on the light of the floor lamp. She looked at her watch. Two minutes after eight. Steve was half an hour late.

She left the chair and went toward the front door along the hall, which was all in shadow now. She heard a crunching sound in the driveway and quickened her step. When she opened the door, she saw that a green sedan had turned into the drive and was now backing out. Apparently it was someone who had picked the wrong house. She stepped out on the brick stoop and looked down Brookside Drive. No sign of Steve's beige Oldsmobile convertible.

Back in the house, she clacked to the kitchen in her sandals and mixed herself a daiquiri. She realized, too late, that she had put in too much rum. Steve always made the daiquiris. She was annoyed with him. He was never late Thursday evenings.

She returned to the living room and began reading again, this time in the latest book club choice. When she looked at her watch the next time, it was eight-thirty. Just where was he?

She felt a rising irritation. He at least could have called to say he would be late. She tapped her foot and, against her will, began dwelling on the little things about her husband that irked her. His Sunday morning breakfast foursomes . . . Those suits he wore, the cut always out of date . . . He played the hi-fi too loudly . . . He looked at her balefully if she interrupted him while he was reading, as though she had committed a discourteous act. Manners! Why, he scratched his rear when he stood up from a chair. Then he had an annoying way of clearing his throat like some pompous, old judge . . . He never hung up the towel after a shower . . . Oh, the list of his tiresome habits! And that she should sit here alone, waiting. Just who did Stephen Greer think he was, anyway? Just because he happened to be a friend of the President gave him no right . . .

Oh, etc., etc., she told herself. She promptly drew a line through his sins, consigning them to the trash heap of spite. He was kind, considerate, and just reliable enough. He was stuffy at times, but those wonderfully nutty streaks made him a dear. He was imaginative, he was fun, he was her man, and she loved him.

When she finished the daiquiri, it was dark outside. She turned on two other lamps in the living room. Her watch showed nine-ten. The sweep of the second hand, newly glimpsed, gave her a start. It was getting late. Where *was* he?

She switched on the light in the hall and stood looking at the telephone for a moment. Then she dialed Steve's law office. She waited through nine rings, but there was no answer. That was stupid, she thought, when she knew he was at the club. She eyed the phone uncertainly. Should she call the club? She had never done it. She detested wives who bothered husbands at these masculine retreats. Still, this was not like Steve. She extended a finger to dial the number of the Burning Tree Club, Washington's all-male golf club, but realized she did not know the number. She retrieved her reading glasses from the living room, then leafed through the "B's" in the Maryland section of the metropolitan phone directory. She dialed 365-1200.

The phone made six anonymous, echoing demands before a man's voice answered.

"Oh, this is Mrs. Stephen Greer. I'd like to speak to my husband please, if he's still there." She felt intrusive, like a woman rapping on a neighbor's door during a dinner party.

"We're about to close up," said the voice. "I'll switch you to the bar." It sounded as though it would rather not.

"Oh, thank you." Why must she feel like an intruder?

The line stuttered a moment, then a heavy voice said: "Nineteenth Hole."

"This is Mrs. Stephen Greer. I hate to do this, but there's a small household emergency. May I speak to Mr. Greer please?"

"Oh, Sue. This is Maury Rimmel."

The voice had a whisky heartiness, and Sue could visualize the tiny purple veins in the moonish face. She knew him only casually, but Maury Rimmel, a lobbyist—was it for steel?—first-named everyone.

"I'm sorry," said Rimmel, "but Steve isn't here. Just Joe Hopkinson and myself, finishing up a gin game."

"I know I'm being a bother, but something has come up and I was trying to locate Steve."

"No bother at all," said Rimmel. "Anything important?"

"Nothing cataclysmic. Just a family thing. Do you know when he left, Maury?"

"No, I don't. Actually, I don't remember him coming back through here, but I wasn't paying much attention. This damn Hopkinson is into me for too many bucks. Steve probably showered without sticking his head in here. Just a minute, Sue . . ."

"Hey, Joe." Rimmel was talking across the room. "When did Steve Greer finish up?"

The answer was indistinct to Sue, and Rimmel said: "Hang on another minute, please."

The minute stretched to three before Rimmel came back on. "Sorry, Sue," he said. "I was just checking with Joe. Matter of fact, we don't remember seeing Steve since we saw him at No. 1 about six. We invited him to make it a threesome, for the front side, but he said he just wanted to knock around a few holes, that he had to leave by seven because he was due home."

"Oh." She had been imposing over a trifle. "Thanks, Maury, I—"

"Hold on," he said. "Why don't I go see if his car is still in the lot. Drives a convertible, doesn't he?"

"Yes, an Olds, beige-colored. Maury, I'm being an awful bore."

"Forget it," he said. "It'll only take a minute. I'll be right back."

But it was a full five minutes this time before Rimmel returned to the phone. She drew up a hall chair and lit a cigarette while she waited. This was odd. She began to feel uneasy.

"Hello? Look, Sue, a couple of things don't quite figure." Rimmel's voice had lost its heartiness. "The car's still out in the parking lot, but Steve's nowhere around the clubhouse. Joe and I checked his locker—they're all open here—and we found his suit hanging in there. On the other hand, his golf shoes are in the locker too. Then Joe remembered that when we saw Steve at the first tee, he was wearing his street shoes."

"Is that peculiar?" She felt a bit lost. Golf was an alien game to her.

"Well, yes, in a way. Steve had on his golf clothes—a polo jersey and slacks, I think—so we wondered why the street shoes."

"But nobody's seen him since six?" She was upset now. "And you're sure his car is still there?"

"No doubt about that."

"Could something have happened to him out on the course?" As she raised the cigarette, she noticed that her hand trembled.

"Oh, I wouldn't think so, not a man in such good shape as Steve. . . . Tell you what, Sue. Joe and I'll get a cart and a flashlight and have a look around. Just to make sure, you know."

"I'll be right out," she said, forgetting for the moment that Burning Tree banned women from its grounds.

"No, I wouldn't do that," he said in words that seemed intentionally slowed. "You just mix yourself a drink and stay right there. You couldn't help us any. . . . Now don't worry, honey. You just take it easy until I call back in half an hour or so."

The instant she replaced the receiver, the thought struck her that Maury Rimmel suspected that Steve had collapsed somewhere on the golf course. That was it. Maury thought Steve was lying unconscious, or maybe . . . dead? . . . and he did not want a hysterical wife around when they found the body. The thought jolted her physically, and she sat for several minutes staring at the telephone. What could have happened? Heart seizure? Stroke? Steve was in excellent health. Still, he was at that age when men suddenly crumple. Susannah walked slowly to the kitchen to mix another daiquiri. The house seemed abruptly and strangely cold, and she crossed her arms and rubbed the sleeves of the blouse. She must get a sweater.

The Nineteenth Hole, Burning Tree's card room and bar, overlooked the eighteenth green on one side and the tenth tee on the other through a wide stretch of window that reached to the ceiling. A wall was covered with caricatures of members, present and past, including Presidents Truman, Eisenhower, Kennedy, Johnson, and Roudebush on the top row. Rimmel and Hopkinson had been playing gin rummy at a padded green table next to the cartoon gallery. Joe Hopkinson, a thin, tanned man with deep-set eyes that seemed to have receded from life, sat shuffling the cards like an executioner. He was far ahead at a penny a point.

"I take it we're going on a sweep and search," he said.

"Yeah," said Rimmel. "Add it up at the end of the last Hollywood and I'll pay off."

"Already have," said Hopkinson. "You're down 3678. Pay to the nearest five. That's thirty-five."

Rimmel took his wallet from a hip pocket, found a twenty-dollar bill, a ten and a five, and spread them fan-like on the table. "To my least favorite charity," he said. "Let's have another look around the locker room."

They went first to a small dressing room with special shower stall that had been built years ago for President Eisenhower. Now President Roudebush had a locker there with a small brass plate which read, "Mr. President." Greer's locker was next to it, and Rimmel and Hopkinson inspected this again. A gray business suit was draped on a hanger, shirt and tie on hooks. On the metal floor were a scatter of golf tees, sweat socks, and golf shoes.

"Can't figure those golf shoes," said Hopkinson.

They walked through the adjacent shower room and lavatory, then looked down the wide aisles of the deserted main locker room. The lights were still on. Colored flags of cabinet officers and military chiefs who had belonged to Burning Tree hung brightly limp from the ceiling. They passed into the lounge and dining room, but found no one. Except for the front desk attendant, the old stone and brick clubhouse was abandoned for the night. Rimmel found a large, red, box-type flashlight hanging in a service closet.

Outside a thin overcast veiled a quarter moon which shed a diffused light as if from a dusty bulb. Rimmel and Hopkinson walked to the cluster of electric golf carts, and Rimmel flashed the light over the buggies, all numbered in the rear.

"No. 10 is missing," he said after a time. "That must be the one Steve took."

They wheeled a cart away from the nest of vehicles, and Hopkinson said: "You drive. If I know we have to do a reconnaissance mission, I don't have the third martini."

"You and me both," said Rimmel. He squeezed his abundant belly behind the wheel and handed the flashlight to Hopkinson, who tried the beam up and down. It was a powerful one. When they reached No. 1 tee, the shaft of light shone a hundred yards down the fairway.

"Let's make the first five and then cut by No. 8 green and come in on 9," said Rimmel. "If he was only going a few holes, that's the way he'd play it. Didn't he say he wanted to practice his irons?"

"Check," said Hopkinson. "I'll sweep on both sides. If we don't find anything, we can come back and try further into the rough."

The cart rolled smoothly on the thick Bermuda turf, but Rimmel sensed the effects of the alcohol. His head felt fuzzy, and the trees bordering the course appeared immense. The light fanning the fairway between the flanking woods could have been a boat's searchlight in a canyon river.

"You think he collapsed out here somewhere?" asked Rimmel.

"What else?" returned Hopkinson. "His car sits in the lot, a cart's missing and his suit hangs in his locker. He doesn't figure to be out here writing poetry."

Rimmel was irritated by Hopkinson's habit of speaking in the present tense as though he were still reviewing a gin rummy play. It seemed inappropriate to the seriousness of their mission.

"You don't sound like a man about to weep."

"I'm not," said Hopkinson. "Greer isn't one of my favorite characters. Knowing Roudebush must have brought him a million in fees, but he acts like he did it all on his own."

"Steve's not a bad guy," said Rimmel. "He's smart. He'd have made it anyway. Having a President as a pal iced the cake. You're envious, Joe."

"The hell I am. You play a Sunday-morning foursome with Greer, and you've got no barrel of laughs, believe me."

"Oh, he's sort of a loner," said Rimmel. "But when he loosens up, with a couple of drinks under his belt, he can be damn funny. Let's face it, Joe. Steve works harder than we do. He doesn't sit around wasting his time at gin."

"Wasting time is the name of the game," said Hopkinson moodily. "If you're not playing around, you're usually trying to screw somebody out of something."

The beam swept back and forth across the fairway, then cupped the first green. Hopkinson shone the light around the lip and into the surrounding trees and the underbrush trampled by erratic golfers.

Along the cart path leading from the first green to the No. 2 tee, Hopkinson lowered the light and played it in a narrow band along the ground.

"What the hell are you doing?" asked Rimmel. The rising breeze had failed to clear the fog from his brain, and he felt vaguely ineffectual.

"Looking for footprints," said Hopkinson. In his lemon slacks and matching polo shirt, he could have been an advertisement for a sportsman's whisky. "Just because a cart's missing doesn't mean Steve's using it. Maybe he walked."

"And lugged his bag?" asked Rimmel skeptically. "Anyway, what's that supposed to tell us?"

"Don't know. You want me to play private eye in the middle of the night, I do it right . . . Hold it." Hopkinson leaned out and picked something off the ground. "Good tee," he mumbled.

Joe's half-squiffed, thought Rimmel. After a ride around No. 2 tee and several futile sweeps of the light, they rolled slowly down the center of the long second fairway.

"Maybe we ought to make the whole front nine," said Rimmel. "He could have changed his mind and gone the route."

"Doesn't figure," said Hopkinson. "If he plays slow, working on his irons, he doesn't have time to do nine before dark. He said he wanted to finish by seven. And if he speeds up, he has to play through us."

They surveyed the second green and the short No. 3 fairway, with its deep dip like the creased abdomen of a fat man, then carted to No. 4 tee. Hopkinson shone his light on the black and red iron standard which supported the ball cleaner and marked the distance: 439 yards, par 4. Nearby nestled a cement marker with the legend "John J. Pelley," eternally commemorating a member who contributed money to improve this section of the course. No. 4 was all uphill, with a dip in front of the green.

"I wouldn't want my name on this one," said Hopkinson. "I par it only about once a year."

"You can say that again."

They drove between the arching guardians of trees, oak, hickory, white ash, and pine, and the smaller dogwood, its leaves already stained with the copper of late August. The cart slid into the little valley, then climbed toward the green. On the orange-striped pin, the triangular red-and-white flag stood out in the stiffening breeze. Hopkinson played the light over the sand trap to the right, an obstacle that always reminded Rimmel of a clothes dummy with truncated arms.

"Look," said Hopkinson, aiming the light.

Behind the trap, halfway to the border of high trees, stood an electric golf cart, empty save for a leather golf bag in the rear.

The number on the back of the buggy was 10. The woods protruding from the nest of clubs in the golf bag wore their brightly knitted hoods like four girls at a skating party.

Hopkinson centered the flashlight's strong beam on the bag. He moved a finger across a small leather label.

"It's his," he said. "S.B.G. What's the 'B' for?"

"Byfield," said Rimmel. "Some family name, I guess. Let's look around. He might have gone to the woods to take a leak."

"Greer would," said Hopkinson. "Anybody else would do it right here."

They walked into a semicircle of trees, Hopkinson playing the light over the underbrush and pine needles. The first few yards of rough were fairly clear, but beyond was a matted tangle of fallen limbs, saplings, weeds, and bushy growth, all partially flattened by the flailing clubs of men who had overshot the green. The steel mesh boundary fence was only a short distance beyond, dividing Burning Tree from homes along Arrowwood Road. There was one gate, but when Hopkinson tried it, he found it locked. They returned to the green. The breeze blew steadier, cooler. Branches creaked and there was a soft rustle of leaves like ripples at the edge of a lake. Rimmel zipped down a pocket of Greer's golf bag and two golf balls fell out, bouncing off the cart.

"Leave the bag alone, Maury."

Rimmel looked up from a squat as he retrieved the golf balls. "Why, for God's sake?"

"Use your head," said Hopkinson. "We don't see Greer, do we? Suppose somebody sneaks up on him and clobbers him. So that means the police, right?"

"Police?" Rimmel's moon face reflected disbelief. "Come off it. Besides, what's that got to do with Steve's bag?" But he replaced the balls, zipped up the pocket, and stepped away from the cart.

"Search me," said Hopkinson. "I just figure we do better to leave things as they are."

They stood for a moment, uncertain.

"He didn't have a caddy, did he?" asked Rimmel.

"No," said Hopkinson. "We got the last one still here. . . . Couple of things . . ." Hopkinson put down the light and shook a cigarette out of a pack.

"What?"

"How far from here to the Burdette Road fence?" asked Hopkinson. He swept the light to a thicket off to the right. The boundary fence made a corner near the intersection of Arrowwood and Burdette Roads, then ran back to the club entrance on Burdette.

"Maybe seventy, eighty yards," said Rimmel.

"Let's have a look."

Hopkinson walked from the green, Rimmel following him through the trees. The flashlight, bent to the ground, threw bright cones over a heavier undergrowth, moldering leaves, pine needles, shrubs, and fallen limbs. The growth was so dense they were forced to detour around logs and to hold branches away from their faces. They skirted the edge of a pit, once excavated for fill dirt for the course, but now a trough for rotting wood. It took them five minutes to reach the steel mesh fence, some six feet high and topped by three strands of barbed wire which slanted outward and upward for more than a foot.

"Well, how about that," said Hopkinson.

He centered the light on the base of the fence between an oak tree and the smooth gray trunk of an American beech. Upended against the fence stood a wooden crate, perhaps two feet high. Hopkinson illuminated the ground, which was springy and moist. He pointed to footprints and a freshly made cut in the earth.

"Somebody was here," said Hopkinson. "And it looks like the box was chucked over the fence from the other side, making that dent here."

Then he trained the light on the ground just outside the fence.

"Those look like heel marks to you?"

Rimmel peered through the mesh. "I don't know. But if he climbed to the top of the fence and jumped, he'd land on the balls of his feet, wouldn't he?"

"Don't ask me. The guy's almost fifty. I don't know how you old men jump." Hopkinson had just celebrated his forty-fifth birthday. "Anyway, it looks to me like that ground has been roughed up—on both sides."

"I'm a lousy detective," said Rimmel. His head began to pound from the fading martinis, and he wondered how he could hoist his 240 pounds to the top of the steel fence and jump clear of three strands of barbed wire. Was Greer in that good shape?

An automobile's headlights came toward them, rising and falling on narrow, hilly Burdette Road, and Hopkinson instinctively clicked off the box light. A screen door slammed in the house across the road.

"Let's go back to the clubhouse," said Hopkinson.

At the electric buggy, they stood for a moment, brushing debris from their clothes.

"I wonder," said Hopkinson. "Steve's a careful player, not good, but careful. He wants to practice, he says, but he doesn't put on his golf shoes."

"Yeah."

"So, a guy takes the trouble to put on his playing clothes, but not his shoes. Then he leaves his car in the lot, and parks his cart and bag right up high behind No. 4 green. And he doesn't start out until the course is almost empty. Then he shinnies over a fence."

"So?" Rimmel was distributing his bulk behind the wheel.

"So, it looks like he intended to walk off the course before he started to play. He's got his street shoes on for walking, no caddy to bother him, and he leaves his clubs and car where somebody will find them for him."

"But why?"

"How the hell do I know?" retorted Hopkinson. "You know the man better than I do."

"I think we ought to continue down No. 5 and then cut back on 9," said Rimmel. He was thinking of the phone call he must make to Sue Greer. "I don't know. Maybe he felt faint, found his cart didn't work and decided to walk back."

Hopkinson snorted his dissent, then got into the No. 10 cart, which held Greer's bag. He pressed the accelerator and the buggy moved ahead immediately.

"Nothing wrong with this one," said Hopkinson. "Maury, use your head. A box by the fence, footprints, the cart and the bag left here. Steve went over the hill, my friend."

"Could be," said Rimmel, "but we ought to look anyway."

"Okay," said Hopkinson as he got into the cart, "but we're looking for a man who isn't here."

They drove the fifth fairway, cut behind the No. 8 green, and headed for the clubhouse, on the ninth fairway. Hopkinson fanned the light back and forth, beaming it into the rough on either side. The watered Bermuda grass lay lush and dark on the fairways, and the breeze stirred in the tree tops. Once a rabbit blinked at the light over a shoulder, then hopped away. There was no sign of a human form.

"Give up?" asked Hopkinson as Rimmel steered the electric buggy past the ninth green.

Rimmel nodded, scratched at his mound of stomach, and halted the cart at the cluster of other buggies. "Shouldn't we go get his bag? Some kid might steal the clubs."

"Leave it," said Hopkinson. "If the bag goes, it goes. No sense in our disturbing things. . . . Say, were the keys in his car?"

"I don't remember."

They walked to the parking lot and found the keys in the ignition switch of Greer's convertible.

Back in the card room, Rimmel said: "Funny, isn't it? The way it adds up, I agree with you. It looks as if he meant to walk off the course from No. 4 green."

"The question is why?"

"I'll call Sue back," said Rimmel, "but I don't like the job."

"Well," said Hopkinson, "you can tell her we're pretty sure he's alive and kicking."

Rimmel frowned. "But we can't be certain. It looks that way, but he could be lying around anywhere out there." He motioned toward the course, black now with no shadowed relief from the hidden quarter moon.

Hopkinson shook his head. "Doesn't figure. My hunch is he's somewhere, God knows where, with two good legs under him."

Susannah Greer slowly replaced the receiver, aware that anxiety was flooding the initial flowering of relief. The golf bag . . . the golf shoes and the street clothes in Steve's locker . . . playing without a caddy. None of the things which Maury Rimmel stressed made much sense to her. And the car keys in the ignition switch? Were they significant? The box by the fence, she thought, could have been placed by someone else, children perhaps. She wondered if she had made the right decision in asking Rimmel not to call the police yet. But she wanted time to think . . . and give Steve time to come home. Could he have had one of his impulses, left his clubs on the course, and walked home? No, that was not reasonable. When Steve appeared to act suddenly, there was usually a design of some kind. He was no feckless small boy. . . . Perhaps he just grew tired of playing, left his golf bag, and went walking through the woods. Soon he would return, wheel the cart back to the clubhouse, and drive home. She looked at her watch again. Eleven forty-five. . . . Yet if Steve had gone walking in the night, he could have collapsed somewhere on the course. She felt suddenly resentful of Rimmel and the other one—what was his name?—Hopkinson. They had searched only a small part of Burning Tree. Why hadn't they gone all the way around? No, that wasn't fair. They were trying to deduce what another golfer would do.

Now what? She walked to the living room and sank into the big easy chair. The open book, but little read, rested on the coffee table, a symbol of her frustration. Call Gretchen? No. It would be thoughtless to upset her when Steve might walk into the house at any moment. She sat quite still, seeking to contain herself and stave off the chill ripples of apprehension. After all, only a little more than four hours had elapsed since the normal Thursday time for Steve's arrival. . . . Yet, suppose Steve was lying somewhere on the ground at Burning Tree, unconscious, in silent need of help. She just had to do something. . . . Or, wait. Could he have been summoned suddenly to the White House? Maybe a messenger came and fetched him from the golf course. Several times Steve had left his bed when the President called. Yes, that might be it.

She walked swiftly to the hall telephone and dialed 465-1414. She felt comforted to hear the warm voice of Hilda, the chief night operator. Hilda seemed to sing the phrase, "White House," a prelude of joy and solace for all callers.

"Hilda," she said, "this is Sue Greer. Do you know whether my husband is around there some place?"

"Oh, Mrs. Greer . . . The President retired early tonight. But just a minute. Mr. Culligan and some others are still here working. Perhaps Mr. Greer is with them."

Sue felt a quick lift of spirit.

"Hello." It was the raspy voice of the White House press secretary. "This is Gene Culligan, Mrs. Greer. Can I help you?"

"Thanks, Gene. Aren't you working awfully late?"

"Speech-wrestling," he said. "We're about to quit."

The "we" buoyed her further. "Is Steve there?" she asked confidently, already sensing an affirmative answer.

"Steve? No, Mrs. Greer. Just me and a couple of speech writers. Why? Is he supposed to be here?"

Her hopes slid downhill. "Well, I thought . . . he was supposed to be home at seven-thirty and I, uh, haven't heard from him."

"Oh, I see," said Culligan. "Pretty late, isn't it? Let me give the agent on the night detail a ring. Maybe Steve's over in the house with the President."

A minute dragged by. "No," said Culligan, returning to the phone. "The President went to sleep some time ago and Steve hasn't been around tonight. I had lunch with him this noon, and he mentioned that he was up to his neck in work. Did you try his office?"

"Yes," said Sue. "He's not there." That sinking sensation again, but also embarrassment. Here she was bothering the White House at midnight. "I'm just mixed on domestic signals. He's probably at some meeting I've forgotten. Thanks, Gene."

"No trouble, Mrs. Greer. Good-night."

Sue walked slowly back to the living room, her arms folded against the night chill and her eyes unaccountably watching each sandaled foot as it moved forward. The phone rang. She wheeled and ran to the hall again, skidding on the waxed floor as she rounded the corner.

"Mrs. Greer?" asked an unfamiliar male voice.

"Yes. This is Susannah Greer."

"Mrs. Greer, I have a message for you. I will read it slowly. Quote. 'Dearest Sue: Please don't worry, Cubby. Have faith in me. I'll return when I can, but it may take time. I love you.' Unquote."

"Who is this?" But in mid-question she heard the telephone click at the other end.

"Hello, hello. . . ." The phone held only the barren hum of an empty line.

She stood for a moment, stunned, then pressed down repeatedly on a button of the phone. No response. She hung up, counted ten, then dialed the operator.

"This is an emergency, operator. I just received a suspicious call. Can it be traced?"

"I'm sorry, madam. Unless the connection is still open, we cannot help you."

She noted her watch as she hung up—12:09. Shouldn't she make sure of the exact time? In case of police—the thought alarmed her—didn't they want to know such things? She dialed the number for time, and heard the flat, recorded voice say, "The time . . . the time is . . . 12:13." Sue adjusted her watch, then calculated the elapsed time since the anonymous call. Two minutes? Three? Probably three. She marked the time of the call in her mind, fixing it at 12:10.

She sat immobile for a moment, then felt the first onset of panic, like cold fingers plucking at her. Her throat tightened and when she fought the sensation, she broke into tears. She wept only briefly, but her shoulders trembled and she became aware of her fright. She forced herself to go upstairs for a sweater, chided herself for not doing so earlier. When she returned to the living room, she was reasonably calm again, but the unanswered questions kept flying at her like swooping bats.

It was too late to call any of her women friends. What could they do at this hour except lose sleep and catch Sue's distress like a contagious disease?

No, the thing to do was to call Gretchen in New York. Gretchen was a steady one, a cut of Steve. Household crises had a way of melting in Gretchen's presence. But Sue was reluctant to call her daughter. There was still that stubborn, if dwindling, hope that Steve would appear at any moment. The truth was, she knew, that she did not want to appear foolishly panicked in Gretchen's eyes. She would feel absurd if she poured out her alarms to Gretchen, only to have Steve walk in the house a few minutes later. But that anonymous call! That must mean that Steve would not return soon. The voice had been brutally curt and yet had used Steve's pet nickname for her. Had Steve been kidnaped and this frightening message was but the first of a series?

She fought with her thoughts and her fears for an hour before she finally forced herself to walk to the hallway and dial Gretchen's number in New York.

Gretchen's voice was querulously drowsy at first, but as soon as Sue explained, in a rush of words, the sleep evaporated.

"Start at the beginning, Mother." Gretchen was in gentle command. "What happened after you called the club?"

The full recital consumed a half hour, for Gretchen insisted on learning each detail, then made her mother retrace the story chronologically.

"Let's see," said Gretchen, "it's two o'clock now. I think you should call that Mr. Rimmel and ask him to notify the police. After all, he's the one who knows about the cart and the box and all. There's a chance that Dad has been beaten up or kidnaped, and if so, the police should get on it right away. . . . I'll take the first shuttle down in the morning, but you call me back in an hour, whatever happens."

"All right, Gretchen."

And so it was with a feeling of relative calm, a subordinate carrying out orders, that Sue telephoned Maury Rimmel at his home, waited for the long rings, and then asked Maury to inform the proper authorities. She wasn't sure. Would it be the Bethesda or the Washington police? Leave that to him, said Rimmel.

Sue went to the kitchen and put a large measure of coffee in the electric percolator. She knew it would be a sleepless night, what was left of it.

It was 3:35 A.M. when an assistant night desk officer at Washington's Metropolitan Police headquarters walked into the littered third floor press room of the limestone building on Indiana Avenue.

Ordinarily the press room would have been deserted at this hour, but an early morning knifing of a pretty government secretary had brought the afternoon newsmen on duty ahead of schedule. Two young reporters of the capital's afternoon newspapers, the *Washington Evening Star* and the *Washington Daily News*, were there. The *Star* man pecked at an old typewriter. The *News* reporter was standing over the precinct teletype machine.

"The name Stephen Greer mean anything to you Pulitzer Prize winners?" asked the sergeant. He leaned in the doorway, mouthing a toothpick.

"Yeah," said the reporter from the *Star*, "if you mean the lawyer, Greer, that friend of Roudebush's. You mean him?"

"That's the guy."

"P.I.?" asked the *News* man.

"No. Missing person. Greer disappeared from the Burning Tree Club tonight. Bethesda just asked our help. Two detectives are on their way to the Greer house now. It's 5814 Brookside Drive in Kenwood . . . in case you're interested."

"Wise guy!" said the *News* man as he left the room one step behind the *Star*'s police reporter. Then he called over his shoulder: "Thanks, Homer. That's one more we owe you."

The first blue-streak edition of the Friday, August 27, *Washington Evening Star*, which reached downtown news stands shortly before noon, carried a three-column photograph of Stephen Greer on page one. The story ran a column on the front page and four more inside.

The article disclosed the disappearance of Greer, a five-hour search of the Burning Tree Club grounds by police, and the surmise of Chief Thad Wilson, of the Metropolitan Police, that Greer probably walked off the course about 8 P.M. Thursday. The story also noted the arrival that morning of Greer's daughter, Gretchen, a New York fabric designer, at the Kenwood home. The writer said that Miguel Loomis, a young friend of the family, had been enlisted as a liaison man between Mrs. Greer and the press. The search by Maury Rimmel and Joseph T. Hopkinson, a Washington broker, was described, and the story stressed the odd circumstances of the golf shoes, the box by the fence, and the keys in the ignition switch of Greer's car.

Greer's description, the story said, had been broadcast on the nation-wide network of LETS (Law Enforcement Teletype System). The *Star* writer described Greer this way:

Greer is a balding, unprepossessing man in appearance with sandy hair, gray eyes, and a slight slouch. He is five feet 11 inches tall, weighs 170 pounds and recently celebrated his forty-ninth birthday. Although reserved with strangers, he is affable with friends and is known for his quick enthusiasms and his zest for occasional off-beat ventures that break the daily routine.

The article reported the widespread police opinion that Greer had disappeared voluntarily. To emphasize that this was no routine missing persons case, the writer described Greer's reputation, background, and standing in the community:

Stephen Byfield Greer is regarded as one of the leading attorneys of the District of Columbia bar and is a senior partner in the prominent firm of Greer, Hilstratter, Tomlin & DeLuca. He headed the United Givers Fund Drive in the metropolitan area four years ago, is a member of the American Bar Association's international law section and a director of the World Law Fund. He has practiced law here since his graduation, third in his class, from Columbia University Law School. He did his undergraduate work at Wesleyan University in Connecticut, and is a native of Dover, Del., where he played third base on the high school baseball team.

A full column of the story dwelled on possible repercussions. The writer summarized the first quick reaction in Washington's political community where every event, from a caustic remark at a cocktail party to a declaration of war, is weighed exclusively on the scales of electoral portent:

> The disappearance, unless quickly resolved, could have national implications in view of the upcoming presidential campaign. President Paul Roudebush is slated to open his campaign for re-election eleven days hence with a Labor Day speech in Chicago. Gov. Stanley Wolcott of Illinois, the opposition candidate nominated at the recent Houston convention, will kick off his campaign the same day in Detroit's Cadillac Square.
>
> Greer has been close to President Roudebush since the President's terms in the Senate. Greer was an adviser during the successful Roudebush presidential campaign, aided in the transition of government, served as a talent scout for the new Roudebush administration, and has since frequently advised on legislation and policy. In addition, Greer is a social caller at the White House, Camp David, and the presidential winter retreat on Captiva Island off the west coast of Florida.

At his desk on the Senate floor, Senator Owen Moffat of Nebraska, a tactician for Governor Wolcott, finished reading the last of the lengthy newspaper story. He leaned toward his colleague on the right.

"What do you make of this Greer business?" Moffat asked.

"It's a puzzler," said the other senator. "Looks as if he planned it, doesn't it?"

"Yes," agreed Moffat. He leaned closer and whispered. "A close friend of a President of the United States doesn't disappear at the outset of a presidential campaign unless he's in very, very bad trouble."

3

I looked at my notes on the square, lined pad. A dozen items all began with the same symbol—G. We were nearing the end of one of the most hectic days in months, and I glanced longingly at the spot where my pack of cigarettes used to rest. I had sworn off smoking two weeks ago, and now the craving was fierce.

"Knock it off, Jill," I said, "and let's get them in here."

As ever, Jill's desk across the room looked like a typhoon had swept it. As ever, she was whispering into the telephone. The long hair dripped to her shoulders, one hand was cupped about the mouthpiece, and the other waved imploringly at me. Three lights winked at the base of the phone, frantic signals from the men who hunted news.

She brushed at the hair, but it cascaded back over the phone, and I wondered again about her attraction for me. She was a baffling girl, an anarchist of the office, yet efficient in her own chaotic way. She addled me, which is to say, I suppose, that she at once triggered my lust and my affection.

Jill finished her low conversation, moved across the room, straightened my desk sign, which read simply, "Culligan," and planted a prim kiss on my forehead. I thought, forlornly, that I was not old enough to be her father and not young enough to be her husband.

She walked to the door with her sinuous, boneless flow. Opening the door, she called, "Press!" in that fey voice of a child, then stepped back quickly to avoid the surging tide of journalism.

The newsmen swarmed around my desk, like a single rubbery body under a forest of heads, then ballooned to the walls. Henry, the civil service stenotype man, growled when a foot struck the three-legged support for his machine. He moved the tripod, glared obliquely at the kicker, and looked over at me with a professional's expression of vigilant boredom. The normal contingent of thirty White House regulars had swelled to more than a hundred men and women of the newspapers, networks, and news magazines. The reason, of course, was Greer.

"No announcements," I said, "except that the President is keeping all appointments on the list." (Arthur Ingram's 4:30 call was off-the-record and thus had not been posted.) "So let's go to questions."

"Greer. What else?" said Dave Paulick, the *D.P.* weekly newsletter man. He had been the first to call me, at 7 A.M., at home. Paulick should have been a sparring partner. He was brusque, sharp, cocky, unrelenting, a mountain of a man with bull shoulders and hands that belonged to a pro football tackle. By rights, Paulick did not even rate a White House press card, for he was not accredited to a newspaper, wire service, network, or magazine. He wrote and edited *D.P.'s Dossier*, a newsletter of fifty thousand circulation which specialized in uncorking Washington scandals. He was as nonpartisan as litmus paper and as incorruptible as Jehovah. He grated on me, probably because I, like all Washington officials, feared him. Yet I respected the bulldozer in him and admired his craftsmanship as I would that of any pro. More than that, I secretly envied him because in Paulick I saw the kind of newspaperman I should have been, but never was.

"We don't know any more about the situation than you do, Dave," I replied. "The President is following the police reports as they come in. We know, naturally, that Stephen Greer has disappeared. Beyond that, we're stymied."

"Is this for direct quotes?" asked a voice in the rear.

"No, the usual paraphrase," I said. "When you can make it a direct quote, I'll tell you."

"But this is big, Gene," complained another.

"Now let's not start arguing ground rules," I said. "They've been good enough around here for three and a half years."

"Has the President spoken to Mrs. Greer?"

"Yes. He expressed his concern to Mrs. Greer and, of course, offered to help in any way he can."

"Will he drive out to the Greer house?"

"No," I said, "but he's invited Mrs. Greer to come here this evening if she feels up to it."

"Look, Gene, can't we quote you direct somehow on just how the President is taking this? After all, the whole country wants to—"

"I know," I said. I glanced at the note pad. The President a few minutes earlier had dictated the sense of what should be said, but had left the phrasing to me. "You can quote me directly on this one thing. I'll take it slow. Quote. 'President Roudebush is deeply concerned. Stephen Greer is one of his best friends as well as a trusted, if unofficial, adviser. Naturally, therefore, the President's concern is a personal one and he looks forward to an early solution.' Unquote."

"That's kind of tame, Gene. Isn't he surprised?"

Surprised? Did that word ever fit any of Paul Roudebush's reactions? I could see the President gazing out of the French doors at the rose garden, and I could see the frown lines of concentration as he talked.

"Yes, of course," I said, "although 'puzzled' is perhaps a better way to say it. None of us knows a thing right now, really."

"Does the President think Greer is alive?" It was Dave Paulick, boring in.

"Yes, Dave, he does. At least, all the early evidence points that way. You've got the police statements. There's no indication of a . . . well, body . . . at Burning Tree, and no evidence on the ground of a scuffle."

"When did the President last talk to him?"

"Tuesday night," I said. I noted a flurry of writing in the raised notebooks. This was the first piece of hard news they had from me. "Greer came to the house after dinner for a talk."

"What about?"

"I don't know."

"Will you check for us, Mr. Secretary?" That was the Baltimore

Sun man. He always called me "Mr. Secretary," mouthing it sardonically as though I did not merit such a lofty title.

"Sure." I made a note on my pad: *Last Talk. Wh?*

"You expect political repercussions?"

I hesitated. I prided myself that never, in more than three years on this impossible job, had I lied intentionally. Several times I relayed information that proved to be misleading, but that was the fault of foul-ups in the system. I could dodge, obfuscate, clam up, but never lie. Actually politics and the campaign had been among my first thoughts when Paulick called me that morning, and they had been on my mind throughout my talk with the President. I had warned him that this type of political question was inevitable. Roudebush merely smiled and said, "Do your best for us."

"I don't speculate on a matter of this kind," I said. "I would hope it would not become a political issue. A man has disappeared and his wife and daughter are disturbed and alarmed."

"You think the Wolcott people won't speculate?" The tone of the question carried its own answer.

"I hope this thing is cleared up very soon, period," I said.

"There's a report that you lunched at Greer's law office yesterday with Greer and Miguel Loomis. What about it?"

The question surprised me. I knew that Miguel, in briefing reporters at the Greer home, had mentioned his own luncheon with Steve, but he had not said I was there. Parenthetically, I was the man who suggested to Mrs. Greer in early morning that she might recruit Miguel to handle the press out at the Greer house, since he was a sharp, competent young man and he knew the family well. Also, I thought the two Greer women could use a man around the house during the trying hours when the publicity would surely attract a flock of crackpots, overly solicitous friends, and curious strangers to Brookside Drive.

I thought fast about the question and could see no reason to evade. "Yes," I said, "I did have lunch with Greer and Miguel Loomis in the law firm's dining room yesterday."

There was another restless stir in the room. This was the second bit of hard news.

"What was the purpose of the lunch?"

"It was somewhat personal on Miguel Loomis's part," I said. "He had a problem and he wanted some advice from Greer and me."

"You say, 'somewhat personal.' Was it also somewhat official?"

"It was at Miguel's request that we met. I think I'll just leave it at that. At any rate, the luncheon discussion had no connection with Greer's later disappearance."

"How did Greer seem to you at lunch, Gene?"

I thought a moment. "Nothing out of the ordinary except perhaps the pressure of time. He spoke of a heavy load of business. Nothing else worth mentioning."

"No tip-offs from him about what happened a few hours later."

"None. I was as surprised this morning as any of you, even though Mrs. Greer called late last night to see if her husband was at the White House. The call meant little to me at the time. But for my reaction this morning, you can check Dave Paulick. He called me out of bed at 7 A.M."

There was a pause, then Paulick said: "Gene, this lunch bit adds mystery to the case. You and Loomis conferred with him on the day he disappeared, but you won't discuss what was said. Why not?"

"Dave, there's no mystery. I imagine Greer talked to a dozen people yesterday on a variety of subjects."

The questions pulsed for another five minutes while Jill stood with her back to the door, guardian nymph of the exit. The inquiries buzzed with irritation, like patrols of mosquitoes. Had the FBI been called in? No. So far no indication of a violation of federal law. Had Mrs. Roudebush called Mrs. Greer? Yes. What was Greer advising on currently? General policy. Had Greer ever been to a psychiatrist? Don't know, but think implications of question are out of order. What did I make of the abandoned golf shoes? Nothing particular. I'd shot a few practice holes myself without changing shoes. Had any tips been phoned to the White House? Yes. Mostly cranks, but the Secret Service recorded them all and passed on a few leads to the police. What did I think of the disappearance?

"He isn't paid to think," said Paulick.

"And that crack sounds as if you've run out of soap," I said with a forced grin. "Thank you, Dave."

"Thank *you*, Mr. Culligan."

Jill, smiling beatifically, opened the door. The herd stampeded to the lobby. Her pale lipstick against white skin made her appear unusually delicate in the rude crush of bodies.

Jill closed the door and turned to me.

"Have I told you today that I'm very fond of you?"

"You sound like my kid sister." Why the hell couldn't she be working in some other office? "Besides, it's not that time of day."

"Tell me more at my place tonight. Butter has a date. Right?"

"Right."

I watched as she settled in her padded swivel chair and faced the phone. The first light winked. "Press," she said. The voice was a feather in a fall of corn-silk hair. She had no business being here, I thought. No business at all.

The buzzer on my green phone, my direct line to the President's office, set off a low, steady drone. When I answered, Grace Lalley said: "Arthur Ingram's waiting. The President says he'd like you in here, if you've finished with the newspapermen."

I turned to Jill. "Front office. Any question about Greer, stick to my transcript. Okay?"

Arthur Ingram was already seated in the oval office when I entered. He nodded to me, curtly, I thought. The CIA director disliked people like me sitting in on conferences involving the Agency. I was half inside, because of my service to the President, and half outside because of my obligations to the press. Although I held top security clearance, I'm sure Ingram considered me a risk, emotional if not patriotic. He sat stiffly upright near a corner of the President's desk. The No. 1 intelligence man was immaculately groomed as always, his trousers sharply creased and his crossed feet shod in cordovans with a gleaming polish. Ingram held his rimless spectacles in his hands, his fingers framing them in a precise, semirectangle. The narrow, tanned face wore an expression of wary confidence as though this were his command post and the President and I were calling at his request. Ingram

was an adroit, intense, aloof man, even though he might conceal
the aloofness behind a shield of congeniality when he entertained
legislators at the Agency. He was also suspicious of others,
whether innately or by the nature of his current trade I did not
know. His personality traits were the opposite of Roudebush's
candor, forthrightness, and warmth. I suppose that is why I always felt on guard in Ingram's presence.

The President was leaning back in his chair, the big hands
clasped on his stomach. His glasses were pushed aloft in the
thatch of gray hair. He grinned at me, but it flashed off quickly.
I sensed a tension in the room.

"Have a chair, Gene," he said. "I've merely told Arthur that I
wanted to discuss the Agency's operations among scientists. Why
don't you just sketch the affair as you did for me yesterday."

"Yes, sir," I said. "Yesterday noon I and Miguel Loomis, the
son of the Educational Micro president, had luncheon in the
Ring Building with Steve, and—"

"Steve?" cut in Ingram. His thin eyebrows were arched.

"Stephen Greer."

"Oh," said Ingram. He managed to impart a dismissive inflection to the word as if to imply that anything involving a man who
vanished in the night was subject to discount. I was puzzled, since
I assumed Ingram had inquired sympathetically about Greer before I came into the room. Thus the name should have been fresh
in his mind.

I told the story as Miguel related it the day before, adding for
Ingram's benefit a few words about the political importance of
Miguel's father, Barney. This last bit was perhaps gratuitous, for
I knew that Ingram followed the nuances of politics as closely as
we did in the White House.

When I finished, Ingram's eyes left mine and went inquiringly
to those of the President. Roudebush lolled informally in his
chair. Ingram sat stiffly erect.

"Well, Arthur," said the President in a pleasant tone, "what
about it?"

"Except for a few unimportant details," said Ingram, "the story
is correct as far as it goes. We initiated the atomic scientists' proj-

ect last fall and used the Spruance Foundation as a conduit for funds."

"I see," said the President. "Does this project have an Agency name?"

"Yes," said Ingram. He colored slightly. "Operation Flycatcher."

I could understand his embarrassment. Both the Agency and the Defense Department had a gift for appending lilting names to their covert undertakings. The blacker the mission, the more euphemistic the label. In this case, one could picture a crested flycatcher standing on a birch limb and pealing his song of spring while young physicists skulked about and conversed in hooded whispers.

"And why was I not informed of this?" asked the President.

"Because of our quite explicit understanding at our first session after you took office," said Ingram swiftly. "I keep a memorandum of our discussion in my desk as a constant guideline. You said you wanted to be consulted on broad policy, on major new undertakings of a sensitive nature, but that you could not and would not deal in day-to-day details of Agency operation."

"Arthur, do you consider the manipulation of young atomic scientists to be a day-to-day detail?" The President's tone was low, curious, rather than hostile.

"I would take exception to the word 'manipulation,' Mr. President," said Ingram. "We supply funds to graduate students who inevitably will swell the nation's reservoir of skilled scientists. In return, we receive—or I should say we are beginning to receive —some valuable information on nuclear developments abroad."

"I don't recall that this ever came before the National Security Council," observed Roudebush.

"No, sir. As I say, I interpreted our understanding as applying to the Council as well."

"Is Operation . . . uh . . . Flycatcher confined to young men, or have you also tried to recruit some of the older nuclear scientists?" asked the President.

"So far," said Ingram, "we have confined it to men working on masters' and doctors' degrees. We hope, of course, that many of these men will continue to serve the Agency throughout their careers. But we did not deem it wise to approach the older physicists, chemists, and engineers at this time. In most cases, their attitudes have . . . well, hardened, shall we say."

"Did you weigh the consequences in the event the Agency's hand was exposed?" asked Roudebush. "The CIA isn't exactly loved abroad as it is."

"Of course, Mr. President." Ingram seldom groped for an answer. "Very few of our recruits yet know the exact connection between Spruance and the Agency, and those who suspect it are, I must say, the kind who place the national interest ahead of personal ambitions in science. Loomis is the first young man to raise a substantial question from an antagonistic viewpoint."

"Who is this Mr. Rimmel, who heads Spruance for you?" asked the President. "A Maury Rimmel is a member at Burning Tree, the one who searched for Steve last night. Is that the man?"

"Yes, sir." Ingram obviously did not intend to amplify that brief answer, but he saw the President's continuing look of inquiry. "A number of businessmen co-operate with us, as you know, some without compensation, some for a fee. Rimmel is paid a fee."

"How much?"

"I don't have the figure in my head, but I believe it is on the order of fourteen or fifteen thousand a year."

"Fifteen thousand to run a nonexistent foundation?" asked the President. "That seems more than ample, to put it mildly."

"He does have to fend off questions about the foundation," said Ingram. He looked down at his glasses as though measuring them. "That takes a certain brand of acumen."

"I see." The conversation lapsed for a moment.

It occurred to me that Ingram would find it quite handy to have a man on a CIA retainer circulating at Burning Tree among its members. The implication was Machiavellian, of course, and I wondered if I were being overly suspicious.

So the President's next comment surprised me.

"I suppose none of Rimmel's fellow members at Burning Tree are aware of his Agency connection," he said.

"I would doubt it," answered Ingram. "As you know, the basic law protects the identity of Agency personnel and, uh, consultants."

"I'm a member, you know," the President said dryly. He paused, then added: "Frankly, I thought the only mystery about Maury Rimmel was whether he really earned his pay as a steel lobbyist."

There was silence again, rather heavy this time. An ordinary American voter, I thought, would never credit this scene: The President of the United States informing his intelligence chief that he was unaware of the CIA connection of a fellow member in a private club. Ingram toyed with his glasses, betraying for the first time a dent in his self-assurance. But he made no comment. The President clasped his hands behind his head and stared up at the ceiling.

"Arthur," he said, "we have more than a question of Intelligence economics here—the value of information obtained per dollar spent, as it were. We have a moral question."

"Just what do you mean, Mr. President?"

"I mean you're in the covert business of twisting young American scientists into something they don't purport to be to their fellows. Science prides itself on open access to all knowledge, from whatever source. Scientists must share, seek, and exchange information in an atmosphere of mutual trust. Now you come along and turn these young men into secret agents whose real mission is to spy on their colleagues, both American and foreign. I'd say that raises a prime ethical issue."

"I disagree with you, Mr. President. The project differs but little from a dozen other highly successful operations of the Agency."

"I wonder." Roudebush studied Ingram for a moment, then turned to me. "How did Mike Loomis put it yesterday, Gene?"

"He said American physics was being 'tainted and corrupted' by the CIA connection," I said. "He contended his friends were being bribed to inform on their colleagues."

Ingram flicked a hostile glance at me. I was the unbidden visitor. "I would say that's a highly emotional verb," he said. "Not very many young men, except perhaps the New Left radicals, would confuse service to their country with bribery. . . . And, of course, in this case, since the boy is half Mexican, I'd say we'd have to consider a latent antipathy for the United States."

"Oh, come now, Arthur." The President smiled briefly. "I don't know the young man, but I do know his father. Miguel Loomis was born and reared here. He's an American who happens to be bilingual because his mother is from Mexico."

"I merely point out a possibility," said Ingram coldly. "I may be doing him an injustice."

"Isn't that beside the point anyway, Arthur?" asked Roudebush. "If there had never been a Miguel Loomis, and I learned of this . . . this venture of yours . . . I'd have very grave reservations."

"I'm sorry we differ, Mr. President," said Ingram.

The President sighed, and I sensed that this abyss between viewpoints was an old one for these men.

"Arthur," said Roudebush, "I can't understand why I wasn't briefed on this operation along with other major Agency undertakings."

"I suppose, Mr. President, I didn't weigh it on the same scales you do." A note of apology slid into Ingram's voice. "In a total budget of a half a billion dollars, some three or four hundred thousand over-all doesn't bulk very large. I assure you, sir, there was no intent to withhold information from you. Perhaps it would be better all around if my future briefings went more thoroughly into minor Agency operations." Ingram stressed the word "minor."

"Yes, I think so," said the President. There was silence again, definitely strained this time. Roudebush arose, pushed his hands into his coat pockets and walked to the French doors. He stood for a moment, gazing at the back of a Secret Service man on duty on the outside walkway.

"Arthur," he said when he turned to us again, "why isn't it possible to obtain the same information you get from the young scientists via normal embassy and Agency channels?"

"I just don't believe we'd get the same kind of result," said

Ingram. "Mr. President, until last fall we had to rely on a rather limited structure for our information on foreign nuclear weapons. We do, of course, have a few—a precious few—agents in nuclear installations abroad. And a number of reputable scientists—again the number is deplorably small—have volunteered information to us after their travels abroad or attendance at international conferences."

Ingram's tone had become confidently professional. He was in his element now. "I am building for the future in Operation Flycatcher."

While I managed to retain a straight face, I wanted to laugh each time I heard that phrase. The thought was a droll one— flycatchers impressed into the muffled legions of espionage—and I wondered what brain at the Agency packaged these dark missions in such festive wrappings.

"I envision the day," Ingram continued, "when vital information will roll into the Agency from several hundred trained scientific agents who have reached top levels of their professions. You must remember, Mr. President, that many eminent American scientists today have a higher loyalty than to the United States. They regard the world of science as a kind of frontier-free society in which information should flow as easily as would commerce around a globe without tariff barriers. We have evidence of imprudent contacts between American and Communist scientists which appear to breach our own security regulations. Frankly, many of these men do not trust any government, including their own. And hundreds of them are still laboring under a guilt complex for having worked on the atomic bomb. I can appreciate this kind of emotional trap, but I can't sympathize with it."

Ingram paused and squared his shoulders. "In sum, Mr. President, I'm trying to indoctrinate a new breed of scientist, with first loyalty to the United States of America. Operation Flycatcher is our vehicle. I think it's an excellent investment of time, money, and energy."

The President had stood by the French doors as he listened. Now he returned to his desk.

"To use your words, Arthur," he said, "I can appreciate your viewpoint here, even if I cannot sympathize with it. Perhaps, from a cold intelligence appraisal, your Flycatcher project makes sense. But I have to look at this from a higher vantage point, one that takes in the whole scope of our relations with the rest of the world. And what I see, I do not like." He looked directly at Ingram. "To be blunt, Arthur, the CIA wouldn't be exactly crippled if we ended this operation?"

"Crippled, no." Ingram flushed under his tan. "Handicapped, yes."

"This thought has been running through my mind," said Roudebush. "Suppose I had a son, and suppose he, as a young physicist, had been approached by your people. What would my son say to me when he found out that the CIA was infiltrating the ranks of his colleagues? And, further, wouldn't he find it incredible when I denied knowledge of the operation? . . . Arthur, there is a corrupting aspect of this that I don't like at all. Not at all. These young men of science are exploring the wide world of knowledge, seeking the essence of matter, the precise nature of the universe. They must be free to test, probe, and weigh. If they are merely to be the subsidized front for old men and old ideas —and by that I mean you and me and our whole generation— then their careers become a sham." The President tilted back in his chair. "I think if I were in Miguel Loomis's shoes, I'd be just as disturbed as he is."

"I take it you want Operation Flycatcher dismantled," said Ingram quietly.

"I do." Roudebush smiled. "Actually, of course, Miguel Loomis has left us no alternative. If CIA support is not withdrawn, he plans to expose the connection publicly."

"He could be handled," said Ingram, leaving the clear implication that President Roudebush could not. "I respect your wishes, sir, and although I do not agree with you, the Spruance support of Flycatcher will be terminated and the project closed down."

Ingram sat perfectly straight in his chair, still framing his spectacles in that neat little half rectangle of fingers.

"Good," said the President. "I appreciate your co-operation, Arthur." The compartment door was closed.

Ingram, sensing it, arose from his chair and folded his unused glasses into the leather case at his breast pocket.

"I'm sorry about Stephen Greer," said Ingram. "I know it must be a shock to you, Mr. President."

I'm the one who felt the shock. It seemed inconceivable to me that Ingram would not have mentioned Greer the moment he entered the President's office.

"Sue Greer is the one I'm worried about," said Roudebush. "So far she's holding up. The whole business is extraordinary. The police don't have a solid clue."

"If the Agency can help in any way, please call me at once," said Ingram.

"Thank you, Arthur. For the moment, I think we should let the police handle the case."

As Roudebush walked Ingram to the door, he indicated by a nod that I was to remain. He returned to sit on the corner of his desk, his favorite informal roost beside the golden donkey pen set. His first remark was unexpected.

"Gene," he said, "I suppose you're going to write your version of this administration someday?"

"I had thought of it, Mr. President. No definite plans, but . . ."

He waved a hand. "I hope you do. You might be the best man. Your position, half fish of the media, half fowl of this office, ought to give you a fairly objective viewpoint. Personally, I can't stand these fawning memoirs that follow the late king like so many paid mourners. Jack Kennedy once said there was no such thing as history. I agree with what I think he meant. But you might come close."

I grinned in relief. "I'm not much for the establishment line anyway."

"Good, I hope you've been keeping notes. On this intelligence matter, you definitely should. I think we're in for quite a time. Who, for instance, would think the CIA director would keep secrets from his boss? . . . Or plant a shifty agent in his locker room?"

We eyed each other. Roudebush grinned, then we both broke into laughter. This man *is* different, I thought. I could imagine the irate explosion of a Dwight Eisenhower or a Lyndon Johnson at a similar revelation. But Roudebush, God bless him, also saw the irony. After our laughter quieted, he became serious again.

"Gene, can you give me one good reason why Ingram should be using graduate students in physics as servants of the Agency?"

"Ingram thinks it's sound," I replied. "But I sure don't. Frankly, Mr. President, in my book that Spruance-Flycatcher operation is a crude, cynical business."

He nodded. "I agree completely with young Loomis. This Flycatcher thing is repellent to me. It's the kind of operation that erodes faith in our own institutions. It is corrupting, and it's nasty, and the man who conceived the idea can't have much appreciation for the values of a free society." He shrugged. "But that's Arthur Ingram. . . . Damn it, just recalling what he said makes my blood pressure go up all over again."

"You didn't show it."

He shook his head. "No, anger is lost on Ingram. We've been over this ground before. He can't see that if we adopt Communist methods in our zeal to contain them, we wind up defeating ourselves, war or no war. What is left of our open society if every man has to fear a secret government agent at his elbow? Who can respect us or believe us when some of our best young scientists go abroad as the instruments of a hidden agency?"

He left the corner of the desk and walked back toward his chair, his head lowered as he scuffed at the carpet.

"The whole CIA has gotten out of hand," he continued. "Subsidizing intellectuals and labor leaders, buying up university research brains, fomenting revolutions, clandestine paramilitary operations—a whole ball of wax that was never contemplated when the Agency was set up to gather vital information abroad. That's its job, and that's all it should be doing. . . . Of course, it's partially my fault. I should have cracked down long ago. But at this desk, there is always some other crisis, crying to be handled at once."

He looked at me as if I could absolve him. Then he smiled

wryly. "And, of course, there's Ingram's personal lobby on the hill and with the press. He's not an easy bird to net for a wing-clipping. . . . What we need is a nice, big, fat victory margin in November. Then we'll see." He paused. "Follow this CIA situation, Gene. Make notes of what I tell you. Someday, when the time is ripe, the country ought to know what went on."

He squared the stack of mail at the side of his desk blotter, a signal that the subject was ended. "Well," he asked, "what questions did the press have about Steve?"

I briefed him on my press conference, but even as I talked, I wondered: Would I have been able to suppress my curiosity about press reactions to the disappearance of an old friend while I philosophized about the CIA? Of course, our talk did involve the son of an influential political supporter. Also, I realized, every President must think and act in compartments like any file clerk or bank vault attendant. First emotions do not necessarily have priority.

There was a knock on the door. The President's stylish, gray-haired secretary, Grace Lalley, tucked her head into the room. "I think you may want to take this one, Mr. President," she said. "It's from Chief Wilson about Mr. Greer." The President nodded, held up a restraining hand when I started to leave, then answered the phone.

He listened a moment, then said as he hung up: "A ten-year-old boy who lives on Burdette Road says he saw a man being helped into a car last night a little after eight o'clock near the Burning Tree fence. The boy isn't sure whether the man entered the car voluntarily or was forced in. He thinks there were a total of three men at the car. The area is not far from the fourth green."

"The fourth is the green where they found Steve's bag," I offered.

The President nodded.

"I suppose that means the FBI," I said.

Roudebush looked up quickly. Apparently he had not considered the implications of the boy's story.

"You mean kidnaping." Roudebush frowned. "Yes, I suppose

it does raise that possibility. Yes, well, I'd better call Deskowicz."

I stood up. "If the FBI comes into it, I'd appreciate a call. I couldn't hold out on the boys on that one."

"Of course not," he said. "I'll get to you in a few minutes."

"Oh, one more thing," I said, remembering my promise at the press conference. "I was asked what you and Greer talked about at your last meeting Tuesday night. Anything I can say, sir?"

Roudebush pondered a moment, the heavy eyebrows knitted. "We talked until late, after midnight. . . ." He hesitated. "No, I think not, Gene. It was a mixture—policy and a personal chat."

"They'll ask, of course, whether there were any indications or hints . . . you know, about anything troubling Steve."

The President pondered again. "Not at all troubled. Full of vinegar and ideas. The same old Steve. . . . You can pass that on if you wish."

"Right."

As I entered my office, Jill handed me a yellow sheet, torn from the UPI ticker.

UPI-184

(Greer-Finance)

New York—Stocks broke sharply today in the wake of the unexplained disappearance of Stephen B. Greer, close friend of President Roudebush.

After drifting lower in early trading, stocks fell in the final two hours under a crush of sell orders.

The New York Stock Exchange composite average dropped $1.37, deepest decline since the airline strike last year. The Dow-Jones averages were off 21.3 points at closing.

Shares on the American Stock Exchange and regional exchanges around the country duplicated the sell-off. Stocks on the West Coast, where markets were still open, were in a steep slide.

Brokers attributed the surge of late selling to the "unsettling Greer news" from Washington, but generally predicted a rally Monday since all business indices still point upward and economists are universally bullish.

8/27—MJJ409PED

"It figured," I said, but I reproved myself for forgetting possible market reactions. I could have at least asked the President whether we should comment.

It was an hour later when I received my expected call from the President. I turned to my typewriter, rattled off my two-finger ballet, then asked Jill to summon the troops again. This time she walked out into the main west wing lobby.

"Mr. Culligan again," she called. The words floated elegantly over the leather lounges. She could have been announcing a fashion show.

The army, only slightly depleted, clattered into my office, emptying the press room and the lobby.

"All in," said Jill from her post at the door.

Dave Paulick stationed himself directly in front of me. "There's a Greer sell-off on the market," he said.

"I know," I replied. "We're not commenting on Wall Street." I held up the sheet on which I had been typing. "I'll just read this."

"Quote. 'President Roudebush has requested the Federal Bureau of Investigation to join the search for Stephen B. Greer. The President made his request after receiving information from Chief Thad Wilson of Metropolitan Police that two men had been observed helping another into a car Thursday night on Burdette Road near the Burning Tree area where Mr. Greer's golf clubs were found. FBI Director Peter Deskowicz has assigned a task force of special agents to the investigation, which is being pursued under provisions of the federal kidnap law. This does not mean that we believe Greer was kidnaped. It is merely a possibility being explored. The President urges all law enforcement agencies to co-operate fully with the FBI.' Close quote. . . . That's it."

"How large a task force, Gene?"

"I don't know yet. Sufficient for the job."

"Who's the special agent in charge?"

"I'll try to get you the name tomorrow."

"You promised to find out about the President's last talk with Greer Tuesday night. Any luck?"

"I don't disclose what the President discusses in private," I replied, "but as for Greer's attitude, the President said Greer was not worried or upset. He was in a cheerful mood and presented his usual quota of ideas. In other words, normal in all respects."

"Will the President receive reports from Chief Wilson tonight?"

"Yes, if anything significant turns up. The same goes for Director Deskowicz."

"Is the lid on, Gene?"

"The lid's on until 9:30 A.M. tomorrow. If that changes, we'll phone the list in plenty of time."

Jill opened the door and squeezed against the wall as the troops elbowed by her. For a change, only one man in the exiting throng took the time to tell her she ought to get her hair cut.

Dave Paulick remained stubbornly rooted in front of my desk.

"I'm giving notice," he said. "You're entitled. I'm doing nothing but Greer for the duration."

"Good luck," I said. "If you hear anything you can't print, let me know."

"I hear lots about an Irishman and a girl who works for him," said Paulick. "I could print something about that affair, but I don't. Shows my deep consideration for my friends."

"Your deep consideration for the libel laws, you mean." I forced myself to grin. "Okay, Greer expert, call me anytime. But not after one at night and not before seven forty-five in the morning."

"I promise nothing."

"You wouldn't."

He half turned away, then checked the swing of those bull shoulders. He stared at me, shaking his head. "I don't get you, Gene. You act like this is just another routine story. I think not. I think it may be the biggest piece of news since I hit this rat-race town."

"Frankly, Dave, I've been too busy to figure out what I do think."

"Yeah," he said, and he left the office trailing incredulity.

But I spoke the truth. And now, free at last and with Jill manacled again to the telephone, I swung around and gazed over the front lawn, shaded by the great elms from the lowering sun. Stephen Greer had vanished, swallowed up by the night at the edge of a golf course! It was preposterous. I reached into my memory for everything I knew about Steve, starting with our first meeting in the campaign and ending with the recollection of his nervousness and his obsession with his wrist watch yesterday. What did I know? I sat for perhaps a half hour before I realized, with a start, that I knew very little about the disappearance or even about the real Greer. For the first time since I came to the White House, a major national event was unfolding far beyond me, as in a distant, misted valley. I had no knowledge, no source, no intuition. It was an unnerving feeling.

"Gene," called Jill softly. "It's time to go. It's almost dark."

The shadows of the great elms were blotting the lawn when we finally closed up shop and went home.

4

Stanley Wolcott fingered the long glass of gin and Bitter Lemon, shook it slightly to make the ice tinkle. He sat in his leather armchair in the study of the governor's mansion at Springfield, Illinois. Despite the even, air-conditioned coolness, he felt uncomfortable. His new role chafed him like an over-starched collar.

Everyone, even his old friends, addressed him with a new restraint, a subtle deference, since his nomination at Houston as the party's candidate to oppose President Roudebush's bid for re-election. The deference was absurd, he thought, as if a plumber were being introduced as a sanitary engineer. For he was the famous "sacrifice" candidate, his chances of defeating Roudebush being rated from minimal to zero. The first postconvention polls, the Gallup and the Harris, were close to agreement. Gallup, as of mid-August, gave him a probable 38 per cent of the November vote, the Harris survey 36.7 per cent. Wolcott was not disheartened. He had expected this. He would do his best for the party without taking any years off his life. He prided himself on being a realist.

So did Matthew Silkworth, his campaign manager, who sat opposite him, hunched over a scotch-and-water. Silkworth was a squat man with wiry black hair and a perpetual jaw shadow. His self-proclaimed pessimism was contaminated by quivering energy. Any man in constant motion must be propelled subconsciously toward optimism. No matter what the mind cautioned, the body demanded action and action sometimes influenced events. Wolcott enjoyed Silkworth's unvarnished estimates of the party's plight. If nothing else, Matty was a reminder to the candidate that the campaign had nowhere to go but up.

"Despite the six-o'clock news," said Wolcott, "I think there's a woman involved."

"Don't be too sure, Governor." Even in thought Silkworth was taut, wary.

"Matty, for the last time, quit calling me 'Governor.' The name is Stan—S-T-A-N."

"All right, Stan, but the first signs in Washington don't read 'broad' to me. This Greer is a cool, steady, uptown operator. If he were involved in an affair, he'd have it with discretion. Hell, he's got too much to lose. The umpteen times his name gets coupled with Roudebush's in the papers is worth three, four hundred grand a year in legal fees."

"You think it may be a kidnaping, then?" asked Wolcott.

Silkworth tilted his head as he reflected. "Could be, but all we've got to go on thus far is a report from some imaginative kid who says he's seen something or other in the half-dark. If it was a kidnaping, why didn't the ground around that fourth green show some evidence of a scuffle? And only psychos would try to kidnap the President's best friend."

"The country has its share of those, Matty."

"Sure, sure, but if it's a kidnaping, we'll find out soon enough," said Silkworth. "If they grab a guy, they want money or maybe revenge or notoriety. Whatever the motive, they've got to let it be known soon that they have Greer."

Silkworth thought a moment, then leaned forward and shook a finger at his candidate. "You know something, Stan? We want to pray it isn't a kidnaping. That's the one thing that helps Roudebush. Dead or alive, a kidnaped Greer creates sympathy for the family and friends, including the man in the White House."

"I wasn't thinking of political advantage, Matty."

Silkworth shot a dubious glance at the governor. Was he serious? He was not sure about this man, even after several years of working with him. These global thinkers became so entangled in a web of altruism and world betterment that sometimes they failed to recognize self-interest when it dangled before their eyes.

"Whatever you think, or I think," said Silkworth, "the case of

Mr. Greer could mean a hell of a lot of campaign mileage for our side. Think a minute, Stan. Why would a pillar of the community suddenly drop out of sight? A broad, maybe. But if Greer ducked out with a woman, it'll be a draw politically. For every housewife who gets riled at the President for having a friend who can't control his glands, there'll be another voter who'll feel sorry for Roudebush. Fooling around with women never hurt a candidate. Remember Harding and Grover Cleveland. . . . But look at the other reasons a guy vanishes. For one thing, he could have blown a fuse." Silkworth tapped his head.

"I'd hate to wish that on Mrs. Greer or Paul Roudebush," said Wolcott. He shifted in his chair.

"But anything mental is a plus for us," said Silkworth. "People get nervous over these psycho cases. They'll wonder why Roudebush didn't discover the symptoms himself and what kind of life-and-death matters this unbalanced guy was advising the President on." He took a swallow of scotch, then lit a cigarette. "Or maybe Greer is ducking some big financial scandal that would ruin him and maybe reflect badly on his friend, Roudebush. This is a hot possibility for us. The newspapers would eat it up. Roudebush would be up to his ass in denials, explanations, and alibis all through the campaign."

"You're a ghoul, Matty," said Wolcott.

"I'm a realist," said Silkworth, "the thing you think you are, but aren't. . . . Oh, there are plenty of other possibilities. Greer's afflicted with temporary amnesia, he's a secret fag who's been found out, or he's a Communist who's defecting to Russia." He swallowed more scotch. "Or he's a practical joker and this is his idea of a gag. Maybe he's meeting secretly with the Black Muslims to try to stave off an armed Negro revolt. Or he could have stopped in at somebody's house for a snort and drunk himself into a stupor. Hell, the list is endless."

"Of course," mused Wolcott, "there's one very likely possibility. Greer might have felt a heart attack coming on, walked out to the road and then gotten picked up by people who robbed him or perhaps even murdered him."

"Could be," said Silkworth, "in which case it'll all be over in a couple of days. But it doesn't look like it. Remember, wearing street shoes on a golf course, the clubs left in plain sight, the keys in the car so it could be driven away. All that looks like he planned to take off."

"I'd forgotten," said Wolcott. "Actually, the clues do point that way, don't they?"

Silkworth nodded. "Which means he's mentally disturbed, there's a dame, or it's money trouble. Personally, I'd give odds it's something involving money. I wish we could get a list of his law clients—and what he really does for them."

Wolcott smiled. "Is the wish fathering offspring now? You may be blowing up this incident all out of proportion."

"Maybe. Maybe not." Silkworth drained his drink. "Look at the market today. This could be big, very big. It's the first campaign break we've had, and Christ knows, we need one."

"With that profane statement, I agree."

"On my horse." Silkworth snubbed out his cigarette and stood up. "I'll put out a couple of lines in Washington. This one we've got to watch closely."

Wolcott arose and placed a hand on his manager's shoulder. "No sensational speculations by our people, Matty. We should be quite circumspect until the facts are in."

Silkworth's shadowed jaw emphasized his grin. "Don't worry. All I want right now is information, so we can be ready when and if."

They parted with a handshake, and when Silkworth left, Governor Wolcott switched on the television set for an eight-o'clock news program. He had to know the latest about Greer. Also, to be honest with himself, he knew he would be dismayed if Greer turned up with an easy explanation. And, as for that thought, well, he was glad that Matty could not read his mind.

Peter Deskowicz sat in his office in the new FBI building on Pennsylvania Avenue. The room was small. There was just enough space between his desk and the wall for the folds of the American flag. On the other side, bookcases huddled comfortably close. On the window ledge, behind his right shoulder, rested a mounted seal of the Bureau, the shield with scales of justice above the words, "Fidelity, Bravery, Integrity." Deskowicz would have felt lost in the baronial sweep which his predecessor inherited from J. Edgar Hoover at the old Bureau quarters. Pete Deskowicz liked to feel snug, his books within easy reach and his caller directly in front of him.

The present caller, Special Agent Clyde Moorhead, held a sheaf of papers on his lap.

"Plenty here," said Moorhead. "Greer had a full field three years ago when the President wanted him cleared for defense policy meetings."

Deskowicz fingered his own copy of the investigative file. He was a stout, wan, deliberate man whose instinct for caution guided him through the reefs of bureaucratic struggle. He had devoted his life to the Bureau before Roudebush picked him as the director. He was without flair, had known few vaulting leaps of intuition, but he was painstaking at detail and acclaimed by his colleagues as the steadiest, most exhaustive investigator in the Bureau.

"I've spent an hour on this," said Deskowicz, "but it doesn't help much. . . . Are we all squared away?"

"Yes," said Moorhead. He was a husky man, a former University of Wisconsin linebacker, an accountant, and a lawyer. Although he joked about his work and bantered with other agents, the Bureau's stamp of competency was solid upon him. "All offices are alerted, and I've picked twenty-five agents for the special detail out of here."

Deskowicz leaned back in his chair. "Clyde, you know how sensitive this is. With the President up for re-election, and Wolcott's people scratching around for anything that might damage Roudebush . . . Well, I don't like it. We're on the spot."

"I know what you mean," said Moorhead. These political cases were always sticky.

"So I want some added precautions," said Deskowicz. "For one thing, you're to report directly to me and not through the usual."

"You mean I'm by-passing Fred?" Moorhead looked puzzled. Special details always worked through Deskowicz's right-hand man, the associate director.

"Yes. I've told Fred and he understands. I don't like these short-circuits, but . . ." He shrugged. "The President will feel more comfortable the fewer people we cut into the Greer case. . . . Also, I want everything passed directly to you. No handing reports around among the agents or cross-checking information."

"Now, wait a minute, Pete," protested Moorhead. "That's a rough restriction. We always get dupes of all reports. In fact, I was going to pick a co-ordinator who could pass on new leads as fast as they come in. It's the Bureau method."

"I know." Deskowicz was torn. "I hate to change the drill, but this is different. Every agent reports directly to you. You're your own co-ordinator. And no cross-checking below you."

"It'll take five times as long," Moorhead failed to keep the reproof from his voice. "And it's bad for morale. The men will feel they're not being trusted."

"I can't help it." Deskowicz's pale face reflected frustration. "Blame it on the White House. I'm not a free agent this time—if I ever was."

"Okay." Moorhead said it with feigned enthusiasm, seeking to dispel his superior's gloom. "What about getting Greer's tax returns from IRS? I always like to start with fundamentals—the buck and the bed. I can handle Greer's bed life, but I need help on his money."

"Umm." Deskowicz made a note on a pad. "I'll have to check that out first with the 'man.'" He thought a moment, then made another note. "Let's call the Greer case 'Ajax.'"

Moorhead stood up. "I'd better get with it," he said, adding caustically, "if we want to clean up Ajax by Christmas."

"I hate to hobble you," said Deskowicz, "but this is sensitive with a capital S."

Moorhead grinned. "Okay. Just remember that I want to be promoted to saint when I come up with the miracle."

The director escorted the younger man to the door. "I want the first break yesterday, St. Clyde."

Hilstratter switched on the muted, indirect lighting. His conference with Tomlin and DeLuca was running late in Hilstratter's paneled office. The only senior partner absent was Stephen B. Greer.

"So we've got three problems," said Hilstratter. He walked to the window ledge and looked out. Below him was the statue of Longfellow in the little triangular park formed by a junction of Connecticut Avenue, M Street, and 18th Street. The sidewalk lights had just come on.

"The Bureau ought to have access to anything it wants in Steve's office," said DeLuca. His dark complexion seemed to blend with the oak paneling.

"Except the file cabinet," amended Hilstratter. "Steve has all the working papers on Ed-Mike's taxes. One look at the figures on Educational Micro's accelerated depreciation, and the government would have a certain tax action against Barney Loomis's company. It could murder our client."

DeLuca shook his head. "The Bureau doesn't work that way, Bill. If the agents give you a pledge to disregard extraneous matter, they'll honor it." DeLuca, a former FBI agent, customarily had the last word on any matter involving his old employer.

Hilstratter, a spare, bony man, tugged at his open shirt collar. "I grant that, Luke, but one agent with a long memory for that file could play hell with us a couple of years from now."

"What else is in the cabinet?" asked Tomlin. "Anybody know?"

There was no response, and Hilstratter reached for his phone. "I'll call Helen," he said. The other two men waited while Hilstratter talked with Greer's secretary.

"There's no reason for any outsider to go into Steve's file cabinet," said Hilstratter when he hung up. "Helen says there isn't a single personal paper in it. All firm business. In addition to Ed-Mike, there's Lennox Chemical and that damned messy Pav-X contract with the Air Force. I, for one, am dead set against opening that file cabinet to any one."

"All right." DeLuca yielded. In Greer's absence, Hilstratter's decision was final.

"So the cabinet's off limits," said Tomlin. "Where's his personal stuff?"

"Helen says most of it is in his desk drawers," said Hilstratter. "But he keeps some things in the small safe. Only Steve and his daughter, Gretchen, have the combination."

"What's in the safe?" asked DeLuca. The former agent's curiosity was quickly aroused.

"His own business contracts and special papers," said Hilstratter. He hesitated, then said uneasily, "And cash."

"Cash!" echoed DeLuca. "How much, for God's sake?"

Hilstratter shook his head. "Helen doesn't know."

"Why so excited, Luke?" asked Tomlin. "What's wrong with cash?"

"Cash in large amounts always looks suspicious to the public," said DeLuca. "Especially for a credit-card man like Steve. . . . I never knew he kept money in his office safe. Did either of you?"

Both men shook their heads. The silence was uncomfortable. A curtain was being drawn slowly from the picture of a man they thought they knew intimately, and suddenly a nick—was it a blemish?—appeared.

"I don't like it," said DeLuca, the firm's spokesman on public relations matters. "I can see the headline, 'Find 50 G's in Greer Office Safe.' . . . We'd look like some crooked union headquarters."

Again there was silence, broken by Hilstratter. "I think we have to leave it up to Gretchen. No reporters or police, but if the FBI insists on looking into the safe, it's up to her. After all, she's the only person besides Steve with the combination."

"I still don't like it," said DeLuca.

"Neither do I, Luke," said Tomlin. "But Bill's right. It's between Gretchen and the Bureau."

"Now what about the police?" asked Hilstratter. "That detective who talked to us today will want to look at Steve's office tomorrow. I'm not happy about two crews—the FBI and the police—making an airport terminal out of this place."

"Still, we don't want to offend Chief Wilson," said Tomlin.

"Why don't you ask the chief, as a personal favor, to let the Bureau handle Steve's office?" DeLuca asked Hilstratter.

"Good idea," said Hilstratter, "but if he gets touchy about it, we'll just have to let them two-platoon us. . . . Okay, now how about the press?"

"I've had at least thirty calls today," said DeLuca. "And already CBS wants to put a camera crew in here for an inside look at Steve's working quarters."

"That's out," said Hilstratter. "This is a law office, not a TV studio."

"A couple of junior partners think it would be good publicity," observed Tomlin.

"That kind we don't need, Tommy," said Hilstratter. "Reading the firm's name in every edition and hearing it on the radio is too much already. Our kind of clients will get the jitters. My feeling is, no cameras or news pictures up here. The building, the hall, we can't stop them. Okay?"

The two other partners nodded. "Now," continued Hilstratter, "anything the firm feels obliged to say, Luke will be the spokesman."

"How about interviews?" asked DeLuca. "If this goes on very long, newspapermen will be trying to talk to everybody up here. Including secretaries, that's fifty-two people."

"We can't repeal the first amendment," said Hilstratter. "No ban on interviews. We'd get a black eye, if we did."

"Agreed," said Tomlin.

"However, Luke," said Hilstratter, "you ought to pass the word tomorrow that we'd appreciate discretion when discussing Greer, with the press or anyone else."

He stood up and stretched, then began drawing up his tie. His two partners made ready to leave.

"What's your guess about Steve, Bill?" asked DeLuca.

Hilstratter thought while he took his suit coat from the hall tree and shoved his long arms into the sleeves. "I really don't have one." He paused. "I thought I knew Steve like a brother. Now I don't know. I don't know at all."

Tomlin and DeLuca returned to their offices, then met by the elevator.

"What do you think, Tommy?" asked DeLuca.

"I'm with Bill. I don't know. All the clues at the club look as if Steve intended to disappear. But those in the office point just the opposite way. Take Steve's desk calendar. It's loaded with appointments for today and next week, all in his own handwriting."

"I know. There's nothing solid."

"That cash in the safe worries me," said Tomlin. "Suppose he has a hundred grand in there?"

"If he does," said DeLuca, "there'll be hell to pay in the papers. In that case, Gretchen ought to take the money and bet a couple of thousand on Stanley Wolcott to win in November."

In many homes around the country that night people studied the television shots and the front-page pictures of Stephen Greer. An AP wirephoto was the most widely used in the newspapers, since it placed the missing attorney in an appropriate environment. The photo showed Greer completing a drive on the first tee at Burning Tree. The No. 1 wood was rising over his left shoulder and he was grinning as though watching a long, straight flight of the ball. But every golfer noted that Greer was off balance. He had probably sliced, they surmised, and promptly lost the grin. Women noticed the high forehead, the beginnings of baldness. They also noted a resolution in the stance, a certain sensitivity about the mouth, and they decided they liked him. Men, with less analysis, felt Greer was a man they might trust.

In a small, stone house of French Provençal style on Battle Road in Princeton, New Jersey, Deborah Kissich showed the picture to her husband, Felix. Shadows from the sinking sun gathered on the gracious sweep of lawn and the great oaks and sycamores began to merge with the coming night. Felix Kissich had worked late at the Forrestal Laboratory that evening, and now he was sipping ale as he sat in his favorite chair, an enormous pit of scarred leather.

She folded the afternoon newspaper into a slab with Greer's picture extending across three columns, handed it to her husband, and stood behind the battered chair.

"Isn't that the man who came here to the house last fall?" she asked.

Kissich adjusted his steel-frame glasses and peered at the picture of the happy golfer.

"It does resemble him remarkably." He still spoke with a trace of Hungarian accent. Years in the United States had not erased it completely. "But no." He pointed to the face in the photograph. "See, Deb, these eyes are different. They are set wide apart. The man who visited here had eyes very close together. And his chin was more pointed. . . . Still, the two men do look much alike. It would be easy to confuse them."

"I'd have sworn it was the same man," she said. Standing behind him, she gently kneaded his neck. "What was his name? That man last fall?"

"Martin, Morton," he said. "Something-or-other Morton, I think. My memory isn't what it was. Mr. Something Morton from the National Science Foundation. And what a crazy idea that one brought. The government wasted our time."

She leaned from behind and kissed his cheek. It was grooved with age now. "You need new glasses again, dear," she said. "If Mr. Greer isn't Mr. Morton, they're twins."

"I doubt it," he said. "You only saw him for a minute before you went up to bed. He and I talked in the den until late." He tapped the newspaper again. "The eyes and chin. Much different."

"Maybe," she said. She sounded unconvinced. "All I know is that when I saw the picture, and then looked at him on television, I knew I had seen him somewhere."

"Probably many times on TV," he said. "A close friend of the President, like this Greer, must be seen by the camera very often."

"Yes," she said. "That's probably it. But I'd know for certain if he were here right now. Every person has his peculiarities—even his own smell sometimes—that aren't forgotten."

He laughed and turned to kiss her. "Yes, that's true. And you, you always smell so wonderful."

"Vunderful," she said, mimicking him, "is such a wery nice
word."

Gretchen Greer helped her mother out of the light green summer coat and gave her a quick, reassuring hug. Susannah Greer
had been quite calm on the ride home from the White House, but
then, as they drove past Brookside's bloomless cherry trees and
turned into the driveway of the house, tears came. Gretchen had
waited quietly in the car while her mother fussed through her
cluttered handbag, searching for a handkerchief.

"You're great, Mother," said Gretchen. "I'm proud of you."

"I'm so glad you're here, Gretchen. I hope you can stay a few
days."

"As many as you need me," said Gretchen. "I called the office
this afternoon and asked to take my vacation now. No problem.
They're understanding people."

"Coffee?"

"Please. And don't forget the cream."

Susannah brewed the coffee and then they settled in the living
room, Sue on the floor and Gretchen in Steve's armchair, where
Sue had huddled last night, waiting. It comforted Sue to have her
daughter near her. Gretchen was almost a young feminine version of Steve, tall, broad in the shoulders, the same light brown
hair Steve once had, the same widely spaced gray eyes, the same
sense of permanence. Gretchen was a stately, sober girl. None of
those zany, wayward fits that seized Steve occasionally. Where
had they gone in the mysterious fusing of the genes?

Sue was thankful that Brookside Drive was quiet now. The
newspapermen had been considerate. Miguel Loomis had reached
an agreement with them. They withdrew from Brookside at nightfall in return for Miguel's promise to see them again tomorrow
morning and report any significant development during the night.
Gene Culligan had been wise, so right to recommend Miguel
for the press chore. The young man handled the assignment
instinctively. She knew she would have come apart if she had to
face the barrage of questioning herself.

And it was thoughtful of the President to order Secret Service protection for the house. Don Sheehan, the quiet, solid chief of the White House detail, had come to the house personally to make the arrangements. She could see a tall figure outside now, strolling back and forth along the curb. She assumed that the Secret Service guard stretched the letter of the law—wasn't it only supposed to protect the President, Vice President, and visiting statesmen?—but when the President extended the offer, she welcomed it.

"Is the President always like that now?" asked Gretchen. "I haven't seen him in more than two years."

"Is he always like what, dear? He couldn't have been nicer."

"Oh, I don't know," said Gretchen. "Kind of distant, I guess. All the time he was trying to comfort us, you especially, I had the feeling his mind was on other things. He wasn't, well, natural, if you know what I mean."

Did Sue know? Paul Roudebush had changed in these last years. More preoccupied, more withdrawn after his first ebullient greetings, less given to banter. But had he been more so tonight? She did not know for sure, although she, like Gretchen, had sensed a certain air of detachment about the President as they talked in the oval sitting room upstairs.

"I suppose the White House changes everyone who lives there," said Sue. "Yes, he is different now."

"I can't stand Ellen Roudebush," said Gretchen. "There's something—oh, I don't know—kind of hollow and phony about her."

"Ellen is always playing a role, dear. She is not quite sure who she is." Sue surprised herself at describing the President's wife so aptly. She had been relieved when Ellen left the oval room after only a few minutes. "She means well."

"That one," said Gretchen, dismissing Mrs. Roudebush from mind. "I don't think the President asked enough questions. After all, his closest friend—to say nothing of your husband and my father—has suddenly disappeared."

"Yes, he did, Gretchen," said Sue. "He wanted to know when you arrived, what I did before I called Burning Tree, why it was

Maury Rimmel who called the police, whether reporters pestered us, all those things."

"But nothing about what we might know or suspect," said Gretchen. "And actually, Mother, he never told us what his own theory was."

No, thought Sue, Paul had not. She had wondered about that as they were leaving and the President, linking his arms in theirs, escorted them to the private elevator.

"Except for the remark about kidnaping," Sue added aloud as a postscript to her thoughts. "He did say that while the evidence didn't indicate kidnaping, he was happier to have the FBI on the case."

"Yes, but he never said what *he* thought." Gretchen balanced the coffee cup and saucer on the arm of the chair.

"I wish you wouldn't do that, Gretchen," said Sue automatically. "It's going to spill all over the rug."

Gretchen smiled. "Same old mother." But she placed the dishes on the occasional table. "And what do you think, Mother? You haven't really said."

Actually, at the moment, Sue was thinking of her daughter. She might have succumbed to panic in this house tonight if Gretchen had not been here with her. Gretchen, so resembling Steve, had seemed totally mature since she was seventeen, more a friend than a daughter, a woman Sue instinctively leaned on. Their exchanges of confidence were those of equals.

"So?" insisted Gretchen.

"I don't know. I'm so confused, Gretchen." Sue lit a cigarette and reached toward her coffee, then changed her mind. She just had to sleep tonight. Not a wink since she awakened yesterday morning. Yesterday? Thursday? It seemed a year ago. Her mind was woolly, her thoughts tangled.

"That anonymous phone call keeps worrying me," said Sue. "I suppose I should have told the President about it. The man frightened me. That curt voice, no name, hanging up right away."

Sue related the details again, including how she marked the exact time of 12:10 A.M.

Gretchen repeated the main phrases slowly: *"Don't worry. Have faith in me. I'll return when I can, but it may take time."* She frowned as she pondered, then said: "But that could have been a kidnaper, or maybe some lunatic who . . . well . . . beat Dad up and then decided to torment you for some crazy reason."

Sue shook her head. "No. You see your father's pet name for me was used. He's never used it in the presence of others. And Steve wouldn't mention it to anyone who took him by force. They would have no way of knowing it."

"What was it, Mother?"

"Oh, it's too silly," said Sue. "It doesn't mean a thing to anybody else. Just one of those nonsense names."

"Oh." A veil lowered between them. It gave Gretchen a start to remember that her father was also her mother's lover. She felt shut out.

"It's not one of those lewd things," said Sue quickly. Not quite, she thought. It was on their honeymoon, wasn't it, when Steve said she tumbled about like a lion cub? So "Cubby" it became.

"Just a nickname Steve has used for years," she added.

"I understand," said Gretchen. But she did not. She had tried that afternoon to piece together an objective picture of her father. All her life Stephen Greer had been a quarter friend to her, a quarter effortless authoritarian, and half stranger. She knew she could never feel as keenly about her father, whether in disappearance or death, as her mother did.

"But you see," said Sue, "the use of that name means that your father was somewhere with people he trusted. And if that's true, then I think, well, he . . ."

"Planned to go away?" asked Gretchen.

Sue nodded and snubbed out her cigarette.

"But why, Mother? Did you and Dad have a quarrel? Was there anything wrong between you?"

"No, no, nothing. Actually . . ." Sue was on the verge of revealing her anticipation last night, but she checked herself. That would mean explaining the whole, intimate Thursday-night mood and routine, and she could not do that, even to Gretchen.

"Actually," she concluded lamely, "Steve and I have always gotten along much better than most."

"And that means? What?"

"Well, as man and woman."

"Mother," said Gretchen sternly, "for God's sake, don't be old-fashioned with me. Do you mean sexually?"

Sue smiled. "What a dreary way of putting it! . . . But, yes, we were . . . are . . . quite happy."

"Then why? Why did Dad just walk off?"

"I . . . I don't know. Oh, Gretchen." Sue's lips trembled, and Gretchen reached down to cup her mother's face in her hands.

There were so many possible answers, thought Gretchen. For hours they had pelted her mind like hail. Some were ugly possibilities for this vulnerable woman below her. Gretchen could not mention them until she knew much, much more.

"What time is that FBI agent coming tomorrow?" she asked.

"Nine-thirty," said Sue. "It will be an ordeal. He wants a couple of hours with each of us."

"Are you going to tell him about the message?"

"Should I?"

"Yes," said Gretchen. "I think you should. Both of us ought to be completely frank and helpful. There's nothing to cover up about Dad, and even if there were, we'd just get trapped trying to lie." She paused. "Except the office safe. I'm not sure about that."

Sue was instantly troubled. "What safe?"

"The one in Dad's office," said Gretchen.

"Oh." Sue felt an odd sinking sensation. Had she ever heard of a safe in Steve's office?

"I suppose the agents will want to look through it," said Gretchen, "but I haven't the vaguest what's there. When Dad gave me the combination, he said I should use it only in case of his death or an emergency involving him. He did say there was some cash there."

"Cash?" echoed Sue. She was mystified. "How much?"

"I don't know. His idea was for payment of funeral expenses and to keep you in running funds until they probated the will."

Sue flinched. "Funeral expenses!" Then she smiled. "How like Steve. Your father thinks of everything." But in her gratitude for his thoughtfulness, Sue was aware, there was a thorn of irritation. Steve could have at least mentioned the safe to her. Did he think her so frail that even the idea of his death would shatter her? Her husband had misjudged her. A drop of strangeness fell.

"But there's plenty of money," Sue added. "Our joint checking account, my household checking, and five or six thousand in my savings."

"Then," said Gretchen, "we won't need the money in the safe. But I suppose I ought to tell the agents about it, and if they want me to, I'll open it up."

"All right. Whatever you say, Gretchen."

And they went to bed, Gretchen thinking of the pet nickname that linked her mother and father in a bond she could not know, and Susannah thinking of the cash in a safe that Steve had never mentioned to her. Had he returned that moment, Stephen Greer would have found himself partially a stranger in his own home.

In bed, drifting fitfully toward sleep, Sue once came awake with a start. She had, she realized, been thinking of Steve—in the past tense.

It was almost midnight as the rented Carey Cadillac left the Thomas E. Dewey Thruway and rolled northeast on the Connecticut Turnpike.

Brady Manship slumped in a softly upholstered corner and watched the chauffeur slide the car into the left lane for the long run to Southport. He was tired to the bone.

He had worked late at the office after the market closed on the final surge of sell orders. As a speculator, primarily in oils and electronics, he had felt the sudden pressure on the blues as he would a heavy hand on the shoulder. Sell Jersey Standard, sell Gulf, sell Mobil, IBM, National Cash Register, and Educational Micro. He had bought on the first downside move, but then the market buckled as though pounded by an air hammer, and he held off. When the market closed at three-thirty that afternoon, he was $45,000 poorer than when he left home.

He switched on the overhead light and took from his inner breast pocket the little black notebook in which he recorded his transactions for the day. What worried him most were the entries under "Dragon," the American Stock Exchange nickname for Educational Micro. The brokers called it Dragon because when Educational Micro shifted, it moved quickly, powerfully, unpredictably, a fire breather on the rest of the market. For one thing, Educational Micro's market was thin for such a large concern. A few individuals held huge blocks of stock from which they traded but seldom and then only in bits and pieces of one hundred to five hundred shares. Another cause for Educational Micro's volatile nature was its ambitious new product research. Some of its discoveries were as spectacular as DuPont's. Others proved to be flops. Either way, when the news came out, Dragon lurched violently up or down. Dragon had been good to Brady Manship in recent months. He had made money on all but a few of its shifts, anticipating correctly in which direction it would move. But today he had guessed wrong. He had bought at noon, after Educational Micro eased ⅝ths in the morning, but Dragon continued to fall, closing at 55⅛th, off two points from Thursday's last quote.

Then at dinner tonight at the Bankers Club he heard disturbing news. The club, normally dead as a tomb at night, had a feverish air. Brokers and traders were working late, tidying up the debris left by the "Greer day," and their faces reflected crumpled weekend plans of the sailors, golfers, and beach club devotees. Manship dined with Bruce Folliard, a specialist in electronics stocks who spent his working days pacing in a small circle near a post on the American floor. Folliard, loosened by a few scotch mists, spoke in his veiled way of special pressure on Dragon. While words became tiny masks for facts when Folliard talked business, he did imply that a single source was selling fifteen thousand Dragon through several brokers. Fifteen thousand shares! In the thin Educational Micro market, where not more than five thousand shares traded on a typical day, fifteen thousand was an enormous block. Brady had to go back many months to recall an offer of that size. This meant that Dragon would continue lurching downside on Monday. Manship managed to conceal his concern from Folliard, but the news struck him like a slug in the stomach. Manship was heavy in Educational Micro.

Who was selling fifteen thousand Dragon and why? This whole Greer day had been nutty on Wall Street, one of those inexplicable psychological movements, like a freak tidal wave from an uncharted storm. All the indices were up, magnets for the long "Roudebush" bull market. Then a friend of the President of the United States disappeared and the traders went crazy, their subterranean fears boiling through a surface fissure. Ignored were freight car loadings, housing starts, steel output, auto production, all up.

But fifteen thousand Dragon? Suddenly Manship remembered a shred of conversation, one of those thousands of facts and rumors that he tucked away in his memory like piled bric-a-brac in a basement. It had been about two weeks ago at lunch at the same club, at a table near the window. Somebody—who was it? Someone knowledgeable, he knew—said he had it from the grapevine that Educational Micro was dickering to acquire Carib Oil. Carib was a small, profitable Caribbean refinery, while Educational Micro, Inc., was the leader of the new glamour industry —micro texts for schools. Microfiche, which could put the whole Bible on a three-by-five card for use in a cheap viewer, had revolutionized the publishing business. The rumor was that Educational Micro, seeking to diversify, would swallow Carib Oil at a bargain gulp. The deal, it was said that day at lunch, would be handled by Greer, Hilstratter, Tomlin & DeLuca, the most politically invulnerable law firm in the country right now. Greer's closeness to Barney Loomis of Educational Micro, thought Manship, was surely reflected today when Miguel Loomis turned up in the news as a spokesman for Mrs. Greer. Did the sale of fifteen thousand Dragon mean that some insider feared the Carib deal might collapse if Greer vanished for good and the law firm lost its tunnel to the White House? But why sell Dragon despite that? Micro's earnings were good and its future appeared limitless regardless of whether it absorbed a small oil company. Was there something else about Greer and Educational Micro? Did Greer do tax work for the company? Always be on the alert for the hidden tax angle. He had better call his man in Washington tomorrow, have him nose around.

Manship gazed out at the turnpike's leafy flanks as the car glided past Stamford and Darien. Clouds hung as if nailed to the hot arc of the night. Manship replaced his notebook and watched the lights of the inbound cars streak by, fiery tusks of lethal monsters. Who would dump fifteen thousand Dragon because Stephen Greer disappeared? He must call Maury Rimmel in Washington.

Dave Paulick could feel the pump of his blood, like a rap on his chest, when he saw the two tall men leave the house and walk to their parked car, a black Ford sedan, in front of 6709 Barnaby Road, Bethesda. His surmise had been right. He was sure they were Bureau men. He could see the living-room light and a woman's shadowed figure in the screened doorway until the sedan moved away. Then the woman shut the door.

Paulick mentally shook hands with himself, a not uncommon event with him. If his guess was wrong, then the FBI obviously was following the same false lead.

Playing the long odds, he had driven out River Road at dusk and turned right on Burdette, the road which led to the Burning Tree Club. He stopped approximately at the spot where Greer was thought to have climbed—or been bundled over—the steel mesh fence, made a note of the mileage on his speedometer, then drove to the nearest airport marked on his map. It was the Montgomery County Airpark at Gaithersburg, a small field for sports planes and light charters. Paulick noted the distance between club and airfield, sixteen miles, and the driving time. Using the expressway and observing speed limits, it took him twenty-one minutes.

Darkness was settling like a hood when he entered the operations building, walked past a deserted recreation room with pool table, and mounted the stairs to the second floor where he had seen a light burning. A man in coveralls stood behind the flight counter. This was a long shot and Paulick had no great hope for it.

"Say," he said, "I'm Paulick of *D.P.'s Dossier*. I'm working on a story and I wonder if you could help me?"

"Doubt it." The man's hands were grease-stained. He was chewing gum. "Everybody's gone except me."

"Did a plane take off from here about eight-twenty last night, give or take a few minutes?"

"You got anything to show who you are?"

Paulick took out his wallet and showed his laminated color photograph over the two-line legend, "News. The White House." The man took the wallet, scrutinized the picture, compared it to Paulick's face.

"Pretty good picture," he said. "Who took it?"

"The Secret Service," said Paulick, hoping the name and the color photo would have the impact of officialdom. Sometimes it did, sometimes not. The airport man looked impressed.

"Looks like everybody wants to know about a plane taking off last night," said the man.

"Everybody?"

"Well, you're the third to ask. Two guys were here about a half hour ago with the same question."

"Oh, sure," said Paulick casually. "FBI."

The man nodded. Paulick hid his elation.

"What did you tell them?"

"Look, friend, I don't want to get mixed up in anything." He eyed Paulick appraisingly again.

"What I hear stays under my hat," said Paulick. He shoved a five-dollar bill across the counter. The man slid it into a pocket of his coveralls.

"Yeah, well a Beechcraft Baron took off at eight thirty-five. Belongs to Brubaker. Said he was going to Raleigh-Durham, I think."

"How about the flight plan?"

"Brubaker files one when he feels like it. Last night he didn't bother."

"Who's Brubaker?"

"Arnie Brubaker. He's a charter pilot around here. Lives over on Barnaby Road in Bethesda."

"When did he come back?"

"He hasn't." The man noted Paulick's frown and added: "Don't mean a thing. Arnie's liable to put down anywhere. Depends on his business."

"Did he have any passengers?"

"Yeah, one. Some fellow named Hendricks, I think he said."

"What did he look like?"

The man chewed hard on his gum, then said: "Search me. Arnie was running up at the end of the runway, and this car drives out and puts the passenger on board out there. Arnie give me the guy's name earlier."

"Isn't that unusual?"

"Naw. Not around here. A passenger has a scheduled take-off time, but he's late, so they wait on the runway for him. This is Washington, brother. Say, what's this all about?"

"I don't know yet," said Paulick. "Thanks again. See you around."

Paulick noted that outside the runway lights had winked on like strings of glowing beads and he surmised that Brubaker and his passenger had taken off on a lighted runway last night. Paulick looked up Arnold Brubaker in the phone directory, then drove to the 6700 block of Barnaby Road. He found his number, 6709, and saw the parked car in front. He drove slowly past, turned around at the end of the block, then parked. It was just as he turned off the ignition switch that he saw the two tall men emerge from the house and felt the jolt of his blood.

He waited several minutes after the other car left, then walked to the Brubaker house. It was a modest Cape Cod, the brick painted green and the base shrubbed with small evergreens and rhododendrons which drooped like basset ears from the August dry spell. Paulick rang the doorbell and heard chimes sound the first bars of "How Dry I Am." The woman who opened the door not more than three inches wore a blue cotton smock and a defensive frown.

"I'd like to speak to Mr. Brubaker, please."

The door held steady at three inches. "I'm sorry. He isn't home."

"I'm here for the same reason the FBI was," said Paulick. He extended his press card.

She glanced hurriedly at it, not really seeing, and shook her head.

"I'm afraid I . . ."

"I just want to know where to reach him by phone," he cut in.

"Please telephone him tomorrow. I'm sure you can talk to him then."

"But I need to talk to him tonight."

"I'm sorry," she said. She closed the door quietly but irrevocably, and Paulick heard the night lock click.

As he drove home, Dave Paulick sorted out his impressions of the long day. By the time he reached the garage of his Connecticut Avenue apartment house, he was reasonably sure of one thing: Stephen Greer had vanished by appointment.

5

Special Agent Lawrence Storm skimmed the Monday-morning *Washington Post* with half his mind, raked his own frustrations with the other half, and so succeeded in slopping coffee and scattering toast crumbs over the paper.

The Greer case straddled the front page for the third successive morning; speculation on political effects, a compilation of editorials around the country, and a main news story. The hard news was notably skimpy. There were interviews with Burning Tree caddies about Greer, a statement from Press Secretary Culligan attempting to calm Wall Street before the market opening, quotes from Miguel Loomis on Mrs. Greer's feelings of the moment. As far as the press knew, Stephen Greer could have dropped off the lip of an unknown canyon.

And, thought Larry Storm, he knew little more than the press did. He had dogged the Ajax case sixteen hours Saturday and as many yesterday without advancing a foot. Oh, he had learned plenty about Stephen Greer, including his pet nickname, "Cubby," for his wife, but nothing about Greer's Wednesday night habits. Mrs. Susannah Greer had told Storm about the Potomac Study Club during their three-hour talk Saturday morning. The fact that club membership and meeting places were secret, that Greer had been attending sessions for a year, that Mrs. Greer knew absolutely nothing about them, all this proved more than mildly interesting to Storm. He had reported promptly via car radio to Clyde Moorhead, the task force chief, and received the green light to check out the study group.

By late Sunday night Storm had seen half the Roudebush cabinet, most of the little cabinet, and a dozen political acquaintances of Greer. Not one had heard of a Potomac Study Club which met Wednesday nights or any other nights. Some informants might have lied to him, but his sixth sense told Larry Storm that the Potomac Study Club was a phantom. Greer, for some reason yet unknown, obviously had lied to his wife. She was a pretty, gracious woman with an inner core of self-reliance. Shook up now, of course, but a thoroughbred, he thought. She could take it.

So now, what? He shoved the stained paper aside, stacked his dishes in the sink, and walked toward the phone in his small apartment to check in with Moorhead. At that moment, the phone rang. Even at 7:45 A.M., it was hard to keep one step ahead of Clyde Moorhead.

"Doesn't sound like much," said Moorhead, "but you'd better check it. A woman called in late last night. Says she saw Greer's picture in the paper. Claims he's the same man she saw a couple of times in an R Street apartment. My memo says she sounded a little whacky, but ready to talk."

Storm jotted down the name and address. "Anything else I ought to know, Clyde?"

"Can it, Larry. You know the drill on this one. Everything goes vertical."

"Why don't you hand out blindfolds? It would make as much sense."

"Sorry about that, pal."

Storm drove to R Street in the mood of a man who has just been snubbed by an old friend. Nineteen years with the Bureau, and suddenly they began to treat him as if he were just out of Quantico training school. And he was in line for an assistant directorship too. That he knew. What a way to handle a major case! Normally he would spend two hours checking through reports of other agents, and by 10 A.M. he would have a dozen leads to follow. But not this time. Oh, what the hell . . .

The Wilmarth was a five-story apartment house two blocks off Connecticut Avenue. It had the air of an aging beauty with new dentures—the lobby had been redone recently—and Storm guessed apartments rented in the $150 to $200 range. Nothing luxurious, but clean and well-tended, a decent if unfashionable address. He rode the small self-service elevator to the fourth floor and walked down the short corridor, sniffing an aroma of bacon and noting that there were only five dwelling units on the floor.

The name plate on 4-C read "Beverly West," and he could hear the throaty plaint of a Latin singer. He made a note on his pad: "8:22 A.M. Loud record player." He rang the bell and stood ready with his black leather pocket case opened to the Bureau card.

The door swung open, then closed slightly with a shake of black hair, obviously dyed, and a blast of Latin music. The partial closing, as if the door had reflexes of its own, had been anticipated by Larry. He had won again, at five to one against himself. He was used to it. He extended the card and said, loudly above the music, "From the FBI."

The woman lowered her head skeptically, inspected the card, his face, hesitated. Then she opened the door for him, closing it slowly behind his back. She handled the door so gingerly, thought Larry, the hinges might have been made of glass.

She wore a loose, white blouse, pink Capri pants that hugged her legs like sausage skins and pink spike-heeled mules. The lax face showed signs of a long night.

"Could we turn down that record player, please, miss?" asked Larry.

She obliged by reducing the volume, then folded her arms and surveyed him, swaying slightly. The whites of her eyes had flecks of red.

"I didn't know they had Negro agents," she said.

"Once a slave, always a slave," he said. "The Bureau has plenty of us now." But he could remember the days when he knew most of them by name.

"Oh well . . ." She coughed, looked at his tie, suit and shoes as if to reassure herself. "Coffee?"

"Yes, thanks. Black."

He watched through the doorway of the tiny kitchen as she spooned instant coffee into two mugs. To one, she added a splash of bourbon, then poured hot water from a kettle into both.

Larry sat in an armchair while she squeezed into a corner of a sofa and tucked the high heels under her. He noted that the furniture was fairly new but splotched by liquids.

Storm took several three-by-five photographs of Stephen Greer from his jacket pocket and handed them to her. Each photo showed Greer's face from a different angle. She glanced at them briefly.

"That's the cat," she said.

Storm took down a brief bio of her, making sure not to press too hard. Intuitively, he felt her past deserved such fragile shelter as it could find. She was twenty-seven, from St. Louis and she worked as a part-time secretary through an employment agency. She was, she volunteered, "engaged," and her intended helped furnish the apartment. She had lived here eighteen months. In his notebook, Larry wrote: "Semi-pro."

"Now if you could just tell me when and where you saw Mr. Greer?" asked Storm.

"Sure." The fresh scarlet had missed its mark at one corner of her mouth. Dark loops hung beneath her eyes. "I've seen him around here three times, I think. Yeah, three. Once last fall, once this spring and once, the last time, just last week.

"The first time, last fall, this other guy, the little one, comes to my door, accusing me of having the record player up too high. Of all the god-damned nerve. Too loud, he says, and it's only nine-thirty at night. What does he think this is, a convent or something?"

She lit a cigarette and flourished it, a glowing exclamation point.

"Pardon me," said Storm. "What other man?"

"Oh, there are two of them across the hall in 4-D," she said, "the little creep and the bigger one, this Greer guy. I never had any trouble with the big one, Greer, but the little smart-aleck made my—if you'll pardon my English—ass tired."

"You mean these two live across the hall?"

She hunched her shoulders. "Don't ask me. I don't ask questions of anybody around here, and I expect to be recorded—I mean accorded—the same courtesy. Anything wrong with that?"

"No," said Storm. "None at all."

"Thanks for nothin'," she said. "How do I know if they live there? I've only seen them at night, three times, like I said."

"Would you mind describing each meeting, each time you saw Greer?"

"That's what I'm trying to do," she said reprovingly. She took a swallow of the coffee and bourbon, then inhaled deeply on the cigarette. "Like I said, I was playing some music about nine-thirty this night, see, when there's a knock on the door and this little character is standing there. He's in shirt-sleeves and he's got big-rimmed glasses, like some jerky scientist on TV or something, and he says, 'Pardon me, but would you mind turning down your television?' I says I don't have no TV—which is a lie, but anyway it wasn't on—and he says, 'Well, whatever it is that's playing music.' Of course, I told him I would, and I did turn it down. Only thing is, the incinerator is down the hall, and pretty soon I could hear this loud banging, somebody slamming the lid.

"So I knock on 4-D, and when the little guy comes to the door, I say, 'Is this a nice tit-for-tat or something, when I turn down the hi-fi, and you start making all that lousy noise at the garbage chute?' 'I'm sorry,' he says, 'but I haven't dumped anything in the incinerator.' 'The hell you haven't,' I said, 'I'll bet your trash basket is clean as a baby's behind,' and I start walking right by him to the kitchen.

"That's when I see this sandy-haired fellow sitting on the sofa. He jumps up, surprised, and I say, 'What's the matter, I'm not that bad to look at, am I?' Let's face it. Just between us, Mr. FBI, and you don't have to write this down, I'd had a couple by that time and . . . well, you know, I'm all alone here, and I like some fun, who doesn't? So I said to these two cats, even if they are older, I says, 'Come on, fellows, let's forget it. Come on over to my pad, and let's have a drink and make up like neighbors should.' At that I introduce myself, Beverly West, but neither of them gives a name. The little one says, 'Oh, thank you, some other time,' and all that crap, and pretty soon he's edging me toward the door. So I could see I wasn't wanted. That was all, the first time. I never saw neither of them until March, I guess it was, some time."

"And what happened then?" asked Storm. Casting a lure here was a waste of energy. The fish wanted to jump into the boat.

"I came home about eight-thirty one night, and the bigger one, this Greer, I know it is now, he's standing at the door of 4-D fiddling with the lock. 'What's wrong, honey?' I asked. . . . I always say honey like that. It don't mean a thing. . . . I said, 'You locked out?' He smiles, a real nice smile. . . . Wait a minute. Let me see those pictures again."

She selected one and held it up for Storm to see. "He looked just like that." The photograph was a news agency shot of Greer leaving a building, walking directly at the camera.

"A good smile. See what I mean?"

Storm agreed. Miss West drained the last of the whisky-laced coffee and dropped the cigarette butt, hissing, into the mug.

"He was embarrassed," she continued. Her scarlet lipstick, pink pants and pink mules registered an overwhelming color scheme at this early hour. "And he said, 'No, I've just got the wrong key.' I said, 'Well, if you can't find the right one, come on over, it's been a long, cold winter,' or something brilliant like that. Then he found the right key and opened the door. He turned and smiled at me again. 'You're very hospitable,' he said. 'Perhaps you'll give me a rain check.' I said, 'Why sure. Any time, honey.' Not a bad guy. I liked him. He had class, if you know what I mean. Anyway, I was glad I had kept the hi-fi down sometimes. I guess you can hear it in 4-D because the two apartments join at the end of the hall where my big closet is over there. That's where I keep the player.

"So that was it until last week one night. I was coming in around midnight and this Greer was just leaving. I said, 'Hello, long time no see,' or something, and he smiled and said hello. For an older man, he sure made a good appearance, not good-looking, but you know. I said, 'Say, do you live here or what, since I only see you about every four months?' He says, 'Oh, I only use the apartment when I'm in town,' he says. 'How about your little friend? Did he move out on you or something?' I asks. 'No, he was just visiting,' he says. And he kind of bows and leaves by the elevator.

"But you know what? That wasn't true, because I was emptying the trash in the chute about an hour later, and who do I see coming out of 4-D but the little squirt again. . . . Anyway, when I saw Greer's picture in the paper, I started thinking. This Greer, a big lawyer and friend of the President, he disappears. Now, I wonder what the runty guy knows about it? So, finally, last night, I called the FBI and told them. And here you are."

"We appreciate your co-operation, Miss West," said Storm. "Do you remember what night it was last week that you saw both men?"

"Call me Bev, honey. Everybody does." She patted reflexively at her coal-dust hair. "Yeah, let's see. It was the night I was over to the Dialogue in Georgetown with my girl friend. Tuesday. No, Wednesday. Yes, Wednesday. Hey, how about that? I saw this Greer the night before he went on the lam or something. Wasn't that Thursday night?"

Storm nodded. "You're sure about Wednesday?"

"Yes, now I am. It was Wednesday all right, maybe just a little after twelve."

"Could you place what nights of the week you saw Greer here the earlier times?"

"You kidding? That was months ago. But the first time must have been a week night," she said, "because I remember what the small guy said about the record player—that it wasn't as if it was a weekend, after all. Which means it wasn't a weekend night. Right? . . . But it still bugs me. Why do two guys make such a fuss over a little music?"

She shook a new cigarette out of a pack, mating it uncertainly to the flame of a lighter, then asked: "Say, is there something about fags, they got to have quiet like a tomb?"

"Why do you ask that?" asked Storm. "Do you have some evidence of their relationship?"

"No," she said. She was dignity affronted. "I'm no Peeping Tom, for God's sake. But I mean, what else? Two guys in a pad where neither of them lives . . . even if Greer didn't seem the type."

"Do you have any idea who the smaller man is?"

"Search me. I've only seen him twice. That's your business to find out, not mine. . . . More coffee?"

"No, thanks." Storm stood up. "I guess that's it, Miss West. We'd appreciate it if you'd keep quiet about this. And call us if you think of anything else that might help."

"Do I get paid?" she asked. She stood up also and folded her arms across her blouse. The lipstick was too vivid against the pale face, like blood on a mushroom. "Aren't there paid informers or something you read about?"

"I'm afraid not in this case, Miss West, but we would ask your further co-operation."

"It's Bev, remember?" She offered her hand, and Storm took it briefly.

"Say, you're a gentleman, like they're always saying about the FBI," she said. "But I swear, honey, I never heard they had colored G-men."

"We're all the same," he said. "Another day, another buck—red, white, or blue."

"You're with it," she said. "If you're not married or something, give me a ring some night. I'm in the book."

"Thanks," said Storm. "I'll remember that—after we find Mr. Greer."

"Business before pleasure, huh? Okay, hon, call me any time."

She saw him out, and his last thought was that if the pink pants had been a shirt-waist, she would have choked to death. By the time Larry reached the elevator, he could hear another surge of the Latin music from 4-C. The piped melody in the self-service elevator was blander, an innocuous poultice for the mind. That, he thought, took care of at least one Wednesday night of the non-studying Potomac Study Club, perhaps three. At the least, the two other nights when the milk-faced broad had seen Greer were weekday nights. He would bet they turned out to be Wednesdays, but the instant the thought occurred, he shelved it. If he had learned anything in his nineteen years at the Bureau, it was never to run ahead of his ticket. "Don't let a hunch become a conviction until the file is closed," Moorhead always said. Good man, Clyde. They had worked some tough ones together in their day.

Storm stopped the elevator at the second floor while he completed his notes . . . Description of the smaller man . . . A reminder that Greer apparently lied to Beverly West when he said the second man was only a casual visitor. Larry checked the note in his pad which quoted Beverly as saying she had seen the shorter man leaving 4-D an hour after Greer last Wednesday night.

Storm's interview with the resident manager went swiftly. He had the grayish pallor of indoors and a mole on one cheek. He did triple duty as bookkeeper, rental agent, and small chores maintenance man. The pictures of Greer evoked no clear response. The manager thought he had seen the face several times around the building, but he could not be sure. Apartment 4-D had been rented, furnished, for $175 a month, for a year beginning last September 1. Lease up day after tomorrow, Wednesday. The leasee was the Crown Arts Co., 939 N. Charles Street, Baltimore, and the signature on the lease was that of David Klingman, same address. Yes, he was a short man with dark-rimmed glasses, probably Jewish, he guessed, kind of a brooding type. Only saw him a few times. Monthly checks? No, the man paid by cash each month. Left it in an envelope in the resident manager's box. No, he hadn't saved any of the envelopes, but he would save the next one, provided, of course, Crown Arts renewed the lease.

"I'd like a look at the apartment," said Storm. "Of course, you're under no obligation to let me in unless I produce a search warrant. If you wish, I could come back this afternoon with one."

"Naw," said the manager. "Anything the FBI wants is okay by me. Here, you take the key. Lemme just buzz 4-D from the lobby. If nobody's there, you're welcome. Just let me have the key back and don't say who give it to you."

Five rings from the lobby producing no response, Storm went back to the fourth floor with the key. The Latin music, this time a mariachi band, still boomed from Beverly West's apartment like muffled thunder. Larry let himself in quickly.

Apartment 4-D had an L-shaped living room, the short leg of which served as a dinette. Storm surmised that one wall of the dinette adjoined Beverly West's large closet, domicile of the turbulent hi-fi. One bedroom opened off the living room. The furniture, barely filling the suite, had the appearance of mail order modern. Most of it was cheap maple with a jaundice-like finish. Storm went slowly through the suite, but found not a single article that belonged to the occupants. The inside of the kitchen refrigerator, which Storm opened with a handkerchief wrapped around his fingers, was antiseptically empty with not even a can of beer on the metal shelves. In the bedroom, the double bed wore a dark green coverlet which was tucked neatly around two pillows. There was a telephone on a bedside table, but when Storm picked up the receiver with handkerchiefed fingers, there was no dial tone. He wrote down the number in his memo pad.

When Storm returned the key to the manager, he asked who did the cleaning in 4-D. The occupants, said the manager. To his knowledge, there was no cleaning woman.

"Only one key to a tenant?" asked Storm.

"No, I gave Mr. Klingman two the day he signed up and paid two months in advance. Every tenant gets two keys."

Storm called Moorhead on the car radio. He was parked near Connecticut Avenue.

"I guess you'll want to check 4-D for prints," said Storm after giving his concise report. "And it might pay to put a man on the building, but my guess is nobody's ever going to show at 4-D. I think that lease has had it."

"Okay, we'll handle the apartment," said Moorhead. "You check out this Klingman."

"Right," said Storm. "Give me a fast count from a Baltimore phone book, will you? Either David Klingman, that's K for kitty, L for long, or Crown Arts Company, 939 North Charles."

"Hold on," said Moorhead. He returned to the phone several minutes later. "No Crown Arts listed in Baltimore."

"It figured," said Storm. "How about Klingman?"

"The book lists two David Klingmans, one David R. and one David W." He gave the addresses and phone numbers. "Good luck, Larry baby, and listen—take your time, huh? We don't need anything nailed down until noon."

"It's discrimination," said Storm. "I get all the tough ones just because my old man lost his color chart."

"Right," said Moorhead. "Wait'll you get black power. Then you can goof off five minutes a day, just like me. Until then, get off the air. You're wastin' time."

"Okay, Mushhead. Don't call us. We'll call you."

Storm mentally plotted the shortest route to the Baltimore-Washington Parkway, then remembered something he had overlooked. He left the car and walked back to the Wilmarth. The manager was sweeping the front steps.

"One thing more," said Storm. "Where's the nearest parking garage?"

"Around the corner to your right."

The young man on duty in the garage's glass cubicle blinked at the FBI card, then officiously held the door open for Storm. The easily impressed kind, thought Larry. The description of "David Klingman" spurred no recollection, but the man offered to call the night cashier. The voice at the other end of the line sounded co-operative though sleepy. Yes, he did remember a small man with dark-rimmed glasses. Thought he used the garage about once a week, arriving in midevening and leaving about one in the morning. Tags? Not sure, but thought they were Maryland plates. Last week? Yes, thought so, but not sure. Storm thanked him and apologized again for interrupting his sleep.

The time-stamped parking cards were sent to the central office the first of each month, said the day duty man, so he still had those for August. He cleared a space for Storm on the small desk and gave him a bundle of claim checks. Each day's packet, numbering about three hundred tickets, was wrapped with a rubber band. They were filed by check-out time, Storm learned, so he culled out the four Thursdays in August.

He had what he wanted in a few minutes. One license number, a Maryland tag, appeared early on each Thursday, at 12:50 A.M., 1:03, 12:57. Last Thursday, August 26, the car left the garage at 1:08 A.M.

Larry walked back to his car and called Moorhead on the radio phone.

"You're gabby today," said Moorhead. "You got Ajax tied up yet?"

"No, Clyde, but I may have his buddy's number. Do me a favor, and ask the Baltimore office to check motor vehicles over there for Maryland tag number MQ 4472. That's M for mother, Q for quack, four, four, seven, two. As you said, I need it yesterday."

"Take five and call me back."

When Storm called again, Moorhead reported briskly: "Maryland passenger vehicle license number MQ 4472 is registered to a Phillip Jacob Lubin. Two l's in Phillip. Lubin is spelled l love, u uncle, b boy, i instant, n nothing."

"Got it."

"The address registered is 3333 North Charles Street, Baltimore, and our Baltimore office says that's near the Johns Hopkins University Homewood campus. Not the hospital med school, Larry. The college proper."

"On my way. Aren't you amazed how fast I changed David Klingman into Phil Lubin?"

"You're the genius type, Dr. Martin Luther Storm. I'd put you down for golden time—if this outfit had any."

An hour later in Baltimore, Storm parked near the N. Charles Street address, another apartment building, this one of Georgian architecture and named the Charles Apartments. The large lobby with Oriental rug was flanked by two sitting rooms.

"Can I help you?" asked the receptionist. She was a middle-aged woman of assured carriage and a blue tint to her hair.

"I'm looking for Phillip Lubin," he said.

"He's on vacation," said the woman. "Would you care to leave a message?"

"No, thanks," he said. No sense using the Bureau identity card when he did not have to. He chanced a shot. "I'm calling on behalf of a friend." That was no lie. "Perhaps I'd better leave word at the university."

"That would be better," she said. "Dr. Lubin gets most of his mail over there."

"Which building is it again?"

"Rowland Hall," she said. "Just ask for the math department's office. May I leave a name for Dr. Lubin?"

He could not resist it. "Certainly. David Klingman."

"All right, Mr. Klingman."

Mister, he thought, in Baltimore yet, following a respectful "sir" in Washington. Maybe times were changing.

The chic little brunette who worked for Dr. Lubin and eight other mathematics professors of Johns Hopkins University was volubly apologetic. Storm knew the type, excessively polite to anyone of darker skin, so anxious to please that her words tumbled into one another.

"Isn't that a shame," she said. "You just missed him, really. He left yesterday, and he won't be back until goodness knows when. He's not teaching next semester, you know, so he decided to take a long automobile trip out West and up into Canada. He's worn out, poor man. . . . But isn't that too bad? Have you known him long?"

"Not too long," said Larry. In fact, he thought, I first became acquainted with him about two hours ago. "Who's head of the mathematics department, miss?"

"He's in Europe on a grant this year, but Dr. Winthrop is acting chairman. If you want to see him, he's down the hall to your left." She pointed the way.

The Bureau card quickly admitted Larry to the office of Dr. Henry Winthrop. He was a lean, well-tanned, and reserved man who shook hands with a firm grip. Larry assumed he played tennis. Winthrop studied Larry's card.

"We get a few of these around here," he said. "Awful lot of security these days."

"Dr. Winthrop," said Storm, "I have to check out Dr. Phillip Lubin rather carefully. I'd appreciate your co-operation for a few minutes and also access to whatever faculty records are available on him."

"I see." Winthrop settled in his swivel chair and hugged a knee. "Is this security? Or is Phil Lubin in some difficulty with the law? That's difficult to imagine."

"No, sir. I'm sorry I can't reveal what this is about. Bureau policy, you know. But the case really involves someone else. Dr.

Lubin is merely a friend. But, of course, in a case of this kind, we have to cover all the friends, too."

"Yes, I suppose so. . . . Would you object if I call the FBI office here just to make sure? Not that I doubt your word, but . . ."

"Not at all," said Storm. "The number is LE 9-6700. I'll wait outside."

Winthrop held up a staying hand. "No need for that." When his secretary connected him with the Baltimore FBI office, Winthrop asked for the special agent in charge and described Storm and his mission. At one point, he hesitated, glanced at Storm and said, "Why, yes." Larry surmised that was when Fairbanks asked if the agent was a Negro.

Winthrop held out the phone. "He'd like to speak to you."

"Is that you, Bob? This is Larry Storm, checking the MQ 44 you gave us earlier."

"On the 'A' case?"

"Right. A for Ajax. Working under Moorhead."

"Okay, Larry. Put the professor back on and I'll soothe him."

After that, while Winthrop was still guarded, he responded to whatever questions Larry asked. Obviously, too, he was trying to puzzle out the purpose of the inquiry.

Storm jotted down his notes. Lubin was listed in Who's Who in America and in the directory of the American Mathematical Society. Born in Nebraska, Phi Beta Kappa at University of Chicago, M.A. and Ph.D. in mathematics at the same university. Taught at Cornell, then came to Johns Hopkins eleven years ago. Now no undergraduate classes. Graduate seminars only in Fourier Analysis and Hilbert Space. Real interest was his own research. Had done projects for several foundations and classified work for the CIA. At this point, Larry thought: If Lubin did CIA work, he must have a file as long as an arm from security investigations. So why couldn't Moorhead get the file and save all this work? But he could hear Moorhead's answer. All right, Larry, but you check out every-thing you can at the university. The Bureau method. Double-check, then triple-check.

Lubin was a linguist. German, Danish, Chinese, French and even a dab of some obscure African tribal tongue, Winthrop thought. Fast, quick, fertile mind, but a bit, well, abrasive as a personality. Had all the marks to be chairman of the department, but uninterested in personnel and administrative minutiae. Winthrop couldn't blame him, really. It was a bore, by and large. Lubin unmarried. Engaged once, he thought, but perhaps intensity of his intellectual commitment alienated women. Lives at the Charles Apartments. . . . Eye trouble. Too much reading. Frankly, thought Lubin heading toward collapse from overwork, so when, about a month ago, Lubin asked to be relieved of duties in upcoming semester, Winthrop quickly agreed. Only thing out of character is his love of automobiles. Likes to drive his Mustang and tinker with engine. Winthrop understood he left on motor tour yesterday, Sunday. Out West somewhere. Of course, he would call in at regular intervals, but doubted that Phil would return to Baltimore until February. Anything else.

"Perhaps later after I look at his file," said Storm. "Just one thing, Dr. Winthrop. This is delicate, I know, but actually the question is routine. Do you have any reason to believe Dr. Lubin's sexual habits are anything but normal?"

Winthrop's amiable smile faded. "That has never been a concern of this department. . . . Really, Mr. Storm, do the government agencies have to dig into a man's sex life? Is it relevant?"

"It is distasteful," said Storm, "but once in a while, it can provide a missing clue. Anyway, Dr. Winthrop, I merely carry out orders."

"I realize that. I didn't mean to accuse you personally. . . . At any rate, I don't think I can be of much help."

"I must ask the question, sir," Larry insisted.

"Yes, well . . ." Winthrop hesitated, eyed the ceiling for a moment. "You used the word 'normal.' As an academic, I regard that word as less than definitive. I suppose you mean something other than heterosexuality?"

"Yes," said Larry. "Any indication of homosexual tendencies?"

Winthrop frowned. "My impulse is to refuse to answer, but of course that would merely prejudice Dr. Lubin in your eyes. Let me think a minute." He did so while Larry studied his face. "I would say not, and I don't wish my hesitance to be construed as meaningful in any way. I was just trying to satisfy myself as to whether I could properly make an evaluation. . . . I can't really, of course, but I can give you my reactions. I've had almost daily contact with Phil for six or seven years. While I'm no expert on such matters, I do notice that in the presence of homosexual men, I feel a chemical recoiling, as it were. I never felt a trace of that with Phil. . . .

"On the other hand, I doubt that Phil experiences strong sexual stimulations. He goes out socially with women a fair amount, but there has been no serious attachment, I'd say. He's a very busy and committed man." He paused with a wry smile. "All I'm saying, I suppose, is that this math department has no expertise in this field."

"I think that's a frank appraisal on your part and that's all I can ask for," said Larry. In his pad he wrote: "No woman-chaser, but W. believes not fag."

"Is that all?"

"One final question," said Larry. "How about his friends? I'd like a list of them for a routine check."

Winthrop named several faculty members, a Baltimore doctor, a blind woman to whom Lubin read once a week, despite his weak eyes, and a number of mathematicians, both American and foreign. Larry noted there was no mention of Stephen Greer.

Winthrop chuckled. "Oh yes, and Eugene Culligan, the White House press secretary. Lubin jokes that he can leave here any time for a plush government job because he has a friend at the White House. Lubin taught a class at Chicago when Culligan was an undergraduate. They've kept in touch."

Storm spent an hour over Lubin's manila folder in the faculty files, filling in dates, degrees, places. Lubin was forty-three years old, had his appendix out, attended a Baltimore synagogue, was the son of a language teacher, now deceased, at an Omaha high school. Ran the low hurdles in high school, but no athletics in college. Salary at Johns Hopkins, $20,000. Drew extra stipends for special research for foundations. Nobel prize committee made inquiries about Lubin two years ago.

By the time Storm finished, it was three o'clock and he realized his stomach was protesting the lack of food. He ate at the Greenway Pharmacy just off campus, and spent the luncheon break reviewing the life and times of Phillip Lubin. It was as he was absent-mindedly paying the check that the hunch occurred to him. At first, it appeared to involve an enormous amount of thankless extra work, yet the more he thought, the stronger the hunch grew.

He reported briefly to Moorhead from the Greenway phone booth, trading but one round of insults with him. Then he drove to the U. S. Post Office and Courthouse Building in downtown Baltimore. He took the elevator to the fourth floor, walked down the dingy hall—why were so many government buildings so depressing?—past the pictures of the ten most wanted criminals in the FBI office.

Bob Fairbanks, the SAC, gave him the office list of all parking lots and garages in the city and use of the visiting agents' workroom. On a map of the city, Storm drew a series of widening circles from the Charles Apartments. Then he plotted each parking facility within the circles.

When he finished work that night, fatigued and out of fuel at 10 P.M., Storm had covered every parking lot and garage in the inner circle. Then he checked into the Lord Baltimore Hotel, had two hamburgers and a glass of milk in his room, and worked until past 1 A.M. on his portable, typing out his notes on Ajax.

He was out on the street again by 8:30 A.M. Tuesday and working his rounds. It was a tedious routine. First show his Bureau identity card to the parking attendant, ask about a Mustang with Maryland tag MQ 4472 being left for monthly storage, then receive the shake of the head, then walk through the garage looking for a Mustang and, when finding one, checking the tag.

His shoes were dirty, his calves ached and he was beginning to doubt his intuition when he entered an underground parking garage called Sol's Metro Park. He walked down the oily ramp, glad to be out of the soggy heat, and looked around for the attendant. It was after five o'clock, Sol's Metro was miles from the Charles Apartments in a sleazy, nondescript section of east Baltimore, and the man on duty looked more blankly sullen than most. When Storm showed his card and asked his question, the fleshy attendant wiped his hands on his coveralls and shook his head with unconcealed disgust.

"Jesus, now you're taking over the FBI," he said. "Next thing, I guess, we'll have one of them new Adam Clayton Powells in the White House."

Storm bit his lip, restraining himself . . . The cheap, unshaven, fat slob . . . But all he said was, "The Mustang's tag is MQ 4472, Maryland."

The man jerked his head to the left. "There it is against the wall. Won't do you no good, though. It's locked. The owner took the key."

Storm checked the plate, looked in the windows, saw nothing except a wire coat-hanger on the seat. When he returned to the grimy office, the sullen attendant was chewing on a broom straw.

"I don't know from nothin'," he said. "You want to look at our half of the claim check, that's your business, but the car came in yesterday and Sunday's my day off."

"Yes, please. I'd like to see the check."

The man fingered a card file, withdrew a two-by-four white ticket, and tossed it wordlessly through the opening in the cashier's window.

Storm recorded the data in his memo pad: Sol's Metro Park. Time-stamped in at 11:52 A.M., Aug. 29. In ink was scrawled: "Mustang MQ 4472. Phillip J. Lubin. Monthly rental, $40 rate. Receipt given for $100 cash deposit. Indefinite storage."

Storm returned the ticket through the slot. "Thanks."

The attendant grunted and shook his head again. His white world was folding like an accordion.

Larry bristled all the way to his car. . . . Just one punch at that beer-fat, whiskered face. . . . But once he was behind the steering wheel, the attendant was forgotten. Instead, the old feeling of elation coursed through him. Another hunch had paid off. These moments hooked him. They were beautiful, like rainbows at twilight, a woman standing nude in a shower or a coolness welling up from the ground at dawn. He loved these moments, and he knew they would keep him on the Bureau treadmill until his legs gave out and they pensioned him off.

His car short-wave radio was out of range of Washington. At the first corner phone booth he saw, Larry called Moorhead.

"More Ajax," he said, trying to keep the flying flags of pride from his voice. "Dr. L. isn't on a motor trip. He stored his car, indefinitely, at a cruddy parking garage in east Baltimore, a long way from home." He telescoped the details.

"Nice work, Larry," said Moorhead. The sincerity was there, the plaudits of one pro to another. Then the needle: "So what have you done for us lately?"

"Nothing. Listen, Mushhead, I'm going to blow my per diem on a lobster dinner at the Chesapeake—with two martinis first."

"Be my guest."

"Clyde, how about checking out the airlines? L. probably flew out of Friendship Sunday for somewhere, or maybe Dulles or National."

"Already got it down. We'll take that from here. After dinner, come on back and take it easy tonight. I'll check with you at eight tomorrow at your place. . . . Say, Larry, we're going through your notes from yesterday. What do you think? Is there a homo angle here?"

"My guess is no," said Storm, "but as Doc W. said, I really have no expertise in that field. Frankly, my taste is women—young ones."

"Don't change." Moorhead laughed. "After your neat job yesterday and today, we want you just as you are, Larry, baby."

But after Storm hung up, the elation ebbed, then vaporized. He realized, again, that Moorhead had not relayed a single item from other agents of the task force. He was working in the dark, blindfolded at that, for the first time in nineteen years with the Bureau. And he did not like it a bit. Not one damn bit.

6

Wednesday morning at the White House press office opened as if jarred awake by a clamor of gongs, and the discord swelled until our shop resembled an orchestra pit seized by mad musicians. Jill's five-eyed phone winked psychotically. The two ghost writers took turns harassing me over the President's Labor Day opener, only five days off. An apoplectic defense man at the Bureau of the Budget accused me of dropping a zero from yesterday's announcement of a cut-back on vertical takeoff fighters. It was a one billion slash, he complained, not one hundred million. Outside on Pennsylvania Avenue, pickets protesting trade with South Africa got into a shoving match with police, and a UPI reporter was belted on the ear by mistake. A bearded, sad-eyed TV commentator from Los Angeles somehow argued his way past the Secret Service into my office. The SS had new men on duty. Don Sheehan, the detail chief, and a couple of the regulars were away, probably on advance work for the President's Chicago trip. The L.A. kook wanted to video-tape me, exclusive on Stephen Greer. We had to call the White House police and have him ejected.

Reston, Alsop, Pearson, Wilson, Alexander, White, and Drummond all had calls in for me. Evans and Novak got their wires crossed. Evans called me from home—Novak from Stockholm. Everyone wanted to talk Greer, Greer, Greer. Except the *Wall Street Journal*. It proposed to do a take-out on me and Miguel Loomis, undoubtedly under the headline, "The Last Lunch." The White House correspondents in the lobby all hammered at Jill, demanding personal time with me, but I put Dave Paulick at the head of the list even though he was not a regular. The reason was simple. He warned Jill that if I refused to see him privately, it would be my neck, not his. Gentle, solicitous Dave.

When we let him in, Dave bruised across the room like a pro linebacker blitzing the passer. He waved off my offer of a chair. Paulick preferred to tower over a man and, by sheer volition, shrivel his foe down to a midget. Funny thing. It sometimes worked. Squirming toward the back of my chair, I felt like saying, "Okay, just hand me the summons and leave."

Instead I said: "Good morning, David. We've missed you—and the humility—around here the last couple of days."

"Where's Greer?" he asked.

"Have you tried his office? Or maybe he's up at the Supreme Court."

He glowered down at me. God, the man was big. With those shoulders, he might have been the front end of a moving van.

"Do you know where Steve Greer is today?"

"Please, Dave. No jokes this morning."

"That won't do. I want a straight answer. Do you know where he is?"

"No. I do not know where he is, was or will be."

"Same house rules. You never lie?"

"If I were bigger, I'd clip you for that." A little of Paulick's browbeating was enough. "I'm leveling with you, and you know it. Now, quit the strong-man act."

He relaxed—slightly. "Well," he said, "I know where he went —or at least where he went part-way."

He flicked his big head toward Jill. She was ignoring her telephone now and she sat with elbows on the typewriter, chin in her hands, watching us.

"Jill stays," I said. "We're a team, and she's the most discreet member of it."

"So I hear." He leaned over and put those ham-like palms on my desk. "Steve Greer flew out of Montgomery County Airpark at Gaithersburg in a Beechcraft Baron last Thursday night at eight thirty-five. The pilot said he was going to Raleigh-Durham, but instead he flew to Atlantic City. Greer, using the name Hendricks, switched planes and flew to Kennedy in a Cessna Sky-night. He left Kennedy at about midnight on a jet cargo job operated by Overseas Quick-Freight, Inc. The flight plan called for a nonstop to Rio de Janeiro. Greer, now using the name Fairchild, was the only passenger."

I was stunned. Steve Greer flying secretly to Rio? Why?

Paulick stared down at me like a great Dane accosting a beagle. His challenge bristled as though I were the sinister mastermind of Greer's disappearance.

"I suppose you checked this out yourself?" I asked, but with Paulick, I already knew the answer.

"Every step of the way."

"Are you printing it?"

"No. The *Dossier* goes in Monday nights, remember? Maybe next week. Maybe not. Depends where this leads."

"Well, what do you want from me?"

"A straight steer—for a change. There's one chance in a hundred I've added wrong. If I have, and you know it, I want to be put straight."

"Dave, I have no idea. I don't know a thing beyond what I've announced. Not one thing. To be perfectly candid, I just assumed Greer was somewhere inside the country. But that was just a guess."

"That's hard to believe—that you're blanked out on this."

"It's the truth, Dave, so help me."

He studied me for a moment, his eyes moving point by point over my face like a buyer inspecting a used car for defects. Then he shrugged and turned toward the door.

"Where you off to?" I asked.

He stopped at Jill's desk and peered at me over his shoulder. "Rio. Where else?" Then he was out the door, which shuddered at his departure.

Jill crossed the room in a silent glide. She wore a high-buttoned shirtwaist with frills at the collar like a turn-of-the-century school-teacher. Her occasional efforts to appear prim, perhaps some private penance for her customary sensuality, were futile. She was about as sexless as Sophia Loren in a negligee.

"Do you believe it?" she asked in that tone of guileless wonder. "Paulick isn't wrong often," I said. "He's a barbarian—but he's thorough."

"What are you going to do?" She asked it as though I could wave a wand and make Stephen Greer materialize from the vapors.

"Tell the President. Aside from that, nothing."

As she looked at me, her eyes took on a distant glaze. "Gee-ene!" It was her little girl's plea for attention.

"Yes, Jill." My staff phone was ringing. I picked up the receiver and held a hand over the mouthpiece.

"Last night Butter and I had a discussion and she said, 'God is a gigolo.' What do you suppose that means?"

"It means you ought to move the hell out on her. . . . What a time to ask a question like that." I took my hand off the mouthpiece and said briskly, "Culligan." Jill, wrapped in her theological quandary, returned to her desk.

My call was from the guard at the side entrance on West Executive Avenue. An FBI agent named Lawrence Storm wanted to see me. I said to send him up. I knew he would take the inner passage past the staff offices and cabinet room. That way he avoided the big lobby where the press camped.

I knew that Larry Storm, a Negro, was one of Deskowicz's top special agents, but I was unprepared for the man who entered via the inner door a few moments later. He was quite wide in the shoulders, then trimly tapered, the build of an athlete. He had skin the color of cocoa, black eyes, and a bearing of serene confidence. That impressed me at once. We were not accustomed to serenity around our yapping kennel. He greeted me and held out his Bureau card. Ignoring it, I shook his other hand.

"I know you by reputation," I said. "It's a pleasure. Have a seat."

Unlike Paulick, he accepted. He settled himself in leisurely fashion while adjusting the pants creases of his subdued gabardine suit. In the exchange of amenities, I decided I liked the man. I assume he reciprocated the feeling, for we were soon first-naming each other. When he looked inquiringly at Jill, I reassured him. Jill was top cleared.

"In fact," I added, "she's so security-conscious, you could dismantle the H-bomb in here if you wanted to. . . . Go ahead, Larry."

"I'm checking out a Dr. Phillip J. Lubin and I understand you know him."

"Sure," I said. "What's up? A full field for some government math boondoggle? He's good at getting the gold-plated deals."

"No," he said. "This is in connection with another case."

With Storm's prestige at the Bureau that meant only one thing. "Greer?"

"I'm sorry. I can't say. Orders." His smile was sincerely apologetic. "It seems presumptuous saying that to the President's press secretary, but you know the Bureau."

I did. Still, I was miffed. My status was dented, and it was an effort not to show it. The next time I saw Pete Deskowicz . . . But I was intrigued. What could fiercely intellectual Phil Lubin possibly have to do with Steve Greer, the lawyers' golden lawyer?

Storm asked me all the usual questions: How long I'd known Lubin, whether we had seen each other recently, how I sized him up, etc. I told him that Phil and I became friendly at the University of Chicago when Lubin was my graduate instructor in a third-year math course. I thought Phil was eccentric, moody sometimes, but undeniably a brain. He impressed me as much as any other young person at Chicago. Of course, he wasn't much older than I, so the gap in our . . . uh . . . mental powers disheartened me sometimes. After college, I lost touch except for a couple of phone calls when Phil came through L.A. Then in the Roudebush campaign, when my name got in the papers as the press man, Phil called on me to offer aid. He had helped form a scientific panel backing Roudebush. We renewed our friendship and, since my arrival at the White House, I'd had lunch or dinner with him maybe once every four or five months. In fact, I had dinner with him not too many nights ago. That was about it.

"Do you recall what night you last had dinner?" Storm looked up from the notebook he had been writing in.

"Jill," I called. "Look in my date book and see when Phil Lubin and I had dinner at Paul Young's. I think it was last week some time."

"August 25," said Jill. "It wasn't Young's. It was the Hay-Adams. I had it marked down for six-fifteen."

"August 25," repeated Storm. "A Wednesday night, wasn't it?"

"Yes," said Jill.

"Yeah," I said. "I remember now because it was the night before Steve Greer disappeared. Things haven't been the same around here since."

"I can believe that," said Storm. He made another note. "Do you recall how long you talked that evening, Gene?"

"Well, let's see . . . Oh, yes. We made it a quickie dinner because he had to get back to Baltimore for some appointment. We broke it up about eight o'clock, I remember."

Storm put a few more general questions, then asked: "Have you ever heard of a discussion group of administration officials called the Potomac Study Club?"

"Nope." The question puzzled me, but Storm did not pursue it. Instead he riffled back through his notes, then tapped his pencil on the pad.

"Gene," he asked, "what do you know about Dr. Lubin's relations with women?"

"What do you mean?"

"The usual," he said. "Does he like them?" Storm's slight smile hinted that he and I shared the same appetite for the female sex, whether Phil Lubin did or not. I was conscious of Jill leaning forward, listening intently.

"You mean is he a fag?"

Larry nodded.

"No, I don't think so," I said. "He's not the big, masculine, aggressive type, but on the other hand I never thought of him as effeminate either. . . . I'd say he's a gentle and considerate man." The questions annoyed me. "Maybe . . . well . . . he's civilized, and as far as I know that's no particular crime—at least not under this administration."

Storm sensed my resentment. "Gene, don't take offense. The question is routine. It has no special significance." He arose and slipped his notebook in his side coat pocket. "I guess that's about it. Thanks for helping."

I stood up and we shook hands again.

"Say, what does all this have to do with Steve Greer?" I asked.

"I wish you wouldn't make that assumption," he said. He looked genuinely distressed. It was obvious he disliked playing games with an aide to the President.

"It was good to meet you," I said. "I hope we can sit around and talk sometime when you're not trying to pick my brains officially."

"You get me a couple of hours off at the Bureau," he said, "and I'll buy you a drink."

I walked over to the door with him, then tried again in a lower voice: "Listen, Larry, I'm really in the dark on this Greer case. I hear a report that Steve flew to Brazil last week. What do you hear?"

I could see the remark jolted him, but he managed to keep his expression reasonably blank. All he said was: "*You're* in the dark!"

When the door closed, I turned to Jill: "Now what do you suppose that last crack meant?"

She frowned, and when Jill frowned, she made a dramatic production of it. "Well, it sounded as though he didn't know anything either."

"But he's got to be working on Greer, and if he is, he must know more than we do."

She brushed the long hair off her forehead. "Do you suppose," she said slowly, "that Dr. Lubin has disappeared too?"

"Smart girl." The thought meshed with mine. "Get Phil's home number in Baltimore from your book. The one at the Charles Apartments, I think it is. If he's not there, try Johns Hopkins. Let me talk to him."

I tried to work on the final, definitive, semi-next-to-last draft of the President's Labor Day speech while she put through one call, then another. Her soft, muffled inquiries merged with the hum of the air-conditioning system. I knew it must be sweltering outside.

"Gene!" She had the wide-eyed, wondering look. "Both the

apartment and the math department say Mr. Lubin left Sunday on a long auto trip out West. They don't know where to reach him."

We looked at each other with shared awareness. Steve Greer and Phil Lubin both gone. . . . Paulick says Greer flew secretly to Rio. . . . Larry Storm, obviously working the Greer case, asks questions about Lubin . . . Raises a fag angle . . . Greer and Lubin? . . . Oh, for God's sweet sake . . .

I called Grace Lalley, asked to see the President soonest—about Greer. She said the Vice President was just finishing, and she'd squeeze me in before the chairman of the Fed. Maybe another five minutes. But I fidgeted for ten minutes before she buzzed me back.

The President was bent over a memorandum when I entered. He bestowed the wide, warming smile as he pushed his specs up above his forehead.

"The Pentagon wonders how you could make a nine-hundred-million error on the VTO fighters," he said. The man never missed a trick.

"Budget already has my hide for that," I said. "I plead guilty. I get confused by those damn two zeroes they tack on after the period—like a woman's $29.95 hat."

"You'll correct it at your press conference?"

I nodded. My first goof in a month. What a morning!

"Grace says you're super-urgent." He came around the desk and perched on the corner beside the gold donkey. It was his way of telling me to relax. In a world of nukes, wars of liberation, taxes and tears, everyone's mission was urgent.

"It's about Steve," I said. I gave him the highlights of the Paulick and Storm sessions. As I talked, he left the desk and walked slowly back and forth, his hands in his coat pockets, his head bent. Through the French doors, the rose garden lay inert, burdened with the late-morning heat. When I finished, Roudebush eased into his swivel chair.

"I'm sorry, Gene." He motioned me to the chair in front of his desk. "Have a seat. . . . That's surprising news. Let's take Paulick first. When do you suppose he intends to print this?"

"He can't for another week. His *Dossier* went to bed Monday night without any new Greer stuff. But my guess is he'll try to spring something big next Tuesday."

"I see. . . . That could be terribly embarrassing." He paused and began tapping a letter opener on the soft green desk blotter. "Is there anything we can do about Paulick?"

"You mean to prevent him from printing what he finds out?"

"Yes." He was utterly serious now.

"Not a chance, Mr. President. One word from me—and he'd just lay it on thicker."

He thought for a moment. "I think I'd better handle this myself. Please get in touch with Paulick. Tell him that before he prints anything, I'd like an opportunity to chat with him. No strings, of course."

I was dumfounded. Paul had laid down a press rule on the first day after his inauguration—no solo interviews. He occasionally saw top correspondents in groups of six or seven for off-the-record guidance sessions, but he believed that single interviews were unfair to the press corps and risky for the White House.

"That will get us in hot water with the regulars," I said.

"I don't think so, Gene," he said. "We can bring Paulick in via the back driveway entrance. The others needn't know."

I did not like it, but neither did I protest. "All right, sir. I'll have Jill find him. It may take a while. I think he's flying to Rio to pick up Greer's trail."

"Mmm." He looked beyond me to the section of the wall where his favorite painting hung. It was a bright water color of the shore of Captiva Island, his winter retreat. "Now, as for the FBI agent, your guess is what?"

"Putting two and two together, after Jill found that Lubin left on an auto trip, so-called, there's at least a . . . well . . . possibility that Greer and Phil Lubin may be somewhere together. Storm's last questions hinted at perversion."

The President leaned forward. "That, of course, is preposterous. . . . Gene, I think it would be wise if you and Jill did not discuss that particular angle. Mere speculation may do a grave injustice to a number of people."

"Yes, sir." I certainly would never mention it again in this room.

"Now, whether Lubin has disappeared too is another matter. I already knew of this development. It was included in Deskowicz's report. The Bureau is checking every avenue thoroughly."

"You could have told me," I protested with more tartness than I intended.

"It was in this morning's Bureau report," he said.

"Well, is it true that Steve flew to Rio?" I asked. He was looking beyond me at the painting again. "Also, I ought to know whether Steve and Phil Lubin know each other."

The President lifted his glasses from atop his head, blew on the lenses and polished them slowly with his handkerchief. It was a favorite delaying tactic which I'd seen many times when a conference funneled toward a presidential decision.

"Gene," he said after an unusually lengthy pause, "I think we had better reach an understanding on this matter. Until all the facts are in, I'd rather not discuss piece-meal aspects. . . . This is a trying period for me personally as well as for Sue Greer and her daughter. It isn't that I don't trust you. It's just that I don't want any of us to become involved, on the basis of fragmentary evidence, in conjectures that might prove both erroneous and harmful." He paused again. "I'm afraid you'll just have to bear with me for a while."

I could feel my temper rising. From the outset of my White House duty, it was understood that certain national security matters were beyond my province. I was not, for instance, to sit with the National Security Council, nor in meetings involving specific details of our defenses such as the command-and-control procedure by which Roudebush kept in constant touch with what Lyndon Johnson had called the "mash button." I was an outside-inside man, and I realized from the start that my dual role would provide some thorny days.

On the other hand, I had always assumed that on all other subjects, no matter how sensitive—and the Greer case was a prime example—I was to be clued in so that I might brief the press with reasonable accuracy and understanding.

"Mr. President," I said, "I figured I was to level with the press on Greer, and to do that I have to know what's going on." I hesitated. "Not, of course, that I have to report everything. After all, we *are* beginning a campaign."

"I'm acutely aware of that, Gene," he said. "Stanley Wolcott's people could cause us endless trouble by some sly use of half-truths."

"But the heat is building fast, Mr. President." I thought of that thicket of unanswered calls in my office. "I can't pretend that Steve Greer never existed."

"I'm hopeful," he said, "that we can unravel this thing before too long and then be able to state the exact facts."

"But in the meantime, sir, I'm on the spot." I could feel the temper simmering and I knew my cheeks were flushing. "I can't handle a guy like Paulick unless I have the picture."

"On the contrary, you can answer honestly that you don't know. If you had fractional information, you might be tempted."

"At the least," I insisted, "I ought to know what the Bureau is reporting to you." This was our first real dispute and I found, strangely, no inclination to yield. I knew I was right.

"I'm sorry, Gene," he said. "That cannot be done at this stage."

"Fine deal."

"Gene, please." He spread the big smile, but I was in no mood for blandishments.

"I don't like it, Mr. President," I said. I almost called him Paul. "And you might as well know exactly how I feel. Suddenly, I'm not your press secretary, I'm a damn palace eunuch."

He came quickly around the desk, threw an arm around my shoulders and, with barely perceptible pressure, began moving me toward the door.

"Please live with it for now," he said, "as a personal favor to me. This should all be cleared up before long."

"If it's tomorrow," I retorted, "it won't be a day too soon."

I closed the door sharply, and not until I heard the slam did I realize what I had said—and done. I amazed myself. I may explode now and then, but I'm definitely not the type who tells off Presidents of the United States.

Jill could read the results on my face.

"Trouble?"

"Yes. He wants me to play deaf, dumb, and blind on Greer. What's more, he won't tell me a thing . . . nothing, period."

"It's Wolcott," she said. "The President is nervous over what Springfield might find out."

"Jesus, I understand that, but that's no justification for holding out on me. Me!" It came boiling out. "Damn it, Jill, what does he take me for? Some two-bit press agent?"

She walked over to me and framed my face in her hands. The fingers felt cool, but I felt ridiculous. The nurse was soothing the fevered patient.

"He thinks you're the best p.r. man in the country," she said. "I think something too. I think you're the greatest."

She kissed me lightly. I folded her against me. Two telephones ignited simultaneously, the buzzer on mine, the lights on hers. The duodenal ulcer shop screamed for its victims.

The rest of the day was a hapless shambles. If anything went by the book, it escaped me. Drew Pearson's assistant tried to check me on a report that a man in dark glasses, resembling Greer, had been seen in Lisbon. Bill White wanted guidance on a column which apparently would state that Roudebush's devious handling of the Greer case belied his posture as a "pragmatic centrist." Dick Wilson fished for reaction to his tip that the next Gallup Poll would show Roudebush down three points. Scotty Reston commanded me to lunch at the Metropolitan Club—when my stomach already was jumping so much I could not digest the hamburger and chocolate shake I had at my desk. Evans and Novak never did get straightened out. When Evans reached me from the Senate press gallery, he asked the same question Novak asked from Stockholm: Was the *London Economist* correct in stating that Steve Greer had become a millionaire on legal fees since Paul Roudebush entered the White House? How the hell should I know? Alsop delivered me an Olympian lecture for five minutes on management of the news. And Jill never did track down Dave Paulick. If Paulick was headed for Rio, he must have been traveling by chartered submarine.

My four-o'clock press conference resembled a bull run in a Portuguese village street. I was the old bull, frayed, weak-kneed, and sick to death of the whole weary business. They baited me, like whooping young men armed with umbrellas, from every wall, stoop, and doorway. What had the FBI reported? Why couldn't they interview Mrs. Greer? What about an AP bulletin that a Pennsylvania congressman was demanding that Congress remain in session until Greer was found? Why had Miguel Loomis skipped his noon briefing at the Greer home in Kenwood? What about the TASS dispatch from Moscow, charging that the law firm of Greer, Hilstratter, Tomlin & DeLuca was in a conspiracy with the White House to suppress the worst financial scandal of the century? Was the President refusing to pass on FBI data to me? (That one made me wince.) If I really knew as little as I claimed, would I welcome a taxpayers' suit to withhold my salary? What about the rumor of a large amount of cash in Greer's office safety vault?

We ended in a swirling row when the Baltimore *Sun* man demanded that I release the verbatim transcript of the press conference. He knew it would make me out a fool at the best, a conniving enemy of an informed press at the worst. I said firmly that we would follow the old ground rules. The transcript was for guidance only, not for direct quotes. The *Copley* correspondent growled that he did not care, that he was taking shorthand and thus had me all on the record anyway. The Chicago *Sun-Times* reporter offered him fifty dollars for a copy. The New York *Daily News* raised the ante to one hundred dollars. Everyone seemed to be shouting at once, and when the Baltimore *Sun* writer finally yelled, "Thank you, Mr. Secretary," a voice from the rear added, "for nothing."

When Jill closed the door behind the last baiter, I knew how the old bull felt when he staggered back to his pen and the last white-shirted youth with an umbrella raised a victory cry in the emptying street. I was shaking, and I wished to God I had a cigarette. For the first time in my life, I wanted to quit.

"Jill," I said, "tonight you're coming up to my place and we're going to fill the martini pitcher right up to the snout."

She shook her head slowly and the hair swung like a sad pendulum. "I'm sorry, Gene," she said. "I'd love to, but I can't tonight. Butter and I have two friends—women—coming for dinner. It's been on for a week."

"And I suppose Butter will brood far into the night," I said, "on such cosmic themes as 'God is a gigolo.'"

"Et cetera."

"Et cetera," I echoed, "et cetera."

That tied it. So I would go home and get drunk by myself. If God was not a gigolo, Greer was a blasphemy on all honest men. I could already feel my splitting headache when I would awaken at 3 A.M., and I could taste the sour grit of the second aspirin.

7

Peter Deskowicz walked down the brightly lighted executive corridor of the CIA building and halted before the purple door.

Doors of the Central Intelligence Agency were individually painted like those of a nursery school, some yellow, some red, some orange. There were blues, grays, pinks and greens. The colors seemed to shout their delight at man's surveillance of man. Intelligence, they proclaimed to visitors, was anything but a shrouded, black operation. Rather it was a festive gambol.

The painted entrances gave a lift to the spirits of those who labored in the vast building. If some dolorous academician, plagued by respiratory allergies and a knobby wife, had to spend his hours tabulating the tonnage, speed, and capacity of the Soviet tanker fleet, he need only repaint the office door a spanking scarlet to brighten the days. Once a clandestine agent, back for a home tour after years in the khaki deserts of the Middle East, painted his door snow white. He said it reminded him of the Vermont winters of his boyhood.

The purple door usually matched Deskowicz's mood on these Thursday mornings. The small black plaque beside the entrance read, "7E26, USIB Conference Room." Deskowicz entered with a sigh, passed through a small reception area into the long room where the United States Intelligence Board held its regular weekly meetings.

At times the FBI director felt that he had spent half his life in this room. The walls were paneled in dark plywood, the green drapes were drawn and the two flags hung in limp folds at their standards. One was the American flag and the other the CIA's banner—yellow-beaked eagle and sixteen-point compass rose against a blue background. Emblems of the government's various intelligence units—DIA, ONI, FBI—lined the walls, and the long, narrow table, curving slightly in the middle, stretched for twenty feet. As usual, white, lined pads and yellow pencils rested before each chair. The table reminded Deskowicz of the gaping mouth of a prehistoric mastodon, white teeth edged with yellowing tartar.

Deskowicz, nodding to Arthur Ingram at the head of the table, settled carefully into the FBI's assigned chair. Although of a graceful, modern design, the chair was too narrow for his beam. Deskowicz eyed the sheaf of slick, duplicated papers he had brought with him. A red box, rubber stamped in the upper right hand corner, read: "Secret, NIE A-4. Copy No. __." The figure 4, inked by hand in the space, subtly reminded Deskowicz of his rank at this morning meeting.

The rating, dictated by the whims of Arthur Victor Ingram, placed the FBI director fourth among ten. Copy No. 1 went to Ingram, saluting not his command of the CIA but his broader role as the government's director of intelligence who shepherded all U.S. efforts to find out what the rest of the human race was up to. Copy No. 2 always was issued to Ingram's CIA deputy. Copy No. 3 went to Lt. Gen. Marvin O. Palfrey, chief of the Pentagon's Defense Intelligence Agency; No. 4 to Deskowicz; No. 5 to Abrams, of the State Department's Bureau of Intelligence and Research; No. 6 to Walton, of the Atomic Energy Commission; No. 7 to Jerome Freytag, of the National Security Agency, at once the architect and saboteur of codes and ciphers. (Freytag's army of mole-like clerks worked in a concrete fortress near Fort Meade, Maryland, behind a double barbed-wire fence upon which searchlights played all night.) Copies 8, 9, and 10 went to the intelligence chiefs of Army, Navy, and Air Force.

By law all intelligence captains save Ingram sat as equals on the U. S. Intelligence Board, which met regularly to survey a fragile globe and America's own insecure stake in the ever-shifting sands of world power. But Ingram, exercising his authority as chief sleuth, issued the numbered copies of any document according to his own estimate of status. Deskowicz resented this arbitrary pecking order. It seemed to rate a man's opinion in advance, each inferior to Ingram's, all nicely in file like geese waddling to a pond, each quack dwindling in prestige down the straggling line. Freytag, of NSA, brought up the rear of the major agencies, just ahead of the subordinate military intelligence chiefs, because—or so Deskowicz surmised—Ingram thought Freytag unduly frivolous for global statecraft.

Deskowicz fingered the sheaf before him, his mind only fractionally on its contents. His thoughts centered instead on Stephen B. Greer, missing now for almost a week, or more precisely, a full week at eight thirty-five tonight. The FBI chief silently reviewed the last bulletin from Clyde Moorhead, phoned to him just before the Bureau limousine ferried him to Langley, Virginia, for this meeting behind the purple door. Deskowicz had read SA Larry Storm's Wednesday night report during the ride out the George Washington Memorial Parkway. He finished just as he spotted the turn-off sign for the CIA, "Fairbank Highway Research Station." He always winced at the sight of the small road marker, regarding it as a coy attempt to mask a building known to every foreign diplomat and intelligence agent in Washington.

"We'll be delayed a few minutes," Ingram's voice, edged with irritation, pierced Deskowicz's thoughts from the head of the table. "Marvin phoned from the Pentagon. He was held up by a call from the White House."

"God disposes, The Man imposes," said Jerome Freytag. The head of the National Security Agency was a slight, fox-faced man from M.I.T. who liked to needle his colleagues. Deskowicz knew that the very complexity of NSA duties, a wilderness of codes, ciphers, and computers which no one else on the board really understood, gave Freytag immunity. Like a man in a sheltered mountain cave, he could snipe without fear of lethal return fire.

Ingram smiled wanly at Freytag. Abrams, of State, drummed on the table with his fingers. Walton, of the AEC, craned his neck for an unnecessary look at the wall emblems. Establishment men all, they viewed Freytag with wary discomfort. He was not properly institutional, and they weighed his iconoclasm as a council of bishops might regard a young parish priest who experimented with a jazz Mass.

"Or perhaps," said Freytag, "Marvin is closeted with his colonels, plotting a coup."

The three military chiefs grinned and Freytag happily saluted them. Then he began doodling on his pad. Deskowicz, sitting across the table, saw that the NSA chief was drawing a Chinese coolie.

Lt. Gen. Marvin Palfrey entered at that moment. His hurried smile swept his colleagues at bargain rates, and he strode to his seat, to the right of Ingram, like a commander to the lead bomber. His seamed face was the kind that had to be stretched for shaving to mow the whiskers out of the crevices. Three silver stars winked at each shoulder. He breathed heavily as he sat down.

"We'll consider the U. S. Intelligence Board in session," said Ingram crisply. His words marched like soldiers on parade. "The sole item on the agenda is, of course, our review of National Intelligence Estimate A-4. It was prepared under the direction of Dr. Geoffrey Page, the Agency's China evaluation chief, whom most of you know. He is here to answer any questions."

Ingram nodded toward Dr. Page, a tall angular scholar wearing a casual tweed jacket with leather patches at the elbows. He was seated alone against the wall and was puffing on a Dunhill pipe.

"Since we've all read the estimate from Dr. Page's group," said Ingram, "I suggest we go straight to discussion."

"Substantive first, or can we raise derivative matters?" asked Walton. The Atomic Energy Commission representative was a pale man, with scanty gray hair, whose habit of peering through the upper lenses of his bifocals gave him an aspect of constant perturbation.

Freytag arched a thin eyebrow without looking up from his doodling. "That question is corrosively derivative," he said.

"What do you mean?" asked Walton.

"I have no idea. What did you mean?"

"Oh . . ." Walton glanced at the ceiling, pleading despair in the face of lunacy. His spectacles were poised on his nose, a tactical defense weapon.

Deskowicz cheered inwardly. Most of Walton's comments were as pointless as smoke, and Deskowicz was always heartened by Freytag's refusal to pretend he understood them. The three military chiefs all grinned, but their superior, General Palfrey, coughed reprovingly. Abrams frowned. Ingram rapped on the table.

"Let's adhere to the regular order," he said. "You lead off, will you Marvin?"

"We have no basic objection to NIE A-4," responded General Palfrey. The "we" went unaccented, but the cathedral tones evoked a picture of numberless Pentagon cubicles, crammed with brush-haired military intelligence officers, all pledging assent. In fact, the Army, Navy, and Air Force intelligence chiefs at the table did nod their approval.

"Basically," he continued, "the estimate takes note of the unusual lull in bomb-rattling by the Chicoms during the last two months. It attributes this lull to an inept, perhaps I should say foolish, attempt to influence the U.S. presidential elections this November." He glanced toward Ingram. "Is that a fair summation, Arthur?"

Ingram nodded. "Yes. Also, of course, it makes the point that Peiping undoubtedly prefers President Roudebush to Governor Wolcott, simply because Wolcott is still an unknown quantity to Premier Wang Kwo-P'ing and the party hierarchy."

"Right," said Gen. Palfrey. "Now, we have no quarrel with that assessment. In the old days, the Russians made similar misguided attempts to influence U.S. elections. While they are too sophisticated now for that kind of crude maneuver, the Chicoms remain fairly primitive in their politics. At least, that's our thinking at DIA, always hastily adding, of course, that politics is not our main dish. We have our own fish to fry."

"You would approve the estimate as written then?" asked Ingram.

"With one addendum," replied Palfrey. Deskowicz noticed one tiny hair in the general's cheek furrow which the razor had missed this morning. He wondered if Palfrey brooded on Chicoms while shaving. "I think the board should underscore the fact that nothing material has changed, lull or no lull."

"Why?" asked Abrams. "I'm not being contentious, you understand. I'd just like to get your thinking."

"Of course." General Palfrey smiled at Abrams, seeming to enfold the doves of State to the iron bosom of the Pentagon. "Two for-instances. DIA has incontrovertible evidence that the Chicoms recently moved carloads of small hardware to the Indian border, including a new line of bazookas which are quite ingenious in their kill ratio per ounce of explosive. . . . A second for-instance, I have information that two ammo factories near Shanghai have gone to three shifts this summer."

"The ammo plant discovery was forwarded to DIA from the Agency," observed Ingram. His stress of "the Agency" was a reminder of the CIA's senior status at this table. "Did you get corroborative data from your own sources?"

The general rifled a glance toward the CIA director, and Deskowicz thought it a balanced mixture of surprise and poison. Freytag grinned.

"We already had the information in hand at DIA," said Palfrey, "but I will say the Agency's paper helped us fill in some chinks."

"First pun of the day, Marvin," cried Freytag. "Even though it was unintentional, you get three points." He motioned in the air, chalking a figure on an imaginary blackboard. General Palfrey's smile was a weak one. Walton shook his head. Abrams scowled.

Ingram, ignoring the digression, moved swiftly ahead on his rounds. "Pete?"

"I'd ditto Marvin's belief that nothing basic has been altered," responded Deskowicz. "Our surveillance of Red China's embassy and of her U.N. delegation shows the same old espionage contacts proceeding as usual. I suppose if we were to graph Red Chinese espionage since our diplomatic recognition three years ago . . ."

"Thirty-one months ago," corrected Abrams of State.

"Yes. Well, I'd say the graph would show a pretty straight line. We could say the same thing for the period since Red China was admitted to the U.N."

The FBI director hesitated. Should he mention the newly discovered Chinese dead drop in New York? In theory, these board meetings were supposed to afford uninhibited exchanges of information, the boots, shirts, coats, and assorted accessories of intelligence being traded as easily as old clothes at a swap shop. In practice, each agency chief jealously husbanded his own wardrobe. The accepted gambit was to reveal just enough to pique his rivals' curiosity, but not so much as to expose a potential line of inquiry which an alert competitor could commandeer for his own use. Deskowicz was proud of the Bureau's discovery of the new dead drop and he recognized, ruefully, a desire to brag to his peers. But he suppressed the urge. His fealty to gamesmanship carried the day.

"Illustrations of continued espionage are plentiful," he said. "There's no point taking up the board's time by describing them."

State's Abrams, an actor already upstaged, came next. He added little except his agreement with DIA and FBI. Walton, of the Atomic Energy Commission, peering gravely through his bifocals, declared that Communist China under Premier Wang still declined to sign the test-ban treaty and continued to detonate nukes of various sizes.

"So," concluded Walton, "I would hope we could agree unanimously this morning without dissent."

"Nothing basic has changed," commented Freytag, "not even Walton's tautology."

"And that not very gentle remark brings on Mr. Freytag," said Ingram.

"I haven't much to add," said Freytag. "As I told you last month, we cracked a senior diplomatic code of the Chinese. They apparently knew it, because they promptly went to a new system which we're still playing with. Lots of flower talk: iris, pomegranate, daisy, sweet pea, delphinium. Sounds like a damn ladies garden club. Our computer's working on it, but so far no pay dirt. . . . But that's beside the point. If it's the consensus to add a Board footnote that nothing basic has changed, I'll go along."

The three service intelligence chiefs concluded the protocol of the morning by agreeing with General Palfrey. Ingram asked Geoffrey Page if he had anything to add, but the China specialist shook his head.

"I have taken the liberty of anticipating the board somewhat," said Ingram. He glanced about the table and picked up a sheet of paper. "I prepared a tentative statement to be attached to NIE A-4 for the information of the President. Let's see if it doesn't encompass all our thinking." He paused, then read the paper:

The United States Intelligence Board, having considered National Intelligence Estimate A-4, approves that estimate.

NIE A-4 notes the unusual cessation of radio and diplomatic attacks on the United States by the government of Communist China. This is the first sustained hiatus in Red China's bellicose attitude since its seizure of power on the Asiatic mainland. The belligerency had continued with but slight abatement despite settlement of the Viet Nam war, despite admission of Red China to the U.N. and despite U.S. recognition of Red China by the Roudebush administration and the subsequent normalizing of diplomatic relations.

NIE A-4 surmises—correctly, we believe—that Communist China is engaged in an oafish attempt to influence the U.S. election. The Chinese know that President Roudebush successfully forced diplomatic recognition of China through a reluctant U. S. Senate and that this year, the U.S. even supported Red China on two minor U.N. votes. Thus far, while he has avoided the specific, Governor Stanley Wolcott of Illinois, the opposition candidate, has questioned the "firmness" of the Roudebush Asian policy. NIE A-4 concludes that Red China hopes by its new muted tone to stave off the election of a commodity unknown to it, namely Governor Wolcott.

This board concurs in this estimate, but wishes to append its unanimous assessment that nothing basic has changed in long-term China policy toward the United States. That policy remains suspicious, capricious, and hostile as evidenced by continued arms build-ups, nuclear intransigence, and espionage on U.S. soil. We therefore warn against any tendency to interpret Red China's temporary noncombative posture as indicating a permanent shift toward peaceful coexistence with the United States.

Ingram removed his glasses, held them in his fingers as though anointing them, and looked about the table for approbation. Deskowicz marveled at the snug fit of Ingram's coat. The CIA chief always looked as though a disembodied valet stood behind him to perform instant pressing services. Deskowicz himself usually felt irretrievably rumpled by this hour of the morning.

"Comments?" asked Ingram. The tone implied he anticipated none.

"I caught the word 'oafish' somewhere, didn't I, Arthur?" asked Freytag.

"Yes. The word is used to describe China's attempt to influence our elections."

"It offends me," said Freytag. "It smacks dangerously of creative imagery in an otherwise orthodox government document. Besides, what the hell does it mean?"

Ingram peered at the paper. The slight lift of his eyebrows betrayed him, thought Deskowicz: The document probably had been drafted by Ingram's deputy.

"In this context, it carries the idea of stupidity," replied Ingram.

"If we mean stupid, let's say so," said Freytag. "Personally, I find the Chinese stupid only in their slavish imitation of Western bureaucracy."

"Thank you, Mr. Freytag," said Abrams, quickly embattled as though the State Department had been slandered by name.

"How about 'clumsy' in place of 'oafish'?" suggested General Palfrey.

Ingram, taking the moment of silence as assent, somewhat reluctantly inked in the new word. "Now, is there any other objection?" Silence again. "If not, we'll consider the Board's addendum as unanimously adopted."

Abrams looked at his wrist watch. "Is that it for the day?" he asked.

"Yes," replied Ingram. "That was the only item on the agenda this morning." He paused, then added as a seeming afterthought: "Of course, I think we'd all like to be brought up to date on the Greer case. It seems to me this very odd disappearance may have implications for the whole intelligence community."

The new silence was disturbing, reminding Deskowicz anew that federal intelligence was less a community than a clutter of fortified and mistrustful fiefdoms. Freytag moistened his lips as if about to speak, but refrained. The shadow of the White House lay upon the room. Several men looked inquiringly at Deskowicz, but the FBI director said nothing.

"I'm not sure Greer comes within the purview of the board," said Walton, conscious as always of structures and channels. "Greer's personal relationship to the President makes it a White House concern."

"Of course," said Ingram. "But since the FBI has been assigned to investigate, there are possibly aspects for all of us." He turned to Deskowicz. "I think, Pete, it would be helpful if you could tell us where the Greer matter stands at the moment."

Deskowicz shifted heavily in his chair, conscious of his excess poundage. He gazed at the sheaf of papers before him, avoiding the eyes of the other men.

"Unfortunately," he said, "there has not been a great deal of progress. I'm afraid I couldn't be very enlightening."

"Well, just give us the results thus far, Pete," urged Ingram.

"I'll have to beg off, Arthur."

"Why?"

Deskowicz glanced about the table. "I'm sorry, gentlemen," he said, "but the President has ordered me not to discuss this case outside the Bureau. The only exception is, of course, the President himself. In light of his orders, you'll have to excuse me."

The silence this time wore the face of shock, clearly mirrored about the table. The rules of the game had been flouted. In this room, a man might treat intelligence as a perishable resource to be doled out frugally. Or he might move cautiously, advancing an item like a pawn in a chess game, so as not to expose his full strategy. But no member of the U. S. Intelligence Board ever before had refused bluntly to honor a colleague's inquiry.

"I can appreciate the President's feelings," said General Palfrey slowly. "However, if his order was intended to include this board, I think it unfortunate. If we can't lay our cards on the table, we must reach conclusions without knowing whether we have a full deck. That's not intelligence. It's guesswork."

"I agree," said Deskowicz. His normally impassive face reflected his turmoil. "I would like to be completely candid here, always, but in this case, I cannot. Of course, we must realize that Stephen Greer's disappearance could become a national security hazard only in the most improbable circumstances."

"I was inclined to agree," said Ingram. He spoke without looking at Deskowicz. "Until this morning . . ."

He paused and the only sound to be heard was the scratch of Freytag's pencil as he doodled on his paper tablet.

"Just before entering this meeting," said Ingram solemnly, "I received information via Agency channels that Mr. Greer last Thursday night flew by stages—involving two small airports—to Kennedy International. He then flew, apparently alone, in a jet cargo craft to Rio de Janeiro."

The silence hung like smoke from a pistol shot.

"That information, if correct, should be given promptly to the President," said Deskowicz, "without discussion by this board."

"We are under no presidential orders on the Greer case," said Ingram. His stare challenged Deskowicz.

"I am," said the FBI director. He returned the stare.

"Perhaps we should stick to the agenda," offered Walton. He looked at Palfrey, beseeching military support for a cease-fire.

"The agenda is completed," said Ingram firmly. "No, I think this board is entitled to know whether my agency's information conforms to that of the Bureau. The fact that Mr. Greer undoubtedly is abroad raises a possible national security angle."

Deskowicz became the target of all eyes.

"Arthur," said Deskowicz, "I must respectfully decline to answer."

Walton wiped his brow with a handkerchief, but Freytag flashed a smile of relish.

"I find this incredibly frustrating," said Ingram. His diction was meticulous. "We are paid salaries to gather and evaluate intelligence, not play blind man's buff."

"I refuse to argue the matter," said Deskowicz. "With all deference, Arthur, I must remind you that my orders come from the President."

"Now, Pete . . ." began Walton.

"Man overboard," said Freytag. He slapped the table. "I move we adjourn."

"I second the motion," said Deskowicz promptly.

Ingram looked about the table. "Obviously, there is no need for a vote." There was frost on his voice. "The meeting is adjourned."

Deskowicz walked to the head of the table and extended his hand. "I'm sorry, Arthur. Nothing personal. I hope you understand."

Ingram shook hands perfunctorily. "The hope is misplaced. I do not understand."

The conferees filed wordlessly from the room, leaving Arthur Ingram at the head of the long table. After a few moments, he walked alone down the corridor to the yellow door of the director's office. The black sign beside the door was as discreet in size as the others along the hall. This one read, "7D60 DCI."

He said a few words to his secretary and entered his private office, closing the door behind him. He had kept this command retreat largely as he had inherited it from his predecessors. The furniture was heavy, male, upholstered in brown leather. The paintings were inoffensive, their hues blending with the drapes and the brown nap of the carpeting. His only addition to the walls was a framed quotation from Dwight Eisenhower. At the building's cornerstone ceremonies in November 1959, the then President had said: "Success cannot be advertised: failure cannot be explained. In the work of Intelligence, heroes are undecorated and unsung, often even among their own fraternity." Ingram took pride in the thousands of undecorated heroes he commanded at home and abroad.

He stood at the long, three-paneled window, gazing out at the hill of elms, beeches, dogwoods, oaks, and maples which placed a leafy barrier between him and the Potomac River. The foliage was glazed with dust from the long rainless stretch and the sun

steamed behind a white rag of cloud. Beneath him in the land-
scaped parking lot reserved for visitors, a hundred cars huddled
like multicolored candy bars. His domain was a magnet for all of
official Washington.

Then he turned to the mahogany cabinet behind his desk
which held his battery of five telephones. Here was his post of
instant contact with his agency and with the world. The gray
phone connected him with his platoon of experts within the
building, scrambling the words in transit into random idiocy, then
miraculously sorting them out again for his auditor. The cream
phone and push-button box was the instrument for ordinary
communications, save for two red buttons which marked secure
channels within the Agency. The black telephone connected
Ingram with the White House switchboard and from there, to
the world. The green phone was his private line to the Pentagon.
At the end of the cabinet sat his small blue phone, the direct line
to the President's office. He lifted the blue receiver. The buzzer
sounded on the desk of Grace Lalley. A moment later, the President's hearty voice said, "Good morning, Arthur."

"Mr. President," said Ingram, "I'm bothering you only because
this is a matter of concern to you. It's about Stephen Greer."

"Oh?"

"We've just concluded board discussion of NIE A-4 which you'll
have in a few minutes on the Xerograph. Just before the meeting,
I received information that Mr. Greer flew to Rio de Janeiro by
several apparently secret stages last Thursday night. I thought
you should know this at once."

"I see," said Roudebush. "What was the source of your data?"

"Regular Agency channels. I was handed the memo by my director of intelligence. We'll have more details, of course, but I
thought you should have the gross, unevaluated material without
delay."

"Yes," said the President. "That was thoughtful of you."

The brief reply left Ingram hanging.

"In view of this development," he said hurriedly, "which puts
Greer abroad, I assume you'd like the full attention of the Agency
from here on out."

There was a moment of silence on the line. "No," said Roudebush, "I think not, Arthur. The Bureau's investigation is quite
wide at the moment. This is all very distressing, both to Steve's
family and to myself, and I just don't think further alerts would
prove helpful at this time. Involving the whole Agency right now
would place too much government emphasis on what is, really, a
private matter."

"It could be done narrowly and discreetly by two or three of
our best agents," offered Ingram.

"No, Arthur," said Roudebush firmly. "For the time being, we'll
rely on the FBI."

"The Agency is not to help then?"

"No, not at this time. If that changes, I'll notify you at once,
naturally. . . . By the way, was Greer discussed at the board
meeting?"

"Yes, sir," said Ingram with just a trace of guilt in his voice.
"Briefly, I relayed my information and asked Deskowicz if it
tallied with his data. He replied that he was under orders from
you not to discuss the case."

"Yes," said Roudebush. "I believe discussion at this juncture by
the U. S. Intelligence Board is unnecessary. Right now, I'd like
the matter confined to one agency. While that may change, I do
not feel justified in bringing the entire range of federal artillery
to bear on this highly personal affair. My own feeling is that Steve
will return in his own good time with a perfectly adequate explanation."

"Yes, sir."

"Thanks, Arthur. I hope you understand."

As Ingram hung up, he realized the phrase was the very one
Peter Deskowicz had used a few minutes earlier—and that he,
the director of central intelligence, did not understand at all.

The gulf in his understanding was widened by the memorandum which Nick, his director of intelligence, had sent him just
before the USIB meeting. The memo contained two separate
items of information. Ingram had intended to reveal both at the
meeting, but changed his mind when Deskowicz took his obdurate,
negative stand. Nor had he discussed the second point with the

President. Roudebush detested interbureau rivalries, and the second paragraph clearly indicated surveillance of one barony of the "intelligence community" by another. Wondering, Ingram unlocked his top desk drawer, withdrew the memorandum and read it again:

From: Nick

To: Vic

1. Stephen B. Greer reliably reported in Rio de Janeiro after three-stage secret flight last Thursday night which took him from Gaithersburg Airpark to Atlantic City to Kennedy International. Flight from Kennedy to Rio made solo in jet cargo of Overseas Quick-Freight, Inc.
2. Little Sister investigating Phillip J. Lubin, Johns Hopkins mathematics professor, in connection with Greer case. Lubin missing from Baltimore apartment since Sunday.

Ingram studied the paper for several minutes, then phoned his secretary in the adjoining office: "Alice, get me a print-out on Phillip J. Lubin, a Johns Hopkins faculty member."

Five minutes later the computer's swift judgment on Mr. Lubin, four feet of paper with perforated borders, was placed on Ingram's desk. He walked down the inner executive hall, softly carpeted, to his private dining room, trailing the sheet like a bride's train. Sunlight poured through the bank of windows, enriching the blue velveteen of the dining chairs and the blue and gray of the grass paper covering the walls. There was a cool, gentle stir of air from the central conditioner. Ingram's lunch was set out for him, Mahattan clam chowder, a corned beef sandwich, the usual glass of skimmed milk.

While he ate, Ingram read about Phillip J. Lubin, four feet of a man's life, 5000 words of degrees, chairs, honors, habits. Lubin was No. 10874 in the CIA's electronic reservoir of scientific talent, already cleared, ready for instant summons in event of war or some specific chore for the Agency. The print-out recorded Lubin's work for GOBLET, a CIA-sponsored research project

which measured Communist scientific advances in relation to
Western progress. A hazy picture of Lubin formed in Ingram's
mind—a short, introspective fellow, somewhat testy, wasn't he?
They had met once in the conference room, or was it twice? At
any rate, Lubin had a high security clearance. Ingram also found
that the Agency rated Lubin among the world's top twenty mathematicians, that his foreign languages numbered five.

Ingram's eyes lingered on the last section, headed PER-
SONAL: "Bachelor. Never married. No known affair with women
since early romance with Helene Wallenstein (dec. 1958) when
both were U. of C. graduate students. Occasionally dines with
women, but appears to prefer company of men, usually fellow
academicians. Basically self-oriented. Known to Hopkins faculty
members as 'loner,' 'fussbudget,' or 'solitary.' Rated as sensitive,
easily offended. Does not smoke. Drinks but little . . ." The report
trailed off into Lubin's taste in clothes, automobiles, and hobbies.
Ingram lost interest.

The director sat thinking of Phillip Lubin and Stephen Greer.
And he thought of Paul Roudebush as he lighted his panetela.
Ingram's anger smoldered with the rising smoke. Twice rebuffed
within a week. First on Operation Flycatcher, a modest but immensely promising venture which he had conceived and in which
he took personal pride. Then to be forbidden to touch the Greer
business! Strange that Stephen Greer, a man whose chief talent
was a fortuitous friendship, should figure in both reverses. Ingram
pondered his duty and his future.

Duty first. He was the commander of a vast, clandestine army
dedicated to amassing information about every foreign nation,
large or small, powerful or weakly inept. This building was his
citadel, his life, almost his home. He had labored through long
nights to forge what he knew to be the largest, most competent,
and painstaking intelligence agency the world had ever known.
He loved the Agency in a way that no other government official
could comprehend. The Agency was a tightly knit family, bound
by common vows of secrecy, by a common purpose, by its clois-
tered separation from the fractures and the turbulence of American life. Here were discipline, commitment, order, composure,

rationality. And yet here also was the excitement of the chase and of discovery. Here was the passion of intricately fitted knowledge and the thrill of solving hidden puzzles that unlocked the doors of diplomacy and power. This was the fascinating inside world, walled unto itself.

Ingram took pleasure in the little physical manifestations of his family empire. When he arrived every morning at eight-ten o'clock, the greeting by the uniformed doorman beneath the angled, concrete portico was a private, knowing one. In the huge pillared lobby, with the great seal of the Agency embedded in the terrazzo floor, he often paused to look at the inscription cut into the marble wall: "And ye shall know the truth and the truth shall make you free. John VIII, XXXII." At the roped barrier, three guards said their good mornings to him. Beyond was his world: a ceaseless flow of workers through the cheerful corridors, every person wearing his identification badge, every door singing its individual song, every office boasting its own cabinet safes with the red "Open" signs, every desk equipped with transparent plastic baskets lettered with a single word in red, BURN. Contents of the "burn" baskets were trucked to the incinerator, where flames each day consumed thousands of confidential memoranda, letters, and scribbled notes.

Ingram took pride in the expensive machinery of intelligence: the giant computers, the code machines, encrypting and deciphering with nonchalant speed, the communications center, where 150 messages an hour chattered in from all continents throughout every day and night, the building's pneumatic tube and conveyor tray systems for swift exchange of documents, the scrambled Xerograph equipment, which permitted secret papers to be transmitted instantaneously to the White House or Pentagon.

It was Ingram's passion that the top echelon of the CIA should know everything that happened in the world which could conceivably affect America and its uncertain ramparts. Information without totality was not intelligence, but merely information. One missing piece in the jigsaw puzzle meant failure, and every

piece had its value. Thus a vanished Stephen Greer, a close friend
of the President, if loose somewhere in the world, held a clue for
intelligence potentially as significant as the last conversation of
the Cuban prime minister or the contents of a Kremlin cable to
the Soviet embassy in Bangkok. Ingram strove to make the daily
bulletins of intelligence, which reached the desks of top government officials every morning, as complete and as accurate as possible. The bulletin was held in type until 4:30 A.M. for late
additions and corrections.

To deprive Arthur Ingram of his right to search, to discover
and finally to know—anything and everything—was to cripple him.
The thought was intolerable. His whole life was this command
in the wooded hills of Langley and he would not live it as a lame
commander.

When he reached his decision, Ingram returned to his office
and placed a call for Senator Owen Moffat of Nebraska, the ranking minority member on a Senate subcommittee of six men, the
silent watchdogs of the CIA. Moffat was one of less than a score
of men in Washington who knew almost everything about the
Agency worth knowing. Ingram reached Moffat in a Senate cloak-
room, stated his need opaquely but urgently. Moffat promised to
drive to Langley as soon as possible.

It was an hour later when Senator Moffat settled into the
leather armchair facing Ingram's uncluttered desk and the battery
of telephones below the CIA's blue seal with its proudly vigilant
eagle.

Moffat was portly, dignified, yet oddly cherubic. He had an
eternally flushed and unlined face that seemed to have escaped
the erosion of time by some private miracle. He exercised daily
in the pint-sized Senate gymnasium and, although sixty years old,
he still paid rapt attention to the way women walked. If it had
not been for women, politics would have been his first love.

"Owen," said Ingram, "I'm perplexed and I need your help."

Moffat smiled, a curved line on a pink balloon. "You need help,
Arthur? That's the first time I ever heard you admit it."

Ingram's face slid into its genial mold. Amiability taxed him, but he knew his man as Moffat knew his.

"Perhaps, Owen, that's because I've always gotten your aid in the past without asking."

"What's your problem, Arthur?"

"Stephen Greer."

"Oh." Moffat showed surprise by a slight tilt of his head. "What about Greer?"

"We're speaking in strict confidence, of course?"

"Always."

Ingram sketched what had occurred, Nick's memorandum, the board discussion, the adamant stance of Deskowicz, President Roudebush's rejection of Agency help.

"Rio, huh?" Moffat's eyes lighted, saluting some half-remembered tryst. "I know the city. Just where in Rio is he holed up?"

"I don't know," said Ingram. "We only know that he landed there by jet cargo."

"So?" Moffat's eyes belied the feigned disinterest of his voice.

"Owen," said Ingram, "there's another point in the memo which I did not mention to the board or to the President. We have learned that the FBI is investigating one Phillip J. Lubin in connection with Greer. Lubin, apparently, has also disappeared."

He described the Johns Hopkins professor, then read the paragraph from the computer print-out which had drawn his attention.

"Very interesting," said Moffat. His restraint underlined the delicate balance between them. It was Ingram's move, not his.

"Look at the evidence, Owen," said Ingram. "A close friend and political ally of the President disappears from a golf course. He flies abroad via several planes, using two little-frequented airports on the way. The President orders an investigation, but through the FBI only. He also orders Deskowicz not to speak to anyone else. The President forbids the CIA to enter the case. Then the FBI, operating in strict insulation from the rest of the intelligence community, makes collateral inquiries about a sexless mathematician who has also disappeared. Doesn't all this strike you as peculiar?"

Moffat pondered for some time. "It would," he said, "if it were not for one major factor."

"The campaign?"

Moffat bobbed his head rapidly. "The second law of politics holds that a candidate for re-election will do anything to insure victory."

"What's the first law?"

Moffat grinned. "That Law No. 2 takes precedence over all others."

"So you think that . . ."

"Arthur," said Moffat, "I think it's time we quit sparring. We've known each other too long for that." He paused, and Ingram's quiet smile was one of assent. "I think exactly what you're thinking, that Steve Greer is in some kind of scandal—money, women, blackmail, sexual deviation, God knows what. I also think that Paul Roudebush knows, or suspects, what this scandal is. Also, in some way we can't fathom yet, the President probably is personally involved. If the facts became known before November second, they might conceivably elect Wolcott, as improbable as that may seem at the moment. Therefore, Roudebush will make every effort to keep the facts hidden until after election day."

"But somehow that explanation doesn't quite fit the President's character," said Ingram. His expression indicated that he was forcing himself to be as generous as possible.

"Ordinarily, I'd agree," said Moffat, "but you forget the second law of politics. We're only two months away from election day."

"So you believe the President is suppressing something?"

"At my age, I believe very little," replied Moffat. "Christ no, Arthur. It's just a guess, a quick hunch that hit me the minute you gave me the news."

"Your hunches are usually good ones, Owen."

"Especially when they agree with yours?" Moffat smiled.

"I think we understand each other." Ingram returned the smile.

"You said you needed my help. . . ."

"Yes." Ingram gazed through the window. Concentration lent weight to his words. "Suppose, Owen, that the Central Intelligence Agency were to track the movements abroad of Stephen Greer. Suppose the President were to learn of this. And assume that subsequently, perhaps after the election, the resignation of the director of central intelligence were demanded. Under these conditions, what might be the attitude of you and your friends on the Hill?"

Moffat crossed his legs and folded his hands at his waist. His smile was a flicker. "Arthur, you really like your work, don't you?"

"I've put a great deal of myself into this job."

"I know you have. I prefer to state cases, positively, Arthur." He paused. "Without answering your questions, let me just say that I think when a prominent American citizen flees—if I may assume the validity of that verb for the moment—flees abroad, the director of the CIA has a patriotic duty to ascertain his whereabouts, his intentions, and his motives. . . . I would further say that such action by the CIA director is a purely routine intelligence operation and would be so regarded—and applauded —by those Senate and House members privileged to oversee the operations of the CIA."

After a silent moment, Ingram said: "Thank you, Owen."

"Thanks are not in order," said Moffat. "And I'm speaking here, not as a campaign adviser to Wolcott, but as an American who happens to be a senior member of the Senate watchdog committee."

"That's all I need to know."

Moffat arose, extended his hand, and gripped Ingram's with an extra firmness. Then he laughed.

"Arthur," he said, "what is there about this place that always makes me think twice before speaking—as though the joint were bugged?"

Ingram shook his head. "That's an old joke here—about the CIA bugging itself. Seriously, this is the one place in town where you can feel safe—to say nothing of me."

Moffat turned with his hand on the doorknob. "I'd appreciate being kept informed of Agency operations as usual."

"As usual," repeated Ingram.

When the door closed, Ingram reached to the intercom box and flicked a switch. "Alice, get me Nick, please."

A moment later a male voice said: "Yes, sir."

"Nick, what was the source of that Greer memorandum you handed me this morning?"

"It came from Lady Y."

"Lady Y!" Ingram's eyebrows lifted. "Both parts?"

"Yes, sir."

"Nothing from the field then on Greer?"

"No, sir."

"And Y's sources would be the obvious, I suppose?" asked Ingram.

"I assume so," said Nick, "but under the circumstances, a public pay phone, we did not feel warranted in questioning her. She gave the information an A-1 rating."

"I see. Thank you."

Ingram's fingers lingered a moment at the box. Then he pressed a key. "Alice, please get me the personal code for John in Brazilia."

Ingram worked for half an hour encrypting a message that was a code within a code, a method sometimes used by Ingram for direct, sensitive dispatches to selected agents abroad. He sealed the paper in an envelope and sent it to the Agency's cryptographic center for routine encrypting. When deciphered by machine a few minutes later at the U.S. embassy's communications room in Brazilia, the message would seem to instruct "John," the CIA station chief in Brazil, to collect some complex statistics on coffee exports. Later, when John applied his own private deciphering key in his office, he would find this message as originally written in the clear by Director Ingram:

John

Brazilia

Stephen B. Greer reportedly arrived Rio de Janeiro 8/27 by Overseas Quick-Freight, Inc. Need detailed cover Greer since arrival, daily movements. You assigned. Hereby detached all other duties until further notice. Solo job. If help needed, request permission first. Your contact here Vic only, repeat Vic only.

Vic

9/2/2037 Z

In his large, shadowed room in the old Senate Office Building, Senator Owen Moffat sat for half an hour, gazing out the window across Capitol Plaza toward the dome of the Capitol. The building lay hunched like an old lion, its great shoulders poised, its head patient and stately. Moffat thought of Greer, Lubin, and Roudebush, was diverted by a fleeting memory of a Rio weekend long ago, then thought again of Arthur Ingram. The CIA chief, he mused with a private smile, was forever the armored knight, riding to battle as if in an ancient tapestry. A knight of restless power, more driven than questing. . . . Oh yes, he knew his man.

Moffat, his course charted, walked swiftly to the door which connected his office with the adjoining staff quarters. He locked the door, returned to his telephone, and dialed the congressional switchboard.

"This is Senator Moffat," he said. "Person to person, please, to Mr. Matthew Silkworth in Springfield, Illinois. . . ."

8

Maury Rimmel talked at the shoulder of Brady Manship in that hooded, conspiratorial manner of his, even though the nearest listeners, a noisy group engrossed in its own gossip, were out of earshot of Rimmel's muffled voice. The two men had the corner table in the old, smoky-beamed barroom of the Union League Club.

The room was thinning out now. It was eight forty-five, the twilight of New York's cocktail hour. In the long billiard hall, an extension of the bar area, two men in shirt-sleeves played listlessly at rotation pool. A Negro, wearing the funereal uniform of the club, was clearing the last of the cheese, peanuts, and pretzels from the snack table.

"My source at Justice confirms your guess," Rimmel was saying into Manship's shoulder. He punctuated his talk with parenthetical glances to each side.

The man's half phony, Manship was thinking, a ham actor. They had met to discuss Dragon, and Rimmel was shooting his informational pellets at Manship like a wary hunter on posted grounds. The New York speculator never completely trusted the Washington lobbyist. Rimmel was an elusive, shifty operator in what remained to Manship essentially a parasitical city. Rimmel drank too much and he dropped renowned first names with abandon. Manship suspected that Rimmel's pipe lines of information were rusting these days, that he knew less than he pretended. The purplish moon face, with its lacework of veins, reflected Rimmel's affinity for the high calorie life. Still, Rimmel did know his way through the bureaucratic bogs of Washington and some of his gossip proved valuable. It was, thought Manship, still worth—

barely—the $20,000 which he paid Rimmel annually, an arrange-
ment unknown to all save Rimmel, Manship and a few clerks of
the Internal Revenue Service.

"It's true Ed-Mike was dickering to acquire Carib Oil," said
Rimmel in a voice just a notch above a husky whisper. "But when
Justice hinted it might nix the deal, Greer is supposed to have
told Barney Loomis he couldn't handle it. Conflict of interest.
The way I hear it, Steve told Paul . . ."

Rimmel dug a finger at Manship's chest. Rimmel never said
"the President" or "Roudebush," always "Paul."

". . . he told Paul he was getting out. That was at that Tuesday night meeting at the White House the papers have been trying to figure out."

Manship felt pinned to his seat by Rimmel. He moved to one
side and held up a finger for the waiter. "Another?" he asked
Rimmel. The lobbyist nodded.

While they waited for Rimmel's Gibson and Manship's scotch
and water without ice, Rimmel realized anew how edgy he felt
tonight. He envied Manship his detachment, his chisel mind, his
long, fit body, the flesh packed tight as a thoroughbred's, his
way of wearing clothes with elegant negligence.

Rimmel himself had begun to feel the pinch he had long
dreaded. Last weekend Arthur Ingram had cost him eight grand,
suddenly closing down half the Spruance Foundation's work
without warning. He had a suspicion that young Miguel Loomis
may have been partially responsible, for he recalled that Loomis
had questioned him recently about Spruance's subsidy of the
physicists. Perhaps Greer had a hand in it too, because Miguel,
the papers said, had lunch with Greer on the day of the lawyer's
disappearance. But not a single word of explanation had been
offered by the CIA director. A cold one, that Ingram. Halving the
Spruance account hurt badly, coming as it did only a few days after the Dolan Company decided it no longer needed a man in
Washington. Now he was down to seven grand from Spruance,
eighteen from Imperial Steel, and the twenty from Brady Manship. He had dreamed last night that he was sliding down a long,
icy hill, accelerating madly in a bitter wind, unable to arrest his

descent. And then that quick, hammering pulse of his eardrums, the old sign of high blood pressure. Now he felt the flick of panic again. He needed that $20,000 from Manship, but he knew damn well he had better not let Brady sense it.

"But one thing's sure," he said, pushing on as if a lapse in conversation could prove lethal. "Carib Oil or not, Steve did plenty of work for Educational Micro. One Sunday breakfast foursome this summer, he talked about how microfiche was revolutionizing education. He claimed the day was coming soon when a school kid could have five hundred textbooks in a small slot in his desk —all for two, three bucks. He said production costs were going down so fast . . ."

The new drinks arrived and when Manship spoke, he seemed to ignore Rimmel's rattle of information.

"I got out of Dragon," he said. "Those 15,000 shares that were supposed to be dumped never showed. Somebody changed his mind, probably waiting for the market to recover. Ed-Mike went back up to fifty-six yesterday and I sold. Cost me a few thousand, but what the hell, you can't win 'em all."

"How do you figure the market now, Brady?" asked Rimmel. He took a deep swallow of the Gibson, hunching forward to avoid spilling the liquid on his shirt front.

"It's back, sure, from last Friday, but still jittery." Manship stretched his long legs. "Business, bankers, the fund managers claim to be for Wolcott, but it's only lip service."

He motioned his head at the group near the bar. A spray of laughter greeted the sally of a thin, white-haired man whose bronzed face spoke of long yachting or golf week-ends. "They're typical," said Manship. "That bunch is mostly insurance. They say they like Wolcott's stand on economy, fiscal tidiness, obeisance to the debt limit, et cetera, but they don't bet their money that way. Roudebush has given the country a breather abroad, brought the balance of payments in line. Sure, he spends too much at home, but what the hell, the Street likes that because it's mildly inflationary." He paused to sip his drink. "So, when the Greer thing is solved, the market is bound to shoot up. Last Friday the market was really saying that it feared anything that might endanger Roudebush's re-election. Believe me, the smart ones aren't putting their money where their mouth is."

"You say 'when' the Greer case is solved," said Rimmel. "Suppose it comes out a nice, fat scandal."

"Then the market will hit the skids. Greer's the key." Manship's eyes questioned Rimmel's. "Listen, Maury, what do you really know about this Greer business?"

"Nothing," said Rimmel. "Nobody in Washington does. I've talked to Sue Greer a couple of times since that first night, and if she knows anything, she's some actress. I don't think she's acting. I think the lady is shattered."

"I never bought that kidnap theory," said Manship. "So, what else? A woman?"

Rimmel shook his head. "I know Steve. He's not the type. I think he's in love with his wife, if you can believe a thing like that today. And you can scratch those stories that he's psycho. Steve's as solid as you are."

"Money?" asked Manship.

"Could be." Rimmel frowned. "Steve has the reputation for probity, chiefly because he has Paul's respect. But, let's face it. Steve's in big-time political law—and some of that's a racket. So, suppose he did something shady, and suppose Paul found out and read him the riot act. Steve might take off."

"You mean the Brazil bit?"

"Right." There was a long silence.

"Do you really believe that, Maury?" asked Manship.

"No, goddam it, I don't," replied Rimmel. "At the top of my head, it might figure. But in my gut, no. I think if a scandal was about to break, Steve would stay and take it. He's that kind."

Manship sat without speaking, his eyes shifting from Rimmel to the drinks to the cluster of men who were now rising from the table near the bar.

"Brazil," he said softly. "I wonder. What if a rumor spreads through the Street crowd over the Labor Day weekend that Greer has hightailed it to Brazil because something big and messy involving him is about to break at Educational Micro. What happens?"

"Ed-Mike takes a dive," said Rimmel, "and I suppose a lot of the market follows along."

"And suppose the word got around that a big trader, a man who knows the score, was selling Dragon short. That would put more pressure on the stock, wouldn't it?"

"Sure would."

Manship gulped his scotch this time. His eyes were alight. "Suppose the man who went short was Brady Manship? Does that name carry enough muscle?"

"Come on, Brady," pleaded Rimmel. "Don't kid with me. What do you want me to say? No?"

Manship ignored the testiness. His smile was remote, brief. He withdrew in thought for some time.

"You know," he said at last, "we're all hung up on instant communications. We get swept away by today's news, tomorrow's forecast. We tend to forget the long haul, even the smartest of us. I was just thinking, Maury—what's the real future for Dragon? Not next week, not the day after election, but one, two, three years from now?"

"I guess it's pretty good," said Rimmel.

"Pretty good is the worst it can do," said Manship. He was speaking slowly and carefully now. "At the best, it could be fabulous. Educational Micro could be another IBM or Xerox. I look for it to go to a hundred next year. Hell, in a couple of years it could reach three, four hundred. That company has got it. Loomis is a bear cat. Nothing is going to hurt Ed-Mike over the long haul." He waved his hand. "Elections, Greer, Carib Oil, all that's immaterial."

"So why did you sell yesterday?"

"Because, as I said, I have the same hang-up as everyone else," said Manship. "I didn't think. I reacted. That may be good for an actor, but it's lousy for a man in the market. . . . Anyway, I'm convinced of Educational Micro's future, and I'm thinking it would be very, very sweet to pick up a nice chunk of Dragon at, say, thirty-five or forty, and ride it way up to heaven. And what's good for Manship is good for Rimmel. Right?"

"Maybe," replied Rimmel. "I get the short selling, but what about the rumors—Greer in Brazil and all that jazz. Are you suggesting I go into the rumor business?"

"I'm suggesting nothing," said Manship. His eyes lined Rimmel like a tape measure. "As I said, I'm thinking, just thinking. . . . Rumor can have a powerful impact on a thin market, and Dragon's market is very thin."

"Short sales, that's market judgment," said Rimmel. "Rumors are something else. They can call that rigging the market and the SEC has penalties for it."

"Hell, Maury," said Manship, "some rumors are like Topsy. They just grow. Nobody has to start them. A guy calls his broker and says, 'Say, I hear Brady Manship is selling Dragon short.' Right away the broker wants to know what's with Educational Micro and the customer says something like, 'You got me. I hear Steve Greer did a lot of work for Educational Micro. You don't suppose he's jumped to Brazil, or something, do you? Anyway, if Manship wants to get short Dragon, that's good enough for me. I want to sell five hundred Educational Micro short.' "

Rimmel raised his Gibson and eyed Manship over the rim of the glass. "Listen," he said when he finished the drink, "if you're hinting what I think you are, I don't want in. Steve's a friend of mine at Burning Tree. We're no buddies, but he's a decent guy. I helped his wife that first night, and I'm not about to start spreading lies about him."

"If I sell short, and you report the fact, that's no lie."

"No, but all that Brazil stuff."

Manship's eyes fixed Rimmel's moonish face, mocking him. "You're getting very Billy Graham all of a sudden. You don't sound like the Maury Rimmel who gets twenty grand a year to sneak me information from Burning Tree—or anywhere else around Washington."

"I'm no Snow White," said Rimmel, "but on this one, I pass."

"Okay, Maury. . . . But let me ask you. How do you know Steve Greer has not taken a powder to Brazil?"

"It doesn't figure."

"It makes as much sense as anything else," said Manship, again looking Rimmel in the eyes. "If a rumor like that started in New York, and you heard it in Washington, could you deny it?"

Rimmel did not answer. He looked down at his wrist watch, then said: "I'd better move it to LaGuardia, if I'm going to make the last shuttle."

"I'm staying here tonight," said Manship. "Sure you don't want to stay over? No trouble getting you a room."

"No, I should be back in Washington."

Manship signed for the drinks, then escorted Rimmel down the curving stairway to the entrance on East Thirty-seventh Street. Two attendants fussed over the departure of Mr. Manship's guest.

"If you change your mind, call me," said Manship.

Leaving through the revolving door, Rimmel could have been a deflated popover.

Manship was dining in his room, lamb chops and broccoli, when the phone rang thirty-five minutes later. He could hear the throb of airplane engines and the collapsing spires in Rimmel's voice.

"All right, Brady," said Rimmel. "I'll do what I can in Washington. And I can call a couple of contacts in Cleveland and Houston."

"Good," said Manship. "I'll handle the rest. We're in business."

The next morning, Friday, soon after the markets opened, Brady Manship called one of four brokers with whom he did steady business and placed an order to sell short two thousand shares of Educational Micro. At noon, he invited another broker to lunch at the Union League and discussed a proposed short sale of three thousand Educational Micro. Manship spoke vaguely of inside information. Of course, he said, it would soon be well known how much Stephen Greer was involved with the company. By the way, he once asked casually, what's this about Greer taking a powder to Rio or someplace in Brazil? No, the luncheon guest had not heard that. A third broker, taken to a late lunch at Pierre's by Manship, was surprised at the speculator's lack of appetite, but interested in the plans to take a heavy short position in Dragon. He asked Manship if it were true that Stephen Greer performed a great deal of legal work for Educational Micro. That was true, said Manship, and he, for one, thought the stock would take a beating when the word got around. Just a professional opinion, of course, but he intended to bet a stack on it. Some of Manship's orders were fulfilled by midafternoon, for the market was moving up moderately and Educational Micro had several upticks, permitting short sales.

And in Washington that hot, humid day, Maury Rimmel called his favorite gin rummy foe, Joe Hopkinson, the broker.

"Joe," he said, "I want to sell 750 Educational Micro short."

"Righto," said Hopkinson. "Anything I ought to know?"

"Just a feeling. I hear Brady Manship's getting short Ed-Mike up in New York."

"Something stirring with Dragon?"

"Not that I know of. It's just all this Greer business and the fact of Steve's legal connection with the company."

"Oh. That's right. He was doing some legal work for Dragon, wasn't he?"

"Some?" echoed Rimmel. "Baby, half his homework was for Dragon."

Educational Micro, the dragon of the American Stock Exchange, closed Friday afternoon off a fraction in a market which moved slightly upward from the Greer lows of the week before.

Rimmel was called by Hopkinson a half hour after the three-thirty market closing.

"Say, Maury," asked Hopkinson, "you hearing the rumor that Greer took off to Brazil?"

"Is that around? Where'd you hear it?"

"One of the guys in the shop hears it out of New York." Hopkinson's love affair with the present tense was fitful but undying. "You sure you don't hold out on me this morning?"

"Not on you, Joe. . . . Hey, if the rumor's true, maybe I got lucky for a change, going short Ed-Mike. . . . If you hear anything more, let me know, will you?"

That evening after work in New York, Brady Manship stopped at a pay phone booth and called his young friend, Eddie Seymour, an investment counselor in Los Angeles. Seymour's mind was swift, skittering. He had been a child prodigy.

"This is confidential, Eddie," said Manship, "but I hear that something's cooking at Educational Micro. I know Steve Greer was doing legal work for the company. Now there's a rumor that Greer's disappearance involves Ed-Mike. Keep me out of it, but I'd like a report. Usual fee. See what you can find out before the market opens Tuesday."

Manship placed two other calls, one to Chicago and one to Atlanta. Educational Micro had factories in both cities. Then, from his pile of dimes and quarters, he telephoned investment men in Minneapolis and Detroit. New York streets were cramped in shadow when Manship walked to the club to meet his Carey Cadillac for the trip home to Southport.

At about the same time, from a pay station in downtown Washington, Maury Rimmel made gossipy inquiries of moneyed friends in Houston and Cleveland.

Then Rimmel walked to the Alibi Club, the narrow, little house on I Street. It was the caterer's night off and the club was deserted. He strolled into the old-fashioned parlor, furnished in Victorian style, and stood looking at the scarred upright piano on which he once belted out bawdy tunes in younger, better days. Fifty members, count 'em, fifty, he thought, all towers of commercial and political Washington like . . . himself? . . . Maury Rimmel, clubman, the Washington *Post* would probably identify him in his obituary. He belonged to all the best, Alibi, Burning Tree, Metropolitan, Chevy Chase, Sulgrave.

He went to the kitchen and took his bottles—Booth's, Noilly Prat extra dry—from the shelf. He mixed a large martini, cooling it on ice for a minute.

He sat down at the round, bare wooden table where Alibi members shucked their own oysters at lunchtime. After the first swallow of the martini, Maury felt the tart sting in his throat. But he also felt that soft pounding in his eardrums like thumbs tapping on a drum. The alarms of high blood pressure came more frequently now. He ought to lay off the booze. But he took another drink of the cold martini. He felt soiled, depressed, and he did not want to go home. The last conversation with Joe had knotted Maury's disgust for himself. Joe Hopkinson, his gin rummy crony.

He had used Joe as if he were a stranger. Damn all Brady Man-
ships.

When the glass was empty, he fetched more ice from the refrigerator, poured from the gin bottle and added a trickle of
Vermouth. He drank slowly this time, feeling the warm virus of
alcohol spread through his body.

And outside his solitary asylum in the Alibi Club, Maury knew,
the virus of rumor was spreading about Dragon.

9

It was Saturday morning. Jill and I were bent over my desk, trying to piece together the semifinal draft of the President's Labor Day speech. I deleted, inserted, and scrawled, while she snipped with scissors and pasted up odd paragraphs. Later she would have one of the girls type a clean copy, which would be torn apart again tomorrow by the professors. I detested this speech manufacture by committee. It was collective insanity.

My green phone buzzed, continuing its steady drone until I lifted the receiver. Grace Lalley put the President on at once.

"Good morning, sir," I said.

"Good morning, Gene," he said. "I'd like you in here. Ingram's arriving out back."

I had only a minute alone with the President before the CIA director entered. Paul and I traded the amenities like men handling fragile glassware. I was still embarrassed over my eruption Wednesday while he, I sensed, wanted me to know that our relationship was back on the old footing. Roudebush told me that Ingram wanted to discuss his briefing of Governor Stanley Wolcott in Springfield, Ill., tomorrow. Under the customary agreement between opposing presidential candidates, Wolcott was to receive a digest of world security intelligence twice during the campaign. Tomorrow's session on the eve of Wolcott's opening speech in Detroit was to be the first.

Ingram saw me the moment he came in the office, and his glance was one of disapproval. He seemed to be saying, mutely, that my presence contaminated the security of his call. The President caught the look, but offered no explanation to Ingram. He merely gestured toward an empty chair as he said good morning. Ingram settled himself carefully, as if the chair were mined.

"Arthur," said the President, "I'd like you to use Air Force One for your flight tomorrow. As a symbol, it ought to reassure Wolcott if he has any doubts about your authority to speak for me."

"That's a gracious gesture, Mr. President," said Ingram. The prospect of flying alone in the President's plane obviously pleased him. Then his narrow face tightened. "I asked for this meeting, Mr. President, because of our recent misunderstanding over Operation Flycatcher—the Spruance Foundation's work with the young physicists. I thought that this time, before I go to Springfield, we should agree on the precise guidelines for my briefing of the governor."

Roudebush tilted back in his chair and shoved his glasses to the perch atop his head. "No problem, really. Stanley Wolcott has a right to know just what we know. While too many details might confuse him, I do want him to have a comprehensive picture."

"I understand," said Ingram, "but there are doubtful areas. As a sample, should he be told about the operation in Nigeria?"

I kept my face blank, but my mind popped. Nigeria? What were we hatching there? The country had a repressive, unstable military government.

"Yes," said the President firmly. "I do not want any replay of that fiasco in 1960 when Nixon had to deny that an invasion of Cuba was planned simply because Kennedy raised the issue. Unless he's warned, Wolcott might, in all innocence, make some troublesome statement about Nigeria."

The allusion sounded ominous, but neither man said anything that enlightened me further. Ingram opened his dispatch case and withdrew a sheet of paper.

"What about this week's NIE?" he asked.

"What about it?"

"Well," said Ingram, "I should think this might embarrass you. If the governor hears our assessment that Red China is pulling its punches in a clumsy attempt to get you re-elected, couldn't

Wolcott use that to his advantage? To me, it seems enormously tempting."

I sat quite still, my attention riveted. This was all news to me.

"I can't help it," said Roudebush. "We gave Wolcott our pledge that he'd receive all vital intelligence. In my mind, that includes our evaluations as well. We have Wolcott's word that he'll use nothing from these briefings. We'll just have to trust him."

Ingram mentioned other developments, including more news for me—that Jerome Freytag's NSA had cracked a Red Chinese code and that Peking now was using a new blooms-and-flowers code which the National Security Agency's computer had not solved yet. In each case, Roudebush said Wolcott should have the information.

"In sum," said Ingram, replacing the sheet in his leather case and snapping the lock, "Wolcott is to get everything the intelligence agencies deem to be important."

"Right."

Ingram shifted in his chair and, for some reason, glanced obliquely at me. "And that, I assume," he said, "includes the Greer matter?"

"Greer?" asked the President in surprise. "Why should he be discussed with Wolcott?" He straightened, tensing. "I don't see the connection, Arthur."

"But, sir, there is a definite connection. As I—"

"Absolutely none." Roudebush's tone hardened. "Steve Greer is not an Agency concern in any way, shape, or form. He is a private individual whose disappearance is being traced by the FBI."

"But, Mr. President," insisted Ingram, "the Agency is charged with gathering intelligence abroad." His calm appeared to be studied. "As I told you Thursday, we have information that Mr. Greer flew secretly to Rio de Janeiro."

For me, the city's name struck gongs. On Wednesday, the President had declined to affirm or deny Paulick's report that Steve had decamped to Rio. Now here was Ingram saying the same thing. The word seemed to be circulating.

"Arthur," said the President, "I told you that the Agency was not to become involved." His voice was cold and I could see that he was making an effort to remain civil.

"But our information flows in every hour from all over the world," protested Ingram. "I can't cut it off on a single issue like Greer without specific instructions to the field—which would stir needless suspicions. I assume you don't want that?"

"Of course not." Roudebush sensed the trap. I could see his anger mounting. "But the Agency is to make no planned effort to gather material about Greer."

Ingram was silent a moment. Then he seemed to brace himself. "Mr. President, I think it is time to be completely candid," he said slowly. "I happen to know that the FBI is investigating a possible homosexual relationship between Stephen Greer and one Phillip J. Lubin, a Johns Hopkins mathematician."

Lubin! I had to hand it to the CIA. It seemed to know exactly what the FBI was doing.

The President rose abruptly from his chair. His face was flushed. He grabbed his glasses and aimed them at Ingram like a pistol.

"That is pure speculation on your part," he said. "I find it personally offensive. . . . What the FBI is or is not investigating in connection with Steve Greer is no concern of yours or of your Agency. I repeat, absolutely no concern."

"Oh, but it is," countered Ingram. The man had poise. He was surprisingly composed before the President's wrath. "You see, Phillip Lubin has important security information. He worked for months on GOBLET, some of which is still highly classified. And Mr. Lubin, like Mr. Greer, has disappeared."

The President seemed to be in momentary shock, but when he recovered, his voice was a near shout.

"Are you trying to tell me that my best friend is a sexual deviate who has had relations with this Mr. Lubin?" He stood behind his desk, raging down at the seated CIA chief. "And that Steve is some kind of sordid security risk? Is that what you mean? I demand a direct answer."

"I never go beyond the facts as I know them," said Ingram with no sign of retreat. "I'm merely trying to point out why the Greer matter is of interest to my Agency."

"Your insinuations are nasty," said Roudebush. "I am ordering you, Arthur Ingram, to stay entirely out of the Greer situation."

"That is a strange order." Ingram pressed against the back of his chair, seeking support for his spine. "It is also odd that for the first time in my memory, the CIA is being denied pertinent reports from a sister intelligence agency. I'm entitled by law to that information as director of central intelligence."

"Only in cases of national security, which this is not." Roudebush towered in fury over Ingram. "Stephen Greer is my friend. His wife and daughter are going through personal torment at this moment. I will not have his name bandied about through the entire CIA network. Greer's disappearance will be solved—and it will be solved within the rules I have laid down."

"That is final?" asked Ingram. God, the man had gall. Never before had I seen the President defied in such manner.

"That is final."

"And I am not to mention the word Greer to Governor Wolcott tomorrow?" Ingram's eyes dueled with those of Roudebush.

"You are not." Roudebush was trembling now. "If Governor Wolcott asks about Greer, you are to tell the exact truth—that Greer's disappearance is not a CIA concern."

"I do not agree. But I will, of course, honor your wishes." Ingram stood up.

"Oh, one item we forgot to cover," he added. His manner and tone were still amazingly cool. "Is the governor to be informed of your decision ending the Spruance subsidy of physicists?"

"I would think not," said Roudebush. "That has no bearing on the world strategic picture—which is the purpose of tomorrow's briefing."

"I disagree," said Ingram. "Had Operation Flycatcher not been closed down, I had intended to send one of the men to an international physics conference at Helsinki. It is opening about now, I believe. Red China is sending a delegation, and our agent might have picked up valuable information on the current situation in China."

"Nevertheless," said the President, "the world picture today is not involved. No, the Spruance—or Flycatcher, if you prefer—matter is not to be discussed with the governor."

"Yes, sir . . . I think, then, that we've covered everything." Ingram bowed stiffly.

Their good-bys were stilted.

Roudebush stood at his desk, watching as Ingram left without a backward glance. Then he sat down heavily.

"Incredible," he said, "incredible." He slumped in his chair as though strings had snapped. He sat for some moments, oblivious of me, and gazed longingly at the painting of his island winter retreat.

"I'd be willing to make two small bets," he said at last. "One, that Governor Wolcott will somehow learn of my orders that Greer is not to be discussed at the briefing. Two, that Wolcott will find a way to tell Ingram that he's to stay on as CIA director if Wolcott is elected."

"You think that Ingram will tell Wolcott about your orders on Greer?"

"No, Arthur is too sophisticated for that." A wry smile, the first in many minutes, appeared. "My guess would be that he'll pass the word discreetly through someone else, a man like Owen Moffat, perhaps. Actually, come to think of it, Moffat would be ideal for Arthur. The senator is close to the CIA through the watchdog committee and, of course, he's one of Wolcott's best strategists."

"It's good Ingram can't overhear you," I said. "It might give him an idea."

"Arthur is never at a loss for ideas," said Roudebush. "He's a very inventive man. . . . Well, remember what you heard, Gene, and make notes on it. If it weren't for the campaign . . ."

His voice trailed away. I made an excuse about the pressure of my work, but he did not seem to hear. As I left, he was staring at the golden donkey with the absurd antenna ears.

By Sunday night I was beat. I was due at Jill's apartment in Georgetown at seven o'clock for dinner for two, Butter Nygaard having decided to stay the night with a "friend." But at seven I was still upstairs in the west wing, cooped up with the two perfectionist speech writers. I was scheduled to fly to Chicago the next morning for the President's Labor Day kick-off, but the speech still was not finished. We were down to nit-picking single words, and my enemy was no longer the opposition candidate, but these two insufferable phrase surgeons. Another ten minutes and my own blood would begin dripping onto the typewriter.

The phone rang. It was a relief to hear the voice of Hilda, the chief night operator, as fresh as springtime.

"Help me, Gene," she said with mock anguish. "Mr. Barney Loomis has called twice from the Coast for the President. I told him the President was resting for tomorrow's trip and could not be disturbed. Now he insists on talking to you. He sounds very upset."

"No sweat, honey," I said. "Barney's always in a flap. Put him on."

Loomis shook the line with the roar of an express train. "Gene," he yelled, "just what in the sweet name of hell are you idiots back there trying to do to me?"

"Anything we can, Barney," I said. "At the moment, we're writing a speech that will promise to fix the economy so bandits like you can get rich all over again."

"You can skip the witty remarks," he said. "Who started those damn cock-eyed rumors back there?"

"What rumors?"

"My God!" He sounded like a man about to rip out the phone. "Have you got wax in your ears? I'm talking about these reports they're trying to murder me with."

"Hold it, Barney. Make sense, will you? Who is trying to murder whom—with what reports?"

"They're trying to ruin *me*," he cried. I held the receiver away from my ear. "They're trying to wreck Educational Micro with a lousy, false slander about Steve Greer."

That figured. Everything was Greer these days. "Just a second, Barney." I turned to the two political scientists who supposedly were absorbed in their word-pruning, but whose ears were flapping. "Could you gentlemen wait outside? This is personal." They withdrew reluctantly, like a wary patrol. "All right, Barney," I said into the phone. "Please explain. I haven't heard the gossip."

"You're about the only alleged insider in the country who hasn't," he said. "There's a story out that Steve Greer went south to duck a major scandal about to break at Ed-Mike."

"Who says so?"

"I don't know, for God's sake." He was shouting again. "If I did, I'd have them in court for malicious slander. Half the brokers and traders in the goddam country have heard the rumor. They say Educational Micro is going broke and that Steve Greer is mixed up in it and that he took a powder before the roof fell in. My God, they'll knock hell out of our stock when the market opens Tuesday."

"Well, *is* Educational Micro in trouble?"

"Trouble!" It was a cry of pain. "Listen, Mister, we're twice as sound as the U. S. Treasury."

Knowing the size of the public debt, I did not think that was the most bullish comparison I had ever heard, but I let it pass.

"Gene," he continued, "we'll make forty-one point eight million after taxes in the first three quarters. We don't owe a cent on long-term paper, and we're backlogged with orders up to our neck. If our books looked any better, we'd be the Chase Manhattan."

He roared on. No scandal, no trouble with any federal agency. Greer quit all legal work for Ed-Mike a month ago. Absolutely no connection with Greer, except for his son, Mike, acting as spokesman for Mrs. Greer—and that was my doing, not the father's. So, who was trying to sabotage Barney Loomis with false gossip and why?

"I don't know, Barney," I said, "but maybe you can help me. If these rumormongers know so much, where do they say Greer is?"

"Rio!" He barked the word. "You know, Brazil, where all the big con men are supposed to go with the loot."

Did everybody in the country think Steve Greer was in Rio? Paulick claimed it. Ingram said the CIA and FBI both knew it.

"Is it true, Barney?" I asked.

"How the devil should I know? Ask the FBI. Now listen, Gene . . ."

What he wanted, it turned out, was a White House statement attesting that the vanished Greer had no connection whatever with Educational Micro and that the President had confidence in the financial soundness of the corporation.

"Now, just a minute, Barney," I said. "You know the White House can't go around endorsing corporations. If you want a commercial, hire an ad agency."

"Steve Greer isn't my friend," he yelled. "He's your boss's. You tell Paul Roudebush for me that he owes me one right at this time—he'll know what I mean—and that if he doesn't bail me out of this, I'll never raise another campaign dime for him."

"Come on, Barney." I tried to play it light. "You know you love to bleed those rich friends of yours."

"This is no time for smart cracks," he said. "You tell Paul for me that . . ."

"Okay, okay," I said. "Let me see if I can reach him. I'll call you back."

He slammed down the phone. If it had been anyone else, I would have dropped the matter right there. But Barney, despite his bluster, was a good friend and a loyal one. Also, it did seem to me that he was getting a raw deal. Hilda put me through to Roudebush in his bedroom.

"Good evening, Gene," he said. "I'm in bed, reading. Is that final draft finished yet?"

I told him of the call and of Barney's demands. He chuckled when I repeated some of the less profane of Barney's comments.

"I think you're laundering Loomis," he said. "I've heard worse than that from him myself." He paused, then said: "Gene, the facts are that Steve came to me about a month ago and said Loomis wanted him to handle legal aspects of some oil company acquisition. We both agreed it would not be proper in view of Steve's policy relationship to the White House. Actually, Steve went further and severed all legal connection with Educational Micro. I saw a copy of his letter to Loomis. So Barney's right, and he does have a point."

"He says something else. He claims you owe him a favor right at this time."

"Yes," he said. "He is doing a special chore for me. Well, let's see, now."

In the end it was decided that if the White House were called, I would state the facts of Greer's severance of legal work for Ed-Mike. The President wanted me to apply the word "baseless" to the rumors about Educational Micro's financial condition.

"If we say that," I countered, "we'll be bailing out the whole boat for Barney. Suppose Educational Micro is in trouble on some other score?"

"No," he said. "I'm willing to trust Barney there."

"All right," I said. "I'll handle the mechanics. You won't be bothered again. Get some sleep before tomorrow, Mr. President."

"I will," he said, "but I'm itching to go. It'll be like old times to hit the road again. A man goes stir-crazy in this place after so long."

I planned my tactics before calling Barney back. To my surprise, he made no protest about the wording of our statement, nor did he object when I told him how it would be put out. He would get more mileage, I said, if there were no formal announcement. But we'd have the comment ready for any newspapermen who called. I suggested he have his p.r. people call the wire services and financial writers and tell them to contact the White House for reaction to the reports.

It was 9 P.M. when I finished with the speech jugglers—final, total, forevermore, end, period. No more revisions except those penciled in by the President himself.

I returned to my own office and almost at once the calls began to come in. First the AP, then the UPI, then the New York Times, the Los Angeles Times, the Washington Post. I read our statement to them: "In response to inquiries, the White House states that Stephen B. Greer voluntarily ended all legal work for Educational Micro, Inc., some weeks ago. This was done with the knowledge and assent of President Roudebush. The President sees no connection whatsoever between Stephen Greer's disappearance and the financial affairs of Educational Micro and he thinks it is unfortunate that the company should be the target for baseless rumors."

By 10:30 P.M., I had had it. I turned the statement over to Hilda and told her to handle the late callers. By the time I finally found time to phone Jill, she said the lasagna was ruined, but she had some cold lamb in reserve. Thank God, I thought. After a week like this, lasagna!

We had several drinks, picked at the lamb and then talked for an hour about almost anything but the White House and Greer. There would be enough of both again tomorrow.

So it was well after midnight when we lay in the narrow bed under the casement windows. Jill's apartment had no air-conditioning, and the windows were opened wide, admitting a spare, hot breeze. These last summer nights were invariably oppressive in Washington, and now the thermometer must have still registered ninety. We were depleted from our love-making, and Jill's long hair lay across my chest. Her head was cradled on my shoulder and, as always at these moments, she was blissfully quiet.

I had to fight to stay awake. I could have slept eighteen hours straight right then, but I knew I had to go home, then be up at eight-thirty for the flight to Chicago. Without enough sleep, I knew, there would be that sharp ache at the base of my skull tomorrow. I dozed off once and when I came fitfully awake, I could hear the drill of the shower and Jill singing a plaintive mountain ballad about two lovers and a killing.

The phone rang. In my groggy condition, I assumed it was the unlisted number reserved for White House business. Now what? Only Hilda would call here at this time of night. That must mean . . . I swung myself out of bed, grabbed the top sheet and draped it around me like a toga. Both phones were on the third shelf of the book case, and I tripped over a light cord on the way, bruising a toe.

I said, "Hello," expecting to hear Hilda's voice. I braced myself for her inevitable crack about sending the house detective to investigate this man in Jill's room. Instead, I heard a voice mumble something. It was a word or just a sound, I couldn't be sure. Then the sound of breathing for a few seconds and the line clicked dead. The voice had been unmistakably male. I looked at the phone as I hung up. I had been wrong. This was not the White House phone. It was the regular line with listed number.

I went back to bed, unwrapped the sheet, and tucked it in at the foot, then lay down and stared at the ceiling. Jill came out of the lighted bathroom, slender and naked. She slid in beside me, nuzzled my ear and whispered, "Still love me?" I kissed her, but said nothing.

A man had called Jill and then hung up when he heard my voice. I had always felt that a moment something like this would come. Here I was, thirty-eight years old. She was a supple, vital, desirable twenty-four. Of course other men were interested in her. Jill had no formal ties to me. Suddenly, I was plunged in private gloom. I lectured myself in quick torment. Now, Culligan, be sensible. It never really figured. But my ego was wounded, ambushed by jealousy.

"What's the matter, baby?" Jill asked.

"Nothing," I said. "Just thinking." I put my arm around her shoulder and she nestled closer.

She nipped me on the chin. "You better not sulk," she said, "or I'll bite you there. And wouldn't you look ridiculous in Chicago tomorrow with teeth marks all over your chin."

"Yeah. Real funny."

"Okay, baby," she said, "you play sullen by yourself. I'm going to sleep."

We lay in our separate silences for a few minutes, but I knew she was wide awake. I could not mask it any longer.

"Jill," I said. "A man just called you."

She moved beneath my arm. "Oh? Who?"

"I don't know. You got a call while you were in the shower. When I said hello, he mumbled something and then hung up like he'd been shot. And it's one-fifteen in the morning."

"He didn't give a name?"

"No. He obviously had no yen to talk to me."

She raised on an elbow and peered down at me. "Now, just why do you assume the call was for me? And not for Butter?"

"How many men has Butter got on the string?" I countered. "I thought she was out with that pothead lover of hers tonight."

"You're jealous." She stared down at me with a happy smile. "You are. The great Culligan. Who would believe it?"

"I'm old-fashioned," I said. "I believe a girl should be content with one man at a time."

"Gene!" This time she shook me. "That call was for Butter. I'd bet on it. She gets calls every once in a while from some admirer. His name is Nick. I know because several times I've answered when he called."

"Nick who?"

"Just Nick."

"That's a likely story. Everybody has a last name."

"All right. If you don't want to believe me, don't." She rolled away from me, her head turned toward the wall. There was another long silence, then suddenly she was back, covering my face with small, brushing kisses. "Gene, I love you so. Let's not fight. Believe me, there's only you."

Love takes its toll of reason. I was persuaded. I held her tightly and mashed her mouth with mine. This girl, this girl . . . A few minutes later, she fell asleep.

I dressed in the shadow of the room, away from the cross of light falling on the bed. The night outside pressed heavily and the cicadas sang their thick, pulsing chant. I tiptoed to the bathroom and turned out the light.

Now Jill rested in a thin amber glow from the window. Her hair curved about her neck. One arm lay outside the sheet and the other seemed to quest toward the place where I had been. Her bosom rose and fell in gentle rhythm. Her face in repose, freshly scrubbed, showed the excesses of love. I had never seen her so beautiful and so vulnerable. I hated to leave, and although it seemed an affront to her in defenseless sleep, I stood there watching her and wondering. Was this the girl I might marry someday? The question seemed rudely out of place. There was a sadness in the room, the sadness of the small death which follows love. Life was so brutally transient and possession such a wild yearning to hold and keep the unkeepable. Then I smiled at the thought that such a young and strange girl could evoke such sorrow. I closed the door softly.

I was several miles from Georgetown, in my own apartment and in my own bed, when I thought of the phone call again. I had been either foolish or groggy, probably both. Why would a man hang up just because another male voice answered the phone? After all, there were two women sharing the apartment and it would be quite normal for them to be entertaining male guests. Unless, of course, the caller knew that Butter was away that night, leaving Jill alone. In that case, Nick, or whatever his name was, would not be calling for Butter, but Jill. The other possibility—a man thinking Butter was alone—did not seem plausible. Butter had but one lover and was lucky to have him. The thoughts festered.

Two o'clock in the morning is no time to ponder a woman's possible perfidy. I burrowed and turned for an hour before falling into a restless sleep and almost immediately, it seemed, the alarm sounded for Chicago and Soldier Field.

10

We were circling at thirty-two thousand feet off the Maryland coast late Monday afternoon. The great white and blue jet, with the Presidential seal at the bow and the American flag at the tail, was in a steady bank. Far below us whitecaps sprinkled the Atlantic. At times the coastline appeared, a hazy pencil line dividing land and sea. A smudge on the line was, I knew, Ocean City, and farther north another speck was probably the sister resort town of Rehoboth Beach, Delaware. The sky was bare of clouds, yet ringed with haze like smoke from a distant fire. Air Force One seemed to be floating on some timeless mission.

I was sitting across the desk from President Roudebush in his private stateroom just aft of the wings. A decor of soft gold and the yellow upholstery of the deep easy chairs gave the cabin a cheerful glow. Behind Paul Roudebush hung the presidential seal and across the aisle was a circular map of the world with Washington, D.C., at its center. Beside me sat Don Sheehan, chief of the White House Secret Service detail, a man who had a close rapport with the President. Sheehan admired Roudebush, appraised him uncritically and tried to emulate him. I had missed Don around the White House during the last week and I assumed he had been out doing advance work for the Chicago trip. Sheehan oscillated in mood, sometimes brimming with the small inside jokes of the White House staff, at other times penned in some private dolor. This afternoon, for perhaps understandable reasons, he had retreated to his cloister. By habit he sat half-turned in the aisle so that he could watch both doors. One connected with the forward, twenty-six-seat passenger compartment. The other led to the President's bedroom. Aft of the bedroom was a cabin for staff and Secret Service agents where I had been sitting until the President summoned me.

Don and I were unlikely auditors for the President at this moment, for Roudebush was speaking—ruminating aloud would be a more apt description—on a subject he normally did not discuss with a chief bodyguard or a press secretary. He was talking about what he called the "insupportable:" the worldwide stockpiles of nuclear bombs which could annihilate civilization within minutes.

If it were not for several unusual and potentially hazardous incidents that day, I doubt that Don and I would ever have seen Paul Roudebush in just that mood or heard him speak in the strangely moving way that he did.

As it was, the scene became imprinted on my memory. It offered a clue to the fascination the American presidency holds for men in our time—the vast powers of office and the equally vast dilemmas inherent in the exercise of those powers. The allure exists for the office's holder and beholder alike. I, for instance, would have sacrificed a year of my lucrative public relations work in Los Angeles for this one half hour in the golden cabin of Air Force One.

The sequence of events which put us in a lazy circle above the Atlantic and which inspired the President's musings was this:

Just before landing at O'Hare International near Chicago that morning, Roudebush received a coded message from the chairman of the Atomic Energy Commission, revealing that Red China had detonated another huge hydrogen device, apparently of about fifty megatons, near Lob Nor in Sinkiang province. The explosion ended a hiatus of several months in Chinese H-bomb experiments. Roudebush appeared surprised and nettled by the news. After a huddle which delayed our motorcade into the city, he had me issue a brief statement again deploring China's refusal to sign the test-ban treaty.

At Soldier Field, where eighty thousand people gathered under a broiling sun to hear Roudebush's campaign kick-off, a weird episode threw the Secret Service into momentary turmoil. The Chicago police, sensitive to their presidential protection duties of the day, apprehended our "nuke messenger" by mistake. This was an Air Force major who that day wore civilian clothes and also, in his lapel, the tiny blue triangular button which was supposed to identify him to all security forces as a Secret Service agent. The major had but a single job: To act as the President's messenger between the speaker's stand and the temporary White House communications center beneath the stadium. While the President had a telephone on the stand, the major was his insurance in event the line failed. Only the President and the messenger carried the brief code by which the President could identify himself to the Pentagon war room in event of a nuclear crisis. The President, and the President alone, could give the signal that released one or more nuclear warheads from missile launching pads, from submarines or bombers.

Our nuke messenger had an unfortunate habit of tucking a hand inside his jacket. A Chicago policeman, who saw him approaching the speaker's platform with one hand hidden, stopped him and demanded he submit to a search. The Air Force officer refused, protesting he was in the President's party and pointing to his lapel pin. The policeman, now joined by two other Chicago patrolmen who also feared a shooting, ignored the major's protestation and began hauling him toward a stadium exit.

Secret Service agents bolted through the crowd to the messenger's side, but the police, adamant in duty, now had too much momentum to be deterred. For a moment there was danger of a battle between agents and police. They argued violently under the stadium while the major stood helpless. The police hotly contended they had orders from higher up. The SS men, ringing the messenger, demanded that the police release him. Luckily Don Sheehan appeared at that moment with a Chicago police inspector in tow, and the custody dispute was arbitrated on the spot. The federals, of course, won the day. Our messenger was escorted back to the speaker's stand by SS men who, in turn, were surrounded by the Chicago police, none of whom, of course, knew the strategic value of their guest. The Air Force officer, a chunky, stubborn man, stood beside the platform through the President's speech, then hovered near Roudebush during the reception for

Chicago politicians at the Sheraton-Blackstone Hotel. Now, fatigued but composed, he was playing solitaire in the staff cabin. When I left him, I noticed that he was fingering a button of his shirt.

Fortunately, although the press had a side-bar story on the hustling of a Secret Service agent by Chicago police, the real identity of the atomic messenger remained under wraps. When questioned, I did not lie. I merely said, "You saw his SS pin, didn't you? We're not giving out the name." In retrospect, the Chicago police could be pardoned their excess of zeal, for when the presidential party entered the stadium, a gang of rowdy teenagers had popped suddenly from the seats. They surged up and down the aisles, shouting, "Greer! Greer! Stole Our Beer!" Police nabbed some and partially quieted the others before the President reached the platform.

The last incident in the three-part drama had occurred a half hour ago on the return flight from Chicago. Air Force One was over Front Royal, Virginia, preparing to let down for its approach to Andrews Air Force Base near Washington, when our pilot was raised on the Andrews frequency. A jet fighter had just signaled an emergency and was expected to crash-land at Andrews. So Andrews was to be closed down, perhaps for as long as an hour. Our pilot informed the President that we could land at Dulles or at Friendship, or as an alternative, we could hold to the east over the Maryland coast. Since airports banned all traffic fifteen minutes before and after a presidential landing or takeoff, diversion to Dulles or Friendship would mean interruption of the heavy commercial schedules. Also, an unexpected "D.V." (Distinguished Visitor) warning always sent airports into a flap. The President, in no particular hurry, elected the holding pattern.

It was natural that the series of incidents should turn the President's mind toward the big bomb and toward his own responsibility. Now, as we wheeled high over the Atlantic, Sheehan was assuring Roudebush that new rehearsals of local police by the Secret Service would be worked out to prevent a repetition of today's abortive abduction of the President's nuclear messenger.

"I doubt if any drill could forestall the possibility entirely," said Roudebush, shaking his head. He was sitting in his shirtsleeves, the collar open at the neck. "Actually, Don, I'm surprised it hasn't happened before. As long as local police can't be told of the major's identity and duties—and that, of course, can't be done—we've got to expect mistakes of this kind."

"But we can reduce the chances," said Sheehan, still in his somber mood. "If I had made sure that inspector had stayed with me, as he was supposed to do, we could have avoided the hassle."

"That crazy Greer stunt in the stands made the cops jittery," I said. I hoped the remark would turn Roudebush's mind back to the big disappearance, for my thoughts and my pockets were stuffed with Greer notes. There were a dozen points that had to be settled soon, preferably before I met the press again.

But the President ignored the opening. He was not to be detoured. "A hundred things can happen to make police jittery," he said. He looked out the window at the Atlantic far below. The plane was still in a steady, gentle bank.

"You see," he mused as he gazed out the window, "the whole day was a symbol of the basic dilemma—how to live with the insupportable." He turned back to us. "The trouble is that the statesmen—if there are any—the politicians and the diplomats all delude themselves into believing the bomb can be lived with. They talk and act as though these dreadful monsters were just another stage in weaponry, fearful, yes, but as supportable as the step-up from bow and arrow to gunpowder. Yet deep within us, we all know this is untrue. The very existence of these huge piles of A-bombs and H-bombs guarantees *Götterdämmerung* someday, just as a Hitler in power once made certain the ravages of the great war. The politicians give lip service to a hope that belies the inner nature of man—a hope that because the bomb is so devastating, it will never be used again.

"How many dreary speeches have we heard about 'the protection of the nuclear stalemate?' Generals talking about the added security of megatons as if each new weapon were a tiny security blanket to nap upon—instead of one more step toward the inferno. And our endless disarmament conferences, each side afraid to yield an inch lest the highway of global destruction be left only part paved. We use comforting phrases like 'nuclear umbrella'—all snug and dry under the shelter of the bomb."

Except for the curiously detached whistle of the engines outside, the cabin was silent. Sheehan was watching Roudebush in mute and clouded absorption. I too was riveted by the President's words, but Don seemed to be actually sharing them.

"But many of the people know. They understand." Roudebush clasped his hands on the card table while he talked. "Many of the people—subtracting the fringe of bomb rattlers—are way ahead of the politicians, far closer to the truth. They know the bomb is insupportable, that man and his civilization cannot live indefinitely with the great thermonuclear weapons. They know that someday—by error or madness, by miscalculation or design —the stockpiles will become fireballs that roast the earth and foul the air. These people are not misled by the argument that just because the bomb has not been used since Hiroshima and Nagasaki, it will never be used. They know man's luck cannot last forever. I think ordinary people all over the world sense this. Children talk about it. Young people feel it deeply. They hate the bomb. I suspect even peasants scratching at the parched ground in Jordan or Pakistan know it. The cashier in the New York bank knows. So does the factory worker in France, in Russia, in China. The bomb hangs over everyone like the shadow of death, not the individual death that each of us must face, but the death of our planet and its wonders."

The President paused, then laughed wryly. "You know, it's phenomenal how far behind the people the politicians are. We professionals of government are mired in orthodoxy, bargaining and clucking and trading over the bomb, as if it were some kind of pagan god that had to be propitiated. No leader yet, and in that I include myself, has had the courage to say very simply, 'The bomb must go. I shall work every remaining day of my life to rid the world of it. Nothing else matters so much, for unless the bomb goes, we all go. From now on, the destruction of all nuclear bombs shall become my first goal as it must become the first concern of all mankind.' . . . Well, maybe not exactly those

words, but something like them. Actually, you know, to say that
and then to follow through on it wouldn't be an act of courage at
all. For the peoples of the world are aching to hear just that. It
isn't so much boldness that is required in a man as it is enough
common sense to look at the nature of the bomb and the nature
of people."

He paused and looked tentatively at us. He had no need to
be apologetic, for this was Roudebush at his most appealing.
Here was his eager conviction that the world could be changed
for the better if we just tried hard enough. I had lost that belief,
but I had to concede that Paul Roudebush at least kindled a
hope.

"Well," he said, smiling, "that was quite a sermon, wasn't it?
Of course, the police seizure of our messenger triggered it. We
do hang by such a slender thread. Suppose I had been faced with
an immediate 'go decision' when the police were wrestling with
the major—at the same time the phone from the speaker's stand
had failed? Suppose, right now, our radio went out and at the
same instant missiles leaped off from Asia toward our cities? Suppose a hundred things. It's all too fantastic, humanity trying to
pick its way across a billion egg shells without cracking them. No
human being is wise enough to make the nuclear decision. And
human beings aren't stable enough—not all of them—to live with
the bomb, fused but unexploded, for decade after decade. The
bomb is insupportable."

There was a knock on the door and when Don opened it, a
flight steward, wearing the ornate monkey jacket favored on Air
Force One, leaned into the cabin.

"Andrews is clear now, Mr. President," he said. "We'll be landing in fifteen minutes."

A few seconds later, the big jet straightened, headed for the
shore line, and began to lose altitude.

"I wish," I said, "we could have had some of that content and
tone in today's Chicago speech."

Roudebush smiled. "At the least, it would have had more impact than what I did say. Several times I had the feeling I was
putting eighty thousand people to sleep."

"That sun was brutal," I rationalized. But privately I was aware that Roudebush had made few hearts leap today. His had been a "review of stewardship"; the steady, climbing economy, respect for the U.S. abroad, not a gun fired by or against American forces anywhere in the world for the last three years, that kind of thing. Reassuring, perhaps, but hardly gutsy.

Sheehan left us to take his usual seat in the forward compartment before landing. Aboard were assorted White House aides and secretaries, SS agents, two wire service reporters, pool men representing radio, TV, and general press, and a senator and five congressmen from Illinois.

"Have you heard anything about Wolcott's speech yet?" asked Roudebush.

I handed him the wire service story somebody had given me at the reception. The President scanned it. It was predictable fare —return the country to government by the people, to fiscal prudence, to less federal regulation, to the rule of reason.

"Stan didn't light any bonfires either," said Roudebush, obviously relieved.

"Look, Mr. President," I said, happy to be returning to familiar territory, "the big sensation in tomorrow's papers won't be Roudebush or Wolcott. It will be a guy named Kulp from Louisville."

"Kulp?" He was puzzled.

"Hillary Kulp," I said, "chairman of the Wolcott-for-President committee of Kentucky. The wires are carrying full text. It'll rip open a hornet's nest. I'll have a swarm of questions on Greer tonight. You'd better read this before we get back to the house."

I handed the President the roll of wire copy dupes which the UPI man gave me just before we took off from O'Hare. Roudebush reached for his glasses in the breast pocket of his jacket, which hung on his chair.

"You can skip the opening," I said. "The meat begins in Paragraph Five."

Roudebush brushed through the opening and began reading where I had indicated.

The gist of Kulp's speech was his expressed incredulity that Stephen Greer could vanish in a country boasting the "most complex and sophisticated communications system" in the world, a country where every man lived within a prison of identifying numbers, from social security and credit cards to those of fingerprints, a country of immense police forces, of tracking computers, and "of devices which search, find, and identify."

Kulp excoriated the President for permitting "eleven long days" to elapse without an adequate explanation to the American people. He hinted that the White House was suppressing information obtained by the FBI special task force, then said:

> We have heard the rumor from Washington, circulating for days among highly placed persons of the Roudebush administration, that investigation has shown a link between Mr. Greer and a mysterious "Dr. X," supposedly a university professor, and that "Dr. X" is nowhere to be found either. Yet, in eleven long days, the White House has uttered not a word about this strange coincidence.

Roudebush looked up from his reading as the flight steward opened the compartment door and said: "Seat belt, Mr. President." The plane was nosed down and the Maryland countryside fled past beneath the wings. Roudebush put down the tissue-thin carbon copy, buckled his seat belt, and began buttoning his collar and hoisting his tie.

"Kulp obviously has learned about Dr. Lubin from some source," he said. "That speech is poisonous stuff."

"It gets worse," I said.

The big plane was shuddering now as the pilot horsed it into position for the final approach. "I'll finish it on the helicopter," said Roudebush. "What's the background?"

"The only thing I know so far," I said, "is that this Kulp was a college class-mate of Matty Silkworth, Wolcott's manager. They're still close friends, I'm told."

There was a slight bump. We were on the ground, speeding at 160 miles an hour. Then came the screech of reversed engines, and we braked to a modest run. Fire trucks and an ambulance, routine precautions for a presidential landing, promptly wheeled into line behind us. Our plane made the second turnoff and taxied toward the apron and three waiting helicopters. Off to the right I saw several trucks and smoking wreckage. Don Sheehan put his head into the cabin.

"That fighter pilot's okay, Mr. President," he said. "It was a wheels-up belly landing. He got out just before the plane caught fire."

"Have somebody find out where he is, Don," said Roudebush. "I want to talk to him."

The four newsmen on the President's plane were waiting for us at the foot of the ramp. The press plane, which had landed ahead of us, was disgorging seventy more reporters, many of whom were running toward us. By the time the President stepped to the ground, he faced a junior mob scene. The first question came in a shout from the rear:

"Mr. President, a Wolcott chairman in Kentucky is charging . . ."

Roudebush held up both hands in a pacifying gesture. "Nothing now, please," he said. "Gene will be available back at the White House. Right now, I want to see the fighter pilot."

The two-star base commander, flanked by three colonels, stepped forward with a smart salute.

"How's the pilot?" asked Roudebush.

"Not a scratch, sir. He's in Operations. He extends his apologies for causing you the delay."

"Ask him to step over to the helicopter," ordered Roudebush. "I'd like to talk to him."

The flyer, a young first lieutenant whose coveralls had a long tear on one sleeve, met the President inside the chopper. Roudebush gave him the big, radiant smile, congratulated him on survival, then questioned him about his life and service record. I took notes for the press, but my mind remained glued to Steve Greer.

Our helicopter rose with that boastful clatter, shaking my teeth, and the President took up the Kulp story where he left off. He read as we racketed over the parkway to the Anacostia River and then turned right along the Potomac.

In the body of his speech, Kulp offered the pretense, always viable political fodder, that he was speaking not as a Wolcott state chairman, but as "an American citizen, entitled by law and by tradition to question those who hold the trust of government for a period of four years." He therefore directed a series of blunt questions at President Roudebush on the subject of Stephen Greer. He asked what the FBI had reported, whether Greer was hiding in Brazil, and what "vital information" was being withheld from the public. In the climax of the speech, which indicated the existence of a reliable source in Washington, Citizen Kulp rolled out these questions:

> Mr. President, is it true that federal agents have tracked Mr. Greer to an airport outside the United States?
> Mr. President, if Mr. Greer is indeed outside the United States, have the worldwide facilities of the Central Intelligence Agency been alerted to discover where he is and why?
> Mr. President, who is the mysterious "Dr. X," what is his relationship to Stephen Greer, and where is he now?
> Mr. President, were national security secrets in the possession of Mr. Greer when he disappeared the night of August 26?
> Mr. President, what is the Roudebush administration hiding and why?
> Mr. President, why the White House silence for eleven long days?
> I am a citizen of a free and open society, Mr. President, and in the name of my fellow Americans, I respectfully request answers.

Roudebush folded the roll of paper and tucked it into his coat pocket.

"A very crafty citizen," he said. "He reminds me of Citizen Genet. . . . Well, that's politics."

He glanced out the window toward the Lincoln Memorial, proudly glistening in the afternoon sun. We were lowering over the Ellipse for the landing on the back lawn of the White House.

It was obvious the President meant to shut a compartment door on Kulp of Kentucky, but mine was wide open—and soon a pack of newsmen would come barreling through it.

"I've got to have something ready for the press," I said.

"We're not going to fall into that trap," he said firmly. "I do not intend to begin answering the so-called questions of Citizen Kulp. . . . Let me handle this. I'll scratch out something in the office. I'll have it for you in a half hour or so."

And when we thumped down on the lawn, he hopped out. The heat was fierce, a last blast of summer. Roudebush promptly shucked his jacket and hung it over his arm. He headed toward his office, loosening his tie as he went, flanked by Don Sheehan and trailed at two paces by the Air Force major whose hand flicked nervously at his shirt front. My mind switched back to the scene in the cabin of Air Force One and the President's soliloquy on the bomb. Good God, what a job he had! Then Greer came battering at me again, and I hurried to my own office.

Jill greeted me with a jumbled handful of slips, her notations of calls for me. There were dozens of them, including overseas calls from three London papers, *Die Welt* in Hamburg, the *Times of India* and *Asahi Shimbun* in Tokyo. Greer had become a torrid international topic. Jill appeared disconcertingly fresh and calm amid the chaos of the office, reminding me of my own sad condition. Three hours sleep last night had been insufficient preparation for Chicago's broiling sun. My skin felt prickly, my head had that dull, solid ache, and my eyes focused on print only with an effort. I resented Jill's cool, refreshed look, a lily to my weed, and I guessed that she had slept eight or nine hours last night. It seemed grossly unfair that love should fail to exact equal physical penalties from both of us.

She moved close for a welcoming kiss, but I merely touched her lips. Why couldn't women keep intimacy turned off until nightfall?

"Throw those notes from London and Tokyo in the waste basket," I snapped. "Let them call their own Washington correspondents. *Asahi* has a half dozen here."

"Please, baby. Don't be mean."

"Don't call me baby around here," I said. She wore a pink shift which hung straight from her shoulders like a tube. "And for God's sake, wear dresses in this office. This is the White House— not Montego Bay."

"You're being contrary. Why?"

"No sleep. S-l-e-e-p. I can still spell it, even if I've forgotten how it feels. Now, please use your head and put those calls in some kind of priority order, instead of handing me a dishful of noodles."

I spoke only half the truth. I was still harried by the thought of that phone call last night and by the suspicion that Jill had lied to me when she said a man named Nick, or whatever, was in the habit of calling Butter Nygaard, not Jill.

Jill folded her arms and surveyed me as she might a familiar piece of furniture newly seen in a fresh light. Will the real Culligan please stand up!

"I should have bitten your chin," she said. "Then it would be a souvenir of your last night in *my* bed."

She wheeled and clacked back to her desk, where she began furiously shuffling the slips of paper.

I held my head in my hands to quiet the throbbing, and tried to concentrate on a copy of Kulp's speech. I had to anticipate the hundred and one questions it would provoke.

Five minutes later there came a soft call. "Gee-ene!"

I looked up to see her posed at her desk like a wistful Madonna.

"It's Kulp, isn't it?" she asked. "You think there's been a leak somewhere?"

"Leak!" I retorted. "There's enough secret stuff flowing out of this place to keep Wolcott's headquarters afloat for two months."

"You don't think it's me, do you?" She was grave and intent.

I was surprised. "You? No. Why should I think it's you?"

"Oh, your attitude, I guess."

"Forget it."

She brooded for a minute. "Gene, you know what I think? . . . I think Arthur Ingram said something to somebody who talked to that Kulp man in Kentucky."

I nodded. "Could be. But how did Ingram learn about Phil Lubin and about Steve supposedly going to Rio in the first place?"

"From one of his agents," she said. She smiled proudly as if the answers were now all tied up neatly with a pink bow on the package.

"Superb deduction, Miss Holmes."

My phone to the President's office buzzed. He was ready, he said.

Roudebush was leaning against the edge of his desk. He handed me a sheet of yellow paper on which he had written in pencil:

The White House declines comment on Mr. Kulp's speech, which was replete with ugly and totally unjustified implications of a type inspired by partisan politics. The FBI is continuing to investigate the disappearance of Mr. Greer. When the case is solved, and a full report made to the White House, the public will be informed.

I felt let down. After a half hour of waiting, I was given verbiage which said nothing. Worse, there was a touch of arrogance in the last sentence which would only inflame our critics, who were growing in number and vehemence by the hour.

"This won't do the job, Mr. President," I said. "They'll crucify me with questions after I put that out."

"You'll have to do the best you can," he said. "I refuse to be put in the position of enshrining every single insinuation—and fishing expedition—on a White House answer."

I looked at him in wonder. Even the most acute and sensitive of men could become woefully insulated in this office. I could already see tomorrow's editorial fires and hear the righteous breast-beating of the Wolcott people. Did Roudebush really comprehend how this Greer case was building up?

"Mr. President, I think it's time to tell the press exactly what the FBI has found out. We have nothing to hide, and everything to gain by playing it straight. But this . . ." I rattled the paper. "This is a lighted fuse. Tomorrow's explosion will be a dilly."

He thought a moment as he leaned against the desk. Then he shook his head. "No, Gene. We can't do that. It wouldn't be fair

to Steve, to his family, to the Bureau, to all concerned. We'll
have to wait. If that means taking a lot of heat . . . well . . . we'll
just have to take it."

And I would be the first to be scorched and fried.

"Of course," I said, "I'll put it out, but as your press secretary,
I have to say flatly that it won't go. . . . There's something else.
The last sentence has a 'public be damned' flavor. Why can't we
soften that?"

"Write something out, will you?"

I drew a line through his last sentence, tinkered a bit, then
printed in my substitute. After reading the new version, Roudebush changed two words.

"Yes," he said, "that is better. Thanks. I guess Citizen Kulp got
my back up. . . . All right. It's yours."

I tucked the paper in my shirt pocket.

"Any guesses as to who tipped Kulp off?" I asked.

He smiled ruefully. "I've got my little list."

"Somebody in the know talked to Matty Silkworth," I said. "It
figures. Kulp and Silkworth are buddies." I nodded my head in
the vague direction of Langley. "Could be our friend across the
river."

He did not pick up the cue. "This kind of thing has to be
expected," he said, "whenever there's campaign mileage to be
made. I can take it, but I'm concerned for Sue Greer and
Gretchen. Some of Mr. Kulp's innuendoes have a gutter smell."
He shrugged. "Well, I suppose you'd better go feed the animals."

About seventy-five newsmen, a huge number for a holiday,
trooped into my office for the press briefing. It was my worst half
hour since Greer vaporized at Burning Tree. Our statement
merely served to raise the pack's hackles. Who was "Dr. X?" Was it
true Greer was hiding in Brazil? What written proof did I have
that Greer severed all connections with Educational Micro? Did
Greer take cash from an office safe for a getaway, as reported? Was
the CIA on the case? I replied, "I have nothing to add to the official statement" so many times that I began to sound like a tape-
recorded answering service. Gradually, the inevitable happened,
and the press corps began to target me as the villain. What was

I covering up? What FBI reports had *I* seen? The Baltimore *Sun* man slipped in a deft stiletto by quoting a freedom-of-information pledge I had made to the American Society of Newspaper Editors three years before. Did I still stand on that? Of course, I answered, but on the Greer case there was no information as yet to be free with. This was greeted by derisive guffaws. I felt miserable, and even Jill's sympathetic thumbs-up gesture at her station by the door did not help.

"Is the lid on until nine-thirty tomorrow, Gene?" someone asked.

"The lid is on until Tuesday, November 2," growled the Cowles correspondent.

The senior of the regulars, the Associated Press reporter, turned on his heel without the customary, "Thank you," and the herd trampled out. Jill did not have to close the door. The last man out slammed it.

A footnote of despair came a few minutes later as I sat eying a pack of cigarettes which rested on a corner of my desk as a memorial to my rusting will power.

"It's Dave Paulick," said Jill, "calling from Rio de Janeiro." I grabbed the phone.

"Gene?" The voice was faint against a wavering hum.

"Yes, Dave."

"What the hell right . . ." The line stuttered and coughed . . . "passport" . . . A string of indistinct words . . . "charter a boat" . . . A rise and fall of cluttered static . . . "American citizen."

The line went dead.

That tied it. My Labor Day, from the nuclear messenger to Citizen Kulp to Citizen Paulick.

Tuesday was another Monday, a day of accelerating frenzy as the public avidly gulped the news provoked by Stephen Greer's descent into nowhere from the fourth green at Burning Tree.

NBC's *Today* program devoted an entire hour to Greer. It ran complete footage of Hillary Kulp's Louisville speech, showed shots of youngsters rampaging at Soldier Field, and wound up with

man-in-the-street interviews around the nation. Gist of the poll-
ing: President Roudebush was protecting Greer for fear that disclosure would help elect Wolcott. One talkative salesman even
exhumed the drab phrase from the Lyndon Johnson era—credibil-
ity gap.

A few hours later, at 11:30 A.M., the American Stock Exchange
suspended trading in Educational Micro after the stock dropped
six points under a crush of sell orders. Our Sunday night statement evidently had only compounded suspicions. The Securities &
Exchange Commission stirred more financial talk at noon when it
announced it had the Ed-Mike rumors under study.

Miguel Loomis called me early in the afternoon. Mrs. Greer, he
said, was nearly hysterical because of radio and TV hints of an
unnatural relationship between Steve and "Dr. X." One commentator even brought up Steve's security clearance with an implication he might be defecting.

The Associated Press carried a midafternoon quote from the
President of the U. S. Chamber of Commerce. He said business
confidence was being shaken and that there could be a "Greer
recession" unless the President quickly cleared up the mystery.
Stocks closed after the steepest slide of the Roudebush administration. Dow-Jones averages were off twenty-eight points for the
day.

My press conference was a wild one. I was handed a petition,
signed by twenty-two White House regulars, demanding a public
session with Roudebush, who had not had one since early August.
The newsmen also insisted on a press conference with Peter
Deskowicz. The FBI director was refusing to talk to the press.
At one point, I was accused of lying. I lost my temper and ordered
every one out of the room. Jill chided me for lack of control. I
lashed back at her in frustration. Then Jill cried and threatened
to quit.

While I was trying to comfort her, the p.r. chief of the Roudebush campaign committee telephoned to report that headquarters was flooded with calls from around the country. Leaders
complained that the White House silence on Greer was turning
public sentiment against the President. Many implored the com-

mittee to persuade Roudebush to speak to the country about Greer on TV.

Then Gretchen Greer called. She said it was vital that the President talk to her mother as soon as possible. Mrs. Greer was in danger of a nervous breakdown over the rumors and uncertainty. I relayed this information to the President. Distressed, he said he would call Mrs. Greer immediately and invite her to dinner at the White House tomorrow night, the earliest his schedule would permit.

Just as Jill and I prepared to close up our lunacy shop for the night, she brought me ticker copy quoting the lead editorial in tomorrow morning's Cleveland *Plain Dealer*. It called for my prompt dismissal on grounds of "ineptitude, dissembling, arrogant treatment of the press, and a flagrant contempt for the public's fundamental right to know." There was one consolation. Jill was outraged by the editorial and now vowed she would never quit as long as I held the job.

At 7:05 P.M. that Tuesday I performed my last chore of the day. I visited the White House clinic, consulted the assistant physician—and left with a packet of sleeping pills.

11

Miguel Loomis and Gretchen Greer found vacant stools near the back elbow of the long bar. It was only nine o'clock, a trifle early for the Dialogue to begin swinging toward its febrile crest of music, talk, and alcohol. Bunched along the bar were attenuated young men of the Georgetown set: tight pants, tight coats, narrow ties, cramped smiles, small talk, brittle greetings. Most of the women sitting on the high stools wore sweaters and abbreviated skirts. A large blackboard on the wall advertised sandwiches, chili, and beef stew. On a rear platform, three guitarists and a trumpet player experimented with a new lament.

"I haven't been here since college vacations," said Gretchen. She felt conspicuous in her dinner dress and lightweight green coat, and she let the coat trail toward the floor. "Nothing's changed, not even the menu."

"Gene Culligan introduced me to this joint," said Miguel. He admired this tall, serious girl beside him. There was a permanence and a tranquillity about her. She was deftly solicitous with her mother, she took command of the household and she had not cracked once since her father's disappearance. "It goes into high gear along about midnight," he added.

"We can't stay that long," she said. "I don't want to leave mother alone in the house."

A White House limousine had called for Susannah Greer early in the evening. She was scheduled to dine with the Roudebushes and later, so the President had assured Gretchen, he would have a private talk with Sue.

"You were nice to take me out to dinner, Mike," said Gretchen. "I suddenly realized that this is the first time I've been away from

Brookside Drive in almost two weeks—except for the morning at Dad's office."

The barkeep, whose black bow tie quivered on an enormous Adam's apple, placed two stingers before them. Miguel touched his glass to Gretchen's. "Here's to your night out."

Two weeks, thought Gretchen, had rubbed the strangeness from Miguel. For his reserve, even somewhat courtly manner toward her, she was thankful. At this time, she knew, she could not have endured one of those young men who practice instant psychological intimacy, an entwining of the psyches into a kind of spiritual pretzel. Miguel had maintained a polite buffer zone between them, and yet the very sharing of the small daily demands provoked by her father's disappearance had linked them in an easy friendship. And she liked the fact that he was handsome. She approved of the black hair, the long, thin nose, the rich ocher color of his skin. In sum, she felt comfortable with Miguel.

They had talked it all out at dinner at Chez Francois and agreed that the disappearance of Stephen Greer was binding them together in small but definite ways. Barney Loomis had called his son twice that day, in a splutter of rage over the plunging of Educational Micro stock, and both times Gretchen caught her share of the wrath by merely answering the phone. Then, when they discussed the meaning of "Dr. X," the mystery man of the Kentucky politician's speech, they found that each of them had been quizzed last week by an FBI agent as to whether they knew a mathematician named Phillip J. Lubin. Neither of them did.

Miguel even shared a confidence that startled her. He had mentioned that at the luncheon on the day of her father's flight Greer had been restless and acutely conscious of time. When Gretchen asked what had been discussed, Miguel told her—after pledging her to secrecy—of the CIA's recruitment of young physicists. Thanks to her father and Culligan, he said, the Spruance training of scientific agents had been abruptly cut off.

Gretchen traded this confidence for one of her own. She told Miguel of the amount of cash—ten thousand dollars—that she had found in her father's safe. And she showed him Greer's handwritten note that had been tucked under the rubber band which held the money: "Dear Gretchen—Take good care of your mother. I love you both. Dad." At dinner, Gretchen and Miguel had picked the wording apart, analyzing it for hidden meaning. Had it been written in anticipation of the flight from Burning Tree? Or was it intended to cover any emergency, as blankly inclusive of disaster as a formal will? While Gretchen had shown the note to Miguel, she had kept it from her mother. Stephen Greer was winding through their lives like a crooked lane, dividing here, gathering there.

"It *is* strange what Dad is doing to us," she said now. "I lied to Mother about the note. I didn't want to . . . well . . . hurt her ego. I'm not sure she ought to know that Dad apparently looked on me as the strong one in the family and that he thought she couldn't take a crisis. . . . And it's not just the note I hate to bring up with Mother. There are other things. This Dr. Lubin, for instance."

"But if the agents questioned us about him," said Miguel, "you know they must have asked her too."

"I know," said Gretchen, "but the whole idea is so revolting. Suppose you were in my place . . . oh, damn it, would you go bringing up some wild gossip that you knew couldn't be true?"

"But the radio and TV have been full of Dr. X," insisted Miguel. "I don't see how you could avoid talking about it."

"She got half hysterical and cried," said Gretchen. "All I could do was try to comfort her. . . . Anyway, my father! Steve Greer! Why, it's ridiculous."

"Sure it is," agreed Miguel. "So why not clear the air with your mother. She's probably brooding herself sick, wondering if you were questioned about Lubin and what you're thinking."

"That awful Kentucky man, Kipp or Kupp or whoever he is. I'd like to get my fingernails on that soft face."

"Politics," said Miguel. But he knew his comment was no consolation. They fell silent as the guitars-and-trumpet group began another sad ballad.

Gretchen nudged Miguel and averted her face. "Don't look now, but someone over there is on the make for you."

Miguel looked across the elbow of the bar. A woman was smiling at him. She had glossy black hair, piled high, a wide mouth rimmed in crimson and obviously enough to drink. Her breasts made curving hills of her sweater, and Miguel guessed that she wore no brassiere. Her smile was as loose.

"Say . . ." The woman's stare became one of proud recognition.

When he frowned, puzzled, she smiled at him again, then slid her drink along the bar in his direction. She left her stool and followed the glass. She sat down beside Miguel and propped her elbows on the bar.

"Sure," she said, "you're the one. Mr. Loomis. I saw your pictures in the papers—out at that vamoosed lawyer's house in Maryland or some place. Am I right?"

"I'm just a guy having a drink," said Miguel defensively. He moved toward Gretchen.

"Okay, so don't admit it, but I know you anyway." She drank to celebrate the knowledge. The glass, Miguel guessed, held straight whisky. "Only thing is, I won't tell you my name either."

Miguel, chalking that up as a minor victory, said nothing. Gretchen leaned forward to appraise their new bar-mate.

"Who's your friend?" the woman asked Miguel.

"Just that. A friend."

"Oh, you've got a thing, huh? Well, don't mind me. Live and let live, I say. If you want to cheat on your wife or something, I couldn't care less." She swayed slightly on her chair. "You look the type, a Latin lover. Not like your lawyer friend, Mr. Greer, if you know what I mean."

"I don't know what you mean." Miguel tried to shut off the conversation.

"Oh, one of those stuffy ones, are you?" She stared at him in quick, drunken belligerence. "If you know so much about Mr. Greer, then what kind of a man is he—or was he?"

"A good guy." Miguel wished there were a house rule against bar-hopping.

"A good guy," she repeated. "And you think he's okay, do you?"

"Right." He addressed his glass.

"He may look okay, but take it from me, pal, you can't always spot the double-gaited ones."

Gretchen tensed. Miguel inspected his bar card with elaborate care. The woman ignored the hint.

"What do you think that Kentucky politician was talking about the other day?" she continued. "A 'Dr. X,' he says. That's a big, fat laugh."

"What's so funny?" asked Miguel coldly.

"If that little runt who was shacking up with Greer at our apartment was a doctor, I'm a mother superior."

Miguel faced her. "What apartment?"

"The Wilmarth on R Street, where I live. Where else?"

"You're smashed."

"Oh yeah? Well, let me tell you, Mr. Smart-ass Loomis. I don't care how much dough your father has . . ."

"You're drunk," he said. "Nobody invited you to sit here."

Gretchen touched Miguel's arm. "No, let her talk, Mike."

The woman made a mock bow. "Thanks, honey." Then to Miguel: "They call you Mike, huh? Okay, Mike, if your friend Greer was straight, then tell me what he was doing so many nights in Apartment 4-D with this four-eyed guy?"

"Where did you hear that?" asked Miguel.

"I didn't hear it, sweetheart, I saw it. And how come I saw it? Because I live right across the hall in 4-C, that's how."

She glared at Miguel, challenging him. The lipstick ran past a corner of her mouth like an unfinished road.

"When was all this?" he asked.

"Three times I seen them," she said triumphantly. "Once inside 4-D when I went in there because they claimed I was playing the hi-fi too loud. They wanted it quiet and cozy. . . . Oh, I kind of liked that Greer. If it hadn't have been for that other bastard, I think we might have become acquainted or something. He had a nice smile, you know what I mean. So that's why I figured he was one of the two-way kind."

"What was the other man's name?" asked Miguel, the starch still in his voice.

"Search me." She brushed back the dyed black hair with a sweep of crimson nails. "When the man comes around asking questions, I quit asking."

"You were questioned? By the FBI?"

"Now, wait a minute. I didn't say who it was that came around. Besides, I was asked to keep it quiet. . . . Anyway, don't try to give me a lot of crap about Mr. Greer because I know better, see."

She drank some more, then put a finger to her lips. "That's between us, right? They asked me not to talk, and I wouldn't have, either, except you were so snotty."

Miguel glanced at Gretchen. She was absorbed, studying the woman's face. Miguel summoned the barkeeper and paid the bill.

"We have to leave," he said.

"See you again," said the woman. "Don't spread it around, huh?"

Miguel and Gretchen walked out swiftly. On the sidewalk, Gretchen found herself trembling. She took Miguel's arm as they walked toward the parking lot.

"A female creep," said Miguel.

"Mike," said Gretchen, "I think you should look up that apartment."

He saw that she meant it, and at the parking lot phone booth, he found the address in the directory for the Wilmarth on R Street. Gretchen insisted they drive there.

At the Wilmarth, Miguel pressed the button under the mailbox for 4-D. The name plate was empty. When his rings went unanswered, he looked for the apartment of the resident manager. The man who answered his knock had a grayish face and a cheek mole. Miguel inquired for Phillip J. Lubin in 4-D. That suite was vacant, said the manager, and the name did not register.

"A short fellow with glasses," said Miguel.

"There was a tenant in 4-D like that until the first of the month," said the manager, "but his name was Klingman."

"Do you know his business address?" asked Miguel.

"Someplace on Charles Street in Baltimore," said the manager. "Say, what's the idea? You guys pumped me enough the last time."

Gretchen was waiting in the darkened, parked car. Miguel told her.

"Why did you say a short man with glasses?" she asked.

"According to the dame at the Dialogue, that was the general idea," he said. Then he added: "Also, the FBI showed me a picture of Dr. Lubin."

"The agent showed me one too," said Gretchen in a small, tight voice. "Mike, I . . ."

She hesitated, visibly trying to contain herself. "We'd better drive straight home," she said quietly. "I want to be there when Mother comes back. . . . Mike, I've got to tell her."

He headed the car toward the District line and the drive to Kenwood. The night was cool, the first token of autumn. Gretchen pulled her coat closer about her. They rode in troubled silence.

Susannah Greer could see the iron railing of the balcony and the broad sweep through the trees to the Ellipse and the Washington Monument. She was seated in the second-floor oval parlor across a coffee table from the President. The high window was open, the air-conditioning turned off, and she could feel the freshness of the night.

She was relieved that Ellen Roudebush had excused herself after dinner, for the meal had been a trial, Ellen rattling along over pebbles of gossip as though Steve had never existed. Paul Roudebush told several lively anecdotes, but his usual amiability seemed forced tonight. Ellen kept darting glances at Sue, trying to gauge Sue's mood and condition as one would with a convalescent.

Not until Sue was alone with the President and riding the snug elevator to the second floor did her tension ease. Roudebush led her down the wide hall, nodded to a Secret Service man on station, and ushered her into the oval living room with its serene décor of soft yellows.

A butler brought coffee in a silver pot, and Roudebush filled the demitasses.

"I'm grateful for this, Mr. President," she said.

"Please, Sue. It's Paul."

"I really can't, you know." She laughed for the first time that evening. Why did Ellen's absence seem to lift a weight? "I do think of you as 'Paul.' I just can't bring myself to say it. . . . Please thank Ellen again for me. I appreciate her thoughtfulness so much."

"Sometimes Ellen . . ." The thought went unsaid. He stirred the coffee with a tiny silver spoon. "Sue, I'm sorry we couldn't do this earlier. I can imagine what you've been through."

"It's been a bad two weeks," she said. "When I'm being honest with myself, I . . . well . . . I think now that I can take anything except the uncertainty. Another woman. Some kind of brain damage. Even embezzlement as they seem to think on Wall Street. Anything, really, anything at all except the strain of not knowing. That's the worst." She found herself hurrying, intent on exposing every facet of her anxiety. "Anything, even what people believe after that horrible speech in Kentucky Monday. I became hysterical at first, but now . . ."

"You mean that dirty business about Dr. X?" he asked.

"Yes. Even that I could take now. That may sound strange, but I mean it. Anything is better than not knowing. You see . . ."

How could she say it? Her thoughts, as she lay sleepless in bed last night, had evoked flashes of memory . . . Steve's passion, his tenderness, the warmth in his eyes. . . . She meant that even if it were proved in a court of law that Steve had loved a man physically, she would not credit the evidence. A mountain of so-called facts could not smother her intuition. So, no matter what others might think they knew, she knew better. And, if that were a ridiculous lack of logic, then logic did not make truth.

Roudebush waited patiently for a moment, then leaned forward. "Sue, that speech is the main reason I wanted you to come here tonight. Even if Gretchen had not called, I would have insisted you come to dinner. . . . You know how cruel politics can be. Charges are made that can't be easily dispelled. But Sue, on that aspect, Citizen Kulp's innuendo about Dr. X, I think I can reassure you."

"You don't have to," she said. "I've known Steve too well too long."

"Yes, I think I do," he said slowly. "No matter what your instinctive feeling about Steve is, it would be bound to erode in time. You'd have little, niggling doubts, small questions that would nag at you. That's human nature, Sue. . . . So let's talk quite frankly within the limits of my knowledge. You see, I'm familiar with the FBI reports, and I can tell you in confidence some things that the country can't be told yet."

She felt the swift exhilaration of good news to come. She drank some coffee and waited.

"First," he said, "there is a Dr. X, although I have no idea how Mr. Kulp learned of him. His name is Phillip J. Lubin, a Ph.D. in mathematics. He's at Johns Hopkins University."

She nodded. "I guessed as much. The FBI showed me a picture and asked if I'd ever known the man as Dr. Lubin or David Klingman. I never saw him in my life."

"I realize that." He smiled sympathetically. "It's also true, Sue, that Steve was seeing Dr. Lubin regularly. They met almost every Wednesday night for a year or so."

"Wednesday night!" She felt betrayed. "Steve told me he attended meetings of some private group on Wednesday nights. He called it the Potomac Study Club."

"Yes," he said. "Well, although this might be difficult for the public to understand, you and I know Steve well enough to realize that he could have been studying with Dr. Lubin."

"Studying what?" Sue felt newly adrift. "And why so secret about it? Why couldn't he tell me?"

Roudebush shrugged and smiled again. "You know Steve better than I do, Sue. You know how he acts. Didn't he take the family off to Harvard one year for—what was it again?"

"Oriental art," she said faintly. It seemed so long ago. "But this time? Does the FBI know what they were studying and why?"

"Phillip Lubin is quite celebrated in his field," said the President. "So, it seems logical that Steve might have been studying some kind of higher mathematics with him."

"He did try Gretchen's new math some years ago," said Sue. "He figured the household accounts in another system—base eight, I think it was."

"You see," he said. "It's entirely plausible."

"I don't know. I find that very strange." Once again her hopes had collapsed. The sensation now had the familiarity of a chronic illness.

Roudebush rose, thrust his hands in his coat pockets, and strolled toward the high window overlooking the back lawn. The great trees were etched by light from the driveway lamps. He stood for a moment, and when he turned back, he spoke quietly.

"Sue, this is a trying time for me as well as for you. Steve, as you know, is my closest friend, but he is more than that. Steve sees the world as I see it, so closely at times that his judgment gives me a kind of second sight. So, I miss him, especially now that we're heading into the heat of the campaign. I know that if he could, he would be here working with me now. The fact that he is not here can only mean that there are good reasons for his absence. I feel confident that these are reasons he will explain someday to the satisfaction of everybody. Sue, I trust Steve implicitly."

He paused. He had a quizzical expression, a seeming fretting of indecision. Sue knew that she was being bathed in words, words that sought to soothe while actually carrying their own burden of doubt.

"Perhaps the best way to approach it is this," he continued. "While the situation is still cloudy, there are certain things you and I can assume without much doubt. First, Steve is not involved in any deviate sexual business. That we both know. No matter what the rumors, we know there can't be any truth to them. As for the gossip, you'll just have to put up with it, secure in your knowledge of the facts."

He returned to his chair. "Now second, Sue, he is not mixed up with another woman." He tapped his finger on a manila folder lying on the coffee table. "Steve loves you. You know the truth of that better than I do, but at any rate, I can assure you there's no illicit romance."

Roudebush threw an arm across the top of his chair. "And a third thing. Steve is not involved in a financial scandal. The checking on that has been thorough."

Susannah wondered at once: Did that mean that the checking on the other phases had been less than thorough? She wished the President would be more explicit.

"This whole wave of rumor about Educational Micro, a good, sound company, is nonsense," said Roudebush. "Steve did legal work for Loomis's company, as you probably know, but it ended some time ago. From every angle, Steve is clean financially. That's definite."

He tapped the manila folder again, and Sue wondered why, if the FBI reports were inside, the President did not summarize them for her. Roudebush gazed at her, weighing her reactions.

"My own belief," he said after a lapse, "is that Steve will return in his own good time, maybe in a few weeks, maybe longer. That is my conviction, and I further think his eventual explanation will reflect nothing but credit on you and Gretchen. I say I believe that, Sue, but I can't promise a thing. I wish I could. But whatever happens, you must continue to be as brave as you are. . . . Frankly, Sue, I admire your courage and your spirit. You're quite a woman."

Where had all this taken them, Sue wondered. Her questions still hovered like shadows, her uncertainty was as vast and as lonely as ever.

"Do you know where Steve is, Mr. President?"

"At this moment, no," he replied. "He has left a trail, of course, and the Bureau has traced some of his movements."

"Is there anything to tell us whether he's outside the country?" She glanced at the manila folder as if it held the answer.

"Yes," he said, "the trail appears to lead to Rio de Janeiro, but as far as the FBI is concerned, there are many leads yet to be checked."

"Do you think he's alive, Paul?" The first name slipped out unconsciously.

"I do," he said. "In fact, we know that he was alive a few days ago, because he was seen. There is no reason to assume that anything has happened to him since."

Roudebush stood up and she sensed that it was time for her to leave.

"I wish," he said, "I could be more helpful, but I can't. Soon, I hope we'll know more. Until then, just share my faith." He patted her shoulder.

As she arose, she said: "I got a message from Steve that first night via an anonymous caller. He used Steve's pet nickname for me, so I was sure it came from Steve. Did the FBI report that?"

He nodded. "Yes, I know all about that. Like you, I see no reason to doubt that Steve was the source."

She picked up her handbag and held it firmly. It seemed to be the one solid thing she could take with her. Roudebush escorted her across the hall to the elevator and once he pressed her arm reassuringly. But at the elevator, she realized she would soon be alone again.

"It's so bewildering," she said. "It makes no sense. None at all."

"We've both got to trust Steve," he said, "and I think you do."

"I try," she said. Then, as the small, old-fashioned elevator began its descent to the main floor, she was alone.

Mother and daughter were seated in the living room of the house on Brookside Drive, Sue on the floor and Gretchen above her in Steve's favorite armchair. When Gretchen finished telling of the woman at the Dialogue and of Miguel's inquiries at the Wilmarth, she clasped her mother's hands in hers.

"That's it, straight, Mother," she said. "I didn't know how else to tell you."

Sue looked up at Gretchen. "And you really believe your father was involved with this man."

"No, I . . . Damn it, Mother, I don't know what to believe any more."

"Your father," said Sue calmly, "is as normal as you and I. He is not a homosexual. I know that chemically as a woman. I know it from the years and the months and the weeks."

"But Mother," protested Gretchen, "how do you explain their relationship, then? Some men are . . . well . . . both. You know that."

"Some men, yes. Your father, no." Her face was drawn, the look of a woman determined to shut out the unwanted.

"I want to believe that, Mother. But how do you explain this Dr. Lubin and secret meetings in a grubby little apartment?"

Sue stared at her daughter. "I find this conversation offensive, Gretchen . . . after all your father has meant to you. But if, like some stranger, you demand evidence, let me tell you what I learned at the White House."

She related what the President had told her, but even as she talked, she found herself stating as fact, as if from an affidavit in the unopened manila folder, what she had heard only as hope and opinion.

"And so," she concluded, "that explains the Wednesday night meetings of the Potomac Study Club." She could not keep a certain tartness from her voice. The memory of Steve's lie was still bitter.

"But what were they studying?" asked Gretchen.

"Well, we don't know for sure. . . . But you know your father. A course in higher math would fascinate him."

"But why couldn't they meet here?" Gretchen was losing patience. "Why all the secrecy? And why an apartment on R Street? . . . Oh, Mother."

"Gretchen," said Sue sharply, "your attitude is hateful."

"I'm trying to understand."

"You are not. You're acting like a prosecutor."

"Don't say that, please." Gretchen left the chair and sat down on the floor beside Susannah. "It's just that this has gone on so long. I think you've got to begin to face some things. And we must try to be honest with each other."

"I'm trying to be honest."

"Where is this Dr. Lubin now?" asked Gretchen.

Sue thought a moment. "I don't know. The President didn't say. But if the Kentucky man is right, I suppose he has disappeared."

"Mother," said Gretchen. "After we came home, Miguel tried to reach Phillip Lubin through information in Baltimore. His apartment says he's away and not due back until February. There's no forwarding address. He left a week ago Sunday, three days after Dad."

"Three days after . . ."

"Yes, on Sunday, August 29."

"That doesn't mean . . ."

"No, it doesn't," said Gretchen. "But we have to face the possibility that they were forced to leave—or wanted to."

"Oh, Gretchen." Sue put her arms around her daughter and buried her head against Gretchen's shoulder. The tears came and she cried with little choking sounds. Gretchen gripped her wordlessly, and she wondered if their world would ever be quite the same again.

It was an hour later when Sue lay in bed, staring into the dark. Sleep would not come. She could see the manila folder resting on the coffee table at the White House, a repository for her doubts. And thoughts of Steve moved through her mind like a train in an endless tunnel. Now her intuition lay discarded, frayed, and limp. In a vivid scene, she could see the small, huddled figure of a man. He crouched beside a mound of some kind and upon it stood Steve. The smaller man reached up and took Steve's hand. Steve smiled. Hand in hand, they walked away. Sue turned roughly on her side.

The bedside phone rang. She groped for it in the dark, could not find it. She turned on the table lamp, then answered.

"Mrs. Greer?" It was a strong, male voice.

"Yes. This is Sue Greer."

"Mrs. Greer, I have a message for you. Please listen carefully. Quote. 'Dearest Cubby: I am safe and well. I plan to be home within a month. We can celebrate our twenty-seventh early with toasts from the stone bottle. You'll find it in the wine room behind the rack of champagne. Until then, all my love to you and Gretchen. Steve.' Unquote."

There was a click on the line.

She scrambled from bed, fumbled for her slippers, pulled a robe from the closet. She raced down two flights of stairs to the basement.

The wine closet, a room made of rough boards, stood across

the basement from the oil furnace. She pulled the light cord. The shelves were well stocked with gin, whiskies, and rum, and in one corner stood a wine rack with several bottles of Moet Chandon. When Sue reached behind the champagne, she found it.

It was a gray crockery bottle, heavy with dust, and she knew it contained ginger beer. Memories flooded through her . . . their June honeymoon so long ago in Nova Scotia . . . the gulls and terns crying in the muffled mist . . . the beat of surf on the rocks . . . the pungent smell of salt and fish . . . the frame cottage near the shore, and their daily walk to the village of Port Mouton, where they always shared a stone bottle of ginger beer . . . the sharp, refreshing taste . . . Steve laughing and saying that when they were old and doddering, they would celebrate some wedding anniversary with ginger beer.

She stood caressing the smooth crockery as dust coated her fingers. How like Steve to keep the bottle all these years without telling her, how utterly nutty and sentimental. She replaced the ginger beer behind the champagne, turned out the light and fairly bounded up the stairs.

She thought of telling Gretchen, but no light showed beneath the door of her daughter's room. Better. She would tell her in the morning. Right now she wanted to savor her excitement alone . . . home within a month. Let's see. This was September 8. That meant October 8, or perhaps he meant only four weeks. That would be what? October 6.

She snuggled under the blanket, thankful that the night air held the tang of autumn. Summer had gone, but Steve . . . Sue slept soundly all night, her first unbroken rest in two weeks.

12

I reached my decision one night in late September. Unless the "crisis" meeting the next afternoon yielded hard facts, and unless Paul Roudebush took me into his confidence, I was determined to quit as White House press secretary.

Three weeks had passed since the night President Roudebush talked privately with Susannah Greer.

While the professional anguish of a press secretary is a mere footnote in history—hardly comparable to the threat of a Secretary of State or Defense to leave the cabinet—in this instance it illustrates a critical aspect of the Greer case. For by this time Stephen Greer's still baffling disappearance posed a dilemma of loyalty and personal pride for officials far more important than I.

News, as I had learned over twenty years of close contact with the business, has a rhythm of its own. After mounting the first wave of public alarm and fascination, a major news story tends to slide into a trough, washing restlessly about until the next wave forms. A sensational murder, for instance, will monopolize the front pages for a week or more, then scatter into little paragraphs near the want ads until the suspect is brought to trial, when another shower of news occurs. It is axiomatic that no national crisis, not even war, can hold the public's attention with unremitting intensity day after day. We all retreat to the shelter of small personal tribulations, gathering a second wind, as it were, for our next mass preoccupation with whatever appears to threaten society's survival, orthodoxy, or comfort.

The Greer case was no exception. After looming above the news like a colossus for two weeks, it receded from the front pages and the evening TV news shows. The crest came with Kulp's speech in Kentucky. When Roudebush declined to go beyond his brief reply, the news faltered, then began to fade. The trouble was that the press had nothing fresh to feed upon. Greer had vanished, but where, how, and why no one knew.

That is not to say that nothing was happening. The nation's collective doubts licked at Roudebush's political support, crumbling soft spots here and eroding supposed hard strength there. We all could feel it at the White House. State chairmen called, agitated and dismayed. Our congressional candidates, whose political future was tied closely to Roudebush's at the November 2 election, voiced private alarms. The national committee's initial confidence gave way to anxiety. The various Roudebush-for-President committees could feel enthusiasm flag and, here and there, large financial contributions failed to materialize.

My own situation, being personal, was more acute. After much pondering and agonizing, I had come to these conclusions:

Steve Greer and Phil Lubin probably were homosexual lovers who had fled the country, where I did not know. I reached this judgment reluctantly and without any of the snide rejoicing which usually accompanies the moral disrobing of a friend. I had known both men more than casually and I liked and respected them. They had been considerate and helpful to me. Still, the more I threshed the evidence, the stronger my belief grew. Also, Miguel Loomis, by now much closer to the Greer family than I was, agreed with me. It seemed unreasonable to me that Greer and Lubin would have gone away together, since a pair is always easier to locate than isolated singles. I surmised they had both fled their separate ways when someone, as yet unknown, threatened to expose their union. It was possible, of course, that they had met furtively on some remote beach or island to while away the sunny hours in arid love. If so, Greer might be financing this shabby idyl with funds mulcted from Educational Micro, for this angle was still uncertain. Or, at the worst, in a mixture of sexual aberration and warped ideology, they may have even defected to a Communist country where, in due time, they would be paraded before TV cameras as examples of Western decadence.

Whatever the circumstances, I was by now convinced that Paul Roudebush knew the precise facts via his FBI reports. He was, I believed, suppressing these facts in a thin hope that he could prevent the scandal from erupting publicly until after the election. What gradually persuaded me was his evasiveness with me on the whole Greer episode and his adamant refusal to link Greer and Lubin in any way as a pair. I was also quite certain, thanks to my loop on the White House grapevine, that the President had taken no staff member into his confidence. In some way unknown to me, I thought, Roudebush had been able to pressure Peter Deskowicz into joining him in concealing the FBI's discoveries. And, while I suspected that Arthur Ingram had relayed what he knew to the Wolcott people, I was coming around to the belief that if Ingram had done so, he had some justification. Indeed, I would not have blamed Ingram if he had started his own CIA investigation in violation of Roudebush's orders.

I had discussed the whole thing with Jill this night, a Tuesday. Jill and I were still tender if disquieted lovers. The incident of the mysterious phone call had been forgotten. That is, Jill had forgotten it while I continued to wonder about it now and then. Still, her insistence that the unknown man, "Nick" or whoever, wanted Butter, not Jill, could not be openly questioned by me without risking a scene.

We talked for hours Tuesday night before I told her of my conditional decision to quit. We were sitting on her old, worn couch under the casement windows of her apartment. Her roommate was still out, but expected home momentarily.

"You're so right, Gene," said Jill. "The President has no business misleading the public like that."

"The public is not my concern," I said. "I don't care what he doesn't tell the public."

"Of course you do." Her indignation was instantly girded. "That's the whole point. . . ."

"It is not the point," I said. "If Roudebush wants to keep something from the country in order to defeat Wolcott in November, that's his business."

"Gene," she said, "I think that's a shocking statement."

"Go ahead and be shocked, if you want," I retorted. Women always seemed more quickly affronted by lapses in public moral standards than by private transgressions. "It's pure self-preservation. He's got an election to win. Every candidate fuzzes the truth, if he has to, when he's going for the big one. Roudebush is no exception. . . ."

"Gene!"

"Let me finish. The country and Culligan are two different things. He can lie by omission to the country, but lying to me is something else: he has no right to fake with me. Either we're in this together; or he can weather it alone."

"You're putting me on," she said. "You have to be. You're playing the role of a supercynical newspaperman. I don't care for it. It's phony and it does not become you."

"I'm not putting anyone on," I said. "I'm trying to level with you. But you persist in floating around on that idealistic cloud of yours. You refuse to look at politics as it is. God, after more than three years in the White House, too. . . . Even a wide-eyed innocent from Swarthmore ought to have learned something."

Instead of bridling, she favored me with a patronizing smile like that of an indulgent maiden aunt. "Oh, you can't fool me, Gene Culligan. You want to appear so hard-boiled. You won't confess to a smidgeon of altruism. But I know better. You're outraged because your hero, just to save his own skin, is suppressing information the public has a right to know. You know that's morally wrong and that's what bugs you."

"Oh, stop it, Jill," I said. "If Paul wants to kid the public, that's his business. But when he tries to kid me, that's my business."

"Baby," she said, "I don't believe you." She was sweetly forbearing. "Why must you disown your own decent motives?"

No amount of argument could persuade her otherwise. I finally gave up, before Butter returned, and went home with my thoughts. Jill's feminine intuition, on which she relied so much, had betrayed her. There was no moral indignation in my decision. I felt that Roudebush was justified in eliding, gilding, yes, even distorting the facts to win an election—as long as the safety of the nation was not involved. Such dissembling was politics, and at stake was the most powerful office in the world. But he was not justified in lying to *me* by evasion or by omission. In so doing, he cheapened my loyalty. He declared, by implication, that I was not a man to be trusted.

But Jill persisted in misunderstanding me. Even now, the next afternoon, as I tried to clear my desk before the big meeting, she said with that grave schoolgirl look:

"Gene, I'm proud of you for what you're going to do."

Oh no! The angel of righteousness was about to be airborne on wings of clay.

Roudebush's genial smile of greeting could have been a lone lighthouse on brooding seas that afternoon. In addition to the President, we were seven men and one woman who headed the women's vote division of the campaign staff. We were all discouraged, with the possible exception of the Independents-for-Roudebush director, a political amateur.

The national chairman was ponderously glum. He even failed to pass around cigars as was his custom. If hard times were coming, the chairman seemed to be saying, he would weather in by hoarding tobacco. The campaign manager, Danny Cavanaugh, a nervous little man who normally hopped about like a jumping bean, was congealed in thought, for him a sure sign of distress. Nor was cheer evident on the faces of the finance major-domo, the youth chairman, the public opinion expert who dealt with charts, depth polls, and computers, and, of course, myself. By the original paper structure of the campaign hierarchy, we should have been nine persons meeting with the President this afternoon. But the ninth, Stephen B. Greer, had been missing for thirty-four days. We could thank Greer for today's gloom.

The opening small talk funneled promptly toward Greer, for the women's division chief came brimming with the latest gossip. The rumor was out, she said, that Hester Portinari, the renowned Washington seeress, had just been blessed with one of her technicolor revelations. This scenario, we learned, focused on a high, jagged cliff from which Stephen Greer was being catapulted, whether voluntarily or not, Miss Portinari could not divine. At any rate, Steve was supposed to be tumbling down into an abyss. (End over end like a keg of ale, I wondered?) Our women's chairman reported breathlessly that Miss Portinari had pronounced Steve dead and was forecasting that the news of his demise would be announced to the world on January 21, the day after the inauguration.

"Whose inauguration?" asked Danny Cavanaugh, deadpan.

Ordinarily the crack would have fetched a laugh, but today nobody made a sound and even Roudebush's grin seemed a trifle strained.

More news on Hester, the lady swami. She was even now being interviewed by the ladies of the press at her baroque workshop of visions and banshees, and presumably tomorrow's newspapers would be draped with Greer's obituary by proxy. The public opinion expert quickly noted that Miss Portinari's batting average on predictions of calamity was only .375, considerably less than the 50-50 split which even random guesses would fetch in her métier. This heartened no one, for Hester's dippy prognostications were taken as Gospel by battalions of women voters around the country.

"Anybody have any good news?" asked Roudebush.

No one did. When the reports shifted from the spectral to the temporal, they got worse. The finance man said that contributions were off markedly. Business was jittery. The Greer mystery seemed to weigh almost as much on the industrial-political scales as all the upthrusting economic indices. The stock markets, it is true, had steadied at a quivery plateau about five points below the level held before the two Greer panic days, but some major stocks were still way off. Educational Micro, for example, was selling at 40, as compared to its pre-Greer roost of 56 and 57. Apparently Ed-Mike would hold around 45, since there were now signs of heavy buying, chiefly by Brady Manship, the New York speculator. Barney Loomis himself was still on the reservation, but his fund-raising results were considerably short of spectacular. And Barney's nose was out of joint because the SEC's investigation of the Educational Micro rumors was a pedestrian one. Some fat cats were shifting to Wolcott, and it was significant that bookies had shortened the odds on a Roudebush victory from August's 12 to 5 to today's 8 to 5.

The national chairman, a lump of pessimism behind his unlit cigar, said morale was sagging at the committee. Volunteers were dwindling. State and county chairmen were grousing and yesterday four men on the Idaho state-wide ticket had wired, asking cancellation of Roudebush's planned speech in the state. When local candidates began to unhitch themselves from the national ticket, look out. That kind of thing can become epidemic. The chairman's recommendation: A forthright TV speech to the nation by Paul Roudebush on one subject—Greer.

The youth representative, who at thirty-nine barely qualified for that cult, could have been colored blue. He said that while both Wolcott and Roudebush were being satirized by the young swingers, the lampoons aimed at Roudebush were dipped in acid. A song entitled, "Old Pal Greer, Odd Man Out," by the Naked Nuns group, was climbing fast on the fifty top tunes. A talk record, which married Roudebush's voice to the questions of Kentucky's Kulp, was a sudden rage. Roudebush's answers, all crudely irrelevant, were plucked from old televised press conferences. Sample—Kulp: "Mr. President, is it true that federal agents have tracked Mr. Greer to an airport outside the United States?" The President's dubbed voice: "The question of sonic booms is under continuing federal study. I assure you I was not elected President to make life miserable on earth just to gain a few minutes in the air."

The youth disciple predicted that the incident during the President's timber conservation speech in Seattle last week would most certainly happen elsewhere. A group of college students had unfurled banners bearing such slogans as "Has Greer Found Judge Crater?," "Immaculate Deception at Burning Tree" and "Dr. X or Heterosex?" Undergraduates on other campuses had improved on the Soldier Field chant and were now yelling, "Greer! Greer! Where's That Queer?" The fun-fun coterie aside, university and youth groups for Roudebush were wavering. Wolcott was winning the campus.

I reported the obvious, that the press had grown sullen about the freedom-of-information issue. Some formerly friendly Washington columnists were now groping for Roudebush's jugular. As for editorial support, we would be lucky to wind up with an even break as against the 65-35 split for Roudebush anticipated in the summer.

The chairman of Independents-for-Roudebush tried to inject some hope. He said there were signs of a sympathetic backlash for Roudebush. But none of us brightened at this, for the IFR man owed his job solely to his wife's friendship with Ellen Roudebush. He was a well-meaning dilettante whose closest brush with politics previously had been soliciting funds for the Boston Pops Orchestra. We valued his judgment about as much as the brass buttons on his blazer.

The public opinion expert, who relished any catastrophe amenable to statistical analysis, served up his news. The next Gallup and Lou Harris polls, due out tomorrow, would show a 45-45 split, give or take a few decimal points, with 10 per cent undecided. This was a drastic shift from the first polls in August. The trend was sobering. Our side had fallen steadily, week by week, while Wolcott's graph was up. The expert's depth interviews invariably fished up some suspicion about Greer.

Curiously, said the pollster, Roudebush was suffering from his own good image. For years the people had regarded Roudebush as candid and reliable, perhaps not the smartest man in the world, but always trustworthy. Now the Greer case was cracking the image. The public thought Roudebush was covering up, hiding something big. Their reaction was one of outrage, as though a father had been caught double-crossing his own children for selfish advantage. The public opinion specialist spoke reprovingly to the President, implicitly accusing him of erecting an unblemished reputation during hours that could have been more profitably employed at routine sinning.

Danny Cavanaugh cleared his throat in quick, nervous gargles. The bird-like hops of his fingers on the arms of his chair were telltale signs. Danny was about to think aloud.

"As I see it, Mr. President," he began, "we are faced with a crisis. . . ."

There was a knock on the door which led to Grace Lalley's office, and after a decorous moment, Grace said: "I was sure you'd want this in here." She smiled apologetically in the ring of gloom.

Roudebush took the sheet of yellow ticker copy and read it briefly as Grace slipped out of the room. His face was impassive, which usually meant one thing—bad news.

"You might as well read it aloud, Gene." He handed me the sheet and I read it to the group:

UPI-131
(Greer)
St. Louis—Stephen B. Greer, the mysteriously missing friend of President Roudebush, apparently met secretly in a Washington apartment with a university professor for a year prior to his disappearance.

The disclosure was made today in a copyrighted story from the St. Louis *Post-Dispatch*'s Washington Bureau.

The newspaper said the professor, whom it did not identify, was the "Dr. X" referred to early this month by Hillary Kulp, Kentucky chairman of the Wolcott forces. Kulp has since alluded twice to Dr. X in speeches.

The *Post-Dispatch* said the meetings of Greer and Dr. X occurred on the average of once a week at night in the Wilmarth, an apartment on R Street in the northwest section of downtown Washington. It said the professor rented the apartment under the name of "David Klingman" of the "Crown Arts Co., 939 N. Charles Street, Baltimore." The story said there is no such company and no such address on Baltimore's N. Charles Street.

The real name of the professor, said the *Post-Dispatch*, was being withheld pending efforts to reach him. The man, a forty-three-year-old bachelor, reportedly left on an automobile tour of western Canada and the United States.

9/29—MJJ304PED

My last syllable was swallowed in silence. While the news was no surprise to me, since Miguel Loomis had told me of his own visit to the Wilmarth and of his futile call to Lubin in Baltimore, it shocked the politicians. They all stared at Roudebush, waiting for some miracle of explanation. The silence quickly became unnerving.

"Do the FBI reports confirm that, Mr. President?" asked Cavanaugh.

Roudebush pursed his lips as he thought. "I'm sorry, Danny, but I'm not in a position to say." He paused, then added: "I have said from the beginning that this is a personal matter, of primary concern to Steve and his family. It is not a political issue and I do not intend to treat it as such."

"But Mr. President!" Danny objected. "It *is* a political issue, in fact the only one right now. It has been *the* issue since that first night five weeks ago. You have no control over it."

"Well," said Roudebush calmly, "I don't intend to throw more fuel on the fire."

Cavanaugh, baffled, looked around the room as if to ask us: What has happened to our sensible President-politician? Has he lost touch with reality?

"I don't think you understand what we've been telling you, Mr. President," he said in an incredulous voice. "You're in trouble. Don't you realize that?"

"I gather, Danny," said Roudebush dryly, "that I've been in better shape."

"But we're not talking about the rub-off of a few percentage points, Mr. President," said Cavanaugh. "We're talking about possible defeat. If you let this thing slide much longer, Stanley Wolcott could win this election."

"That I don't believe," said Roudebush. He lowered his voice as Cavanaugh's went up in pitch.

"It's true," insisted Danny. "Another month like this one, and we could be licked."

"Oh, come now, Danny. You're just trying to frighten me into doing what you want me to do."

"You're damn right I am," said Cavanaugh. He was simmering like a hot kettle now.

Roudebush folded his arms and smiled.

"Just what is it you want me to do, Danny?" he asked.

"I want you to go on TV," said Cavanaugh, "and level with the country about Steve Greer. Tell 'em everything you know about the case."

"Even if I don't have anything definite yet?"

"It doesn't have to be solid," said Cavanaugh. "Just a heart-to-heart talk, being as frank as you can, the kind of President Roudebush the people are accustomed to."

Roudebush thought a moment. "No, Danny, I can't do that."

"Why not, sir?" Cavanaugh would not back down. I was surprised. I had never seen him push the President like this.

"Because," said Roudebush slowly, "there are still too many unknowns. Partial disclosure now—and that's all we'd have—could be terribly unfair to Steve."

"Steve isn't the candidate," said Danny. "He's . . . he's a ghost."

"I can't do it, Danny."

"In that case," said Cavanaugh, "I can't be responsible, Mr. President, for what happens from here on in. I can carry a lot of things—but not a ghost on my back."

The President tried banter. "A live ghost doesn't weigh much, Danny."

"This one weighs a ton."

The aging youth leader spoke up. "If you can't tell the country yet, Mr. President, couldn't you fill us in—for background guidance?"

Roudebush shook his head. "This hasn't been that kind of investigation. I just don't think an exchange of conjectures at this stage would be valuable for any of us."

The expressions on the ring of faces showed injured pride. These people were the sinews of the campaign. They had been working themselves ragged for this man, and now he denied them the common courtesy of confidence. He had shut them out, slamming the door.

The meeting lasted only a few more minutes. It was agreed that Cavanaugh and two others would accompany Roudebush to Omaha next week for his farm speech. The finance chairman and the youth mentor made vague pledges of renewed endeavor. The group filed awkwardly from the room, and Roudebush's parting handclasps did little to buoy the dispirited captains of his campaign.

I remained behind, unbidden. The President was surprised to see me still standing in front of his desk.

"Is there something further, Gene?" he asked.

"Yes, sir." I braced myself. This was the most trying moment of my White House years.

"I'm quitting as your press secretary, Mr. President."

He frowned, then stared at me, uncomprehending, like a man who does not believe what he has heard.

I rushed into my speech. I said it poorly, but the nub got across: He could play games with the public if he wished, but not with his friends who were carrying the burden of the campaign—and especially not with me.

"That may not be a very lofty motive, Mr. President," I concluded, "but that's how I feel."

"Please sit down again, Gene, will you?" he asked in a fatherly tone

I did so. He left his swivel chair and came around to sit on the corner of his desk, his favorite place beside the golden donkey. He swung one leg free.

"Just what is it you want to know, Gene?"

"Everything you've learned from the FBI, Mr. President," I said. "I'm entitled to your trust, sir. I think the others are too, but I speak for myself. I've been working my tail off in this campaign. You've put me in an impossible position with the press . . . and . . . well . . ."

I drew my finger across my throat. "I've had it up to here, Mr. President."

He smiled. "You think I'm allowed to withhold information from the public, but not from you. Is that it?"

"That's it exactly." I had intended to tell him my conclusions about Greer and Lubin too, but somehow I could not bring myself to say it now. "If you won't trust me, then my usefulness to you is ended."

"You know that if you resign now," he said, "it could be immensely damaging to me and to the party."

"I'm not so sure of that," I said. "It would be a one-day story. Also, I could give excuses—breakdown, ulcer, fatigue, something like that. But whatever comes later, I can't go on like this, Mr. President."

"Irish pride?"

"No." Normally I would have flared at that, but now I felt no anger, only a dry sorrow. I merely wanted to get it over with. "Human pride. If you don't understand that, Mr. President, words are useless."

"Yes, I suppose they are." He looked at me with that old mixture of affection and respect. Then, impulsively, he reached out and gripped my shoulder.

"Gene," he said, "I know what you're thinking. You think the FBI has come up with something which is morally damaging to Steve, and that I'm hiding it from the public because I'm afraid the disclosure might defeat me in November."

"I do," I said, "but that's still not the point, Mr. President. My point is that I should be cut in, regardless of what the story is. Frankly, I don't give a damn what the facts show."

"I'm not sure I believe that," he said with a thin smile. "You're not being very charitable with yourself."

I almost laughed. Neither my girl nor my boss would credit me with a big, normal, selfish motive. How could a man level with himself if his best friends refused to do so? Did my mask really look that benign to others?

Roudebush reached across his desk for a calendar.

"September 29," he said. "Gene, will you give me ten more days?"

I was taken aback. The idea of compromise had not occurred to me.

"I'm not sure I know what you mean," I stalled.

He fingered the calendar. "Ten days," he said. "Give me until October 9. On that day you can either have all the FBI reports you want—or you can quit and take a full page ad in the New York *Times* to tell why."

"I don't get it," I said. "What will I know ten days from now that I can't be told now."

"Gene, you were right, you know. I am worried about the effects on the election—a lot more worried than I was willing to confess at the meeting. But the way this thing is shaping up—and the FBI reports confirm my hopes—I think we can lay it all out pretty well in about ten days."

"By then you could be a defeated candidate, no matter what," I said. "I don't think you realize how fast we are slipping."

"Thanks for the 'we,'" he said with a smile. "But as I understand you, that's not what's bothering you. You want me to confide in you—and I'm bargaining with you. Give me ten days, and I'll do just that."

"Well . . ."

"I think that's reasonable, Gene," he said quietly persuasive. "After all, we've been together for more than four years now."

"I'm really not asking much," I said. I could feel myself weakening. "I just want to be cut in on the facts, good or bad."

"And I'm saying you will be within ten days," he said, "or you can gather up all your secret papers and fly them out to Springfield."

He was flashing the big, radiant smile now. The warmth was irresistible. My resolve melted.

"Is it a deal?" He held out his big hand.

I shook it reflexively. "All right, Mr. President."

And soon I was out the door and walking in a half-trance to my office, proving, I suppose, that even a determined man is easy prey for presidential cajolery.

Jill stood up to face me, her hands on her hips.

"Somebody hypnotize you?" she asked.

"That's a good word for it." I walked to my chair and sat down as though someone had pushed me.

"Do I start cleaning out my desk?" Jill asked.

I shook my head. "We're not leaving."

I told her what had happened, both at the meeting and at my private session with the President.

"Baby, you've been had," she said. The long hair framed her disapproval.

"No, it's a compromise—for ten days."

"Gene," she said, "you're rationalizing. You said you were going to quit and you didn't."

"It's not that simple," I said. "A President is different. You can't just quit flat, not when he . . . well . . . pleads with you."

"You didn't stand up for what you believe is right," she lectured. "You let yourself be trapped with flattery."

"Well, what would you have done?" I demanded.

"Quit. I'd tell him I couldn't work for a man who lied to the people—exactly the way you feel about it."

Now I was being accused of deserting a principle I never held. Her illogic was maddening.

"You would," I retorted. "You're twenty-four years old, you don't know what you're talking about and you don't understand politics."

She studied me a moment, then sat down and began beating furiously on her typewriter. She rattled away, yanked out the paper, clacked across the room, handed me a typewritten sheet and then beat a tattoo of heels back to her desk. The message read:

9/29
Nuthouse
Washington, D.C.

Dear Sir:

I am sick and tired, not only of the hypocrisy of this place, but of its atmosphere of timidity and cowardice, which *some* people mistake for loyalty.

I do not like rubbery spines.

I despise self-deception.

I am glad I am 24 and still in possession of some values.

This place is for weirdo has-beens only.

I hereby submit my resignation as of Wednesday, November 3, which is my wedding day. I intend to be married in the chapel of the Washington Cathedral at 3 P.M.

Yours truly,

Jill Nichols

P.S. I am marrying a character named Eugene Culligan in the dim hope of making a resolute man out of him—and an honest woman out of me.

I felt faint. I had envisioned this hour of decision as being several years distant in a very vague future.

"Like The Man said, I'll let you know in ten days," I said.

"You don't have any choice," she said. "And I don't plead with anybody."

"But your folks," I protested feebly. "What will your mother think about you marrying an aging cynic who started cheating at dice before you were born?"

"She'll probably resent you for the rest of her life," she said, "and that's exactly the kind of mother-in-law you deserve." She rattled a batch of papers. "And now back to business, which you're always so fond of doing. My slips are all in order. You have five important calls to return. Also, two hundred students from American University are threatening to picket the White House tomorrow. They're already painting obscene signs about Stephen Greer. The press wants to know what you're going to do about it."

"The sidewalks are free," I replied. I still felt lightheaded. "But District ordinances prohibit lewd placards in public places. I suppose I'd better talk to the Secret Service. Get me Don Sheehan."

"Yes, sir."

I passed the next few minutes in a daze, dimly aware of Jill's soft voice on the phone.

"They say Don Sheehan's out in Omaha," she said, "advancing the President's speech."

It occurred to me that Sheehan was out of town a great deal recently. It was unusual for the chief of the White House detail to do so much of the advance work himself. I was irked. I needed his advice. These screwball college kid demonstrations could get out of hand.

"Okay," I said. "Then get me whoever is acting head of the detail."

She did as asked. I spent the next few minutes planning how to squirm my way through my 4 P.M. press conference without getting maimed. The college demonstrators could be handled later. Right now my main problem was what to say about the St. Louis *Post-Dispatch* story. Ten days—until October 9—seemed like a decade.

"It's four o'clock," said Jill in a mock tone of the crisply efficient secretary. "I'll call them in."

But she paused with her hand on the doorknob. "And Gene . . . tear up my letter, huh? . . . I want to be asked when you're ready. . . . It's just that you made me so mad."

"Don't worry. You can't be married until you're asked," I said. "I'll let you know in ten days—and not by an anonymous phone call." I could not resist the needle. "In the meantime, let's keep the daylight hours for work, shall we?"

She nodded, and still with her hand on the doorknob, she surveyed me gravely as though I were an uncertain juror.

"I wish I knew," she said, "what love really is."

Was the generation gap a chasm?

She opened the door, and the herd thundered in.

13

Larry Storm locked the car, took one purposeful step, then stopped. He leaned against the front fender and surrendered momentarily to the golden afternoon.

It was the last day of September and perhaps the last of this brief, tawny Indian summer. The sunlight shed a lazy warmth, he could see the slow flutter of a mocking bird's wings as it maneuvered for a perch on the telephone line, and from afar came the bubbling cries of small girls at play.

This was his second visit to this street, Battle Road in Princeton in the block between Olden Lane and the dead end which sloped into the meadowy reach of the Institute for Advanced Study. Battle Road at once consoled and vexed him, for this was the kind of neighborhood that existed only in dreams when he was a kid in Newark. . . . The dingy, Newark walk-up apartment, with its stench of overrun toilets, the scraps of food ground tight and black in the cracks of the living room linoleum, and the braying radio competing with the old man's foul, if virile, shouts at his mother.

If men cursed their women on this serene block, he thought, they must do so after midnight, when the neighbors were asleep, and then only in well-bred, modulated tones. For here were grace and ease . . . the immense oaks, the foliage of the sycamores along the curb, mottled now with yellow, the long, cool lawns, the clipped shrubbery, the homes all withdrawn from the road as if aloof from the combat and commerce the street implied. This was a white man's block, and Larry could not approach it without a twinge of resentment.

The Bureau had been his refuge from the abrasions and wounds of race. Inside the Bureau, color was only a whetstone on which he and Clyde Moorhead could hone their ribald taunting of each other. Inside the Bureau, he was Special Agent Larry Storm. There were some agents as good, but none better, white or black. The Bureau, an exacting master, consumed his waking hours, drained his energy, and left him exhausted but proud at night. The Bureau was more demanding than a woman, and thank God for that.

But now he was weary, bone tired, after more than a month of Ajax. Eighteen-hour days and not a single day off yet. Up and down the Eastern seaboard, following, asking, checking leads, some of them crazy, far into the night. The only breaks had been his two trips abroad. At least he had been able to sleep on the planes.

First had come Rio and the surprising trail which led him to the waterfront. There, after two days of digging and disconcerting linguistic skirmishes with his interpreter, came the discovery that Stephen Greer, or an American bearing an uncanny resemblance to him, had chartered a boat and sailed from Rio in the evening hours of Saturday, August 28. Larry could still feel the thrill of that discovery. The boat, a lobster trawler, 110 feet overall, was named the *Casa Alegre*, and the trawler and her Brazilian master had not been heard from since. Larry recalled his narrow escape from an unwanted encounter. Approaching a wharf early one morning, he saw an enormous, wide-shouldered man—an American, he guessed—questioning a longshoreman via an interpreter. Storm faded behind a shed. He learned later that the man was the Washington newsletter editor, Dave Paulick. This information surprised Clyde Moorhead almost as much as the news of Greer sailing aboard the *Casa Alegre*.

Then came his second trip, the flight to Helsinki, and the painstaking checking of airline tickets out of the Finnish capital. He had tracked his man, then lost him.

Now here he was back on Battle Road, Princeton, after two weeks in which his patience with the Bureau had worn as thin as his nerves. He looked again at the stone house. It was an agreeable sight, steeply peaked slate roof, ancient chimney, black door, and matching shutters behind the carefully tended shrubbery. The two dormer windows above were so widely spaced, they gave the house the appearance of a wondering child. Larry hunched his shoulders, ending the reverie, and walked through the drowsy afternoon sun to the home of Felix Kissich.

He knew almost everything about Felix Kissich now. He knew Kissich was a Nobel Laureate in physics, a research specialist in plasma physics at Princeton University's Forrestal campus, a refugee Hungarian from the World War II period, a naturalized American citizen, a gentle man of sixty-six years, and a scientist admired by colleagues throughout the world. The only thing of significance that Larry Storm did not know about Felix Kissich was where he was.

Storm rang the doorbell. In a moment, the narrow, black door opened, and the same little woman with the shy smile stood in the doorway. The summer screen door blurred her features, but Larry caught the look of apprehension. Deborah Kissich reminded him of a doe on a hillside, gracefully poised, yet atremble for any sign that might put her to flight.

"Oh, Mr. Storm," she said. "I didn't expect to see you again. Is something . . ."

The sentence hung on the warm air. She opened the screen door as if wary of an unseen intruder. He remembered he had been puzzled the first time until he understood. Mrs. Kissich was instinctively chary of investigators.

"May I?" Larry put a foot on the doorsill.

"Oh yes. Do come in. I'm sorry. I'm afraid you startled me. I thought . . ."

Again the diffident, unfinished sentence. Larry stepped into the snug living room, seemingly a room scaled down in size to fit its occupants. Felix Kissich, Larry knew, was but five feet six inches tall, and his wife was even shorter. She brushed nervously at a loop of gray hair at her temple.

"Please sit down, Mr. Storm." Her voice was as fragile as she was, bred of the same gentleness. He did not want to alarm this woman.

Storm seated himself on a walnut chair upholstered in fading needlepoint, avoiding the deep, battered armchair that he knew must belong to Felix Kissich.

"This isn't easy for me, Mrs. Kissich," he said. "I know you must be wondering why I'm back so soon."

"Yes, I am surprised." She sat quite primly in a spindle-backed rocking chair and folded her hands in her lap.

"Mrs. Kissich," he said, "I must ask you bluntly whether your husband returned home from Helsinki and whether he is now at home?"

He already knew the answer, for he had spent the last several hours on the James Forrestal grounds on Route I, questioning co-workers of Felix Kissich at the Plasma Physics Laboratory. There a team of government-sponsored scholars sought to tame the frightening power of the H-bomb for peaceful uses.

"No, Felix is not here," she said. Larry noted that she tensed.

"And my other question," he said quietly. "Did he return here from Helsinki?"

"No," she said, dropping her glance. At their first session, two weeks ago, she had said Felix intended to fly home directly the day the conference ended on September 20.

"Mrs. Kissich . . ." He hesitated to press this frail woman. Pursuit was not always a heady game. ". . . have you heard from your husband? Before you answer, let me tell you that Mr. Kissich checked out of his hotel in Helsinki two days after the conference opened."

Larry could see the date, the times, the places as though on a file card held before his eyes. Felix Kissich had flown from New York to Helsinki on Sunday, September 5, arriving in time for the opening of the International Congress of Plasma Physics on Monday. Plasma physics, Larry had learned along with a host of other matters, did not involve human blood, but dealt with the properties of hot ionized gases and their potential for fantastic energy. Felix Kissich checked out of his hotel on Wednesday evening, September 8, a full twelve days before the congress was scheduled to end. Storm had tracked the physicist to Paris, then to Rome and Cairo by commercial airlines, but in Cairo the trail evaporated. Felix Kissich had vanished somewhere in the Egyptian city.

"My husband called me one night from Helsinki," said Mrs.

Kissich guardedly. Larry saw that she was twisting a handkerchief in her thin fingers.

"Was that the last time you heard from him?" asked Storm. "By phone, wire, cable, letter, anything?"

"I've received one letter, that's all," she said. Her voice was faint, and Larry had to lean forward to hear her. "It came a week, I think, after you were here."

"I see." There was no need of spoken reproof. They both knew she had failed to keep her promise to co-operate further with the Bureau. "That would have been September twenty-third? I was here on the sixteenth, you know."

"Yes," she said hurriedly. "Yes, the twenty-third."

"And the postmark? Where was it mailed from?"

She hesitated, her face coloring. "It was mailed from New York the day before. Felix didn't say where he was. He just said a friend was flying to New York and would mail the envelope there . . . to save time, you know."

Larry, avoiding her eyes, made notes in his pad. He did not like this at all. The quarry was too vulnerable a thing to be hunted.

"Mrs. Kissich," he said, "you do not have to comply, but if I may, I would like to see the letter."

She shook her head. Trouble deepened in her eyes. "No, if you don't mind, I'd rather not. . . . It is very personal. . . . But I can tell you, I think, what you want to know. He said he had left Helsinki early and was traveling around Europe for several weeks before coming home. He said he was tired and wanted to be alone." She speeded her words, but the voice remained faint. "Felix is the sort who needs to be alone sometimes, you see. So much pressure, so many conferences. Ever since the Nobel Prize they won't leave him alone."

"I understand," said Larry. "And that is the only communication you've had with him since he left home? No phone or cable?"

"Nothing else," she said. There was silence in the room for a moment and Larry could hear, through the screen door, the far, piping cries of the children at play.

"Mr. Storm, can't you please tell me what all this means. I don't understand at all. Felix does almost all his work for the government. He has given our adopted country everything, so many years of his life. So many questions, so many forms . . . now this. Why must Felix be hounded as if he were a spy or committing treason or . . ." Her voice faded.

"I wish I could tell you, but I can't." That was not all, thought Larry. He himself did not know. First Greer, then Lubin, now Kissich . . . and not a single explanation from Moorhead. The dark chase at night, the restless shadow of not knowing. "You see, Mrs. Kissich, I'm only an agent. I'm only told what to do, not why."

Her look was one of sympathy. "Would you like some iced tea, Mr. Storm?"

"Yes. Yes, I would."

He made more notes while she was absent in the kitchen. She returned with two tall glasses in which ice tinkled. After handing him one, she noticed that the sunlight from a west window struck his eyes, and she lowered the shade.

"Thanks." He sipped at the cool liquid in the new shadow. He smiled at her and they sat quietly a moment. Then he drew a picture from his jacket pocket and handed it to her.

"Have you ever seen this man?" he asked. On his first visit, Larry had been ordered by Moorhead not to mention others involved in Ajax. Now, with Kissich certainly missing, the orders had been changed.

She studied the photograph, then shook her head. "No, never."

"Does the name Phillip J. Lubin mean anything to you?" He tucked the picture away.

"Lubin." She tested the name. "Phillip Lubin, the mathematician?"

Storm nodded.

"Yes," she said. "I've never met him, but I have heard of him. He's quite well known in his field. I think Felix knows him."

"Did your husband ever mention him that you recall?"

"Probably. He knows so many of the famous men of science. So many come to Forrestal."

He handed her another picture. "How about this man?"

"Of course," she said promptly. "That's Stephen Greer, the

President's friend who has been missing so long. I've seen his picture a great deal recently."

"Have you ever met him?"

She did not reply at once, but lowered her gaze to the glass of iced tea. She shook the glass and the ice clinked.

"I thought so, but Felix said I was mistaken." She hesitated again. "That first night after Mr. Greer disappeared, I showed Felix his picture in the paper, and asked if Greer weren't the same man who came to our house last fall. It was in November, I think, at night. But Felix said no, that man's name was Martin or Morton, from Washington. He said they looked a great deal alike, but they were not the same person. I remember our discussion."

"Were you sure it was Greer?" asked Storm. "Last November, you say."

"Yes," she replied. "I was sure until Felix said that our visitor was a Mr. Morton. I wasn't convinced, but of course Felix should know to whom he talked, shouldn't he?"

"Yes, he should. . . . Did you ever discuss it again?"

"No. Of course, Felix left the next week for the Helsinki conference."

"Has Mr. Kissich taken these solitary trips before?"

"Yes," she said. "Not often, but sometimes. He has the need to be alone." She tapped her head. "These men who live in the mind, you know."

Storm studied his notes, thought of what else he should ask. He could think of nothing. He drained off the last of his tea. Mrs. Kissich stood up. The handkerchief was crumpled in her hand.

"You know your visit has worried me, Mr. Storm. Can't you tell me, please? What kind of trouble is Felix in?"

"I'm not sure he's in any trouble," said Larry. "As I say, they don't tell me why, only what."

"But your questions about Mr. Greer and Dr. Lubin," she said. "I've read in the papers about a 'Dr. X.' Is that Dr. Lubin? And what has Felix to do with it?"

"I wish I knew, Mrs. Kissich. I'm sorry."

She came to the door with him, then folded her arms. The gentle look was gone.

"Sometimes I loathe governments," she said. "All governments. They demand, they extract and they pry."

"I know what you mean." Larry sensed his own fatigue again and felt a quick stab of resentment against the Bureau.

She put out her hand in parting. The bones were slim and the hand was cold. Larry pressed it.

"I must ask you again for co-operation," he said. "If you should hear from Mr. Kissich, we'd appreciate knowing promptly. You could call this number."

He handed her the special task force number in Washington. She looked at the card, then at Larry.

"This time I promise nothing, Mr. Storm."

"I understand," he said, and he walked down the path toward the row of guardian sycamores along the curb.

There were a few more interviews: two faculty friends of Kissich on the Princeton campus proper, the desk man at the Nassau Club, where Kissich sometimes lunched. Nothing significant was added. This was the tacks-and-hammer phase, nailing up the box after the contents were placed inside. Very thorough, the Bureau methods.

That evening Larry ate alone in the stag room of the old Nassau Inn. He tucked himself into one of the high-backed booths at a table grooved with the initials of a hundred forgotten undergraduates: BFD '39, WA '41, SMJ '57. The walls reeked of Princeton, framed photographs of championship teams, an oar from a famous crew, a basketball player with "42" on his jersey, probably Bill Bradley, Larry guessed. There was a picture of Hobie Baker, the legendary athlete of F. Scott Fitzgerald's day, and above the bar hung a row of old pewter mugs. The male conversation under the low-beamed ceiling had a hearty sound, a ring of confidence, of Princeton, of status, of certainty. Several of the older voices had the curious intonation of the "old tigers," a blend of pseudo-British and Boston Brahmin, a kind of nasal speech which clung to the roof of the mouth as if fearful of venturing far from the cloister.

Larry drank two daiquiris and let the fatigue seep away until he felt a pleasant tingle. He ordered the prime ribs and a lettuce salad with Italian dressing, then followed with a flan and coffee. He knew that with the cost of his room here, he would exceed his per diem, but why should a bachelor worry? What was money for, anyway? Scrubbed and assured Princeton was a long haul from Howard University and night accounting classes at Benjamin Franklin in Washington.

"Another tiger come back to the womb?" It was a big voice with a rocky base.

Storm looked up to see a man with bull shoulders and a huge head. He held a glass in his hand and he was grinning knowingly. Storm knew the face. He had seen it on a wharf in Rio. It belonged to Dave Paulick, the Washington newsman. A card file flashed in Storm's mind. *D.P.'s Dossier* . . . the bane of Washington officials . . . a tough man who worried a story as a dog shakes a rat.

"Have we met?" asked Storm.

"Almost," said Paulick airily. "In Rio, I think, from what I heard. You're Larry Storm." He put out a large hand. "I'm Dave Paulick, *D.P.'s Dossier*. Mind if I sit?"

"Have a seat." Larry refrained from saying "delighted," because he was not. So Paulick knew about Kissich too. Why else would he be in Princeton? The man got around.

Paulick sat down so heavily on the opposite bench, the booth shivered. He took a large gulp of his amber drink.

"I hope you had more luck with Deborah Kissich than I did," he said. "Felix went to Helsinki, period, she says."

"Kissich?" asked Storm casually. "Felix?"

Paulick boomed a laugh. "Knock it off, Larry. Who you think you're kidding? One of Pete Deskowicz's top special agents in Princeton. It's got to be Kissich. What else?"

The man was huge. He seemed to engulf the booth, and the hand gripping the drink could belong to a hockey goalkeeper.

"I just came from Battle Road," said Paulick. "I gather you got to the little lady first. Shy thing. I hated to bore in, but what the hell. What you don't ask, you don't find out."

"Would you mind telling me what you're talking about?" asked Storm.

Paulick laughed again. "Sure. Everything fifty-fifty. You tell me and I'll tell you."

"You know better than that, Paulick."

"Make it 'Dave,'" said the big man. He paused and shot a shrewd glance at Storm. "You know, we might be able to help each other. If you claim this thing hasn't thrown you, you're bluffing. Greer to Lubin to Kissich, right? It sounds like some goddamned triple play combination."

"I'm sorry, Dave." The man's zest was infectious. "You know the rules. I couldn't talk if I wanted to."

"Some do," said Paulick. He took another swallow of his drink and banged the glass on the initial-furrowed table. "I've gotten a few tips from the Bureau, but I must say I do a lot better with the Secret Service. I'll tell you what. Let me tell you some things I've found out. I'll watch your face to see if we jibe. Okay?"

"I never refuse to listen," said Storm. "That's what they pay me for."

"Yeah, well . . ." Paulick raised his eyes to Storm's. "We both know Greer chartered a tub called the *Casa Alegre* out of Rio. But if you know where he went from there, you're one up on me."

Storm faced Paulick's stare without wavering.

"Now Lubin, that's something else," said Paulick. He lowered his voice. Storm recognized the sign. This was a man who loved the clandestine. "After all those weekly meetings, or whatever they were, with Greer in that R Street apartment, this Lubin flies to London on the Sunday after Greer disappears. Then he catches Iberian Airlines to Madrid. So where does he go from Madrid?"

Storm smiled, hoping it did not reveal his satisfaction. Newspapermen did pretty well, but they were not in the same league with the Bureau, especially on those missions abroad where the FBI identity card opened many officials' doors.

Paulick's reaction to Larry's smile was predictable. "Say," he asked, "how about buying you a drink?" He glanced at Larry's used dessert plate and the coffee. "A liqueur?"

"No thanks," said Storm. "I had enough before dinner. Long day tomorrow."

Paulick nodded, one professional to another. "Okay . . . now this Kissich, the big Nobel prize man. I was late latching on to him. He meets Greer and Lubin once in the R Street apartment in mid-August. He already knew Greer, because Greer visited him here on Battle Road last year."

Storm kept his face blank, but he thought: Very good, Paulick. He realized that Paulick was working alone, one brain, single pairs of eyes and legs, while Larry benefited by a thousand scraps of information funneling into the Bureau. Moorhead might not tell Larry the whys, but he did tell him many whats, wheres, and whos—what to ask, where to go, whom to see. Larry looked at Paulick with new respect.

"Then," continued Paulick, "ten days after Greer disappears, Kissich gets into the flying act. On a Sunday, a week after Lubin supposedly left on his non-auto auto trip, Kissich flies to an international physics congress in Helsinki. Very convenient, it seems, because a couple of days later, Kissich checks out of his hotel and flies to Paris. Right?"

"You're wasting your time asking questions." But Storm smiled again. "I'm just a man who's had a good dinner."

Paulick shrugged off the rebuff. "Then Kissich flies to Rome, and then to Cairo, all commercial single hops."

Paulick raised his glass for another drink, watching Storm as he did so. "And then, finally, Kissich makes the flight by charter to Cape Town."

Storm kept his smile fixed and neutral, but he could feel the accelerated pump of his blood. Days of digging had not turned up that fact. And if it were known to the Bureau, Moorhead had not indicated it by so much as a whisper. Larry hoped his elation did not show.

"And so strangely enough," continued Paulick, "Mr. Kissich also finds his way to a waterfront. Imagine that. A frail little man, sixty-six years old, goes down to the sea and hires himself a boat, just like Steve Greer. And what happens after he puts to sea in this beat-up old lobster boat, the *Mary L.*? Does he have some

great yen for lobsters or what? When a man goes all the way to
Cape Town, South Africa, for lobsters, he must have an almighty
passion for them."

Storm's pulse was racing now, and he fought to conceal the
soaring flags within him. Paulick could be lying, of course, but
that did not seem likely. Everything else he said duplicated or fit
neatly into what Storm knew. Larry's thoughts shot back and
forth between dates, times, places. That old elation, the flowering
of discovery, enveloped him.

"I've changed my mind, Dave," he said. "I will have that drink.
Make it a cognac."

Paulick shot him a quick, appraising glance, then ordered the
liqueur. "And bring me another scotch," he said to the waiter.
When the drinks arrived, the two men raised their glasses.

"*Salud*," said Storm. "To a pretty damn good operator." And
when Paulick grinned his thanks, Storm added: "And that is all
the comfort I can give you, Dave."

"If it means what I think it does," said Paulick, "that's all I
need."

He traced one of the carved initials with the heel of his glass.

"What gets me," Paulick said after a moment, "is this Lubin
guy. He flies to London and then on to Madrid, for no discernible
reason. There he drops out of sight. What's it all about? . . . If
Lubin's a gay boy, with the hots for Greer, like Kulp in Kentucky
keeps hinting with his 'Dr. X,' why does Lubin go to Madrid while
Steve goes to Rio? And another thing. Why would two fags ring
in another man, and an aging scientist at that?"

Paulick studied Storm's face as though the answer might be
written there. "It doesn't figure, does it? Something is up all
right, but it ain't sex—with or without broads. Am I right?"

"That won't work, Dave. I hate to do this to a good guy, but
you started it. I didn't . . . I can't talk, period."

They fell silent and Paulick looked moodily at his glass. Storm
sipped at the cognac. He felt heady and yet guilty. He was a man
who had received five good ones for his counterfeit five-dollar bill.

"You know how I dope it out?" asked Paulick.

"No. How?"

Paulick looked up quickly with a broad grin. "Oh no. Two can play that game. What I got figured out, I'm not telling."

"I don't blame you."

Their talk dwindled into small exchanges over Princeton, the Bureau, *D.P.'s Dossier*, women and politics. After a courteous interval, Storm paid his check and excused himself.

Storm forced himself to walk slowly. He wanted to run to the elevator. The thought was boiling now. Seaport towns! Coastal cities on the South Atlantic! He had known it for days about Greer and Lubin, and now Dave Paulick added Kissich and Cape Town, another city with a bustling waterfront and ship traffic to the world.

At his third-floor room, Larry fumbled the key in the lock, grinned at his haste. Inside the room, he shot the night bolt on the door, lowered the blind, turned on the light, tossed his coat over a chair and took a thin brief case from his overnight bag.

He withdrew two large colored maps from the case, unfolded them, placed them on the floor and fitted them together. Joined, they formed a map of half the world, that half knitted by the Atlantic Ocean: Europe, Africa, South America, the eastern half of North America, Greenland. He had clipped the maps from his atlas at home and used them to plot the recent travels of Greer, Lubin, and Kissich. Colored lines traced his men, red for Greer, green for Lubin, plain black pencil for Kissich. He swiftly ran his eyes along the lines once again.

Larry stared at the maps while his mind sped once more over the pattern. Lubin and Kissich had conferred at least four times in the past year that he knew of, the last time in a car near the Princeton campus about a week before Steve Greer disappeared. Greer had met Kissich but twice in the past year, one night last November at Kissich's Battle Road home and then again in mid-August at the Wilmarth, where all three men were present. But there had been a number of long-distance calls from Greer to Kissich. As for Greer and Lubin, they had met weekly in the Wilmarth on R Street in Washington, always on the Wednesday nights of the "Potomac Study Club."

Larry squatted on his haunches, staring at the lower South Atlantic map. His thoughts coursed over the puzzle, seeking the key. . . . Three prominent men along the eastern seaboard, a lawyer, a physicist, a mathematician, all acquaintances who had conferred frequently, disappear from their homes within ten days. All fly by staggered routes to South Atlantic seaports. Why?

He crouched, studying the maps, until his legs ached. Then he lay down on the floor on his stomach and concentrated on the South Atlantic map. His eyes searched the long west coast of Africa, the great humping eastern coast of South America, the vast reaches of ocean in between and the scattered dots of islands.

Then Larry scrambled to his feet. The sudden thought triggered sensations which went bowling through his body like a ball crashing into tenpins. The old thrill of discovery by deduction. His fatigue was forgotten. He was beside the room telephone in two long strides. Then he checked himself. No, not through the hotel switchboard, not this call.

He straightened his tie and slipped on his jacket. He replaced the maps in the brief case, put the case inside the bag, locked the bag and left the room. Not waiting for the elevator, he went down the stairs, two at a time. He glanced at the lobby phone booth, but turned away. Paulick might come by.

He walked from the inn into the night, which was still heavily fragrant with the aroma of Indian summer. He walked across the little wooded park to the stores of Palmer Square, searching for a phone booth. He could see none. He turned left on Nassau Street, walked past strolling Princeton undergraduates and a racketing knot of teenagers in front of a brightly lighted stationery and paperback store. No phone booth. He looked at his wrist watch: 10:20 P.M. Moorhead would be at home, but reachable through the task force switchboard. Larry turned left on Witherspoon, past an all-night laundry where students pored over books in front of gleaming automatic washers. God, didn't the people in this town ever use a public phone? At last, at a gas station a block down Witherspoon, he found the familiar glass cubicle, a random funnel for the billions of coins which dropped, like pennies for Jesus, onto the great tambourine of A. T. & T. and its three million stockholders. The overhead light popped its halo above him when the booth door closed. He dropped in his dime and made the call collect. Within a minute, he had Clyde Moorhead on a relay to his home.

"Clyde, this is Larry. More Ajax." He said it in his agent's treadmill tone, muffling the pride, the cool pervasive until it was time to drop the bomb.

"Princeton?" asked Moorhead.

"Yeah. Talked to Mrs. K again. Also buttoned up the others. No big score."

"So why keep me from my sleep? Maybe you can cat around all night, but I've got to be at the shop at seven forty-five."

"Listen, Mushhead," said Larry. "This could be big. I think I've got it."

"I'm listening."

"Clyde," said Storm slowly, "D.P. is in town, the one who's been dogging Ajax on his own. Got me?"

"Sure. Go ahead."

"Well, you know he's been all over hell and gone. . . . Tonight, while I'm finishing dinner at the Nassau Inn, he suddenly bobs up, comes over and sits down. We've never met, but he knew me."

"I don't care for that," said Moorhead.

"Couldn't help it. Anyway, all I did was listen. He knows all about K and he's talked to Mrs. K. . . . But Clyde, this guy knows something I didn't."

"Yes."

"He claims . . ." Storm slowed his speech even more. "He claims K flew to the big town in the republic of S.A. . . . Got it?"

"No. I don't think so."

"The dark continent, you know, like me . . . S.A. . . . the last one down, all white, like you . . . or at least all white at the power level. . . . C for the big town."

"Right, right," said Moorhead. "Check."

"Well, he claims K also hit the water at C in something called the *Mary L.*"

"I got it now. Very interesting."

"Okay, Clyde, I think I'm on to something big, as I said, but I need help."

"Always glad to oblige, Larry. What do you want? A raise in grade?"

"Can it. . . . I know you've been checking plenty at the other end on K. Tell me, is D.P.'s information accurate? Do we check out total with him?"

There was no answer for a moment, then: "Please, Larry. Don't ask that. You know the drill on Ajax. No feed-back."

"But this is different. If I knew for sure, I might crack it for us."

"Sorry about that, pal." Moorhead was striving to keep it light. "Orders from The Man. You know that."

"But Clyde, if I knew," pleaded Larry, "we might be able to wrap it up fast."

"Larry, please," Moorhead pleaded in turn. "Don't make me go through that again. We've been over it a dozen times."

"Goddam it, Clyde . . ." A surge of anger left him speechless.

"Sleep it off," said Moorhead, not unkindly. "Lots of nerves are wearing raw around here too."

"Sleep won't help." The penned frustrations broke forth. "This is the worst lash-up in all my years in this racket. Jesus, you'd think I was some rookie cop. How the hell am I supposed to work in the dark with a pillow case over my head. . . . I'd like to see the great Clyde Moorhead try it. Just once, man, just once."

"Easy, Larry. I didn't make the rules. Don't forget, you're not alone on this. We're all going through the grinder." He paused. "So now, what's the hunch?"

"The hell you say," barked Storm. He thought of beleaguered Mrs. Kissich and her remark about loathing governments at times. "If you don't help me, I think by myself. Besides, if D.P.'s lead didn't check out, I'd look like a fool, to say nothing of the wasted time. No thanks."

"Better go to bed," replied Moorhead. "Call me in the morning when your ulcer's not jumping. And then bring in your written report on Mrs. K. We need it soonest. Okay, sweetheart?"

"Okay."

Larry replaced the receiver automatically, and he had opened the door before he remembered to reach back in the slot for the dime refunded from his collect call.

He walked slowly back to the inn, his hands jammed in his pants pockets. The elation was gone, pulverized by the Bureau's bull-dozer. His shoulders sagged and the tiredness became a numbing ache in his back. The warm night was a delusion. Summer had died and with it the vaulting joy he had known on other cases. Why not face it? He was just a hack detective on a routine beat, untrusted, perhaps even unneeded.

His room was hot. He stripped to the skin, ignored the clean pajamas in his bag and rolled into bed with only a sheet over him.

His thoughts retraced the paths they had beaten a dozen times. Why? Why? Why should he be forced to work in total darkness on Ajax, first time ever at the Bureau? Had The Man really issued such orders? Probably. Paul Roudebush, politician above all, feared for his election undoubtedly, and he was determined to keep the lid on until November 2. But suppose Moorhead was lying? Suppose the drill actually originated with Deskowicz? It seemed unlikely, Pete being the cautious type who played by the rules. But what if Deskowicz, for some obscure reason of his own, wanted Roudebush defeated? Then, wouldn't he try to cripple The Man by holding out on him? What if the real solution was a nasty one and Deskowicz intended to slip it all to Wolcott's people at the proper time?

Still, his own hunch . . . What should he do?

Then, turning restlessly in bed, he thought of that morning, a month ago, when he had interviewed Gene Culligan about Lubin. The press secretary had been friendly, had invited him to come back and chat someday. Culligan was the only person he knew at the White House. And perhaps, on a matter this impor-tant he should go to the White House, to a man close to the President.

Of course, he thought at once, that would scuttle him at the Bureau. At the Bureau, few ever went outside of channels. To do so was to ask for the ax. Ask for the ax . . . the ax for Ajax. At last, he was growing sleepy.

Just before Larry Storm fell asleep, he made his decision. Tomorrow, instead of checking in at the Bureau, he would take what he knew—and his hunch—to the White House. As for the ax, he would chance it.

In another room at the Nassau Inn, a floor above Larry Storm, Dave Paulick faced his own decision.

Time was pushing him now. The St. Louis *Post-Dispatch* story yesterday showed that it was only a matter of days until the whole press linked Dr. X to Phil Lubin. Of course, Paulick was still miles ahead. He knew of Kissich, of the meetings and the disappearance of three men—not two. He conjectured that he knew what no other newspapermen knew: that both Greer and Kissich had sailed from seaports in small ships. Lubin's trail, to be sure, had vaporized in Madrid, but Paulick assumed that if he had the time to pursue Lubin, the mathematics professor would lead him to Greer and Kissich. The three men, he was fairly sure, were somewhere together.

Why?

While the key still eluded him, he had his surmise now, a strong one. The homosexual possibility was foreclosed. Never persuasive, it collapsed altogether when Kissich, the elderly wizard of plasma physics, was added. As for Greer running away with a dame, why would he take two scientists along with him? Forget it. A financial scandal was even less credible when one reviewed the evidence. Greer maybe, but not Lubin or Kissich. Neither one cared much for money, and whatever involved them also involved Greer.

No, his hunch was more sensational. It had first struck him in Cape Town just a few days ago. A husky young seaman, who had made a number of voyages on the *Mary L.*, told him that last year the *Mary L.* had provisioned a Russian trawler which worked the spiny lobster beds of the South Atlantic. The remark sparked a parallel thought in Paulick, for earlier in the month, the shore log of the *Casa Alegre*, out of Rio, showed that she had twice recently carried fresh meat and vegetables to a Soviet trawler fishing the same lush beds. And so the hunch: Greer, Kissich, and Lubin, all in possession of national security information, had boarded a Soviet vessel clandestinely somewhere in the South Atlantic.

True, it was only an informed guess, but the evidence was tantalizing. Of one thing he was reasonably certain. The FBI knew everything he did and more. That meant that the Greer case could explode in public any day—unless, of course, Paul Roudebush managed to suppress the story for political reasons. Considering his own competitive position, Paulick, the hard competitor, had to break his story soonest. And the soonest for the *Dossier* was Tuesday. When the *Dossier* went to bed next week, Paulick intended to double the usual eight pages and spread his Greer story through the entire issue.

But first his promise to Culligan. The press secretary had finally reached him Tuesday, after his return from Cape Town, and exacted a pledge that before Paulick printed anything, he would visit the President. Exacted? My God, he leaped at the chance to put his evidence before Roudebush and to tell him the conclusion he had reached. He wanted to see the President's face when he told him. And whatever Roudebush said or did, it would make copy, for no president could ever tell Dave Paulick what to print and what not to print in *D.P.'s Dossier*.

So there was his decision. He could not hold the story any longer. Whether his belief was right or wrong, the facts alone would make fascinating copy, Paulick's biggest exclusive of his career. Tomorrow: Culligan and Roudebush.

14

I was finishing my coffee and the routine skimming of three news-papers in my apartment on Cathedral Avenue that Friday morning when I received an oblique, if insistent, phone call from Princeton.

It was Larry Storm, the Negro FBI agent who had questioned me about Phil Lubin a month earlier. He alluded to that meeting, and although he did not mention Lubin, he said he wanted to see me on a phase of the same matter. He stressed urgency, saying he was returning to Washington at once, but his language was guarded, self-protective. I replied that while my office was a junior madhouse right now, I would make time for him. He said he preferred not to come to the White House, so I offered to meet him somewhere for a quick lunch. That did not satisfy him either. He said his problem involved a security angle and should be dis-cussed in private. Could we meet at his apartment or mine this afternoon? It would take several hours.

I told him—thinking of the flying debris of the Greer case that would pelt me throughout the day—that that was impossible. I suggested instead that we meet at my place that night. We could have a drink and order in some Chinese food. He was reluctant to delay that long, but finally agreed to meet at my apartment at 8:30 P.M. The man obviously was under unusual strain, which made two of us.

Jill already was enmeshed in her communications web when I arrived at the west wing office. The American University students would mount their "Where's Greer?" picket line at 10 A.M.—with-out the suggestive signs. Miguel Loomis reported that Susannah Greer wanted to sue one of the networks for slander. It had identified Phil Lubin as "Dr. X" and linked him with Greer in an un-subtle homosexual implication. Mike was trying to talk her out of it. Reuters also had a story which named Lubin as Dr. X. The British news agency said that Lubin once worked on a secret, CIA-sponsored project and hinted that Greer's disappearance might yet rival the old Profumo episode in Britain as a security scandal. The second wave of Greer news was building swiftly and by midmorning my head began to throb.

Dave Paulick made his explosive entry shortly before noon. He was not unexpected, since I finally had reached him Tuesday and got his promise to call on the President before printing anything. We arranged to have him admitted through the rear driveway, thus avoiding a passage through the lobby where the press camped. The big man's usual cargo of self-confidence was annoy-ingly excessive today. He was tanned, buoyant, and pugnacious. I knew he had been traveling, to Rio and God knew where else.

"Reporting in as promised," he said when Jill closed the door behind him.

"You could have given us a couple hours' warning," I com-plained. His combative air made me testy.

"Couldn't," he said. "I just got in from Trenton and beat it over here as soon as I phoned." He could not have gloated more if he had obtained an exclusive on the Second Coming.

"Trenton? What's with Trenton? Hessians again?"

"My understanding was that I was to speak to the President," he said with a patronizing grin. "I've got no agreement with press slaves."

"Right," I said, "but you could at least explain that nutty call from Rio de Janeiro. You sounded as if you were gargling soap before the line went dead."

He inclined his head toward Roudebush's office. "Not until I talk to him. First things first."

"All right." I reached Grace Lalley on the direct line and asked her to inform the President that his excellency, David Paulick, awaited his audience. I expected that Dave would be allotted a half hour sometime at the tail end of the afternoon. To my sur-prise—a rather consistent reaction these days—Grace said, after a lapse of not more than a minute, that I was to bring Dave right in.

We went through the back door, down the inside corridor to the President's office. For once Roudebush's radiant greeting was outshone. Paulick beamed with the triumph of a gladiator who has just polished off both lions and Christians. He stood a full four inches taller than the President, and his manner implied that his advantage in the room was more than physical.

"Gene," said the President after the preliminaries, "I think I'd better chat with Mr. Paulick alone."

Once more the door had slammed in my face. I could not complain this time. I had asked for it when I made my ten-day bargain with the President. Still, it hurt, and my feelings were not mollified by Paulick's smug look as I left the room. God, the man was cocky today.

As busy as I was that noon, I kept glancing at my wrist watch from time to time. Paulick's talk with the President stretched to an hour, then more. I had lunch at my desk, a chocolate malted and a lettuce, bacon, and tomato sandwich from the staff galley. It was a full two hours before Paulick returned to the press office.

The change in the man was extraordinary. Jill noted it the moment I did, for after glancing at him, she gave me a private, puzzled look. Paulick walked slowly over to my desk and stood there uneasily. He was frowning and newly humbled. He might have visited an old friend about to undergo a critical operation.

"Well?" I asked. "When does the *Dossier* shoot the works?"

He shook his head. "It doesn't."

"What! Why not?"

"You'll have to ask him." He tilted his head toward the President's office.

It made no sense. "You mean you're not printing anything about Greer—after all these weeks of digging?"

"That's right." For the first time since I had known him, the big man looked shaken, almost contrite. It was difficult to hide my feeling of satisfaction over his unaccountable humility. When the mighty tumble, the cheap seats love it.

"I won't be bothering you," said Dave. "I'm turning the *Dossier* over to my assistant. I need a vacation."

"Vacation!" In the middle of the biggest story in years? The idea was preposterous. "Dave, what the hell is this all about?"

"Ask The Man," he said in a subdued tone. "I'll see you in a couple of weeks. . . . I'll go out the back way."

With that, Paulick turned and left the room without even his customary parting jest with Jill. She sat mute in her chair, watching his exit, as dumfounded as I was.

"Well," I said, "how do you like that?"

"Things get curiouser and curiouser." She shook her head in wonderment. "First the great press secretary gets talked out of quitting. Then Mr. Competition decides to stop competing—on what he said might be his biggest story ever. Paul Roudebush must be using the rack for his arm-twisting."

"Not the same thing at all," I said. "I work for the President. Paulick works for Paulick."

"Scratch the shell of all you he-men," she said, "and what do you find? Putty, no?"

"Putty yes, not putty no." My head felt unhinged. "Stop bending the language like a pretzel."

She was about to retort, but my direct phone to the President's office buzzed.

"Yes, dear," I said to Grace Lalley. But it was not Grace. It was the President.

"I want you in here at once," he said. The voice that brushed off my "dear" was harsh. . . . Trouble.

I double-timed it to his office. He was standing by the French doors when I entered. He wheeled and strode toward me. His face was set without a smile. I recognized the signs although I had seen them but infrequently. Roudebush was furious.

"I don't understand about Paulick . . ." I began.

He chopped at the air with his hand. "Later," he said. "I want to talk about you."

Me? What had I done—lately?

He stood facing me, his eyes boring into mine. There was no polite offer of a chair.

"Gene," he said, "I thought we had an understanding. We were, or so I thought, to proceed as usual at least until October ninth."

"That's right, sir."

"Then, will you kindly explain how the Wolcott people learned of our private conversations?" His voice was low as if under pressure, and he stood there, challenging.

"Mr. President, I'm sorry, but I don't have the least idea what you mean." Things were happening too swiftly. What kind of crime had Paulick charged me with, anyway?

"Danny Cavanaugh called," he said, his eyes searching for my reaction. "If Paulick had not been here at the time, you and I would have had it out right then."

"Mr. President, please. I honestly don't know what you're getting at."

"Danny," he said, brushing past my disclaimer, "has word from his inside source at Wolcott headquarters that a speech is being prepared by Kulp, their Louisville hatchet man, which will divulge the most confidential details of our Wednesday strategy meeting here, point by point. Kulp is to make the speech within a few days."

My mind raced. Danny, I knew, had a secretary planted at Wolcott's headquarters who provided discreet tips on the opposition's plans and tactics. Always forearmed, Danny. But, obviously, so was Matty Silkworth. Somebody inside our group had leaked. Who?

"There were nine of us at the meeting," I said, "but subtracting you and me and Danny, that leaves six persons who could have . . ."

"That's not the point, Eugene," he said. The formal "Eugene" chilled me. "Kulp will also tell of your threat to quit and of our ten-day bargain. What's more, he will repeat specifics of our conversation."

Now I understood. Only two people were in this office during that conversation. I felt suddenly naked and defenseless.

"Mr. President," I began, coloring under the stress of being the accused, "I don't know what to say. I realize . . ."

"I do too," he shot back. "It is quite apparent now why you were so anxious to quit."

His attack was two-sided as if from ambush. I lacked bearings and I froze mentally for a moment. I just looked at him, stupidly, I suppose.

"Mr. President," I said at last, "I'm not that kind. I don't play that way."

"So you made abundantly clear the other day with your protestations of loyalty. There's just one trouble with that, Eugene. We were, if you recall, alone here during that conversation. The others had left."

"I know that, sir," I said. I was recovering now and groping frantically for the explanation.

"There is something else," he said. His voice had the coldness of metal in winter. "In thinking back, I find that several items in Kulp's first speech undoubtedly came from inside this office. Two things, specifically . . . the disappearance of Dr. X, as he called him. You learned about the FBI's investigation of Dr. Lubin, and I confirmed it for you. Second, the report that Steve went to Brazil. You knew that too—from Paulick, as I recall."

He flung the sentences at me, each a charge in an indictment, then stood coldly, waiting for my answer. My thoughts went back to that first week after Steve's disappearance—it seemed years ago now—and I began to sift, recall, sort out.

"Mr. President, I talked to no one about any of that," I said. "Nor about our talk on Wednesday. That's all I can say, sir."

"No one! That is patently false."

Then it struck me. My God, I told her almost everything. In the emotional tension of the moment, her name came out involuntarily.

"Jill," I said weakly.

He looked sharply at me. "Jill Nichols?"

"Yes, sir . . . I . . . well, it never occurred to me. She hears a lot of what goes on here. . . . We've been . . . But I can't believe it."

Words were useless. I knew he had suspected our intimacy for months. Now he could realize just how intimate we were.

"I think we had better get her in here," he said.

"Please," I protested. "Under the circumstances, I'd rather talk to her alone."

He looked at me without a touch of sympathy. His face was still set in grim lines.

"No," he said. "I want Jill in here with both of us." Then he added with only faintly veiled sarcasm: "Under the circumstances, the person with the most to lose right now happens to be me."

That was a not very subtle manner of announcing his mistrust of me. But I was helpless. His mind was made up. He flicked a switch on his intercom. "Grace, have Jill Nichols come in right away."

Jill, entering, could have been a college girl on the way to an interesting class. All she lacked were the books in the crook of her arm. She had that beguiling smile and her long hair swayed with her gliding walk. Then she became aware of the President's expression—severe, reproachful—and she looked at us both with wonder.

The President pointed to a chair. "Please, Miss Nichols." He motioned me to another chair, then walked around behind his desk. We all seated ourselves self-consciously.

"Miss Nichols," said Roudebush, "there has been a serious breach of confidence in the White House. The evidence indicates that only three people could have been responsible. One of these is myself. Since the disclosure could be politically damaging to me, I'm obviously not the person. That leaves Gene—and you."

"Yes, sir." Her voice, trembling, seemed to issue from a tiny cave.

As I watched her, affection warred with outrage. I had been falsely accused, but Jill, obviously, had to be guilty. I had told no one save Jill. All those hours of love . . . her fey, innocent demeanor . . . the confidences I had shared with her . . . Betrayal, thy name is love. . . . I watched her in fascination, wondering what outwardly guileless form her denial would take.

The President related, quite calmly, the substance of Danny Cavanaugh's message. Jill's eyes widened.

"I don't think that's proper, Mr. President," she said, utterly artless. "If we don't want Wolcott's people spying on us, then we shouldn't spy on them."

I was flabbergasted. At her own trial for sedition, she came morally armed to indict her prosecutor. She was either a perfect actress, or her innocence was boundless. The President too was stunned.

"The ethics of a political campaign are hardly at issue here, Miss Nichols," he said after a moment. "What is at issue is the loyalty of two of my staff members."

He reminded her of Kulp's first speech a month ago and pointed out what he had to me. The leak, he insisted, had to have come from one of two persons, Eugene Culligan or Jill Nichols.

"Gene tells me he has spoken about these matters to no one but you," said the President.

Jill's brief glance at me was reptilian.

"I don't break confidences, Mr. President," said Jill softly but with exquisite firmness. "I've heard all kinds of secret things around here—missile submarines and radar nets and dismal things like that—but I keep them to myself. Of course, Mr. Greer is different, but I haven't told what little I know about him, either."

"You have not discussed Mr. Greer, or any of the connected matters with anyone?" pressed the President.

"No, sir." She faced him with an unflinching stare.

"One of you has lied to me," said Roudebush. "You're quite sure it isn't you, Miss Nichols?"

She shook her head. "I have not talked about Mr. Greer to any one." She paused, then added: "Except Butter, of course. I talk about a lot of things, even Gene, with Butter."

With the pronunciation of the name, there came a slow dawning in Jill's look of wide-eyed wonder. And the name triggered a scene for me. . . . That phone call. The male voice. Jill in the bathroom. Her protestation, which I later disbelieved, that a "Nick" sometimes called Butter Nygaard.

"And just who, if you please, is Butter?" The President's expression was one of harassed bewilderment.

"Butter Nygaard," said Jill promptly as if the whole world knew the identity of Butter. When she saw Roudebush's baffled look, she added: "She's my roommate."

"I see," said Roudebush. "And you discuss all the confidential matters of the White House with Miss Nygaard?"

"Oh, no sir. Nothing about security—the bombs, the planes and all that. I never mention those. But Stephen Greer is different. It has all been so strange. The whole country is talking about Mr. Greer. . . . I didn't realize we weren't even supposed to mention him."

"Well," said Roudebush. He appeared deflated, like a man who strikes at a foe and finds he is punching a pillow.

"But if Butter said anything to anybody around Governor Wolcott," said Jill hurriedly, "I'd be terribly surprised. Butter has no interest in government, and politicians bore her. She's very apolitical, Mr. President."

"Or she keeps her politics to herself," said Roudebush.

"No, honestly, sir. All she really cares about is art and music and existentialism. Why, Butter does pop sculpture in iron. Actually, she's kind of beat. . . . She smokes pot sometimes."

"A pot smoker?" Roudebush smiled, faintly, for the first time.

"Yes, sir. Marijuana, you know."

He chuckled. "Don't worry, Jill. I'm not that far behind the times. I know what pot is."

"Butter calls it grass," offered Jill.

"In my youth they called it tea." The President's severity was easing. He looked at Jill, half frowning and half smiling, and finally he laughed. It cracked the tension like a bursting balloon. Jill and I joined in, somewhat haltingly, it is true. Still, all three of us were laughing.

"Undone by a marijuana smoker," said Roudebush. He shook his head, mock sad, and wiped at an eye. "What a world. I never did like that weed. I'd better have the Narcotics Bureau tighten up."

He was silent a moment, regarding Jill with a kind of bemused sympathy. The man had to be admired. Even in a time of political peril, he could laugh at himself. I could think of presidents who would have fired Jill on the spot. But when Roudebush spoke, he was serious again.

"From this moment on, young lady," he said, "you are not to discuss White House business with anyone outside the staff—and I mean anyone."

"Yes, Mr. President." She was quickly contrite again.

"Jill," he asked, "did you tell Miss Nygaard about our strategy meeting here the other day?"

"Yes, sir." Her face flushed. "You see, we got to talking about Greer, and I happened to mention how seriously it was being taken at the White House, what with the meeting and then Gene's talk with you and all."

"That was extremely indiscreet of you, Jill," he admonished severely. "I can understand how you might naturally talk over your speculations about Steve, but to tell an outsider about a private White House meeting . . . well, I find that an incredible lapse, frankly."

"I can see that now, sir," she said. "It's just that I never imagined Butter caring enough about political gossip to repeat anything. And I thought it was understood between us that talk about the White House never went beyond our apartment. Even now, it's hard to believe it. If you knew her, Mr. President, you'd understand."

He remained clouded in thought for a time.

"Jill," he asked, "what does Miss Butter do for a living?" He added tartly: "Peddle marijuana? Or sell her sculpture?"

Jill shook her head. "No, she's a paid secretary, kind of an executive secretary, I guess, for the I.C.E.S."

"I.C.E.S.?" repeated Roudebush.

"Yes, sir. The International Cultural Exchange Service. That's the private organization that brings foreign artists and musicians over here, and sends ours abroad, you know."

Roudebush frowned. "And how long has Miss Nygaard lived with you?"

"Actually," replied Jill, "I live with her. It's her apartment. I moved in with her, oh, about two years ago, I'd say, when my first roommate got married."

From then on, the talk went somewhat easier, although the President never let us forget that he was the injured party, wounded by his friends. Roudebush finally suggested that, in view of Jill's position at the White House and the increasing pace of the campaign, it would be wiser if she made other living arrangements at once. Jill hastily agreed. The lease was Butter's, she said, and Jill would pay a month's extra rent and move out tomorrow—if her boss would give her the day off. I assented to that with alacrity.

There was discussion of Miss Nygaard. She obviously had talked directly to the Wolcott people or to someone who had. The method of communication made little difference. The main objective was to plug the leak. Thus, the President favored a hands-off policy with Miss Nygaard. The harm was done, but she would be unable to injure us further. But I insisted I had to find out more about Butter. The thought of that stony-chinned dilettante —in all my meetings with Butter, I had never warmed to her— putting both Jill and me on the spot was an infuriating one. The President finally consented to an investigation by me, provided I did not waste too much time on it. He was more concerned over Kulp's forthcoming speech. An accurate description of our "crisis" meeting would reveal our sagging morale. And a recital of my threat to quit would only aggravate matters.

"You'll have a hard time finessing that, Gene," said Roudebush.

"I've already got my line," I said. "Mr. Kulp has no credentials inside our camp. His malicious and self-serving intent is apparent on the face of it. We don't comment on political charges of the opposition, no matter how grotesque. Period."

"I hope that gets by." He was clearly skeptical.

He left his swivel chair and came around the desk to shake my hand.

"I apologize, Gene."

"I couldn't blame you," I said.

Jill put out her hand tentatively. The President grasped it and patted her shoulder as well.

"No more Butters, Jill," he said. ". . . And no more loose talk."

"From now on," she said, "I'm not even talking in my sleep."

The instant we were back in our office, Jill let me have it.

"Fine, trusting lover, you are," she said. "The minute you're blamed for something, it's my fault. Why did you assume I was the one who goofed? How many other people did you talk to?"

"I talk in confidence only to people I think I can trust," I said, "which is more than I can say for you, big mouth. . . . Butter

Nygaard, of all people to blabber to! . . . Jesus, Jill, haven't you learned a thing on this job?"

"I've learned a lot about you, Gene Culligan. It seems that you're very quick to suspect your friends."

Her logic was monstrous, and I did not propose to be diverted by it.

"And when did you spill this last bit to Butter? Last night?"

She folded her arms and glared at me. "I don't have to answer that, but I will. We talked the night before last, after the 'crisis' meeting and your putty act. Last night, for your information, Butter was out of town."

In that case, I thought, Jill might have called and asked me to come over. The thought irritated me almost as much as her spurious claim that it was I, not she, who had erred.

"Where did she go?" I asked.

"I have no idea."

"Well, get Miss Butterball's office on the phone. I want to talk to her pronto."

She threw me a rancorous look, but turned to her desk and busied herself as ordered.

"She's not back yet," she said after a few moments. "Her office says she's due in at National at six thirty-two, Eastern Flight 702 from Charleston, West Virginia."

My old police beat training nudged me. "Find out where Eastern 702 into Charleston comes from."

She had the answer shortly: "Huntington, and before that, Louisville."

"Louisville!" I echoed. Jill's discerning look told me that the same thought hit both of us. "The plot, let us say, gets very juicy."

"Butter Nygaard," said Jill softly, and there were small daggers in that whisper.

We worked for a time and then Jill came over to my desk.

"Can I apologize?" she asked. "I ought to have my head examined, talking like that to Butter. . . . But I thought it was as safe as when you and I talk. . . . It won't ever happen again, Gene. Forgive me?"

"Yes," I said. I curbed my impulse to lecture her again. A reprimand from the President, thrice reiterated, was enough for one day. "Let's forget it for now. I want to hear what Butter has to say for herself."

I was determined to meet our bony, pot-smoking friend at the airport. I came through my afternoon press conference with no more than the customary contusions and abrasions of these days, then went to my own car in the West Executive Avenue parking area. While I rated a White House automobile and driver, I seldom used them. I pretended I liked to drive, but actually the sacrifice made me feel virtuous, a sentiment I was not otherwise overburdened with. I drove across the Potomac, relishing the burnished autumn afternoon and the brisk breeze which whipped the river. Since I had a few minutes, I stopped at the duck sanctuary, just off the National Airport's flight path, and watched a mixed colony of blue-winged teal, ruddy ducks, and mallards bobbing in the estuary. The late sun flashed alternate purples and mauves on the glossy green heads of the mallards, and somehow the brilliance, mingled with the placid behavior of the ducks, made me forget the clatter of the press conference.

Flight 702 was on time. I glanced through a late *Star* as I waited just behind the grill at Gate 12.

Butter came down the ramp stairs about midway of the file of passengers. She wore her hair skinned back in a pony tail. Her lips, as usual, were bare of lipstick, and her face had the uneven texture of a pebbled driveway. She wore loafers and a soiled trench coat. Butter was one of those women who make themselves as physically unattractive as possible, daring men to love them for the soul alone.

I moved forward, then noticed that Butter paused at the foot of the ramp and looked behind her. A man soon fell into step beside her. He was elderly and plump with a flushed, unlined face that I had seen dozens of times around Washington. He was Senator Owen Moffat of Nebraska, a leader of the opposition and a top tactician for Wolcott.

I turned at once, climbed the stairs and went to the portico just outside the long hall where passengers picked up incoming baggage. Butter and the Senator came in together, picked out their bags and then headed for the cab line. With their air of casual rapport, they could have been grandfather and granddaughter. I slipped into my car, parked in a metered space on the inside circle, then followed at a discreet distance when Moffat and Butter moved off in a taxi.

Across the Fourteenth Street bridge, their cab cut through the grounds of the Washington Monument and went up Fifteenth Street. It swung right into G Street, and Butter alighted with her bag in front of the old Albee Building. She waved good-by to the Senator and walked—or with those loafers, I should say she scuffed—into the building. I swung around the block to a parking garage on F Street, then walked back to the Albee Building.

I found the International Cultural Exchange Service listed on the wall directory and took the elevator to the fifth floor. I did not care much for this since the Albee Building held a number of newspaper bureaus, each member of which knew me by sight. All I could ask for was luck.

My luck was more than I hoped for. Searching for 513, I got the wrong side of the hall and 512 instead. A small sign under the number, a metal plate hardly wider than a strip of adhesive tape, read "Spruance Foundation." My pulse quickened. There was no bell at the doorway, and I tried the door. It was locked, apparently for the night. A few knocks brought no response.

I turned to 513 across the hall. Its plaque, proclaiming the occupancy of the International Cultural Exchange Service, was a large one of polished brass. I stared at it a moment, my mind on Spruance . . . Miguel and his fellow physicists . . . Operation Flycatcher . . . the CIA. But Miguel had said the Spruance Foundation was located in New York. My confrontation of Miss Nygaard was becoming a more fascinating project by the minute.

The Cultural Exchange entrance had a doorbell. I pushed it twice. The door opened, and there stood Butter in a pink blouse and a corduroy skirt that ended an inch above her knees.

"Haven't you got the wrong girl?" she asked. Her smile was a faint, knowing one, as if sharing a secret. Butter, I had always surmised, enjoyed vicarious titillation from the alliance between Jill and me.

"Come in," she said, quite pleasantly. "I don't think you've ever seen my office."

She led the way past a couple of vacant desks to an inner office which was papered with a bizarre design of hatched bamboo poles, all purple, and nestling pink doves. One wall held a floor-to-ceiling bookcase which stepped upward like a jagged pyramid. On a window ledge sat a row of tubby pre-Columbian figures of reddish clay. Several leered as though observing some lewd spectacle. Butter's desk was heaped with pamphlets, newspapers, and letters.

Across from her desk was a suite of thin, twisted iron furniture, a cobbler's bench, two chairs, and a glass table supported by a single spike of iron. Butter lit a cigarette as we sat down.

"What's your problem, Gene?" she asked. "Domestic trouble, and you need to talk to big sister?" Butter was twenty-seven.

"No, no heart burns," I said. "This is something else. Have you got a few minutes?"

"Sure." She looked moderately curious.

"Okay, then." I looked around. "Say, this is a nice spread. How long have you worked here?"

"About three years," she said. "It's not too bad. A lot better than working in some moldy government crypt."

"That's right. You used to work for the government. What department was it, again? I think I used to know, but I've forgotten."

She flapped her hands dismissively. "I loathe mentioning it, it was so dreary. It might as well have been the I.C.C. . . . No, I really like this place, Gene. Lots of types come through here. Always a new kick."

"How's it supported?" I asked. "Individual contributions?"

"Some," she replied, "but we get foundation money mostly."

"Any Spruance?" I hoped my tone was one of casual interest.

She frowned and inhaled quickly on her cigarette. "Why, yes. How did you know that?"

"The old two-plus-two. I saw the name across the hall on 512."

"Oh." Her expression was one of unconcern, but I thought she tightened somewhat.

"I thought the Spruance Foundation was located in New York," I said.

That surprised her. "It was," she said, "but they moved it down here last month."

"I don't know much about it," I said. "What is it? Some family deal?"

"No." She sucked at her cigarette. "Businessmen, largely, who have a passion to purge their consciences with good works. The director is a Mr. Maury Rimmel, a sort of man about town. He's not around here much, though. They manage with one secretary over there."

"Oh, sure. Maury Rimmel. He's that moon-faced guy who searched for Greer that first night at Burning Tree."

She nodded. Her face, without a trace of cosmetics, had a gritty look, and I wondered, irrelevantly, whether any man had had the courage to make love to her recently.

"That's the one," she said. "Rimmel's not my type, frankly, but he goes along with our plans without fussing."

"Actually, Butter, that brings up what I wanted to talk to you about—Steve Greer."

That brought results. Her face hardened and she took two rapid puffs on the cigarette. "Yes?"

I chanced a shot. "Would you mind telling me what you were doing in Louisville yesterday and today?"

She flared. "Who said I was in Louisville?"

"Never mind. The question is, what were you doing there?" I asked.

"It's none of your business where I was or what I was doing." She snubbed out her half-finished cigarette with a flourish and glared at me. "Just what is this, Culligan?"

"Did you travel alone?"

"You've got your nerve," she said shrilly. "If this is supposed to be an inquisition, McCarthy is long dead, thank you."

At this point I expected to be ordered from the room, but beneath her anger, I could sense the virus of curiosity working.

"Butter," I said firmly, "this country happens to be in the middle of a presidential campaign, and I have reports that you've been doing business with Governor Wolcott's top people."

"That's a laugh." She sniffed. "I don't give a damn about politics. I've never been mixed up in it and I don't intend to. . . . Not that it's any of your business."

"I don't believe that. I think your off-beat, apolitical, arts-and-crafts pose is a phony. I think you've been to Louisville, in the company of a prominent Senator, to put a few little vials of poison in the hands of Mr. Hillary Kulp. I also—"

"That's enough." She got to her feet and folded her arms across her pink blouse. This time the order came. "You'd better leave."

I arose slowly.

"You may get away with laying my roommate," she said, "but trying to abuse me is quite another matter."

"Very sweetly put." How did one duel with a woman? It seemed absurd to try.

"One thing you should know, Butter," I said. "Jill is moving out of the apartment tomorrow. She has no intention of having any more of her confidences from the White House being peddled by you to Owen Moffat, Hillary Kulp, or Matty Silkworth."

"Jill Nichols is perfectly capable of telling me her plans herself." She cocked her head, her arms still folded. "As for your innuendoes, they're slanderous. If I were you, I'd watch my step. Any more accusations like that, and I'll tell a few *facts* about the White House press secretary and his Lolita."

"I couldn't care less," I said. "But that's right in your line, telling everything you know."

"Culligan," she said, "you're a fink."

"Oh, you can do better than that, Butter," I said. "That's pretty old-fashioned talk for a hippie."

"Get out of here." The venom needed no fangs.

"I'm leaving." But at the door to the outer office, I turned.

"Who's Nick?" I asked.

She was astonished, and then so quickly furious that if she had had an object handy, I believe she would have thrown it at me. She mumbled something. It had the sound of, "get lost"—laced with profanity.

I looked at her a moment. The bare, mottled face was stiff with anger. Then I walked through the outer office and out the door. I should have felt relieved after our skirmish, but I did not. Somehow, to tongue-lash a woman is seldom satisfying, even if they do own two-thirds of the country.

Save for several night-watch Secret Service agents and White House policemen, the west wing was deserted when I returned. Jill, the staff, and the press had closed up shop for the night. I reached the President by phone in his bedroom where he was changing for dinner. He listened without interrupting me.

"So it seems apparent," I concluded, "that Miss Nygaard has been feeding Wolcott headquarters and, today, probably Kulp in Louisville as well. Also, I think there's a strong possibility that she's an informer for the CIA. Paid by Spruance, and probably directly on the payroll, as well."

"This is simply incredible," he said. "I had Arthur's word that Spruance would be closed down."

"I don't think so, sir," I corrected. "As I recall, that promise involved only the subsidy of the physicists. You remember? He told us Spruance's support of the scientists would be ended. It didn't occur to me that Spruance might have other jobs."

"Yes, you're right. Arthur slices things very thin at times."

The enormous implication suddenly struck me in full: The President of the United States was being spied upon in his own house by one of his own agencies via a kind of human wire tap.

"Maybe I have this all wrong," I said. "It seems pretty weird. Perhaps I ought to check Miss Nygaard's previous government job. My guess is she worked directly for the CIA. Do you want me to make some inquiries?"

He was silent a moment. "No, Gene. Let me handle this personally." He sighed. "It would seem we have a pretty big overhaul job facing us after the election."

He said it as though a favorable outcome of the November 2 voting was a foregone conclusion. I did not share his confidence. We exchanged the parting amenities before hanging up.

I sat staring at my desk, pondering the freakish complexities of the U. S. Government. . . . A President under surveillance by a subordinate, via Butter Nygaard, of all people . . . Jill had roomed with Butter for two years now. Were a hundred shredded intimacies, to say nothing of official indiscretions, stored on the electronic tapes of the CIA?

The more I thought of the possibilities, the angrier I became. And why wasn't Paul Roudebush equally incensed? If our roles were switched, I would be hauling Arthur Ingram on the carpet right this moment. . . . Then I thought of the forthcoming stormy scene between Jill and Butter. Jill should be warned first.

I dialed Jill's unlisted number, but there was no answer.

Then, suddenly, I remembered Larry Storm. I looked at my watch. It was 8:10. He was due at my place at 8:30. I grabbed my coat and left.

I never did call Jill again that night. I forgot her completely in my intense absorption of the next seven hours.

15

Larry Storm and I hit it off at once. We had much in common. We were both bachelors of about the same age. Having just turned forty, he was two years older than I. We were about the same height and build, and we had both been the small men—at six feet even—on our college basketball teams, he at Howard and I at UCLA. As we were to find out, we both came from dreary homes where our parents festered in alienation and blamed their inadequacies on each other. We were both government employees at an upper level, not dealt in on high policy, yet stuffed with miscellaneous information denied the great, gray mass of civil servants. About the only difference between us, aside from my one marriage, was our color. Larry was coffee and I was that timid Irish white that scorches mercilessly in the sun.

I assumed that Larry had come to talk about some aspect of the Greer case. If so, despite my liking for him, I was determined that this time I would keep my ears open and my mouth mostly shut. Butter Nygaard was tormentingly fresh in my mind.

I had arrived at my apartment at 4101 Cathedral Avenue just in time, for Larry was standing hesitantly by the door after several rings without response. We agreed at the outset to postpone business until we had drinks and dinner. I laced him with three daiquiris, his favorite drink, while I managed two martinis on the rocks before dinner, if you can use that word for Chinese food arriving in paper buckets.

So, by the time we stretched out in the living room, we had covered a lot of small talk, including our school days, our politics, our pet aversions, and even the fact that we agreed Richard Burton was still a better actor than his wife. My living room had two long facing sofas with a low, brass-studded chest between. The chest served as my dumping ground for magazines, newspapers, and government documents. He took one sofa and I the other. We had long since shed our coats and loosened our ties. We both propped our feet on the chest and mine came to rest against the five-pound budget of the U. S. Government. I detested the big, brown object. It was a reminder of the infinite, faceless, expensive, and often futile complexity of governing a society such as ours. The paper cover was stained by countless rings of glasses and coffee mugs.

"Okay, Larry," I said. "Let's have it."

"It's understood that anything said in this room tonight stays here?" He knew the answer, but he was a Bureau man, forever rethreading his caution.

"Absolutely." I made it sound as though he were to be entrusted with my confidence, but I intended to play it close.

I could see he was as edgy as I was. Larry did not smoke, and I had gone nearly two months without a cigarette. One more day, tomorrow, and I would have it made—until the day after tomorrow. But we both had mugs of instant coffee and we kept lifting them like crutches.

"Gene," he said, "I've been working the Greer case for five weeks, and not once in that time have I seen a single report of another agent. Nor have I been supplied with one scrap of information not directly connected with my job of the moment. I'm not allowed to exchange leads with other Bureau men. I'm not permitted to inspect the files. For the first time in nineteen years, I'm working blindfolded."

Larry was blindfolded! He should be a press secretary. "How does that differ?" I asked. "How do you usually work?"

He described the Bureau procedures at some length and, to illustrate, he went into detail on a kidnaping that he and Clyde Moorhead were instrumental in solving. At the beginning, he said, it bore many resemblances to the Greer case.

"And so the Bureau method is one of intricate cross-references," he said. "Hell, Gene, on other cases I've spent two or three hours every morning going over the reports of a dozen agents before I left the office. Every investigation follows that routine. But not Greer. On Greer, I'm shut out."

He gave me the core of his problem. He was told that the orders for the new "freeze-out" were issued by President Roudebush. That seemed plausible enough, he said, considering the sensitivity of the case in the middle of a presidential campaign, but the more he learned, the more he wondered. Actually, he surmised now, the order could have originated with Peter Deskowicz, who in turn was withholding information from Roudebush. Storm's old pal, Clyde Moorhead, might be lying to him, or more probably, Moorhead himself had been deceived by Deskowicz as to the source of the orders.

"I had no idea the Bureau was working under a new drill," I said. "I just assumed it was the same old FBI, plugging away."

"You see why I'm confused," he said. "If it's The Man's order, okay, fine. But suppose it isn't? If not, I think he ought to know what's going on. Somebody in the Bureau could be double-crossing him in an attempt to elect Wolcott. That's hard to believe, but it's possible."

My mind jumped to the natural conjecture: Were Arthur Ingram and Peter Deskowicz in some kind of plot to funnel information secretly to the Wolcott people? I wanted to level with Storm, tell him about Butter Nygaard and the Agency, but I smothered the urge. I did not intend to be burned twice.

"And so that's why you came to me?" I asked.

He nodded. "I've never before talked about a case outside the Bureau. But this involves the top man. If the President is being had, he should be warned."

I sensed that Larry assumed I had read all the FBI reports and that I could tell him precisely what the President knew and did not know.

"This may seem strange to you," I said, "but I haven't been cut in on the Greer case. The President takes the position that if I don't know anything, then I won't be tempted to mislead the press."

I told him, honestly enough, that my own theory about the Greer case was almost totally conjecture. I told him, for instance, that I learned about Phil Lubin only through Storm's questioning of me. I had picked up stray scraps of information around the White House and from Miguel Loomis. I did not, naturally, mention my suspicions about the CIA, my quarrel with the President, or my brittle visit with Butter Nygaard that afternoon. In short, I talked at some length without saying a great deal. I was not going to give the President another chance to score me as a White House gossip.

"I'll be damned," said Storm. He stared at me, studying me for signs of dissembling. He was apparently satisfied, for he said: "And I thought they were holding out on me."

"It's all guesswork on my part," I said, "and from what I can piece together, it doesn't make sense. I suspect that Greer and Lubin are probably fags, even though that knocks hell out of my judgment of men. But yet, if they are, why did they both take off at the same time—or maybe even go someplace together? That seems to be the most stupid thing they could do."

Storm shook his head. "They didn't go together. Greer went to Rio de Janeiro. That's not where Lubin went."

"No?" I waited expectantly.

But Storm studied me again, intently this time.

"Are you leveling?" he asked after a moment. "You really don't know about Lubin?"

"I know he disappeared from Baltimore," I said, "but where he went, no."

"Do you think the President knows?"

"I really can't say, Larry." I puzzled on that a moment. "My guess would be no, but it's only a guess."

"You haven't seen any of the Bureau reports?" he asked.

"No. None."

He rose from the sofa, shoved his hands in his pants pockets, and walked about the room a bit. Then he turned to me.

"Gene, you put me on the spot," he said. "When I asked for this meeting, I assumed you knew everything the President did."

"I know practically nothing for sure," I said. "I think your assumption is wrong, Larry."

His large brown eyes were fixed on me. He was weighing me again. "Yes, well . . . I don't think I'd better say any more. You understand, I'm sure . . . It's . . ."

I waited while he struggled with himself. He paced a bit, then resettled on the sofa.

"What's your problem, Larry?"

"I had intended to match my information against yours," he said. "If my suspicion proved to be wrong, well, I'd go on home to bed and forget it. But if what you knew seemed to bear out my belief, then you could take the whole story to the President."

"But what's the difference? You tell me whatever it is that's bothering you. I assume it's a strong case. If so, I tell the President. If not, as you say, we forget it."

"But if you told the President, who would you name as your source for the information?"

"You, of course," I said. "Larry Storm of the Bureau."

"No," he said. "I think my hunch is right, but if it isn't, I could look like a fool."

"All of us are proved wrong now and then. What's so terrible about that? . . . Are you sure that's all that's worrying you?"

He frowned, but said nothing.

"Afraid you'd be fired?"

"No, damn it," he said, "but you know the Bureau. If they found out I'd talked—even to you—they'd bury me in the finger print division for life. Nobody talks outside the Bureau and gets away with it."

I sympathized with him, but my real concern was for myself. My curiosity, of course, was boiling, but more than that, the weeks of not knowing were an insult to my ego. Here was a man who knew a great deal about the Greer case. As between an FBI agent and a White House press secretary, the agent ought to be persuaded to talk.

"Let's recap, Larry," I said. "As I understand it, the real reason you're here is that you think Pete Deskowicz is withholding information from the President and you think the President should be alerted to the fact. Is that right?"

"Yes, that's it."

"Okay, but what kind of information? Is it something important, or just a lot of interesting, but inconsequential details?"

"Important!" he repeated. "If Wolcott's people were supplied with it—and I think they've already been slipped a piece of the story—it could murder your man at the polls."

"So, why the hell should you care?" I asked. "Roudebush, Wolcott, what's the difference to the FBI? Like old man river, it just keeps rolling along."

"I'd think that would be obvious," he said.

Then I realized. It was obvious—with Larry. Roudebush had not an ounce of race prejudice in his being, and Negroes knew it. He treated them as Americans, with dignity, without any pandering to them, and without a cloying pretense that equality of rights means an equality of aptitude for every task. Wolcott, on the other hand, was an uncertain quantity. He might be another Roudebush on race, but again, he might not. It was that simple.

"Frankly, Larry, that's your problem, not mine." If I was to learn anything from this man, I had to press my advantages. "As I get it, you won't tell your story because you don't want to be disclosed as the source."

"It would ruin me at the Bureau."

"But," I said, "I could ruin you right now. All I have to do is call Pete Deskowicz and say I've got a talkative agent here who's trying to tell me the FBI director is double-crossing the President of the United States."

Storm forced a smile. "You gave your word we were talking in confidence."

"Sure, I did," I said. "So why not trust me all the way? You came here thinking I could tell you whether your suspicions made sense. I can't. I'm closed out on Greer. But I'm a reasonable man, so why can't we work out an understanding?"

"What do you mean?"

"Look," I said. "You tell me everything you know. If it hits me as it apparently has you, I take the story to the President tomorrow. I will tell him without giving my source. If he demands to know, I will tell him only on condition that he won't reveal your name and that there will be no interference with you at the

Bureau, and no reprisals. What's wrong with that? . . . You know
Roudebush is a man to be trusted."

"I'd sure be putting myself in your hands."

"You would," I said. "But don't forget, you're already pretty
vulnerable—just calling me and coming here."

"Yeah." He pondered for some time.

"Okay," he said at last, "it's a deal." He appeared to be relieved.
So was I. Pulling psychic teeth was not my trade.

"Gene," he said, "to begin with, your friend Lubin went to
Africa—to Angola."

"Angola!"

"Yes, to Luanda, the capital."

"I'll be damned."

"And do you know where Kissich went?"

"Kissich. Who's Kissich?"

Storm scrutinized me closely. I could have been a suspect being
grilled by the police.

"You honestly never heard that name?"

"No, never," I replied. "Sounds as if he were some kind of rug
merchant."

"Felix Kissich," he said slowly, apparently satisfied that my
ignorance was not feigned, "is a Nobel prize winner."

"Don't sound so reproving. There are dozens of them. Very
few of them know me."

The attempt at humor failed to fetch a smile from him. "Kissich
is a research professor in plasma physics at Princeton. He disappeared too, on September eighth, from an international meeting in Helsinki. We don't have two missing persons, Gene. We
have three."

"The things I don't know." I shook my head and I could feel
another swift surge of resentment over the wall that the President
had placed between me and the Greer case. "Maybe I'd understand all this better if you'd start with the night Steve disappeared."

Larry began with his first talk with Susannah Greer, his investigation of the nonstudying Potomac Study Club and gradually
worked his way around four continents. It was a fascinating de-

tective story and my admiration for FBI thoroughness mounted by the minute. He told how he located Lubin's car, how he was switched back to Greer and his trip to Rio. He expressed his belief, parenthetically, that the continuing shift of assignments was a manifest attempt to prevent him from learning too much about any one angle of the case.

In Rio de Janeiro, Storm covered some sixty hotels and rooming houses with his Portuguese-speaking interpreter before he found a clue to his man. An American, generally answering to Greer's description, had registered at the *Balde Azul,* a small hotel for seamen, late Friday, August 27, about twenty-four hours after Greer disappeared in Washington. The man registered as "Stewart Wolford," which was close enough to the name of the Governor of Illinois to indicate that Greer might be indulging in whimsy, subconscious or not. When, about a week later, Larry showed Greer's picture to the hotel proprietor, the Brazilian was uncertain. The picture might be one of "Wolford," but then again, *quem sabe?* The proprietor did recall that the captain of the lobster trawler the *Casa Alegre* called at the hotel and talked for some time with the American. The next evening the "happy house" sailed with "Wolford" aboard. The log of the admiral of the port showed that the *Casa Alegre* had no fixed destination. Instead the trawler would work the South Atlantic lobster beds for an estimated two months. Larry said he had one close call in Rio: he had narrowly escaped being seen by Dave Paulick of *D.P.'s Dossier.*

I wanted to break in here and tell Larry of Paulick's session with the President this morning and of his astounding comment afterward that he was going on "vacation" without printing anything about Greer. Instead, I merely told him about the mysterious call I had received one day from Paulick in Rio.

"That has bugged me ever since," I said.

"I think I can make a guess," said Storm. "You see, Paulick probably thought at first that Greer had hired the 'happy house' to case the coastline for a safe hide-out. I don't think he believes that now, but he must have then because Paulick tried to charter a coastal fishing boat. The Brazilian authorities told him that, as an alien, he would have to wait a week for processing of his papers. He got sore and went to the U.S. consul, as I found out, and tried to throw his weight around. When that didn't work, he must have called you."

"Some operator, that guy." Dave's gargantuan zest for the chase always made me vicariously weary.

Storm continued his story. What happened to the *Casa Alegre* and Greer, he had no idea, for he was ordered back to Washington and put to work on more background investigation of Greer. Among other stints, Larry laboriously checked out every long-distance call that Greer had made for a year, using the neat stack of monthly bills which Greer kept for his tax records. These showed a dozen calls to Princeton, a few to the home of Felix Kissich, but most to the Plasma Physics Laboratory where Kissich worked.

When Storm learned that Kissich also had left the country, ostensibly to attend an international plasma physics conference in Finland, Larry made an appointment with Clyde Moorhead to discuss the possible connection of Kissich with the Greer disappearance. He saw Moorhead at seven-thirty one morning at task force headquarters and found his friend bleary from lack of sleep. Moorhead told him that he had worked until four o'clock before collapsing on the cot in his office. This fact, related Larry, gave him an unauthorized glimpse of the Greer case, for if Moorhead had been his usual contained and alert self, the incident would not have occurred.

Moorhead, ragged and red-eyed, was having coffee at his desk. They traded a few of their customary insults, then Larry placed a manila folder, crammed with material on Felix Kissich, on Moorhead's desk. The conversation, Larry now recalled, went about like this:

Storm: "There it is, Clyde. After you look it over, you'll see why there's a nice, long trip indicated. And I think I'm the man to make it."

Moorhead: "Trip? You've had one junket, and already you want to go sight-seeing again. But where the hell would you go?"

Storm: "Where? Don't kid me. That's obvious."

Moorhead ignored the folder Storm had placed on his desk. Instead, he picked up a clipboard file, flipped back the cardboard cover and began reading the top sheet.

Moorhead: "Let's see now. The summary says he left Baltimore August twenty-ninth. Flew to London. On August thirtieth flew to Madrid. Switched airlines and flew to Dakar. Lay-over in Dakar, then flew to Luanda, Angola. All commercial. Last seen Thursday night, September second, in Luanda, although not positively identified. Believed to have sailed on motor vessel, *Nova Coimbra*, carrying mixed cargo to Accra. Believed ship actually sailed elsewhere."

Moorhead closed the cover of the clipboard and shoved it aside.

Moorhead: "So, Larry, what do you propose to do? Go cruising around the Atlantic for a couple of weeks, looking for Lubin?"

Larry was amazed. Phil Lubin in a ship out of Angola? Moorhead was grinning at him, but Larry noted that almost at once, the grin began to fade.

Storm: "Clyde, I take it you're talking about Phillip Lubin. You haven't had me on Lubin since before I went to Rio. I'm on Felix Kissich, the third man theme."

Moorhead looked stricken. In a spasm of confusion, he wiped at his eyes, jerked the manila folder toward him, then grabbed at his coffee and took a hasty swallow.

Moorhead: "I'm sorry, Larry. No sleep, no brains. . . . Forget you ever heard that, will you? If Pete ever heard of that goof . . . well, you know the drill. Jesus, I—"

Storm: "Quit worrying, Clyde. We've worked together too long for that. But I would like to point out that this would not have happened if we'd been following the regular procedure. Hell, we'd both know everything. . . . But forget it. What I hear, I keep to myself. Now about Felix Kissich."

But Moorhead never recovered his aplomb at that meeting, and when they finished, he begged Storm again to forget what he had heard about Phil Lubin.

"I'm not sure even now just what the pitch was," Larry told me. He hunched forward on the sofa as he reconstructed the scene.

"Did Moorhead really goof, or was that his way of telling an old friend what he wasn't allowed to tell him under the drill? My guess is it was a real blooper. Clyde isn't that good an actor—and he was really shook up that morning."

"You think the dope on Lubin is accurate?" I asked.

"The first part checks," he said, "with what Dave Paulick found out. Paulick told me in Princeton yesterday that he'd trailed Lubin to Madrid, then lost him."

"What's this about Paulick and Princeton?"

"I'll get to that," he said. "Let me go ahead with Kissich."

Moorhead, he said, assigned him to find and interview Kissich, so he went to Princeton for several interviews, including the one with Mrs. Kissich. The next day he flew to Helsinki. There he learned that Kissich had left his hotel with no forwarding address on September 8, long before the meeting was scheduled to end. Kissich's fellow physicists whom Larry interviewed understood that Kissich had become suddenly ill and had gone home. The hotel night clerk reported that Kissich complained of dizziness and stomach pains. But Larry discovered that Kissich had flown to Paris, then Rome, then Cairo. Larry lost the trail in Cairo, where he spent three futile days checking. When he telephoned Washington for instructions, Moorhead ordered him home for more interviews in Washington, Baltimore, and Princeton. Larry assumed that another agent took up the search for Kissich in Cairo, but he had no certain knowledge of this.

Larry described his chance meeting with Paulick at the Nassau Inn, his conversation with Moorhead and his decision to bring his hunch—as well as his doubts and suspicions—to me instead of to Moorhead. Today had been difficult for him. Returning to Washington in early afternoon, he called Moorhead and pleaded complete fatigue. The task force chief pressed him for his written report on Princeton, but Larry managed to stall him off until tomorrow.

Storm arose from the sofa, flexed his shoulders and walked about the room. He had been talking steadily for two hours. "Get me some more coffee, will you?" he asked. "Then I want to show you something."

I put an electric burner on high, brought a pot of water to a boil and made two more mugs of coffee. The time was approaching midnight. Larry sipped at the fresh coffee. Then he went to his jacket and pulled out two thick sheets of paper from a pocket. Unfolded, they were two large maps of the Atlantic area, one north and one south. Larry placed them on the floor and fitted the two halves together. The break came just south of latitude twenty degrees north which grazes our Guantánamo naval base in Cuba and runs eastward to the Sahara in Africa and cuts the Red Sea about in the middle.

"Come here." He motioned me to the floor beside him, and we placed our mugs of coffee on the rug. Two more stains would not be noticed.

"Now," said Larry, "I've assumed that what Moorhead inadvertently told me about Lubin's travels is accurate. I've also assumed that Paulick wasn't lying when he said he had tracked Kissich to Cape Town. Now look."

He pointed to the maps. "The red line is Greer," he said, "the green line is Lubin and the black pencil is Kissich."

Greer's red line ran from a point near Washington, to Atlantic City, to New York, then straight southwest, across Trinidad and the hump of Brazil, to Rio de Janeiro. There was a short red spur into the sea and a question mark.

Lubin's green line formed half of a large square. It ran from New York across the Atlantic to London, south to Madrid, southwest to Dakar on the bulge of Africa, then southeast to Luanda, the port city of Angola. A short green spur ran into the sea, ending in another question mark.

Kissich's black line was more jagged. It ran from New York northeast to Helsinki, southwest to Paris, southeast to Rome, farther southeast to Cairo, then south to Cape Town. The pencil line then ran out to sea and was punctuated with a question mark.

"Greer winds up in Rio, a seaport, and he boards a boat," said Storm. "Lubin winds up in Luanda, a seaport, and he boards a boat. Kissich winds up in Cape Town, a seaport, and he boards a boat too."

My mind, trying to understand, was stretched as tight as a rubber band. I was sitting cross-legged on the floor, and the lines Larry had drawn seemed to thrust outward from the maps in a three-dimensional effect.

Larry stared at the lower section for a bit, then pushed the top one aside. "We only need the South Atlantic, if my theory is right," he said. He drummed on the colored chart with his fingers, and, hunching over, I saw a printed legend about in the middle of the wide blue expanse:

The horse latitudes, calms near the Tropics of Cancer and Capricorn, are regions of light, variable winds. In contrast to the doldrums, the air here is fresh and clear.

"A meeting in the horse latitudes?" I asked.

Larry sat back on his heels and looked at me with a frown of concentration.

"Maybe, maybe not." He moved into a more comfortable position.

"What have we got, Gene?" he asked. "Here we have three men, a lawyer, a mathematician and a physicist, all prominent and one of them a friend of the President. They all disappear within a few days of one another. They all fly by staggered routes, obviously trying to make tracking difficult, to South Atlantic seaports. They all sail, secretly they think, aboard fairly small boats, seaworthy all right, but hardly big freighters. None of these vessels has any fixed route or schedule. Each man goes aboard a few hours after he reaches the waterfront. That indicates advance arrangements—in fact, one hell of a lot of planning."

Larry took a swig of his coffee and his eyes questioned mine.

"So who does this planning?" he asked. "It's pretty obvious it wasn't done in person by Greer or Lubin, for neither had been out of the country for many months. Kissich, it's true, traveled a lot abroad, but there is no evidence he ever left the cities where scientific meetings were held, except for the last time at Helsinki. And none of those meetings were in Brazil, Angola, or South Africa. They might have planned it by mail, of course, but there is no trace of that. Besides, arranging voyages on small independents, each registered in a different country, would be an impossible headache by mail."

He paused a moment. "No, I think someone else, some third party, lined up those boats for them and laid out their complicated travel schedules. Who?"

" 'Who' is only part of it," I said. "The bigger question is why?"

"Right." Larry nodded. "Who and why. . . . Well, one thing's sure. Whoever made the arrangements is somebody who can move fast and move on the q.t. over a hell of a big area." He swept his hand over the map. "At first, I thought it might be President Roudebush. Greer is his best friend and Greer talked to him a length two nights before the vanishing act. But nothing starting from Roudebush made any sense. Why would a President send three men in secret to distant ports and put them aboard three tubs? A meeting? Hell, he could hold a secret meeting in the White House any night. An oceanographic or scientific expedition? If so, why secret and why a lawyer present?"

Here Larry detoured to cover his speculations about Roudebush and possible motives. He discarded them all, he said, because each seemed terribly risky in a year when Roudebush was battling for re-election. Any secret move, whatever the goal, would alienate uncounted voters. And the proof of that now was the polls, which showed Roudebush's expected runaway victory turning into a real horse race. The Greer case was hurting Roudebush badly.

I wondered. Roudebush's compromise deal with me—he was certain he would have good news within ten days, eight now—nagged at me. And how about Dave Paulick today? He charged in a lion and came out a lamb, and when one has seen Paulick meek, just once, it makes an unforgettable impression. And Susannah Greer? I did not know what the President told her that night in early September, but she had been fairly calm ever since. No hysterics, no attacks of nerves. Miguel reported her as quite cheerful, even serene at times, save for her understandable threat today to sue a network.

I described Sue Greer's attitude since her call on the President. I assumed that Larry knew it anyway.

He nodded rapidly. "You can easily explain her state of mind. When she returned from the White House that night, she got a phone call. A male voice gave her a message from her husband, using a pet nickname and telling her not to worry, he'd be home in a month—also something about an anniversary present he had been saving for her. When Mrs. Greer told me about it, I instructed her to keep it to herself. She had already told her daughter, Gretchen, but I'm sure Miguel Loomis doesn't know of it. Mrs. Greer is satisfied she's going to see her man before long."

The things I was learning. This whole scene seemed weird to me. Here sat a special agent of the FBI, unfolding his story, like a mystery writer, to an aide of the President. Outside we could hear the first sharp night wind of autumn, moaning at the corners of the building, whistling as if through tunnels.

"But you know something?" asked Larry after a pause. "I don't think Mrs. Greer is going to see her husband for a long time— if ever. As for the President, he puts up a brave front in public, a bluff really. I suppose he's betting on the character of his good friend, Steve Greer. He has faith in him and he believes Greer will show up shortly with a tidy explanation. I think it's a forlorn gamble by the President. He's going to lose."

"Why?"

"Because I don't think Paul Roudebush knows what is happening. He's not getting all the Bureau reports. Pete Deskowicz, I strongly suspect, is holding out on him, winnowing the file. If that's true, then Deskowicz is probably feeding Wolcott, and one big fine day soon, they'll spring the sensation that will bury Roudebush."

"That's hard to believe," I protested. There was, I thought, the amazing Paulick incident this morning. Also, I was pretty sure that any feeding of Wolcott's people was being done by Arthur Ingram—thanks to Butter Nygaard.

"I'm certain of it," he said. "I'll bet money right now that the President never heard of Kissich. But Kissich is the main clue."

"How so?"

Larry took his mug of coffee, cold now, raised himself from the floor and returned to the sofa where he had been sitting. I went back to the other sofa, glad of the chance to move. My knees were stiff.

"Gene," said Storm, "this Kissich probably knows as many Soviet scientists as any Westerner. For years, he has promoted an exchange of ideas and social contacts with them. The plasma physics lab invariably has a couple of Russians working there. Kissich goes to all the international physics meetings, not just in his own plasma specialty. He's been in and out of the Soviet Union so many times, he might as well be a diplomatic courier.

"But there's another thing about Kissich. He's a peace disciple who believes the Soviets are ready and we're not. He believes, very deeply and passionately, that the Russians are ready to make book that would end war in our time—a permanent *détente* the diplomats call it. But he also believes that the United States won't buy it, won't move off the dead center of the old cold war. He thinks the reason is the influence of the huge U.S. defense industry and its hold on Congress. He thinks this freezes every U. S. President into inaction. Kissich's idol as a young physicist was Leo Szilard, a fellow transplanted Hungarian, who secretly fought the dropping of the first A-bomb on Hiroshima. Kissich is a very sincere man who thinks the fate of the world hinges on a settlement with the Russians. He thinks the Russians want to settle now—but that his adopted country never will agree in his lifetime."

"If that's true," I said, "he's mistaken. Every year we make some new accommodation with the Soviets."

Larry shook his head. "Not fast enough, or basic enough for Kissich. He doesn't believe these treaties we've signed approach the heart of a true settlement. . . . But right or wrong, Kissich has had enormous influence on both Lubin and Greer. Take Lubin first. He's a brilliant man, with interests far beyond mathematics. I found out quite a bit about your friend Lubin that I bet you didn't know. He's a committed internationalist. He does not believe in national sovereignty. He thinks the world has moved beyond that."

"No doubt about his internationalist bent," I said. "I've heard him on the subject, but I never heard him go so far as to contend that nations were outmoded."

"Well, I'm sure he believes it," said Storm firmly. "Both Lubin and Kissich belong to the breed of scientists who want to combine their knowledge with social action. They're not sure they can save the world, but they're going to try."

He lapsed into thought for a time, then continued. "Now Greer. I'm sure those weekly meetings with Lubin were study sessions. I must confess I can't explain why Kissich wasn't present. Maybe Kissich isn't very articulate, or the inconvenience of travel, something. Anyway, Kissich and Greer did talk a fair amount by phone. The meetings, I think, were preparing Greer for the big step.

"You've got to understand Greer. Beneath his exterior of the steady, conservative lawyer, he's a man who loves adventure and is given to the sudden, unorthodox—call it offbeat—tangent. And Greer too has been bitten by the internationalist bug. In recent months he had begun to brood about how little we're doing in the United States to avert a world disaster. I found out from Mrs. Greer and through other interviews that Greer had become deeply concerned and alarmed about world problems. He wanted to become an activist."

Larry propped his feet on the chest again and eased deeper into the sofa. He shifted his gaze to the ceiling and said nothing for a bit. He seemed to be ordering his thoughts.

"You know," he said pensively, "a guy gets to be a psychologist in this business. It happens to many agents, but maybe I've done more of it because a lot of my cases have been internal security jobs. They usually stretch over a long period and you find yourself analyzing the mind of your suspect, trying to outguess him on his next move. I've spent a lot of nights trying to get inside Steve Greer's mind, and I tell you what: I'm convinced the guy is laboring under a guilt complex. Greer is a decent man, a hard worker, but in the last few years he's made a ton of money without doing very much for it. . . . The old Washington political law racket . . . He's known as a close friend of the President, so business comes piling into his law firm, more than it can handle. Greer, I think, got to brooding about this, and finally decided, hell, he wanted to do something big with no selfish return. So, after months of listening to Kissich and Lubin, he was ready for the big gamble, and screw the consequences. . . . All of which brings me to my hunch, and here's what I think the pitch is, Gene."

Larry leaned forward, an eager, strained look on his face. I could sense what was coming.

"These three guys," he said, "are heading for Russia. They sailed secretly, after reaching the ports by devious zigzag routes, and I'm convinced that they boarded one of those large Soviet oceanographic ships in the South Atlantic. I think they are on their way right now to the Soviet Union."

The long-deferred revelation was anticlimactic. And it lacked plausibility. Steve Greer a possible defector! Too many pieces did not fit, too many bridges thrown across unknown rivers. I was frankly surprised at the solidity of Larry's conviction.

"I can't buy it," I said. "Defections are out of style. Hell, man, there's no need to defect these days. A man can argue his piece in either country. . . . Larry, you Bureau men have a hang-up on the Russians and the espionage and defection bit."

"You don't know what we know," he said. "In the Greer case, everything fits the pattern, the deviousness of the three disappearances, the complicated flight schedules, the secrecy, the small boats. That has Soviet Union written all over it. The Russians love that kind of covert operation. I'll bet the Soviets did all the advance work for the three men. I can't prove it, but consider two small clues I ran into. The *Casa Alegre*, out of Rio, had done a couple of provisioning chores for Soviet lobster trawlers. Then in Cairo, I found out, from a reliable Egyptian source, that Kissich was visited at his hotel by a KGB agent. Small signs, and not conclusive, I know, but they fit. . . .

"Look at some other things," Larry continued after a pause. "Those two phone calls to Mrs. Greer, giving her messages from her husband. Both male voices. That sounds like a typical Russian ploy. . . . Greer climbing over a golf course fence. Is that the way we'd do it? Hell, no. If it had been left to Greer, he'd have probably packed his bag for a business trip to Paris or Rome, then got lost over there. And what have Pravda and Radio Moscow been saying about Greer's disappearance? Nothing. Every other news organ in the world is playing up the Greer story, but from Moscow, nothing."

"That's not right, Larry," I objected. "TASS had an early story."

"I know," said Larry, "but that could have been a slip. You haven't heard a damn word since then about the vanishing American imperialist or the millionaire's scandal."

I shook my head. His theory seemed incredibly thin. "Hell, Larry," I said, "why go to all that trouble just to get to Russia? Intricate air schedules, boats, all that crap. Why didn't they just take off and fly to Moscow straight?"

"I think the Russians were testing them and baiting a trap at the same time," he said. "Try thinking like the Kremlin for a minute. Three big shots agree to come over to the Communist side, but how to insure that they actually defect? If they fly in commercial, straight, then change their minds, they can just leave, announcing they were there on business, research, anything. But once the Russians get Greer, Lubin, and Kissich involved in this furtive maneuver, climaxed by sailing back on a Russian ship, they're totally compromised. They've got no out."

"You're still not persuading me," I said.

All three men were accustomed to dealing with Russians. They knew their way around, Kissich and Lubin in the academic world, Greer in the political. Larry's conjecture lacked plausibility with Greer especially. Greer was a sophisticated man who had observed the inside of international politics for years. Still, the new knowledge that the three men had sailed off into nowhere—three men in three tubs—was almost impossible to assimilate. And, actually, I knew so little about this triple disappearance, while Larry had not only worked the case for more than a month, but he was an expert in Communist intrigue and internal security counterespionage.

My quandary must have been reflected on my face, for Larry studied me for a while before continuing.

"You see, Gene," he said, "I'm convinced that Deskowicz is deceiving the President. Just how it started, I'm not sure. My guess is that the minute Pete heard about Greer's disappearance, and was placed on the case, he smelled something fishy and clamped a tight lock on all his agents to make sure none of us knew too much. Maybe, at the beginning, he briefed Roudebush in full. Then, as the information began to flow in, and it looked more and more like a security problem, he may have told the President his suspicions.

"Roudebush may have gotten mad, refusing to believe that his friend Steve would defect. Then, probably, Deskowicz came back to Roudebush several times with more damaging evidence. But the President still wouldn't listen. A guy like Pete will buck a President only so far. After a couple of rebuffs, Deskowicz would clam up, letting the President have only what he thinks Roudebush wants to hear. That's what I think happened. . . . But, of course, it's remotely possible also that Deskowicz cut the President out right from the start, convinced that Roudebush would never tell the country the truth in the middle of a campaign.

"Just what went on, I can only guess. But I'm sure that right now the President doesn't know half of what you've just learned. As I said, I'll bet he doesn't even know about Kissich. . . . And so, at the right time, maybe this weekend, Deskowicz adroitly leaks the story to the press. The Bureau has its means, you know. Or he might slip it to the Wolcott people. Either way, you've got a dead candidate in the White House."

"You really don't think Greer is coming back?" That central point, like a bone in the throat, would not go down.

"No, I don't," he said. "I think we're going to see these three men using Moscow as a world platform for their views. Maybe a big splashy press conference at which Greer, Lubin, and Kissich contend that the United States is a militant, unyielding barrier to world peace."

"Are you talking about defection?" I asked. "If you are, I can't buy it with Steve. Kissich and Lubin, I'm not so sure, but Steve, no."

"They might be defecting outright, then again maybe not," said

Storm. "They might say they're in Moscow as a form of protest, or that they're going to stay in the Soviet Union until the U.S. comes to its senses. But that's all speculation. . . . What I do feel sure about is that these three men are playing a very serious game with the Russians right at this minute."

I thought for a while, looking bleakly at the tumble of magazines and documents on the chest. Larry's theory was fantastic, and yet . . . what did I really know? If someone had suggested yesterday that the CIA's Arthur Ingram was monitoring the White House through Butter Nygaard, I would have said the idea was a lunatic one. Now, here was a patently sincere Larry Storm linking duplicity by the FBI director to a breach of allegiance by the President's best friend. For all of my supposed intuition about government and politics, I was lost now and I knew it.

"So you want me to tell the President the whole story?" It was a limp restatement of the obvious.

"I do," he said. "And I want to be protected."

"Don't worry about it. I've given you my word. . . . Larry, your theory seems far out to me. On the other hand, I owe it to the President to tell him. I'll try to get to him the first thing in the morning."

We both looked at our watches. It was 3:25 A.M.

"Can you be in your apartment along about ten?" I asked.

"Yes. I have to go to the Bureau first, but then I'll go back to my place and wait. I'll be there from ten on."

I walked him to the door, carrying my burden of frustration and doubt. The enormity of what he had been saying, coupled with the whistling wind at the window ledges, framed the night in unreality.

"You can't be right, Larry," I said. "If you are, Roudebush is a defeated President."

"Maybe not," he said. "At the least, he can be the one to tell the facts to the country, which might create some sympathy for him. Certainly, it would be better than having the news come from Mr. Kulp in Louisville—or from Moscow."

"Hell," I said, "it's death either way. Either he hangs himself, or somebody hangs him—if you're right."

"I think I am," he said, "and bad as it is, the President ought to know."

We said our good nights and I closed the door.

I saw the President at nine-fifteen that morning. Even compressing the story, I talked for a half hour. He listened without interrupting me, grave and troubled.

"Gene," he said when I finished, "that is an incredible story. Precisely who was your source for it?"

"As I told you at the outset, Mr. President, my source fears reprisals if his identity were revealed. He told me only under the condition that I would not compromise him."

"But it's a fantastic tale," he said. "Certainly I deserve to know the source. Consider the implications to the country, to the party —to me."

"I gave my word, sir."

"But I want to question this person myself," he said.

"He told me I could give you his name," I said, "only if we have your pledge that no one else will learn of it."

"Of course," said Roudebush. "You have that pledge—without qualification."

"In that case, his name is Larry Storm, one of the FBI special agents who has been on the Greer case since the start."

"Storm," he said. "Yes, I've heard good reports about him. Where is he now?"

"He's either at his apartment here in town, or will be there shortly. I was to call him after you and I talked."

"Get him here at once," he said. "Have him come in the rear driveway."

"Yes, sir."

He flicked a switch on his intercom. "Grace," he said, "a Mr. Larry Storm of the FBI will be here in a few minutes. I want a messenger to wait for him at the rear driveway and bring him to my office at once."

The President thanked me as he escorted me to the door. He was agitated, distracted, and there was not the customary pleasantry on parting.

Larry was waiting for my call. When I told him of the President's promise and of his urgent request, Larry said he would leave for the White House immediately.

And that was the last I heard from Larry Storm. I expected him to call me within an hour or two, but there was no word from him, no fill-in, no explanation, nothing. I began calling his apartment at noon and continued through the day, but there was no response to any of my rings. Just before leaving the office in the evening, I asked the operator to check his phone. It was in working order, she reported. It just did not answer.

Jill spent a hectic Saturday following a barely endurable confrontation with Butter Nygaard. Jill moved her things to a temporary room in the apartment of two other White House secretaries. Then she came to my place that night for a late dinner. We dissected Miss Nygaard to the marrow, but shied away from any talk about the White House. Both of us still felt the sting of the President's reprimand.

I excused myself several times and tried to reach Larry, the last call at midnight.

Like Dave Paulick, Larry Storm had simply disappeared. As far as I was concerned, we now had five missing persons.

16

He walked along the deck, scanning the horizon to the east. Spray burst over the rail with each lunge of the ship. Westerly winds lashed at the stern in gusts. The *Pedro Alfonso* was being driven faster than the eighteen knots which the compact motor freighter had maintained on the long reach from Rio de Janeiro.

It was foul weather for these latitudes and this season. October was the second month of spring in the far South Atlantic, but the blow carried the sting of winter. The sun had risen two hours ago, yet only a pale light touched the leaden overcast.

He opened a door, stepped into a passageway, and climbed the stairs to the sheltered bridge. The captain nodded to him, then pointed ahead through the thick storm glass.

Bill Hughes, looking where the captain pointed, saw the shape, a burr on the dirty wool of the sky.

"That's it," said the captain in Portuguese. "Six days. Without the engine trouble, we'd have made it in five as I promised."

Bill Hughes replied in Portuguese. "Stinking day," he said.

"We'll be at anchor offshore in another hour," said the captain. He had a face of cracked leather and a stubble of beard. He wore a knitted cap and a heavy convoy coat. Despite the glass enclosure, the bridge was chill and damp.

Hughes took a pair of binoculars from the chart table and focused the lenses as he sighted over the bow. He was a chunky man with black hair, green eyes, and a scalloped nose that had been broken twice. His plump, flushed cheeks were those of a man who ate and drank well. He wore trousers and a jacket of yellow oilskin with a cowl thrown back over his shoulders. He was well padded beneath, long underwear, khaki pants, flannel shirt, and a turtleneck sweater.

"I can see the volcano now," said Hughes. He laughed as he lowered the binoculars. Hughes, the captain had found, laughed a great deal, often for no apparent reason.

"There will be no jokes after we anchor," said the captain. "No islander will put out in a small boat in this weather."

"Then I'll use one of the Pedro's lifeboats to go ashore," said Hughes.

"You'll go alone. That island has a couple of drownings every year." The captain's tone was one of rebuke. This American was a madman, he thought. Who else would pay $28,000 U.S., cash in advance, for a round-trip voyage to the remote island of Tristan da Cunha, more than two thousand miles from Rio? And who else would brave the surf on Tristan's treacherous rocks?

The island gradually took form during the next hour as the *Pedro Alfonso* bucked through the seas to the southeast. First loomed the volcanic mountain which, Hughes knew, rose to 6700 feet. Its peak shouldered into an overcast that had movement now, gray, billowing clouds that fumbled about the black flanks of the mountain. As the ship drew nearer, the mountain walls showed ribs of green, the shrub foliage of spring. And then, later, Hughes could see the small plateau and its field of meadow grass bending before the wind. The level area was Lilliputian —not large enough for an airfield. At last appeared the tiny settlement of Edinburgh, a cluster of about seventy-five stone, thatched-roof cottages on this most lonely and isolated of British islands.

Hughes speculated as the freighter drove through the seas. Would he find his man here? If so, would he be a lone visitor and what would his explanation be? And why the silence of Tristan's radio, the island's only link with the world save for the occasional mail ship out of Cape Town?

The *Pedro*'s captain hove to a half mile off Tristan da Cunha's miniature harbor where a half dozen small boats, apparently none longer than twenty feet, huddled in the lee of a jetty of volcanic rock. The *Pedro's* anchor clanked down, seeking a footing on the island's narrow underseas shelf.

Hughes went on deck, raising his oilskin cowl against the wind. The air was cold, moist with the tang of salt. He studied the harbor through the binoculars. Waves beat at the jetty, raising fountains of spray. Within the small harbor, open rowboats and two motor launches thrashed at their moorings. The waves in the sullen stretch between the *Pedro Alfonso* and the island reached four to five feet in height and were crested with curling white water.

A crowd of some two hundred people, many of them children, had collected near the jetty. Hughes could make out white "kappies," kerchief bonnets of an Afrikaans style, on the girls. The men and boys wore sweaters or jackets and peaked woolen caps. All faces were turned toward the ship.

A tall man in a windbreaker stepped from the crowd and raised a bull horn to his mouth. Hughes assumed it was battery-powered, for he could see the man holding a small box and a wire connection.

The captain appeared at Hughes's elbow with the *Pedro's* megaphone, also electrically amplified. Hughes thanked the captain and waited.

"Who are you?" The question, in English, boomed across the water, vying with the wind.

"The *Pedro Alfonso* out of Rio," replied Hughes. His words sounded strange to his ears as though a giant had seized his voice and hurled it toward the island like a series of boulders.

There was only the whistle of the wind for a moment, and then from the shore: "Are you bringing cargo?" The accent, Hughes felt sure, was American.

"No," replied Hughes. "We have a passenger to put ashore."

"That is impossible," came the answer. Each syllable was enunciated separately and precisely. "A small boat landing here will be broken up. Surf is running too high."

"We will risk that," said Hughes. He hoped he gave his reply a bantering inflection. "This is an emergency."

"There is no doctor here." The booming statement was pre-emptory, less a factual observation than a warning.

"We don't need one," said Hughes. "Our man wants to feel dry land under him."

"He may be killed on the rocks," called the voice from the shore. The unmistakable American accent was probably eastern seaboard, thought Hughes. "We warn you. We will not risk lives here for rescue."

"I am coming anyway," returned Hughes.

"You are a fool."

"Always have been, Mac," called Hughes. The bull horn carried his jesting tone. "But I'll wait a bit. This wind may ease off."

Hughes condensed the conversation in Portuguese for the captain. "The blow will pass to the east later today," said the captain. He pointed to a rift of blue in the woolen sky. "If you wait until tomorrow, the sea may be like glass."

Hughes shook his head. "My job won't wait, Skipper."

He busied himself for the next fifteen minutes in his cabin, tucking personal belongings into his clothing beneath the oil-skins. Toothbrush and paste went into an oilskin pouch which he buttoned into his hip pocket. He wrapped his passport in plastic and placed it in his shirt pocket. Pipe, tobacco, and razor were wrapped and tied to his belt. A special oilskin pouch was reserved for his wallet. When Hughes finished, he felt like a stuffed owl. But he congratulated himself on his planning. He had spent a whole afternoon in Rio, after his talk with the Pedro's captain, trying to anticipate any eventuality on the harsh shores of Tristan da Cunha.

When Hughes emerged on deck, the captain and two crewmen stood beside one of the ship's four lifeboats. The tarpaulin had been pulled off and the men were at the davits, ready to lower the boat.

"You're crazy," said the captain. "If you wait until evening, it will be much calmer."

"No, now's the time. You forget. I'm lucky."

"But is my lifeboat?" asked the captain. "If it is lost, you owe me another thousand dollars."

"Bill me, you robber," said Hughes cheerfully. He squinted at the captain, then slowed his Portuguese so there would be no mistaking his words. "You wait until I'm back aboard. It may be one day—or two. That was our bargain. Was that not our agreement?"

The captain pushed his knitted cap to the crown of his head and jerked his thumb toward the lifeboat. "You go. I'll wait."

Hughes climbed over the rail and the gunwale of the lifeboat, seated himself on the middle thwart and grasped one of the oars. The boat lowered with a creaking of the davits. When it reached the heaving water, Hughes unfastened the hooks at bow and stern and was promptly thrown off his feet as the boat dashed against the hull of the small freighter. The captain, leaning over the rail, cursed in Portuguese while motioning wildly with both arms. Hughes got up, shoved hard against the ship with an oar, then fixed the oars into the oarlocks and began to pull for shore.

Within a minute, he wished that he were back on the *Pedro*. Water sloshed into the boat, waves tilted the bow skyward and, while each straining heave on the oars advanced him several yards, the wind on his quarter seemed to hurl the boat almost as far sideways. Hughes was one man attempting to do the work ordinarily performed by four oarsmen. When he glanced behind him at the island and corrected his course with more weight to the right, the left oar tended to flail the air. The *Pedro*'s crew lined the rail to watch the contest.

After fifteen minutes, Hughes had covered less than half the distance to the narrow mouth of the harbor. Once a large wave slapped the starboard side of the row boat, flipping it like a cork. Water poured over the gunwale and swirled about his leather boots. His back ached and his arms felt weak. Beneath his heavy clothing, he was sweating, yet the wind whipped at his face like frosty thongs. Still, Hughes knew his luck was holding. Yesterday or the day before he would have capsized in wild seas, had he had the temerity to attempt the haul, for this westerly had been blowing for three days. This morning the waves, while still angry, had abated somewhat. So had the wind. Hughes guessed it was scudding over the ocean at about ten knots with occasional gusts to fifteen or more. The boat lurched forward, slanting up the side of a wave, then nosing into the trough. By the time the boat reached the projection of the old lava flow, which formed a natural arm of the harbor, a half hour had elapsed. The harbor's other arm was a man-made jetty of volcanic rocks. Hughes pulled through the opening and was about to relax in the somewhat calmer waters of the protected moorage. The tall man with the bull horn stood on the beach.

"Pull to your right, quick," he called.

The warning came too late. The bow of the wooden boat struck a great lump of volcanic rock and the following wave twisted the boat parallel to the stony beach. Hughes lost an oar, the stern struck another rock and the rowboat crunched at the middle. Hughes was flung into the water about fifteen yards from shore. The next wave carried him shoreward like a bundle of wash. His shoulder hit a stone, then the momentum of the wave rolled him side over side. He managed to get to his hands and knees and dig in like an animal to resist the rush of receding water.

The tall man in the windbreaker, discarding the electric megaphone, ran toward the water. Hughes felt an arm go about his waist and found himself being dragged high on the graveled beach.

After a moment, he wobbled to his feet. The wreckage of the boat and the two oars was being thrashed against the jetty in showers of spray. There would be new planks, Hughes guessed, for the salvage-built houses of Tristan. He pulled back his oilskin cowl and felt at his forehead. The right temple had been cut. Blood seeped beside an eye.

"We'll get you first aid for that," said the stranger.

A torrent of Portuguese poured across the water from the *Pedro*'s bull horn. Hughes listened, then shrugged.

"The bandit," he said. "Already screaming for money for his lifeboat. About me, not a word."

"Well, how do you feel?" asked the stranger. He had a long, full face, lightly tanned. A city man, Hughes guessed. He wore a new canvas rain hat and his partially unbuttoned windbreaker was fleece-lined.

Hughes grinned, patted his arms and legs, and took several tentative steps. "All here. No missing parts."

"You know you're a damn fool. You could have been killed."

Hughes automatically tried to narrow that accent by geography. A soft slur might indicate Delaware or Maryland, but with the high mobility of today's America, he could not be certain.

"I'm usually lucky," said Hughes. He was breathing hard. "I believe in luck."

The man retrieved his megaphone, then led Hughes up to a gray lava road, stepping carefully on the slippery rocks which made a stairway from the beach. The great mountain stood only a short distance away, its rude flanks softened by curling patches of mist. Across the scanty plateau, Hughes could see an ox pulling a wooden cart loaded with stone. The animal had lowered his horns and the man beside him, wearing a rough woolen cap and heavy sweater, also leaned to the wind.

The islanders were gathered in the meadow several hundred yards from the harbor. All faced the newcomer.

"Tristan's welcoming committee," said the tall man. He handed a handkerchief to Hughes, and they stopped on the road while Hughes pressed it to the cut on his forehead.

"Haven't I seen you somewhere?" asked Hughes.

"Maybe, maybe not," said the man. "I know I've never seen you." He put out his hand. "Call me Joe."

"All right," agreed Hughes. "But what's your full name?"

"I said you can call me Joe." It was put firmly, and Hughes sensed that further inquiry would be futile. An unpromising start, he thought.

Hughes looked again at the face. It bothered him. Although undistinguished and lacking some special promontory or cleft to aid the memory, it was nevertheless vaguely familiar. Where had he seen it? The States? Brazil? Europe? He knew the face would nag him, hour after hour, until his memory tagged it with a country, a city, an occupation, a name.

"And what's your name?" asked the man.

"Bill Hughes. The Bill is real. So is the Hughes—Joe."

"What's your business here?"

"Government business."

"Which government?"

"You don't know? With my accent? The United States, of course."

"Oh," said Joe. He pointed to the ship, rolling in a nest of whitecaps. The braying of the bull horn had ceased. "How about the *Pedro?* Does she stay?"

Hughes, still pressing his forehead, nodded. "Until I'm back aboard. I hired her. One hell of a hunk of change, too."

"She can't remain here," said Joe. "She'll have to leave at once." He raised the megaphone to his mouth and flicked a switch.

"No good, unless you speak Portuguese," said Hughes. He grinned again. "Nobody aboard the *Pedro* speaks English."

Joe held out the horn. "Then you tell them. Tell them you're staying on the island, and the ship is to go home, to Rio or wherever she came from."

Hughes did not take the megaphone. "Sorry. I gave my instructions. She's to remain near Tristan until I'm back aboard. . . . Why can't she stay?"

Joe ignored the question. "There's no way for you to leave here. No islander will risk his neck ferrying you out there."

"There'll be better weather soon," said Hughes with bright unconcern.

"I believe in luck too," said Joe, "and luckily Norman Green, the mayor—or headman, they call him here—speaks enough Portuguese."

A quick gust buffeted them and scratched at Hughes's oilskins. "Come on," said Joe. He led his uninvited guest down the road to the knot of villagers. They were waiting in silent curiosity, every face tanned and now damp from the wet wind. Hughes was equally curious, for he knew that many of these people had fled the island during the 1961 volcanic eruption, only to return two years later. They were, he knew, a tough, earthy, and hospitable breed.

"This is Mr. William Hughes from the United States," explained Joe to the crowd. "He will be our guest for a time."

Hughes waved a greeting. "Hello, everybody." There were a few hesitant, answering salutations and several small girls giggled.

A short, scrubby man stepped forward. Black-gray whiskers draped his face like Spanish moss. A front tooth was missing. He wore a heavy blue sweater and short-visored woolen cap.

Joe introduced him to Hughes as Norman Green, headman of the island. Hughes knew the name from his reading. Green was a descendant of one of the first families to settle the island a century and a half ago. He spoke an odd, archaic English and he spoke with pride. He was the island's top politician, his constituency embracing all 250 inhabitants of Tristan.

"Norman," said Joe in a low voice after the amenities, "our new friend refuses to order the *Pedro* to leave." He handed the megaphone and battery to the headman. "You tell 'em in Portuguese that Mr. Hughes is staying on indefinitely and that they're to sail back to Rio. Okay?"

"Okay," said Green.

"Let's go, Hughes." Joe grasped the protesting newcomer firmly by an arm and propelled him across the green meadow where long grass bent to the wind. "We're going to my place."

Behind them, they could hear Green calling single, halting Portuguese words out to sea.

"Chilly spot," said Hughes. "Not the kind of tropical isle I'd pick for a vacation. Besides, I'm wet."

"You can have a hot bath and some dry clothes at my house."

They walked in silence. Hughes could feel the nip of the wind on his face. High in the east, there was a dull glow where the sun made a futile effort to pierce the morose overcast.

"Where's Steve Greer?" asked Hughes.

Joe did not break stride. He merely glanced at Hughes without surprise and said: "I ask the questions here. You don't. . . . But later. After you're dried out."

"You mean I'm a prisoner?" Hughes grinned again.

"That idea seems to appeal to you."

"I've been around. There are times when all you can do is relax and enjoy it."

"Well," said Joe, "you're on this island until I say you can leave. Unless, of course, you like to swim."

Joe's stone cottage, half hidden behind a stand of New Zealand flax which served both as a wind fence and as eventual thatching for the roof, nestled in a hollow. A stone chimney framed one end of the house. A few yards distant squatted a stone outhouse. At the door, they turned to look back toward the shore. The villagers still stood in a cluster. From the *Pedro Alfonso* came the sound of curdled Portuguese.

Hughes laughed. "I don't think he'll leave. The pirate wants his money for that lifeboat."

The interior of Joe's one-room cottage was fashioned from the driftwood and fittings of vessels wrecked long ago. Planks lined the walls. Beams, painted green, supported a wooden ceiling. The furniture was crude, a few wooden chairs, a pitted table with sawhorse legs, and two single beds. The fireplace was bare. Wood was agonizingly scarce on Tristan. Heat came from a kerosene stove whose fumes were thick in the room. While the house looked snug, Hughes wondered if it ever really warmed up.

Joe rummaged in a metal box, found an adhesive bandage and applied it to the cut on Hughes's forehead. Then he pointed to a blanket which hung from the ceiling at one end of the room.

"There's the bath. You'll find a fresh towel back there. I'll heat some water for the tub, but you'd better rub down first."

While Hughes shucked his clothes, Joe put two buckets of water on the stove. Then he laid out dry clothes and thick woolen socks on a chair.

"You can put these on while you're waiting," he said. "We usually make do with one bucket of water, but as a new guest, you get two."

There was a knock on the door and Norman Green entered.

"The *Pedro* lifted anchor and is heading to the northwest," he said. "We'll not see 'er again."

"How'd you work it, Norman?" asked Joe.

"I told him he'd best sail," said Green. He had removed his

woolen cap and stood fingering it. "I said his man was injured and needed care here for a long time."

"That sounds too easy."

"Aye. Musta been the lifeboat and the storm. . . . I told him Mr. Hughes refused to pay for the lifeboat, cause of rotten planking. Then I told him our radio reported a norther, sixty knots or more, would strike us in the night." He motioned his head toward the sea. "Them Brazilian masters don't like northers—not in this latitude."

"You're a genius, Norman," said Joe. "I hate to ask this, but I need another favor. Could you crowd one more in at your place or at your cousin's? I have to move Delaney out to make room for Mr. Hughes. I want our visitor under my roof."

Green nodded. "Send Delaney to my house. We've got one more cot."

Hughes, who had donned dry clothes during the exchange, came from behind the blanket as the whiskered headman left.

"Obliging little liar, that one," he said.

"He's co-operative," said Joe.

"So you chased the *Pedro*, my home away from home." Another wide grin creased Hughes's melon cheeks. "Now I'm really a prisoner."

"Don't you ever stop grinning?"

"Never." Hughes tamped tobacco into his stubby pipe, applied a match to the bowl, and began puffing strenuously. "Brought it strapped to my gut," he said to Joe's unspoken question. "Thanks for the clothes—warden."

"I'll fix us some drink," said Joe. "On this island, that means tea."

After making the tea, he handed Hughes a cracked cup without saucer.

"All right," he said. His long face was unsmiling. "Who do you work for?"

"As I said, the U. S. Government." Hughes had tiny wrinkles about the eyes which gave him the look of a man perpetually and privately amused. "My boss is one of the major wheels. Lots of wheels in Washington, though. I don't like the place."

"There's no point in playing games here," said Joe. "You're 1500 miles south of St. Helena and 2000 from the nearest mainland."

"On an island where no plane can land and that no ship can approach closer than half a mile," added Hughes. He waved his pipe. "I know all that. . . . Tucked away in the South Atlantic, far from traffic jams, TV, and the neuroses of affluence. Kind of a relief, actually."

"Please, no games. It's a waste of energy here."

"It's all a game, according to the psychedelic apostles," said Hughes. "I suppose they're right, you know. I've spent half my life, Christ can testify, at the puzzle game. . . . Now, you, for instance. You're my warden and, I suspect, Steve Greer's guardian. Am I right?"

"It won't work, Hughes." Joe appeared to be enjoying the fencing despite his stern look. "I told you that I ask the questions here."

"Mmm." Hughes sipped at the tea. "I suppose you do. . . . Call me Bill, by the way. This is hardly a formal salon, you know."

"You said Bill Hughes is your real name. Is it?"

"Sure. Sorry I don't have a card. Never carry one. All I need is my pipe and money, the taxpayer's money, thank God. The best kind. . . . Oh, I wouldn't try a pseudonym with you. No use, really. My passport's in my shirt pocket, wrapped nicely in plastic. . . . Anyway, I imagine you have very ingenious communications with the outside world, carrier pigeons, bottle in the sea, all that kind of thing, not to mention a damn good radio transmitter. A transmitter, by the way, that doesn't transmit much. We tried to raise Tristan from the *Pedro* four times this morning. No answer."

"I like to know exactly to whom I'm talking." Joe placed his cup on the floor and leaned forward, crossed arms on his knees, as he studied Hughes. "My guess would be you work for the CIA. Am I right?"

"Not allowed to answer that question. No sense to it, really. Cops and robbers stuff. Still, games are games and you have to play by the rules. Let's just say that I'm personally acquainted with Arthur V. Ingram—in case you know the name—and in a professional capacity. Does that satisfy you?"

"No," said Joe. "With that answer, you could work for almost anyone, the FBI, State Department, even Treasury."

"Not Treasury, for God's sake," said Hughes with mock alarm. "Big, gloomy damn place. Always running a deficit. Can't see how it keeps the country from bankruptcy with all those Harvard men around. I went to Penn, myself." He sucked at his pipe, drank more tea, and managed to grin through both operations. "Well, Warden, what are your ground rules? If left to myself, I'd look up Mr. Greer and maybe a mathematician named Phil Lubin, ask them what in bejesus they're up to, and then zip off a fast radio message to my boss."

Joe shook his head. "Nobody uses that radio unless I say so. And you will not be permitted to go near it."

That face, thought Hughes, where have I seen it? His mind groped for the slot where Joe belonged.

"Pretty arrogant, aren't you?" he asked. "After all, this is British territory, and Radio Tristan receives and sends under the jurisdiction of the poor old Empire."

"You've heard the first of the ground rules. No radio."

"But, my God. They'll think I've drowned or bought the farm somewhere. You could lose me my job, you know."

"Not all luck is good, Hughes," said Joe. "You've run into some of the bad."

"Can't buy that, pal. I always manage to run before the wind." He relit his pipe and puffed like an engine to renew its circulation. "Look at my landing on Tristan! Damned spectacular, if you ask me. . . . Besides, Joe, I'm not the enemy, you know. Unless I've got your accent dead wrong, or unless you're a damned clever linguist, we both pay homage to the good old U.S. and A., the stars and stripes, home, hot dogs, and mother. Also, I see you're a man of reason. So why can't we make a sensible arrangement? You do your job, whatever it is, and I'll do mine. And call me Bill while we sign the treaty, will you?"

"All right, I'll call you Bill. Put a little hot tea in you and you chatter like a sewing machine." Joe smiled for the first time. "But before any treaty signing, I want to know just why you're on Tristan da Cunha."

"You don't pronounce that name right, you know," chided Hughes. "Very insular, most Americans. I speak four languages myself. Not all well, of course, but enough to do business with any whorehouse madam. . . . Now what am I doing here? Well . . ." Hughes shrugged. "God, this place is clammy. I think I'll take that bath. You mind?"

"Go ahead." Joe poured the buckets of hot, steaming water into the galvanized tub. He handed Hughes a bar of soap.

Behind the blanket, Hughes sloshed in the tub and promptly renewed his running commentary. "Damn cramped quarters here. Next trip out, bring a portable shower back, will you? . . . Why am I on Tristan? Well, let's see. I am looking for a prominent Washington attorney named Stephen Byfield Greer. Got a third cousin named Byfield. Lusted after her once. Beautiful woman, but too horsey. I've learned to avoid horsey women. All that bouncing about over the fields and fences takes their minds off men. Hard drinkers, too. Seem to prefer the grog to sex. Never knew a horsewoman who could concentrate on routine adultery. . . . Oh, well. . . . Now, Steve Greer. I'm supposed to talk to him and his friend Phil Lubin from Johns Hopkins. It seems they maintained a little R Street menage in Washington for about a year, and then, presto, they both take off. You know all about that, of course, Joe. My superiors had me packing around Brazil on one errand and another when this Greer went flying down to Rio. So, I tried to locate the follow. Not easy, let me tell you. Finally discovered that he sailed on a trawler called the *Casa Alegre*. No idea where. But, at last, the *Alegre* put back into port, and I got the captain snockered. Tough man, but corrupt. . . . Thank God for corruption, or we'd all be out of business. Imagine you've run into your share on your job?"

"No," replied Joe, "you won't find out about my job that way. Corruption? Yeah, I've run into some here and there."

"Then you know. The corrupt are the lubricant of honest commerce. . . . God, this is a small tub! How the hell am I supposed to get at my plumbing fixtures?"

"Stand up," said Joe.

"Say, that's a grade A idea." Hughes arose, lathered and splashed himself, then stepped from the tub and began rubbing briskly with a towel. "Anyway, the Brazilian skipper talked for one grand of our best tax dollars. I'm a taxpayer too, so I never squander more than I have to. The captain tells me he took Mr. Greer to the island of Tristan da Cunha. . . . Notice how I pronounce that name? Proper way. . . . The *Alegre* had to stand off this island for a day because of dirty weather, but the captain finally put his man ashore. So, after hearing that, the next day I hired me a small but fast one, the *Pedro Alfonso*. She can bull along at eighteen knots. Japanese built. Damn good shipwrights, the Japanese. Damn smart people. . . . Well, anyway, the engines were fine, but the Brazilians are less than perfection as maintenance men. The master promises me a five-day run, but we break down for a day somewhere up the line. So, the *Pedro* fetched me here in six days of wretched food and lousy conversation. Then, down on the beach of Tristan, I met this affable host in a windbreaker, a real, hospitable type. Tea, bath, clothes, all on the house. Only thing is, he stole my ship."

"Untrue. It was sent away for safety's sake."

"Same thing," said Hughes with cheerful unconcern. "Oh well, what you make on the merry-go-round, you lose on the ferris wheel." He padded across the room, dressed in sweater, pants and sweat socks. He picked up his pipe and tamped tobacco into it. "Not surprised, really. That bandit was probably eager to trade the price of a lifeboat for a quick trip back to Rio. Can't blame him . . . Well now, Warden, how about telling me something? What in the hell is Mr. Joe anonymous doing here? Keeping house for Greer and Lubin? And by whose orders and for what purpose?"

Joe stretched his legs and appraised his guest anew. "You're a cool one, Bill. I like you, even if you are a nonstop yakker. I'll leave the talking to you. As for me, I'm under orders and I obey them."

"Dull kind of life," said Hughes brightly. "So what am I supposed to do now?"

Joe shook his head. "That's your problem. All I know is that you're not leaving this island until the rest of us do. There are people here right now who are only temporary residents of Tristan. You may recognize one or two." He paused. "We can work this one of two ways. Either you give me your word that you'll abide by my rules, or we'll have to lock you inside this house under guard. If you give your word, you can wander about a bit —within certain, definite limits."

"The old games within games, what?" The steady grin did not flag. "And what is off-limits?"

"First," said Joe, "you are not to speak to anybody on the island except Headman Norman Green and myself. Second, you are not to take notes of any kind. Third, you are not to enter the radio shack. That's the house with the antenna on it. Fourth, you are not to approach a house known as the Mabel Clark. If you're wondering, it's called that because it was built from salvage of a sailing vessel of that name wrecked here a century ago. I'll point it out to you. . . . Oh, yes, Number Five. If a ship should pass or approach the island, you are not to signal it in any way. . . . Otherwise, the island's yours. Of course, it's small, and we'll be watching you."

"Thanks a lot." Hughes puffed a ladder of smoke circles. "And if I don't give my word as a gentleman, however we construe that word, then I have to stay inside this clammy joint—with no central heating and no indoor plumbing?"

"That's it. We'll give you chow, clothes, and books. But inside you'll stay, except for guarded trips to the can."

"How long?"

"I'm not sure. We may be able to leave in a few days and we may not."

"It's not a fair trade," said Hughes. "I tell you the works. You tell me nothing."

"That's the way it is."

Hughes smoked his pipe, studied the ash in the bowl.

"I opt for freedom," he said. "All freedom is relative anyway, isn't it? If it isn't a woman, a boss, a phobia, or some vestigial man of the Gospel circumscribing your movements, it's an island. All right, I'll take the island." He stood up and bowed with simulated formality. "You have my word."

Joe nodded. "All right. Those are the rules. But one slip, Mr. Agent, and back you go into this pokey."

They sealed the bargain with a handshake.

"And now," said Joe, "put on your clothes and I'll show you around. You might like to pick up a little island history from Norman Green."

They walked through the little settlement, to the shore and then to the meadowed slope which rose to the jagged walls of the mountain. A solitary islander was returning from the cliffs, carrying two large birds. Joe explained they were the prized yellow-nosed albatross, which made a tasty dish when cooked in the Tristan manner.

Later Hughes had a long, rambling talk with Norman Green. He learned much about Tristan da Cunha, but heard no hint whatsoever about the identity of "Joe" or other current visitors. The headman, he sensed, felt himself to be an ally in their enterprise, whatever it might be. Norman Green was polite, wry, and garrulous, but when he referred to "the others," as he called them, he spoke with a special respect and restraint. Was it from awe, gratitude, or perhaps fear? Hughes was unsure.

Later he walked to the harbor, noting that the wreckage of his boat already had been pulled to high ground. Near sundown, he went back to Joe's cottage for a nap.

That night he dined with Joe on lobster, island potatoes, and canned peas. Joe was the listener, Hughes the talker. Joe did offer him one dubious compliment. His guest, he said, was the most formidable monologuist he had ever heard. When the dishes were cleared and washed, Joe went out again. He had work at the Mabel Clark, he said.

It was well past midnight when Joe came back, and the two men stood for a few minutes outside the stone cottage. The wind still blew, moist and steady, from the west, but some of the overcast had rolled back, baring a black roadway of sky on which stars lay like phosphorescent pebbles. It was strange, thought Hughes, that he felt himself a friend of this tall, contained man who had not yet disclosed a single thing about himself. The only barrier between them, Hughes intuitively realized, was the caution thrust upon Joe by his Tristan duties.

"I find it impossible to grasp the idea of infinity," said Hughes as they gazed at the night sky. "If there's no end to it all, where does it go? Matter without end is too large a thought for my brain."

Some one approached them in the darkness. He walked with a long stride, but when he saw Hughes, he slowed his pace. He looked from one man to the other, reluctant to speak.

"That's all right," said Joe. "What Mr. Hughes hears, he can't repeat."

"Well . . ." The newcomer was still uncertain. His hands were buried in the pockets of a leather jacket.

"Go ahead, Delaney," said Joe impatiently. "What's up?"

"Somebody's trying to raise us," said Delaney. "They're sending blind without a call sign."

"At this hour, we answer no one, unless it's clearly identified from Tower."

"I know that. This isn't Tower. He's a big one, though. Lots of power. I just thought you ought to know."

"I don't like it," said Joe. "Any idea who it is?"

"No," said Delaney. "First time this has happened."

"Well, nothing to do but keep to the book."

"Right. We won't open up except for Tower and the regular morning exchange with Cape Town."

"Okay. See you in the morning."

The man loped off, cutting behind the cottage in the direction of the radio shack. Joe turned to his guest.

Now, in the dark, for a fraction of a second, something about Joe triggered Hughes's memory. His mind seized on the face, raced for the name tag, then lost it. But the reaction reassured him. He knew he would place the face soon. If not tonight, tomorrow.

"So the idea of infinity bothers you?" asked Joe.

" 'Bother' isn't the right word. Infinity makes me brood, and I don't like to brood. The astrophysicists and the mathematicians contend that they understand infinity. I wonder if they really do?"

"Why do you say that?"

"Well, if there is no end, how could there be a beginning?"

They both stared up at the ribbon of sky where the stars shone with an intensity Hughes had seldom seen in northern latitudes.

"I know a man who thinks the beginning is still ahead of us," said Joe.

"You mean here on earth?"

"Yes." Joe scuffed at a piece of volcanic rock. "He's a remarkable man, but a practical one."

Hughes shifted his gaze from the sky and glanced at Joe.

"Unless you tell me otherwise," he said, "I'd swear I saw two Chinese walking through the village this evening. Did I?"

Joe merely smiled.

"Chinese on Tristan da Cunha," said Hughes. "Communist or Nationalist?"

Joe shook his head. "Sorry, Bill."

"Is one of them your remarkable but practical man?"

Joe put his hand on Hughes's shoulder. "You're forgetting who asks the questions here," he said.

They stood for a moment, then Joe stretched. "Time for bed. We're up too late tonight."

And Joe led his guest back into the stone cottage while the west wind tugged at the thatched roof and whipped across the dark meadows.

Arthur Ingram lingered over his coffee. He had dined alone in the director's private corner of the CIA building in Langley, Virginia. Two tall candles flickered beside the center bowl of yellow chrysanthemums. The gray linen tablecloth was a pleasant complement to the room's grass wallpaper, now laced with soft lights and shadows. The long window offered a view of the dark hills of Langley, and across the Potomac, Ingram could see the household lights of Maryland and the glow over Washington. He lit an after-dinner panetela and smoked quietly for a few minutes as he pondered the messages. Then he switched on the overhead indirect lighting, adjusted his reading glasses, and once again went through the deciphered file.

From: John, Rio
To: Vic, Washington
    Captain of *Casa Alegre* knows Greer whereabouts. Asks $1000. Request permission for payment.
    9/26 1803 Z

From: Vic, Washington
To: John, Rio
    Granted. Hereafter use station funds as necessary. Urgent.
    9/26 1849 Z

From: John, Rio
To: Vic, Washington
    Casa Alegre captain says he transported Greer to island of Tristan da Cunha. My evaluation 1 A. Can charter 18-knot motor vessel to Tristan. Instructions.
    9/27 1411 Z

From: Vic, Washington
To: John, Rio
    Proceed Tristan at once. Report soonest.
    9/27 1501 Z

From: John, Rio
To: Vic, Washington
    Sailing Tristan within hour. Charter cost, round-trip, $28,-000. Ship *Pedro Alfonso*, Brazilian registry. *Pedro*'s radio not reliable. Will report on arrival island via Radio Tristan. Sailing time, five days. Expect my report night of Oct 3 latest.
    9/28 0915 Z

Ingram tapped his glasses on the little stack of messages. Here it was Monday night, October 4, and not a word from "John." He was twenty-four hours past the promised deadline. Ingram smoked some more, savoring the fragrance as a haven from his anxiety, then gathered up the papers and walked down the carpeted hall to his office. The night duty officer nodded as Ingram passed. Otherwise the executive complex was deserted.

In his office, Ingram turned on the desk lamp and sank into one of the brown leather easy chairs. He glanced, as for reassurance, at the eagle and compass emblem of the Agency and the framed quotation from Eisenhower: ". . . heroes are undecorated and unsung . . ." He sat for a while, ordering his thoughts, then walked to the cream-colored switchboard box and buzzed for the night duty officer. In a few seconds a young man stood in the doorway. He was in his shirtsleeves and, in the dim light, he looked both wan and serious.

"Dick, did you ever hear of an island named Tristan da Cunha?" asked Ingram.

"I think so, sir, but I couldn't tell you where it is."

"It's a British possession in the lower South Atlantic. A few hundred people live there. It has government radio facilities. Tell communications I want them to get the call sign and wave length and then see if they can make contact. If so, report back to me."

"Yes, sir."

"And, Dick. I want the contact made direct without identification on our part. Do not go through the British."

"Yes, sir." The young duty officer walked off quickly.

Ingram sorted out his thoughts as he waited. Lady Y's cover had been blown by Gene Culligan, that annoyingly brash White House press secretary. While Culligan had made no specific charge to Miss Nygaard, he obviously believed she worked for the Agency. For one thing, he mentioned the name "Nick" to her. For another, the next day, Saturday, Culligan's secretary, Jill Nichols, moved out abruptly from Butter Nygaard's apartment.

Culligan most certainly had informed the President of his suspicions about Miss Nygaard's connections, but yet . . . why

no word from Roudebush? It was exceedingly strange that Paul
Roudebush, a very direct man, had not called Ingram in three
days. No irate presidential demand for an explanation, no reprimand, no explosion, nothing. Anticipating a summons to the
President's office, Ingram had projected the scene in his mind,
and he knew that no explanation of his would suffice.

No man, even a president, could appreciate the ruthless demands of intelligence unless he had spent years in the craft. An
intelligence agency, to operate effectively, must strive to know all,
everything. It could not be content to hold a mere majority of
the pieces of the puzzle. Intelligence was the most exacting of
professions, far more than the law, medicine, or even the physical
sciences. It worshiped only at the altar of information, and all
human alliances—friends, relatives, lovers—were but conduits for
that devotion. Ingram could see the inscription on the lobby wall
which he passed each morning and night: "And ye shall know the
truth and the truth shall make you free." The God was truth
and His altar was total information. And in his quest, a con-
secrated one, Arthur Ingram knew that he would use and sacrifice
anyone, his own wife if need be.

President Roudebush, of course, would not recognize the need
for such implacable commitment by the intelligence priesthood.
Roudebush would see the Lady Y affair as but flagrantly disloyal
snooping in his own household. He would not appreciate that the
method differed but little, really, from the Agency's operations
on Downing Street, at the Vatican, or inside the Kremlin. Nor
would Roudebush properly weigh the fact that Arthur Ingram
had not intentionally installed a syphon for White House information. The development had been fortuitous, actually. Lady Y's
task was to report what she gleaned from the international
goings and comings of artists and writers at the Spruance-financed
cultural exchange. It was only happenstance that later Miss
Nichols became her roommate. Butter Nygaard was a conscien-
tious, discriminating reporter. She relayed everything of significance and discarded the dross. Indeed, she would have been guilty
of neglect of duty if she had failed to pass on vital information
from any conversation, including those of Miss Nichols.

That, Mr. President, thought Ingram, is the way of intelligence. It is not an odious enterprise, nor a criminal pursuit, but one of diligent craftsmanship . . . yes, of patriotism. . . . And yet, he thought, could he thus explain this case to Paul Roudebush? Of course not. Roudebush was not of the calling.

And what of Stephen Greer? Actually Ingram knew very little, even now. The presidential prohibition had forced him to forgo a general Agency investigation. Ingram had dared use only John, but John, his best South American agent, had been hobbled. Even the best could do little when deprived of leads winnowed from a mass of Agency sources. Ingram knew, via Miss Nygaard, that Dr. Lubin had vanished from Baltimore after almost a year of secret meetings with Greer in an R Street apartment. Now this facet had become the property of the press as well. Ingram also knew that Roudebush withheld contents of FBI reports from his own staff, and that Gene Culligan had threatened to resign over the issue, then agreed to hold off for ten days—Ingram glanced at his desk calendar—five now. What could that mean?

All of this, Ingram recalled, had impelled him to suggest that Miss Nygaard accompany Moffat to Louisville to brief Hillary Kulp for his television speech. President Roudebush, obviously, was going to extraordinary lengths to maintain rigid secrecy on the Greer affair. And if Kulp were to accuse the President of the United States of duplicity, then Kulp's facts must be precise. Ingram believed, and Moffat agreed, that the telephone should not be used. Rather, Butter should talk in person to Kulp so there would be no ambiguity, no errors of fact or assumption. And the trip would have gone off smoothly and discreetly, thought Ingram, if it had not been for Culligan. . . .

There was a rap on the door. It was the young duty officer.

"Radio Tristan does not answer, sir. Communications thinks Tristan may not keep a twenty-four-hour watch. Of course, we could try through the South Africans. I'm told Cape Town has daily contact with Radio Tristan."

"No." Ingram shook his head. "Perhaps tomorrow. . . . And Dick, there's no need to mention this to your relief when he comes on duty."

"How about the office log?"

"No. That won't be necessary."

"Yes, sir."

After the duty officer left, Ingram sat thinking for a few more minutes, then dialed the number of Senator Owen Moffat's home.

A half hour later the Senator entered the office. His smooth face had its usual pink gleam and his suit fit his portly body as neatly as a glove on a hand.

"The nights are getting chilly," he said after the greetings. "I could use a drink."

"The usual?" At Moffat's nod, Ingram went to the cherry table, with marble top, and poured two scotch and sodas. He handed the one of darker color to Moffat. The men seated themselves in two leather armchairs faced toward the long window and its view of the wooded hills and the lights of Washington in the distance. The desk lamp's stunted glow left most of the room in shadow.

"Any word from Roudebush yet?" asked Moffat.

"Not a word," said Ingram. "I'm at a loss to explain it."

"I think it's plain enough," said Moffat. "If he were to face you with Miss Nygaard's activities, the affrontery to him would be laid bare. As a human being, he couldn't take that. In a word, he would be forced to fire you. And that, at this stage of the campaign, Paul Roudebush can't afford to risk. You're too popular with the Congress and the country."

"But the silence," insisted Ingram, "does not fit his character."

And what about Arthur Ingram's character, thought Moffat. He had known the director for many years, but only in recent days had he come to understand the depth of Ingram's obsession for his office. Ingram appeared willing to go to any length in this weird Greer case—even permitting Miss Nygaard to accompany Moffat to Louisville for the briefing of Hillary Kulp. What was Arthur's hidden, driving motive? Was it professional outrage at being forbidden to join the FBI hunt for Greer? Some deep antipathy for Roudebush personally? Or a monumental zest for collecting information?

In the rules of politics, he, Moffat, could do anything, from fair

to almost foul, to defeat Paul Roudebush. That was the way the
game was played. But Ingram! After all, Arthur was Roudebush's
intelligence chief, a member of the President's National Security
Council, a shining adornment of the official White House family.

"What about the Kulp speech?" asked Ingram.

Moffat ignored the question, continuing to study his man.
Stanley Wolcott had given his secret pledge to Ingram to retain
him as CIA director in event of Wolcott's election. But, wondered
Moffat, if Ingram would betray Roudebush now, what might he
do at some future date with a new president—Stanley Wolcott?
Moffat was not at all sure now that he had been right in urging
that Wolcott make the pledge to Ingram. An Ingram disloyal
once, an Ingram perhaps disloyal again.

"The Kulp speech, Owen," insisted Ingram.

"Oh yes," said Moffat. "Sorry, Arthur, my mind was on something else for a minute. . . . Well, this second postponement was
at my insistence. I thought it would be unwise to go off half-
cocked when there was a real possibility of something definite.
But it's all arranged now for Thursday night. All networks at
seven o'clock eastern daylight. Prime time. . . . Now it all depends on you—and 'John.'"

Ingram shook his glass as he held it on the arm of his chair.
"That's my trouble, Owen. I haven't heard from John. He's far
overdue."

He described the Agency's unsuccessful effort to make contact
with Radio Tristan.

"I'm in the dark," said Ingram. "Perhaps John is on the island,
but the transmitter is out. Perhaps he never reached Tristan. Perhaps . . . well, I don't like it."

"How about talking to that ship? What's its name, *Pedro* something?"

"I tried that earlier." Ingram shook his head and brooded over
his whisky. "John warned me that the ship's radio was not reliable. No contact. Of course, we could query the Navy's seascope
in Norfolk for the *Pedro Alfonso's* position, but under the circumstances, I think that would be highly inadvisable."

"You're right. Not only inadvisable, but hazardous. . . . Arthur, are you sure that other ship, the *Casa* what's-it, took Greer to Tristan? How can you be positive?"

"I trust John," said Ingram. "He gave the information the highest evaluation, 1 A. As you know, that means he places top confidence on the reliability of his source and on the accuracy of the information itself. After all, he paid $1000 to the *Casa Alegre*'s captain, who said he took Greer to Tristan and whose obligation to Greer was ended. The captain might have lied, but John can spot a liar in four languages."

"Tristan," mused Moffat. "I've read everything I could find about that island since you told me. It makes no sense at all. Why would Greer and Lubin go to some God-forsaken hunk of lava, a thousand miles plus from nowhere?"

Ingram made a cautioning gesture with his glass. "Careful, Owen. We have no knowledge that Lubin went to Tristan da Cunha. In fact, we have no idea where he went. All we know is that he disappeared, and that the FBI is following him as closely, apparently, as it is Stephen Greer."

"Yes," said Moffat. "And, of course, how do we explain Roudebush's apparent confidence that he will have good news in a few days? His treatment of Culligan surely points to that."

"You know my theory, Owen," said Ingram.

And once again Ingram reviewed and updated his hypotheses. Stephen Greer and Phillip Lubin were homosexuals who had carried on a secret liaison for a year on R Street. Somehow Paul Roudebush had learned of this, had summoned Greer to the White House that Tuesday night in late August, confronted his friend with the evidence. Both men knew that a public revelation would severely damage, perhaps destroy, Roudebush's re-election chances. Greer, in an emotional welter, agreed to break off the liaison. Then, two days later, Greer collapsed under the tension and fled the country. Lubin, distraught, unable to work, also decided to go away. Greer, taking a large amount of cash from his office safe, intended to hide out in Brazil. But when the FBI —reluctantly assigned to the case by Roudebush—trailed him to Rio de Janeiro, Greer chartered a lobster trawler and sailed for the lonely island of Tristan da Cunha. There, through money or threats, he persuaded island authorities to keep his presence a secret. But President Roudebush had learned from the FBI where Greer was hiding, had dispatched someone to bring him back to the United States. If successful in persuading him to return, the President would announce that Greer had been on a secret mission for him—a president had an infinite range of missions to choose from. But if he refused to return, Roudebush would be forced to tell the country the truth about his friend, hoping for a surge of sympathy for the President among the voters. So, either way, Roudebush expected to be able to clear up the matter within a few days.

"You know I don't hold with that," said Moffat when Ingram finished. "It takes no account of Dr. Lubin. Why would Lubin disappear just because Greer did, even assuming your analysis of their relationship is correct? . . . No, I still think there is either an imminent financial scandal involving Greer, Lubin, and Educational Micro in some bizarre way, or both men are engaged on some secret mission for the President, the results of which Roudebush is about to reveal triumphantly to the country."

"The world has become too small for secret missions," said Ingram. "It would be impossible to carry on that kind of thing without some glimmer reaching this agency. . . . As for the financial angle, Owen, there is just not a shred of evidence."

Moffat took a swallow of his scotch and soda, then leaned forward and tapped his glass on Ingram's knee.

"The fact is, Arthur," he said, "that we know very little for certain. In such a situation, Stanley Wolcott must protect himself against all possible developments. I've talked this over carefully with Matty Silkworth and we are agreed. Actually, Arthur, I was about to call you when you phoned. Matty thought it was vital that I talk to you tonight." He paused. "There is only one weapon that can give Wolcott full protection at this time. . . . And it is a weapon that only you, Arthur, can provide."

"And what is that?" A taut, wary look took over.

"Your resignation," said Moffat.

"Resign!" Ingram looked like a man singled out for human sacrifice.

"Yes, resign," repeated Moffat in a firm voice. This was the instant of test, he thought. If Ingram agreed, abandoning the Roudebush administration to which he owed allegiance, Moffat would never trust him again. And if he refused, Moffat's covert political link to Ingram would be severed.

In the silence, Moffat watched an expression of consternation settle on Ingram's face. Moffat sighed. He knew that Ingram would have to accept. Ingram was in too deep now. He had dealt secretly with the opposition and, in so doing, he had rendered himself pitifully vulnerable. The name of the game, thought Moffat with a twinge of regret, was blackmail. An old-fashioned word, but apt.

"I'm afraid I don't understand," said Ingram.

Oh, but you do, thought Moffat. You understand perfectly. He felt like a judge passing an already anticipated sentence on the convicted man.

"You see, Arthur," he said, "since we know few facts, we must base our case to the public on the perfidy of Paul Roudebush. His best friend has fled abroad. That, at least, is one fact we can use. Stephen Greer, entrusted with vital security information, has abandoned his country. In this crucial situation, President Roudebush relies entirely on the FBI, a largely domestic agency, to trace his friend. Why hasn't he enlisted the services of the one organization, the Central Intelligence Agency, equipped by statute and by long experience to gather information outside the United States? Why has he rejected the offer of the eminent director of this agency to muster the far-flung and superb talents of the CIA in the search for Stephen Greer? Is Paul Roudebush endangering the security of the United States just to protect a friend and win an election? . . .

"Arthur Ingram asked himself this question and then—patriot that he is—when no answer came, he submitted his resignation. He could do no less. Arthur Ingram could not live with his conscience or his honor were he to remain passive and silent when a president flouted minimum precautions for this nation's security."

"You sound as though you're delivering Hillary Kulp's television speech," said Ingram. He nervously moistened his lips, then took a sip of his drink.

"I am." Moffat smiled. "Matty and I lined up a few key points on the telephone. Kulp will announce, subject to your assent, of course, that you submitted your resignation to President Roudebush just a few hours before Mr. Kulp went before the television cameras. . . . Then you can gain us more mileage, speaking for yourself, on a Sunday panel show." Moffat leaned toward Ingram again. "As I say, as a man of honor, you can do no less, Arthur, and you know it."

"I hadn't considered such an extreme move," said Ingram. In his voice was the flaking of dry leaves.

"That surprises me, Arthur," said Moffat. "You have put your best years into this splendid agency. Your offer to throw the worldwide energies of the CIA into the search for Greer has been spurned by Paul Roudebush. My formal language may have sounded overly dramatic. But it did not misstate the facts."

"That's all true." But there was no pride in Ingram's expression. He was a man in distress.

"Politically, of course," pursued Moffat in a confidential tone, "your resignation could just be the one event that put Wolcott over the top. You know, without my telling you, of your standing with Congress, with the men who mold the news in this city, yes, with the public. I am not appealing to vanity when I say that no other . . ." The word "defection" came to Moffat's lips, but he repelled it. ". . . no other resignation in the Roudebush administration would have the shock value of yours. Frankly, Arthur, it would be a sensation."

"Does Stanley Wolcott know of this . . . uh . . . suggestion?" asked Ingram.

"No, the idea was worked out by Silkworth, Kulp, and me. I think Wolcott will be as surprised as the country. But pleasantly surprised, of course. He has given you his word that you will be his CIA director. In essence, then, you will merely take a vacation of a little more than three months, a vacation you deserve, Arthur."

Ingram arose and walked to the long window overlooking the parapet of the building and the dark hills.

"Of course, we should realize," said Moffat dryly, "that if Roudebush is re-elected, your vacation would be considerably more extended. The exact word is 'permanent.' After the episode of Lady Y, to say nothing of Maury Rimmel, the locker room secret agent, I would think Roudebush would fire you within days of his re-election."

Ingram stood with his back to Moffat, shaking his glass slightly. He was silhouetted in a fringe of light from the low desk lamp. Ingram took a long swallow of the scotch and placed the glass on the window ledge. He turned to face Moffat.

"Give me until tomorrow morning to think it over," he said. "This is quite sudden, Owen."

Moffat shook his head. "I'm to call Matty with your answer by midnight. If you say no, well then, we'll have to make other arrangements. We would feel compelled to tell the country our source for certain information. You and I know who that source is. . . . There isn't time, Arthur."

Moffat avoided looking at Ingram. He knew there could be but one answer. Moffat was no sadist. He had no desire to witness the crumbling of a man. The dead quiet was unbroken for a long minute.

"All right, then," said Ingram. His voice was flat, dry. "I'll resign this week. I leave it to you and Silkworth as to the day and hour."

Moffat reached out his hand. The clasp was only momentary and for once Ingram's grip was less than firm.

"Thanks, Arthur," said Moffat. "We'll never forget what you've done."

Never, thought Moffat, never. He left the room across the soft, deep carpeting. In the outer office, he passed the hooded typewriters, the locked safes, and the translucent trash baskets with their admonition, BURN, in red letters.

In the brightly lighted corridor, Moffat turned to look at the director's yellow door and the discreet, black sign, "7D60, DCI."

This yellow door had opened on the eyrie of Washington's

second most powerful official. It had closed on a man dispossessed. Politics had its brutal, naked moments. Moffat shrugged. He had done what he had to do. Arthur Ingram was in his pocket.

Senator Owen Moffat walked swiftly to the elevator, his footsteps echoing in the corridor.

17

Captain A. Harry Cooledge, USN, stood on the port wing of the bridge, bracing his legs to accommodate the slight roll of the big carrier. Through his aviator's sunglasses, the sea and sky had an amber cast and he could feel the rush of salt air on his face. The temperature was sixty-seven degrees, the sun shone high and huge in the east, the choppy seas frisked like white rabbits before a following breeze, and the air was newly gentle and fresh. It was a spring morning in the horse latitudes and, since he had crossed these seas only once before, years ago, Captain Cooledge felt the pleasure of rediscovery.

To his right was the vast, open silence of the South Atlantic, relieved only by the familiar shape of one of his flanking destroyers and by the hiss and splash below as the *Franklin D. Roosevelt* carved through the water at the high speed of twenty-five knots. The ship vibrated with its steady effort and Cooledge could feel the quiver in his legs. From below the carrier's island came the rattle of morning chores along the reach of the flight deck. Harry Cooledge leaned over the rail and looked down on the roof of his domain.

Once again he studied the extra planes, an unusual addition to CVA 42, whose normal complement was four squadrons of jet fighters and attack bombers. Aft of the ship's island, tailed out over the starboard deck edge, two large transports were blocked and tied. They were strange obstacles for a carrier deck, but positioned as they were, limited flight operations could still be conducted. When and if flown, the transports could be wheeled aft and their takeoff assisted by JATO gear. Once aloft, they could not return, for their undercarriage was not built to withstand the shock of flight deck landings.

Near the passenger planes, three helicopters were tethered, their great blades poised above the mole-like fuselages. The choppers had spent most of the nine-day voyage from Mayport, Florida, below decks and had been brought up only yesterday. The transports, however, had made the trip on the open deck, for their wings, unlike the folding species of carrier planes, were rigid, the span too wide for the ship's elevators.

Cooledge glanced at his wrist watch. The Officer of the Deck, although engrossed in the conn of the ship, caught the captain's movement and volunteered: "It's eleven hundred, sir."

Cooledge nodded. . . . 1100 Greenwich time. By the navigator's calculation, they should be reaching Point Alpha about now. Yes, any minute now, if the navigator had correctly judged his winds and currents, they should reach Latitude 30 degrees south and Longitude 15 degrees west.

A minute later, the navigator, a tall commander who, like his captain, wore his khaki shirt open at the neck, appeared at Cooledge's side.

"Point Alpha, sir," he said, "give or take a quarter of a mile."

"Good," said Cooledge. "Round up the exec and come along to my in-port cabin."

Cooledge, followed by his omnipresent Marine orderly, walked aft along the carrier island and down four decks to the quarters where he lived and slept. The Marine took up a guard position outside the door.

The cabin was decorated in rich browns, the bulkheads paneled, and the heavy furniture bolted to the deck with brass fittings. Beside his desk stood a small safe. Cooledge turned the dial to the proper combination and took out a long envelope. In one corner was a stamped, red legend: TOP SECRET. The envelope was addressed to "Captain A. Harry Cooledge, USN. To be opened on arrival at Point Alpha."

The Marine orderly entered and saluted. "Commanders Fifield and Ogden to see you, sir." Cooledge nodded and called toward the door: "Come in, gentlemen."

He motioned the officers to chairs. "Now, let's see what this mystery is all about."

He slit open the envelope with a dolphin-shaped letter opener, took out a single sheet of paper, and silently read:

From: Chief of Naval Operations

To: Commanding Officer, USS *Franklin D. Roosevelt* (CVA 42)

Subj: Operations CVA 42

1. By separate correspondence you have received orders to proceed at best speed to Point Alpha.

2. If you have received duly authenticated orders to the contrary prior to reaching Point Alpha, disregard and destroy this letter. Otherwise you are to:

    A. Proceed to Point Bravo, a point 30 miles due north of the island of Tristan da Cunha. Maintain a position within 25 miles of this point while remaining outside visual range of the island.

    B. Proceed in order to arrive at Point Bravo at 060900 Z October.

    C. Maintain complete electronic silence until further advised.

3. Amplifying instructions will be sent you at Point Bravo.

                          M. R. Freestone

Cooledge pulled a nautical chart toward him, studied it a minute, measured with thumb and forefinger, then telephoned the Officer of the Deck on the bridge: "Set a new course of one-seven-zero and reduce speed to 20 knots."

The captain handed the sheet of orders to his executive officer. "Read them aloud, Fife," he said. "There's no ban on briefing my staff."

The executive officer read slowly without emphasis. He could have been ticking off a grocery list.

"I estimate it's roughly 480 miles to the island," said the captain. "Reduced to 20 knots, we should reach Point Bravo about oh-nine-three-oh Zulu tomorrow. That sound right to you, Pat?"

"Let me see, sir." The navigator bent over the chart, slipped a pair of dividers from his shirt pocket and ran down the line of the ship's new course.

"That's about it," he said. "Maybe a few minutes later if we get the expected westerlies farther down instead of this breeze from the north."

"Well," said Cooledge, "let's keep 20 knots for the time being. Then you work out our course and speed to have us reach Bravo on time."

Cooledge leaned back in his chair. "So what do we make of it?" he asked. "I must say I expected more definite word on reaching Alpha. Now, as I get it, I'm supposed to tread water near Tristan da Cunha until Mal Freestone decides to let me in on his secret."

"My first blind voyage," said the navigator.

Cooledge cocked an eyebrow at him. Commander Ogden, he knew, was a mystery story addict whose cabin was stocked with paperback whodunits. He suspected his navigator deplored the lack of intrigue in shipboard routine.

"Yes," said Cooledge, "mine too. But I can't say I like it. Twenty-six years out of the Academy, I prefer facts to guesswork."

They speculated on possibilities. Captain Cooledge wondered if some antarctic expedition were being assembled. But if so, why the secrecy? The navigator mentioned two African bush wars. Perhaps a space capsule of advanced design had been launched surreptitiously, offered the exec, and the carrier was to stand by for recovery operations. The suggestions were all vaguely dissatisfying. None had the print of reality.

"Or maybe it has something to do with Stephen Greer," said the navigator.

"I thought of that," said Cooledge, "but what would be our connection?"

The three men looked at one another, but the question went unanswered. The Greer episode, which figured daily in the ship's radio news digest, seemed a thing apart, bizarre, alien to Navy business.

"It's pretty obvious," said the executive officer, "that we may be asked to launch the transports. You suppose we may ferry some people from Tristan da Cunha in the choppers, then transfer them to the transports?"

"Mmm." Cooledge swung his flight glasses in a slow arc. "It's true Tristan has no airfield, but there's no problem with choppers."

"But how do the new passengers fit into the deal?" asked the navigator.

Cooledge looked at the exec. "Yes. When are they due, Fife?"

"Couple of more hours," said the exec. "Fourteen hundred, to be exact. . . . A bit hairy. With no position reports from us, CNO had to trust us to make Alpha on schedule."

There was the smallest of rebukes in Cooledge's glance. He was always on schedule, radio blackout or not.

"Two men, is it?" he asked.

"Two men, sir. No names. They're being flown from Rio in two twin-seat attack planes with extra fuel tanks."

"Damn peculiar," said Cooledge. "What they've got to do with this mission is beyond me. . . . Well, maybe they can enlighten us. If not, we should learn something tomorrow morning."

"Unless CNO lets us circle around for a week without orders," said the navigator. The prospect seemed to please him.

"Mal Freestone wouldn't do that to me," said Cooledge. But his quick frown hinted that he was less than certain. "So much for guesswork. . . . What does the weather look like farther down, Pat?"

"Pretty good, according to aerology," replied the navigator. "It was blowing some, but I understand the winds have calmed."

Cooledge stood up, signaling the end of the meeting. "Back to the salt mines," he said. "Twenty knots and present course until you work it out, Pat. Then let me know."

Alone again, Cooledge reread his orders once more, then placed them back in the safe. After puttering about his desk for a few minutes, he climbed the four flights to the bridge and stood watching the long swells of the sea.

Now what? From the moment he prepared to sail, this had been a strange voyage. First, at Mayport, the special passenger planes were hoisted aboard and the ship provisioned for a long trip. He had been informed he was sailing for protracted training exercises off the Florida coast. But, the second day at sea when the air wing flew out to join the ship, the wing commander came immediately to his cabin and handed him sealed orders. When Cooledge opened them, he found that this was no training cruise. Instead he was to set a course for the southeast, destination Point Alpha in the far South Atlantic, which he was to reach about noon, Tuesday, October 5.

This meant twenty-five knots, a high speed to maintain continuously for nine days, especially for an elderly carrier like the FDR. The orders also imposed a strict radio silence on CVA 42, an extraordinary restriction for a carrier in peacetime for so prolonged a time. . . . And inside the orders was the special top secret envelope, to be opened only at Point Alpha. That too was highly unusual, encountered frequently enough in war games, but never to his knowledge on such a solo voyage.

The huge, factory-sized crew, numbering 3700 hands when air wing personnel were added, buzzed with rumors. The men studied the daily bulletin of news from the carrier's radio, seeking a framework of international crisis for the *Roosevelt*'s swift, unknown, and silent mission. For the men soon learned that the ship's radio was not transmitting. It received, of course, but it did not send, and the crew could not answer emergency family messages. Cooledge noted that men eyed the bridge more frequently these days as if a glimpse of the captain might provide some clue.

And still another odd order. He was instructed to avoid being sighted at sea if at all possible. Several times, when the radar picked up a ship that would intersect the FDR's course, Cooledge had veered off, temporarily altering course, then increasing speed to compensate for the detour.

So what could his mission be? Like his navigator, Captain Cooledge could not shake thoughts of the baffling Greer case. It continued to dominate the general news which Navy radio dispersed daily to the fleet. Was Greer somehow involved in an international incident that was simmering toward a climax outside the public's ken?

The air wing which flew aboard off the Florida coast had surprised Cooledge. It was composed chiefly of veteran pilots, most of whom had flown in combat. Actually, the wing was the most highly skilled outfit in the Atlantic fleet. Furthermore, his ammunition, both for the planes and for the ship's guns, was a wartime allotment. CVA 42 was ready for battle. . . . Yet, what of those two transports? They were new, capable of extended range and speed. Could they be masks for his mission? Certainly, if action came, the passenger planes would have to be flown off at once.

Still, Cooledge realized, he really knew very little. His good friend, Mal Freestone, the chief of naval operations, had sent him speeding off to the south, to the balmy horse latitudes and thence to the waters of a small, lonely British island. And what was he to do there?

If an important aspect of his trip was total blackout, he was in luck. The FDR had not been sighted visually by a single ship since leaving U.S. coastal waters. He may have been picked up by radar, but he doubted it. His radar could outrange those of all but a few ships at sea. When a blip appeared, he had changed course at once. That probably meant he was unreported and not appearing on the seascope at CINCLANT's Movement Reports Center in Norfolk. He was a ghost ship hurrying toward a tiny island in far southern waters.

Cooledge stared at the seas, empty save for the escorting destroyers and their wakes. The sun flooded the sky into a bowl of hazy white. There were no clouds and hardly a trace of blue. Tomorrow, his station near Tristan da Cunha.

It was a routine Tuesday afternoon at the Movement Reports Center of the Atlantic Fleet in Norfolk, Virginia.

Lieutenant (jg) Preston Armitage, USN, sat in his dark cubbyhole before the seascope and ran through his daily exercise. The

screen before him was about the size of a large household television set. The work was tedious and young Armitage fought to
suppress a yawn.

By the press of a button, Armitage could bring into focus any
section of the vast Atlantic expanses, from an area as large as half
of the North or South Atlantic to one as small as one hundred
miles square of ocean. The seascope was the visual funnel from
the huge "160" computer which digested all marine reports,
from whatever source, and calculated the position of every ship
afloat in the two Atlantics, hour by hour. A staff of young officers
programmed the position reports into the computer from a host
of sources—commercial departures, radio relays of sightings at sea,
S.O.S.'s, and, the great bulk of traffic, the position estimates sent
at regular intervals by all ships large enough to carry radio trans-
mitters. In an emergency, such as the Cuban missile crisis of 1962,
the seascope became a valuable intelligence aid. In a war at sea, it
would prove a bulwark of U.S. defenses. But in the ordinary, long,
dull days of peacetime, the seascope served chiefly as a facility to
hasten the rescue of disabled ships and as a training device for
its operators.

Lieutenant (jg) Armitage's task during his two-hour shift—two
on and one off to guard against drowsiness—was to report to the
operations desk any ship movement which seemed to him to be
other than routine. The seascope had no miraculous powers of
vision. It merely reflected on its screen the calculations of the
computer. But an alert officer could sometimes find an unusual
pattern on the scope. In more than a year on the job, Armitage
had met with such success just twice. Once he had deduced that
two Russian submarines, one traveling south and one cruising
north, probably would meet for maneuvers off the North Carolina
coast. As a result, Navy antisubmarine patrol planes were dispatched to the area to play cat-and-mouse games with the Soviets.
Again, Armitage had divined that a British freighter, unreported
off the Azores for a full day, might be in distress with her transmitter out. Investigating planes from the Azores found the ship
wallowing out of control, fighting a fire. All hands were rescued,

and Armitage received a letter of commendation for his service jacket. But these were the exceptions in the long, dark hours hunched over the scope. The trick was to stay taut and to remember that only he could supply the human intuition to the computer's cold, diagrammatic pictures. With every flick of the button, focusing on a new area of ocean, Armitage forced himself to ask the same question: What is peculiar about this picture?

This afternoon Armitage was making his methodical sweep of the South Atlantic in blocks of five hundred miles square when, in the block just east of the remote island of Tristan da Cunha, he saw two objects that caught his interest. Ships appeared on the screen as dots with accompanying arrows indicating the ships' courses. Each dot also carried a letter-number designation assigned to it by the computer.

Now Armitage saw the two dots east of Tristan. They were about two hundred miles apart. One dot was moving to the west, the other to the south. The course arrows indicated the ships might be headed for the island of Tristan. One dot bore the designation X 114, the other M 276. The computer assigned X to warships, M to merchant vessels. It occurred to Armitage that he had encountered one of these ships before and had queried the computer about it. He could not be sure. In a day, he scanned hundreds of ships. Still, there was that nag of memory.

On the side panel keyboard, Armitage pressed the X button, then the figures one, one, and four. This was equivalent to asking the computer: "Please give me your stored data on Ship X 114."

A reply appeared almost instantaneously in a corner of the seascope's screen:

X 114. The Szerzhinski. USSR guided missile cruiser of the Sverdlov class. Nine 6-inch guns. Twin guided missile launchers. 15,500 tons displacement. Left Gulf of Finland Sept. 18, destination unknown. Three visual sightings. (Here the computer gave latitude and longitude of the three Atlantic sightings.) South Atlantic course about 180. Estimated speed 23 knots. Maintaining radio silence.

Armitage copied the information on his scratch pad, then pushed another set of buttons on the side panel. Again the computer answered within a second, flashing its information in white letters on the gray screen:

M 276. The Ho P'ing Hao, People's Republic of China merchant vessel, Diesel-powered, 15,000 tons. Sailed Shanghai Sept. 11, cargo unknown, destination unknown. One sighting South Atlantic. (The position was given.) Course 269. Estimated speed 14 knots. No recorded radio transmission.

Armitage copied this message verbatim, then flicked the scope back to the five-hundred-mile square block to the east of Tristan. He pondered the picture. Only two vessels in the area, both Communist ships, both strangely far from home, both avoiding use of the air waves and—yes—both apparently headed for the island of Tristan where, save for an infrequent South African freighter bringing mail and supplies, only fishing vessels and lobster trawlers normally cruised.

Armitage turned the scope over to his assistant, an ensign, and walked up to the operations balcony, where officers worked behind a glass partition.

At the duty officer's desk, Armitage handed his slips of paper to the lieutenant commander. The duty officer looked up inquiringly after reading the two notes.

"Both ships are in the block east of Tristan da Cunha," said Armitage. "They appear to be converging on the island. Could be chance, of course, but also it might be funny business."

The duty officer scratched at his chin. "Yeah," he said, "those two babies aren't renowned for joint maneuvers—and a cruiser and a freighter at that. You suppose they're going to have a Red picnic on that island? British, isn't it?"

Armitage nodded. The duty officer picked up his phone and dialed a number.

"Captain Jetter? . . . This is Frazier, sir, on the ops desk. Our eagle-eyed jg, Armitage, has spotted something peculiar on the one-sixty." He explained, then read the computer's data on the two ships. "Yes, sir. . . . All right, sir."

328   VANISHED

He looked up at Armitage. "He's going to query the British liaison officer. Hang around. Let's see what's up."

The two officers passed a few minutes in desultory conversation before the lieutenant commander's phone rang again.

"I see, sir. . . . Of course." He placed his hand over the mouthpiece. "Any other ships in the area?" he asked Armitage. The younger officer shook his head. The duty officer conferred a moment longer with his superior.

"The captain," he said, "wants you to re-cover all sides of Tristan. See if there's anything else around."

Armitage returned to his screen and focused the scope on a large segment of ocean surrounding Tristan da Cunha. His survey this time embraced a huge square, 1200 miles on a side, with Tristan in the center. He made one inquiry of the computer, jotted down his notes, and reported to the duty desk.

"Only one other ship within six hundred miles of Tristan," he reported, "and that doesn't seem to be involved. It's a small motor job named the *Pedro Alfonso*. It's on a probable course for Rio and is almost out of the area. It got off one weak position report to Rio a couple of hours ago. Having transmission trouble, I guess."

The duty officer relayed the information to his superior, then listened again with the receiver propped between ear and shoulder while he doodled on the edge of a chart. "Yes, sir," he concluded.

"Problems," he said to Armitage. "Captain Jetter says British liaison reports Tristan's transmitter is apparently down. . . . You're to give extra attention to that sector, reporting anything new on M 276 and X 114."

"Right," said Armitage. "But I'll bet that's all we'll get. The ships aren't sending and there's nothing else afloat around there to report on them."

"Well, do your best," said the duty officer. "The way to keep me happy, Armitage, is to keep the captain happy. Happiness is a soft, warm topside."

"Happiness," amended Armitage, "is thirty days leave. I'm overdue."

This whole exchange had been attentively followed by an Air Force major at the next desk. He was the liaison officer at CINCLANT's Movement Center who represented the DIA— Defense Intelligence Agency. The major, a tub of a man who waged his private war against calories, was entitled to all information flowing through the center, but experience had taught him that he often learned faster by eavesdropping than he did by formal request. The Navy tolerated him as a bureaucratic interloper and often took its own good time clarifying marine matters for a landlubber.

As Armitage walked back to his dark cubbyhole and his tryst with the computer, the major picked up his direct phone to DIA, the Pentagon, Washington. He turned his back to the Navy duty officer and spoke in a low voice.

"Let me have General Palfrey, please." He waited a moment, then said: "General? This is Major Spear at CINCLANT. The Navy has spotted a couple of Communist ships, one Soviet cruiser and a Chicom merchant vessel, apparently making for an island called Tristan da Cunha in the South Atlantic." He repeated the descriptions, course, and speed of the vessels as best he could remember. "It's got the Navy in a minor flap, sir. They've queried British liaison and found that Tristan's radio is out of commission. I'll get the whole poop later, of course, but thought you ought to know soonest. . . . Yes, sir. . . . I'll keep on top of it, sir."

And below the gallery, beyond the glass partition, the 160 computer toiled away, its electrical charges hurrying through a million invisible gates, entering this one, shunning that one. It went tirelessly about its task of monitoring the two Atlantics, tracking all the ships at sea. Or, as Captain Cooledge of the *Franklin D. Roosevelt* had surmised—almost all the ships at sea.

Arthur Ingram was listening intently to his Chinese evaluation chief, a tall, bony professor who spoke to the point with none of the ambiguities common to the jargon of fellow government theoreticians.

From the battery of telephones on the cabinet behind Ingram came a demanding drone. Ingram knew the sound. It was his green phone, the direct, scrambled line to the Defense Intelligence Agency at the Pentagon.

"Pardon me a moment, Jeff," said Ingram.

Without further sign, Dr. Geoffrey Page, the Chinese specialist, left the room, closing the door behind him.

Ingram lifted the receiver and heard the cathedral greeting of the DIA chief, Lieutenant General Marvin Palfrey.

"What do we know about a couple of Communist ships, one of them a Soviet cruiser, heading toward the island of Tristan da Cunha in the South Atlantic?" asked the general.

Tristan! The name jarred Ingram. He hesitated while his mind made swift adjustment to the news. "Nothing, Marvin," he said. He hoped he did not sound testy, but it annoyed him to confess less than omniscience to a rival intelligence baron. "Could you explain, please."

Palfrey relayed the information given him by his Air Force major. "Apparently it has the CINCLANT boys in a mild panic down there," concluded Palfrey.

"I shouldn't wonder," said Ingram, stalling. His mind raced now. Stephen Greer on Tristan . . . the island's radio either out of commission or pointedly refusing to receipt for messages . . . no word from John.

"Do these ships fit any pattern you have in your shop?" asked Palfrey.

"No," said Ingram. That, he thought, was no lie. There had been no Agency assessment, no formal amalgam of information, no estimate. He had only his private communications with John —and his hunch.

"Don't you think we'd better scrape together whatever we have?" asked Palfrey. "I'd like to be prepared in case the President calls. And he may, you know, what with Norfolk in a sweat. . . . Of course, it may just be coincidence. It's a helluva big ocean. Still, it smells a little strange. Don't you think so, Arthur?"

"I do. Tell you what, Marvin. Let me put out a dragnet right now, and I'll get back to you as soon as I can."

"Fine," said Palfrey. "I've got a golf date at 4:30 out at Burning Tree, but I'll have a messenger stand by at the clubhouse. I can be back at the phone within ten minutes."

"Don't worry." Ingram was as relieved at the prospect of the general's golf as Palfrey seemed pleased. Ingram wanted to pursue this new line quickly and independently. "There's probably some answer to this. At any rate, I'll see what we have."

"Thanks, Arthur," said Palfrey. "We don't want to get caught out in the rain with no clothes on."

When Ingram hung up, he walked to the door and beckoned Geoffrey Page from the outer waiting room. The Chinese expert's analysis now assumed new significance.

Page, thought Ingram, was one of the few truly brilliant men he knew. Still under forty, indefatigable, surgically clean in his logic, infused with a youthful zeal, Page was Ingram's own find. He was proud to have lured Page from Academe to the Agency.

"And so," said Page in his clipped accent, "there appears no doubt that the Defense Minister and General Feng are operating in concert. One of two possibilities seem clearly indicated. First, the minister and the general are mounting a power display to impress both the people and the Premier that strength and truth —truth as revealed in the old Gospel according to Mao Tse-tung —are in their possession. If that possibility is the correct analysis, then we're in for a lengthy period of unrest while the three principals maneuver for public support. . . . The second possibility is that the minister and the general are prepared for a military coup that could materialize at any time."

"And you favor the second line?" asked Ingram.

"I do, Arthur," replied Page. "If we analyze this week's reports from our agents on the ground, we find that five of the six mesh almost completely—and frankly, my confidence in Number Six has never been overwhelming."

"Nor has mine."

"Good man for collecting the obvious," said Page, "but less than adequate when it comes to motives and clashes of policy. . . . But our five are persuaded that the Premier's line since late June of relative friendship toward the United States—and in present-day China a lack of belligerency must be so interpreted—has left the people confused. It came too suddenly. Also, it has enraged General Feng and the defense minister, old Maoists to the core. Furthermore, all five agents believe that the general and the minister have the heavy backing of the armed forces and that recent moves indicate a coup could be imminent. I must say that I agree."

"You never hesitate to stick your neck out, Jeff," said Ingram with admiration.

"It can only be chopped off once," said Page. He grinned. "And I'd rather leave the Agency bloodied than bland."

"Why do you think the Premier has indulged in this long calm? We're into the fourth month now without the propaganda bomb-rattling of Peking—and with only one nuclear test."

"I think Wang Kwo-P'ing is a man of wisdom and sanity," said Page. "The Premier believes it is time that Red China cease flirting with global obliteration."

"But," protested Ingram, "you guided the preparation of the NIE last month, and that concluded that Wang's government was trying to help re-elect President Roudebush."

"Right," said Page. "But the Premier's politics on this point stem from his deeper hankering for peace. As I say, he's a wise man. . . . And don't forget, Stanley Wolcott is an unknown quantity to him."

Ingram had an impulse to ask Page's advice on this newest, confusing development . . . a Chinese merchant ship and a Russian cruiser heading toward a lonely island where Stephen Greer undoubtedly could be found. But Ingram resisted the impulse. There were too many facets, too many personal conflicts. He would have to think this through himself.

"It's a pity that Freytag and his NSA magicians haven't been able to break the new Chinese codes," said Ingram instead. "If so, we might have some confirmation of your analysis. If a coup is imminent, there must be telltale messages on the military radio."

"Agreed," said Page. "And I might add that the President's cancellation of Flycatcher has left the Agency with a deafened ear. It's not only our lack of contact with the few physicists who manage to get into China, but with those scientists around the world who keep abreast of Chinese politics. Flycatcher was paying off. We were getting some valuable tips."

Ingram nodded. "President Roudebush, I'm sorry to say, does not understand the first elements of sound intelligence," he said grimly. "But what's done is done." He pondered a moment.

"Jeff, I think we'd better have a crash NIE on this China situation. Could you muster your crew and give us a working paper by—let's see—tomorrow noon?"

"Sure," Page's assent was enthusiastic.

"Good. If a coup is probable, the President must be informed at once. But I don't want to cock the hammer unless we're sure of ourselves." He smiled. "You know, you could be wrong, Jeff— for the first time. At any rate, I'll feel better with a formal assessment and concurrence by the intelligence board. Noon tomorrow, then?"

"Can do."

And Dr. Geoffrey Page was happily out the door and on his way to his tidy empire of files, documents, computers, and deciphered messages from the Agency's "black" operatives in China.

Ingram instructed his secretary to call the offices of all U. S. Intelligence Board members and notify them that an emergency meeting would be held in the board room at 1 P.M. Wednesday. "All except NSA," he added. "I'll handle Freytag myself."

Ingram placed his scrambled call to the National Security Agency.

"Freytag," said a voice after a moment. "What's the bad news today, Arthur?"

"Good afternoon, Jerome." Ingram could visualize the fox-like face, the satiric smile. "I'm scheduling a 1 P.M. board meeting tomorrow. China again."

"I'll be there. Anything else?"

"Any luck yet on the Chinese flowers?" asked Ingram.

Freytag did not answer immediately.

"The new codes," prompted Ingram.

"Oh yes," said Freytag. "Progress, Arthur, progress. Like General Electric, that's our chief product around this factory. As a matter of fact, it begins to look promising. We may have something for you soon."

"I could use it today," said Ingram. "We're hurting right now, Jerome."

"Do my best, Arthur. . . . Too many of my men are tagged with a genius I.Q., and you can't light a fire under the ass of a genius. I know. I've tried. . . . Well, see you tomorrow at one."

Ingram sat for half an hour, thinking, piecing, conjecturing. Greer on Tristan . . . Tristan's radio down . . . John where? . . . A Russian cruiser and Chinese freighter steaming toward Tristan da Cunha.

Then he placed a call to Senator Owen Moffat and reached him after a few minutes of search at the Metropolitan Club. Congress finally had adjourned for the year that morning.

"Owen," said Ingram, "I think we'd better have another talk immediately. I've changed my mind as to motive on the basis of new information. . . . Owen, I think Greer is defecting."

At that moment, in his office within the barbed wire enclosure near Fort Meade, Maryland, the director of the National Security Agency was studying a sheaf of messages.

Jerome Freytag had lied to Arthur Ingram.

He had reported "progress" on the decrypting of the new Chinese codes and ciphers. Actually, the proper word was success —a sheer, complete and stunning triumph.

After weeks of labor, Freytag's cryptanalysts and computers had cracked the Chinese codes. The exasperating profusion of floral growth—the tangled messages blooming with delphiniums, violets, buttercups, roses, marigolds, and jonquils—was now transformed into orderly rows of the Chinese language. The NSA specialists knew precisely what Peking was saying, and the facts were so bewildering that Freytag still did not credit entirely the contents of his pile of messages.

A remote island in the South Atlantic, Tristan da Cunha, finally had yielded the prime clue. It was axiomatic in the code-breaking trade that the best way to unscramble the language and find out what the antagonist sought to conceal was to narrow the search to a single area or subject. If, for instance, a submarine at sea surfaced each night and transmitted its position reports in the same code night after night, the decrypting experts eventually could identify such words as "latitude" and "longitude" and the accompanying numerals, thereby grasping the key to unlock the entire code. Or, if encrypted messages were being sent to and from a military ammunition depot, where the officers, type of ordnance, location, and patterns of requisition were already known, then the code wreckers could swing the iron ball of intuition and demolish the façade of secrecy.

And so it was with Tristan. First had come the puzzling discovery that Radio Tristan, which for years had talked to Cape Town in simple English, was exchanging masked messages with someone in Washington via the U. S. Navy's communications center at the Pentagon. These dispatches were baffling, since they contained a code within a code. Then a single, enigmatic encrypted dispatch from Tristan, apparently destined for a city other than Washington. Then, surprisingly, two messages from Tristan in the Russian diplomatic code. And, finally, a brief series of heavily veiled exchanges between Tristan and Peking. The common denominator of all these dispatches was their use of the same code within a code. Light began to penetrate the dark puzzle with the probable identification of "Tower," of "Rock," and of "Alpha." All this developed in fits and starts Sunday and Monday. Then, this morning, came several assumptions by Freytag's chief cryptanalyst, assumptions readily digested and verified by the computer—and suddenly the Chinese code shattered like pottery after a sharp blow.

At the time Arthur Ingram called, Freytag had spread on his desk the full run of intercepted and decrypted messages to and from Tristan da Cunha in the past month. There were not many, only nineteen in all, but their cumulative voice was so astonishing that Freytag had decided that he must report his discovery to but a single person in the U. S. Government—and that person was not Arthur Ingram.

For Jerome Freytag had come to the inescapable conclusion that the "Tower" of the Tristan messages was President Paul Roudebush.

18

Jerome Freytag rode in the rear seat of the director's limousine, his right arm encircling a thin, locked dispatch case. In the front seat, the driver and a guard of the National Security Agency both wore service revolvers in shoulder holsters concealed beneath their suit jackets.

The morning rush hour traffic was subsiding now as the car rolled toward the capital on the Baltimore-Washington Parkway. Freytag had left the NSA building, and its protective barbed wire fence, at nine-fifteen and he was due at the White House at ten. The sun, steaming off the first frost of autumn, glinted on the burnished foliage of the parkway. The solid green was turning to yellows, browns, and russets and, within a few days, the stretch from Fort Meade to Washington would become a wave of copper. The tang of early fall was in the air and Freytag welcomed the warmth provided by the car's heater.

If someone had spoken to Freytag at this moment, he would have replied with a waspish remark or a witticism, automatic responses of his protective shell. But within him, Freytag felt the tug of conflicting emotions. There was pride certainly, the soaring satisfaction of the professional which, had it prevailed, would have lifted him to a peak of euphoria. There was also a troubled wondering, a kind of sparring with the unknown.

And then the guilt. Curious, that guilt. It coursed through him like an underground stream, lapping at his pride and at his confidence. The self-recognition brought a wry smile to his face. He, Jerome Freytag, the iconoclast, the man who ridiculed the elephantine ways of government and who concocted satiric, ribald ballads about the establishment, now felt guilty because he was circumventing the regular channels. Instead of reporting to Arthur Ingram as he was charged with doing by both law and custom, he was ignoring Ingram and going directly to the President.

And why? There had been no signpost to guide him, no diagram or map to chart his way. He knew that Ingram disliked him as the CIA director would dislike any man who punctuated the litany of intelligence with frivolous or heretical remarks. Yet, he had worked smoothly enough with Ingram despite the evident animosity. As far as he could recall, he had never tampered with the truth in his dealings with Ingram.

Until yesterday afternoon. Then he had lied to Arthur Ingram, by implication at least, when he reported "progress" on breaking the Chinese codes at a time when the codes lay stripped before him.

At this hour, thanks to the keys supplied by the Tristan messages, a platoon of Freytag's cryptanalysts was busy programming the computer whose memory embraced thousands of flower-strewn dispatches from Red China's internal traffic and embassy circuits. Freytag knew that by tonight the computer's clattering print-out machine would have unrolled a half mile of Chinese messages in plain English. The heart of official China would lie exposed.

Freytag was exhilarated by the feat and proud of his specialists, yet he had not told Arthur Ingram, the chief of the intelligence community, despite Ingram's hunger to know what Red China was saying to itself in the new flower code. That refusal had stemmed from instinct, but now as he analyzed himself, Freytag had less trouble isolating and identifying his reasons.

They centered on the U. S. Intelligence Board. First was the scene of that meeting more than a month ago, clearly fixed in memory, when the FBI's Pete Deskowicz refused to tell Ingram or any other member of the board what his investigation of Stephen Greer had produced. Then, at two later meetings, Ingram's tart comments made it plain by implication that President Roudebush had specifically forbidden the CIA to join the search for Greer. Yet, yesterday, Freytag had become convinced that Greer was on the island of Tristan under the code name "Flag," and that Greer's whereabouts was known to President Roudebush, the "Tower" of the Tristan file.

And so Freytag had made up his mind. He would take his sheaf of messages directly to President Roudebush and request instructions on what to do with them. When he called yesterday evening, the President set up a 10 A.M. meeting, enjoining him to discuss the subject with no one in the meantime.

The car entered the rear of the White House grounds from the East Executive Avenue gate and halted beneath the balcony. As Freytag left the limousine, two Secret Service agents stepped forward and escorted him through the rose garden to the long portico. President Roudebush walked from his office and, flexing his arms in the morning chill, extended a hand in greeting. Within a few seconds, Freytag was seated inside the President's office.

"You're to be congratulated on solving the Chinese code," said the President.

Freytag noted that Roudebush, who usually trimmed the opening of any conference with peripheral chitchat, went straight to the point this morning.

"Thanks," said Freytag. "It was due largely to a group of messages to and from Tristan da Cunha. In view of their startling nature, Mr. President, I thought I should short-circuit the usual channels and bring the file directly to you."

"I'm glad you did."

Freytag unlocked his brief case and laid a manila folder, filled with messages, on the President's desk. Roudebush began reading the file, page by page. He showed no surprise. Rather, it seemed to Freytag as if Roudebush were reviewing material already known to him. Save for one brief smile, he was serious, absorbed. When he finished, he arranged the sheets neatly and replaced them in the folder.

"Has the breaking of the Chinese code revealed anything else of significance?" asked the President.

"The print-out should tell us by this evening," replied Freytag. "My men are programming the computer with new instructions right now. We'll have all the recent traffic soon."

"What's your normal procedure when you break a code?" asked Roudebush. "What do you do first?"

"Well, of course, sir," said Freytag, "our cryptanalysts at NSA are merely burglars. They break and enter codes. Normally, today's entire decrypted traffic would be delivered to Arthur Ingram as head of the intelligence community. After preliminary evaluation and filing at the CIA, copies of the messages would be distributed by Ingram's people to various intelligence units according to their area of competence, DIA, Atomic Energy or what not."

The President, after a moment of thought, said: "In this case, Jerry, I want all the Tristan messages, as well as the entire Chinese file, held at NSA until further instructions from me."

"I take it," said Freytag, "the subject is not to be discussed with Mr. Ingram."

"Nor with anyone else for the time being," said Roudebush. He hesitated, surveying Freytag. "Jerry, I think you're aware that these Tristan messages pertain to a highly unusual event."

Freytag nodded in agreement. "I guessed that, of course, although I have no idea of the exact nature."

"As it happens," said Roudebush, "secrecy is mandatory for some time yet. That's why I'm asking you to postpone your normal procedure."

"Understood," said Freytag. "I will hold all recently decrypted traffic under top classification at NSA until further word from . . . well, from 'Tower.'"

Roudebush smiled. "Jerry, I wonder if you could explain to me the exact mechanics of code-breaking? I confess I have only the vaguest ideas about it."

"When you ask a shop foreman to explain his work, Mr. President, you're really asking for it."

Freytag tried to clarify the mysteries of the trade. The President leaned back in his swivel chair. Freytag, noting Roudebush's interest, went into as much detail as he thought a layman could absorb. He rattled on for seven or eight minutes without interruption.

Then Grace Lalley suddenly walked into the room without knocking, went to the President's side and whispered in his ear.

"No, we'll speak in Chinese," Roudebush said aloud to his secretary. "Hold the call and explain that we'll have an interpreter in a few minutes. Get Ned in here right away."

Miss Lalley hurried out.

"Premier Wang is calling from Peking," Roudebush explained to Freytag. "No, there's no need for you to leave. You've already got a pretty good idea what's up. . . . Go ahead with your explanation, Jerry, until we're ready."

Freytag, trying to appear unperturbed, took up where he left off, but almost at once, Roudebush cut in.

"Tell me, Jerry. What did you make of the inner code in the American messages?"

"Well," said Freytag, "you realize I only had a few messages to work on. I decided rather early, of course, that 'Tower' had to be you."

"I cooked that up myself," said Roudebush. "As a rank amateur at such things, I wondered how long it would take the director of NSA to figure it out."

"And," said Freytag, "I have a pretty good idea who 'Flag' is, but I'm perplexed by 'Strangler' and 'Barge.'"

Roudebush smiled. "You'll know soon, I hope."

Grace Lalley opened the door to admit a thin young man. He was quite business-like and formal in manner. The President introduced the newcomer as "Ned Young," and Freytag guessed he was of Chinese-American stock.

"Please make yourself comfortable by that phone, Ned," said the President.

Young pulled a chair to the side of Roudebush's desk and sat down. Roudebush handed him the phone, then called: "All right, Grace. We're ready."

"Ned," he said to his interpreter, "please begin by thanking the Premier for his call and expressing my hopes that he and his wife are in good health."

Ned Young began speaking in Chinese. To Freytag, the cadenced greeting seemed unnecessarily lengthy.

Young listened for a time, then said to the President: "Premier Wang says he and his wife are fine and he trusts that you and Mrs. Roudebush are also in excellent health."

A fairly long and banal exchange followed. The President asked about the weather in Peking. The Premier said a light rain was falling and he hoped the weather was better in Washington. The Premier also hoped that his call proved no inconvenience to the President. On the contrary, the President deemed it a privilege to converse with the Premier at any hour. Freytag wondered, irreverently, how much per minute this small talk was costing the People's Republic of China.

"The Premier," reported Young in a brisker voice, "says an embarrassing international situation has arisen in the People's Republic. The defense minister and General Feng are misinterpreting the Premier's policy of good will and forbearance, and they are playing on latent fears of the people. The matter could become critical. Therefore the Premier wishes to beg the indulgence of the President to consider an alteration in the agreed program."

Roudebush thought a moment. "Tell him," he said, "that I'd be honored to consider any change the Premier might suggest, as long as the goal remains the same. . . . What does the Premier have in mind? . . . But Ned, please phrase that question very politely."

Young spoke in Chinese and, after a minute of listening, said: "The Premier wishes to suggest that speed is now a primary consideration from his viewpoint. Would an accelerated plan embarrass or inconvenience the President?"

"Not at all," replied Roudebush promptly. "Tell him the sooner the better—as long as it's feasible."

Young translated the reply into the phone, then made several notes on a pad as he listened.

"In that case," he said, "the Premier suggests that the Peking presentation be made as originally planned, but that the Washington program be staged as quickly as possible. He notes that Washington can act more swiftly because of the less complicated transportation involved. If you agree, sir, he wants to know how soon could Washington present its part?"

"Tell him that if all goes well, the Washington phase could take place tomorrow noon, Washington time, I think. Ask him if that would be satisfactory?"

Young translated, listened, then reported: "That would please the Premier very much. In that event, would it be completely understood that no official blessing by the People's Republic of China would be stated or implied?"

"Understood," said Roudebush. "Tell him that has been our agreement from the start. The precise statement would be that while Premier Wang Kwo P'ing looks with favor on the general goal, he can no more commit his government in advance than I can. Then ask him: Is that clear and is that satisfactory?"

"That is both clear and satisfactory," said Young after an exchange in Chinese. "At the same time, the Premier wishes to go forward with the Chinese phase of the arrangement as planned. He hopes the President will permit 'Mercury' to travel to Peking via the *Ho P'ing Hao* and then by aircraft as originally planned."

"Yes," replied Roudebush, "that will be fine. . . . Now, Ned, so that we can be doubly certain, ask the Premier if he intends that all phases will be carried out as agreed—with the sole exception of the speed-up in the Washington schedule?"

This time, after translating, Young listened for several minutes, checked several words back with the Premier and made shorthand notes on his pad.

"The Premier agrees completely," he said. "There remains then, he says, but one problem. The Premier does not wish to slight or offend Moscow." Young consulted his notes. "On the other hand, he feels communication by him with the Kremlin at this moment would be difficult because of differences on other matters." Young paused. "So, would the President be kind enough to make the proper explanations to Moscow?"

"Ned, let me mull that over a bit," said Roudebush. He turned in his swivel chair and gazed toward the back lawn. "Yes," he said after a lapse. "Let's see, Ned. . . . Tell him I will be glad to conduct . . . uh . . . negotiations on the changed plan with Moscow. But ask him, does the Premier wish me to state the exact reason to Moscow, or would he prefer that I resort to the language of diplomacy."

Young performed his translation chores, then smiled at Roudebush. "The Premier laughed," he reported. "He says he admires you as a diplomat and he prefers that you use the language of diplomacy, which you are so superbly equipped to handle."

Roudebush looked at both Freytag and Young, smiled, then said: "Tell him I'm not sure whether that's a compliment or an accusation."

"It's a compliment," said Young after a short exchange.

"Then thank him for his confidence in me," said Roudebush. "Express my hopes that the Premier will surmount his internal difficulties and that he will approve of our Washington effort."

Young smiled faintly after talking with Premier Wang. "The Premier says that if you can handle Governor Wolcott, he can handle his defense minister and General Feng. . . . In closing, he wishes to extend his sincere thanks for your understanding and sympathy and for your appreciation of his difficulties."

Several more minutes were taken up in felicitations and goodbys.

"Thanks, Ned." Roudebush shook the interpreter's hand. "That was a good job."

After Young left the room, Roudebush relaxed in his chair and grinned somewhat self-consciously. "I'm just as glad you were here, Jerry. I may need a witness to that conversation if things don't pan out right."

"I think, Mr. President, that I've got an inkling now."

"Well, keep it to yourself, please," said Roudebush. "I said tomorrow noon, but that depends on a lot of things. . . . And now, in addition, the Russians. I'll have to attend to the Russians right away."

"Just one thing before I leave, Mr. President," said Freytag. "Arthur Ingram has scheduled an emergency U. S. Intelligence Board meeting for 1 P.M. I'll be asked about the state of our work on the Chinese codes, and—"

"An intelligence board meeting?" The President was startled. "On what subject?"

"Ingram said it involved a crash NIE on China. In view of developments, I assume that means an assessment of the military pressures on Premier Wang."

"That will have to be canceled. I'll do so immediately. . . . Jerry, no matter what happens, I want you to sit on that Chinese traffic and especially the Tristan messages. No hint is to leave your office."

"Yes, sir."

As Freytag left the room, the President already was reaching for his phone.

On the drive back to the NSA building at Fort Meade, Freytag jotted down notes on the conversation between the President and the Premier. At his office, he summoned his computer programmers, ordered them to restrict the print-out of Chinese dispatches to one copy only. This was to be delivered promptly to the director and was not to be shown to anyone else. Then Freytag bolted his office door and spent an hour transcribing and amplifying his notes on the typewriter. He signed his name and typed in the date and time—10/6/1351 EDT.

Freytag clipped this memorandum into the loose-leaf notebook which contained his Washington diary and placed the book in the drawer of his office safe which he reserved for his personal papers. Then, from a stack of Tristan messages, he selected the eight dispatches handled by the Navy's communications center at the Pentagon.

In view of the President's telephone conversation with Premier Wang, Freytag assumed that all would be clear to him sometime tomorrow. But his professional curiosity would not tolerate a delay of twenty-four hours. He had to try to understand now. In

the manner of a puzzle addict heartened by a new clue, he again
reread the dispatches in sequence:

To: Tower
From: Angel
  Preliminary Alpha under way 1000 Z without Mercury. Rock
secure. Flag requests reassurance Pennant.
  9/8/ 1808 Z

To: Angel
From: Tower
  Notify Flag. Pennant flying after talk with Tower. Good luck.
  9/9/ 0412 Z

To: Tower
From: Angel
  Mercury arrived safely. Alpha smooth. Request: Mercury
to leave by Barge? Plan unsure here.
  9/17/ 1200 Z

To: Angel
From: Tower
  Mercury by Barge, yes. Need ETD Alpha, please?
  9/17/ 1314 Z

To: Tower
From: Angel
  ETD Alpha 10/8 to 10/10 rough.
  9/17/ 1524 Z

Freytag noted a lapse of ten days before the next message:

To: Tower
From: Angel
  ETD Alpha now 10/7.
  9/27/ 1705 Z

To: Angel
From: Tower
  Good. Monster due Rock 10/6.
  9/28/ 2018 Z

There was another lapse, of six days, before the final message in the group:

To: Tower
From: Angel
    Strangler here via *Pedro Alfonso* from Riverhead. Plan 4.
ETD Alpha now 10/6.
    10/4/ 1320 Z

In late afternoon, while Jerome Freytag was still puzzling over the riddle of Tristan da Cunha, an assistant came into the room. "Here are three more for the Tristan file."

Freytag added these new messages to those on his desk:

To: Tower
From: Angel
    Monster at Rock. Instructions, please.
    10/6/ 1507 Z

To: Angel
From: Tower
    Evacuate entire Alpha to Monster immediately. Plan Overhead. Change requested by Mountain and agreed Tower. Speed utmost. One exception. Mercury via Barge as planned. Request departure time.
    10/6/ 1622 Z

To: Tower
From: Angel
    Lifting to Monster per your 1622 Z. ETA Tower early 10/7. Mercury awaiting Barge. This last from Rock.
    10/6/ 1740 Z

Twilight coated the office of the NSA director with shades of amber as Freytag continued to work over the sheaf of messages. He had far more than an inkling now, yet full clarity still eluded him. He tapped at his forehead with a pencil and frowned at the last three dispatches.

A group known as Alpha obviously was leaving the island of Tristan and flying to Washington by orders of President Roudebush. Plans had been accelerated at the request of the Premier of Communist China. But precisely who, what, and why was Alpha?

19

Jill walked back to her desk and slumped in her chair with her arms on the typewriter. She was a drooping pennant.

"Gene," she said in that soft, small voice, "if I weren't so beat, I'd cry."

I understood. We had been forced to lock the door of the press office soon after lunch that afternoon. Our little command quarters for official information—or more properly, these days, non-information—had become a beleaguered outpost, under attack from the press and completely cut off from the commander-in-chief. Every phone line into our room, five at Jill's desk and three at mine, was jammed with backed-up calls. Reporters invaded our office at will, ignoring the rule that entrance was by appointment only.

When Jill finally turned the key in the lock, we heard the door rattle and then a hammering on the panel. We were under siege.

I walked over to Jill and kneaded her shoulder. She gave me a frail smile.

"Thanks," she said. "Sometimes I wish Steve Greer had never been born. How many more days of this I can take, I don't know."

"It's my fault, Jill. If I'd made up my mind—or excuse for a mind—we could have had an assistant in the next office to take some of the heat. Now it's too late. It would take a week just to bring him up to date on what we don't know around here." I continued to massage her shoulder. "Why don't you go down to the staff lounge and lie down for a while?"

"No. I'll be okay in a minute. Just an attack of jitters. Don't worry."

She straightened up a few moments later. She eyed herself in a compact mirror, put on some new lipstick, and brushed the hair from her eyes. Then she pushed one of the winking buttons and said, "Press." Her voice had a forlorn, defensive note as if this were the rear guard of a retreating army.

We were not retreating. We were sinking under a deluge of demands. Somewhere, somehow, a dam had burst. The city was awash with rumors and it seemed that every newspaperman and radio and television reporter in town had found at least one.

ABC wanted confirmation of a report that a Russian armada was suddenly loose in the South Atlantic. The New York *Times* heard that a hastily convoked meeting of the U. S. Intelligence Board had been canceled. *Newsweek*'s Pentagon correspondent demanded comment on his story that General Marvin Palfrey, the Defense Intelligence Agency chief, had wrathfully accused the Chief of Naval Operations, Admiral Freestone, of withholding vital information from him. NBC had its own rumor: that Hillary Kulp, in his all-network speech for Wolcott tomorrow night, would charge that Greer and Lubin had defected to Russia. The Los Angeles *Times* wanted to check a rumor that an FBI agent named Larry Storm had been fired because he knew too many seamy details about the Greer case. The editor of a small-town Colorado newspaper called in with the most bizarre story of the day. He heard from an "unimpeachable" source—nobody impeaches a source on a hot story—that Dave Paulick of *D.P.'s Dossier* had been murdered by the same conspirators who kidnaped Stephen Greer. When I said the story was patently crazy, the editor angrily demanded proof that Paulick was alive. I realized then that I had no idea where Paulick was, dead or alive.

The press aside, there were developments that exacerbated the raw nerves of Jill and me because none of them could be checked with the front office. As far as we were concerned, the President was incommunicado.

A White House staffer who normally had quick access to Roudebush called to complain that he could not reach the President. The Securities & Exchange Commission was readying a report that would accuse Maury Rimmel and Brady Manship of rigging the price of Educational Micro stock. It was asking presidential permission to release the findings. Could I get to the President, please? No, I could not. . . . Miguel Loomis called me at noon from the Greer residence to report that Susannah Greer was suddenly transformed from a calm but lonely wife into a chattering, ecstatic female—all within an hour. Miguel guessed that she had heard good news about Steve, but she balked at Miguel's questions. So, what did I know? Nothing. . . . The White House switchboard girls normally screened out nut calls, but somehow a wacky dame named Beverly West got past them and was connected with me. Miss West said she had informed the FBI that Greer and Lubin were pansies who shacked up at her apartment building, the Wilmarth, and why was the President suppressing the goddamn facts, etc., etc. She sounded smashed, but her vituperation was so unhinged that I reported her name and address to the Secret Service. . . . Then, Danny Cavanaugh, the party's national chairman, called. He was in a snappish humor. Danny said it was vital that he speak to the President, but that Grace Lalley would not put him through. The Governor of Montana, a Roudebush stalwart, was about to switch sides and come out for Wolcott because of the shrouded Greer case. Danny wanted Roudebush to speak to the governor at once and try to dissuade him.

"Grace won't listen to me, dammit," shrilled Danny. "What's going on over there? Has the President vanished too?"

I could not help Danny. All I knew about the front office today was that Jerome Freytag, the NSA director, had called in person this morning. I knew that only because Grace told me when I tried to reach the President. Roudebush had been unavailable to me all day.

My first order from the President's office came at 3 P.M. and then it bristled. "The President wants you to come in," Grace informed me without her usual banter. "When?" I asked. "Right now," she said and slammed down the phone. Everyone, it seemed, was stretched tighter than a drum.

The President looked up from some papers as I walked in, motioned me to a chair and promptly resumed reading. He failed to flash the usual radiant smile. He was serious, but by no means grim. He flipped impatiently through the last pages of the document.

"I'm sorry I haven't been available, Gene," he said. "Too much happening too fast. . . . I wanted you in here because our friend from across the river—Arthur—will be here in a minute. I tried to put him off. I really don't have the time, but he was especially insistent. Said it was urgent. . . . I'd like you to listen to the conversation and write up a memo of it. No notes in here, of course. Just . . ." He smiled briefly. "Just use that famous reportorial memory of yours."

I was about to reply that the memory was not as sharp as it used to be, but the door opened and Grace Lalley nodded to the President. Arthur Ingram entered. Grace withdrew, closing the door quietly.

"Good afternoon, Mr. President," said Ingram. His eyes swept the room, rested on me. Again that look of annoyed surprise, as though I were a servant who did not have the manners to leave when family business was about to be discussed.

Ingram was dressed like an investment banker. His brown suit was pressed to crisp edges, his tie neatly knotted above a collar clasp, his expensive cordovans agleam with polish.

"Hello, Arthur," replied Roudebush. "Pull up that other chair, won't you?"

Ingram seated himself stiffly like a man with back trouble, then shifted slightly in his chair so that he was turned an inch or two away from me.

"I would prefer to speak to you in private, Mr. President," he said.

"Oh, don't mind Gene," said Roudebush. "He's become my liaison man, as it were, on policy concerning the Agency."

"This is a personal matter," said Ingram. He sat tensely, gripping the ends of the arm rests.

"Nothing to do with the Agency?"

"The Agency is, of course, involved," replied Ingram, "but I regard my call as essentially a question between you and me."

"I think it best that Gene remain." It was not a suggestion. It was a decision.

"Do I take it that I am to be monitored?"

The President flicked a dry smile. "If so, Arthur, I hardly think we could even the score at one sitting."

This less than oblique reference to Butter Nygaard chilled the already cool atmosphere. Ingram looked as though he had been sculpted to his chair.

"I recall a remark of yours once," said Roudebush, "to the effect that less than total knowledge is not intelligence, but merely information. I must say, Arthur, that you've spared no pains to make sure that your knowledge of this office and its conversations comes under the heading of intelligence."

"That can be explained, Mr. President, perhaps not to your satisfaction, but explained nevertheless. It was never my intention—"

"Not now, Arthur," Roudebush interrupted. He raised a restraining palm. "We'll have ample time for all that later. Right now, I'm under considerable pressure. You said your business was urgent?"

"Yes, sir." Ingram folded his arms as if to fortify himself. "I am here, Mr. President, to tender my resignation."

"I see." Roudebush leaned back in his swivel chair, an ounce of relaxation for Ingram's pound of tension. "As of when, may I ask?"

"Effective tomorrow. I have put it in writing."

Ingram drew a sheet of paper from his inner breast pocket, stood up, and handed it to the President.

Roudebush put on his glasses, scanned the paper—from where I sat there appeared to be only a single typewritten paragraph— and tossed the sheet at his desk. It turned full around, fluttering, before settling on top of the document Roudebush had been reading. The President pushed his spectacles up to their roost in the thatch of gray hair.

"May I have the reasons, please?"

"Certainly." Ingram was again rigid in his chair. "You have

specifically forbidden my Agency to join the search for two prominent missing persons, despite the fact that one of these men has been outside the United States for some time and despite the fact that both men possess information vital to the security of this country. This exhibits a distrust, a contempt—or a fear—of my Agency that completely vitiates my usefulness."

"And why do you think I issued that order?" asked Roudebush.

"I have no certain knowledge. I can only speculate."

"And the speculations center on politics, I suppose," said Roudebush dryly. "A candidate fearful that disclosure might harm his chances for re-election. Is that it?"

"The situation is obvious. We are both aware of it, Mr. President. However, the word 'harm,' I'd say, is putting it mildly."

"Thank you." Roudebush compressed his lips and looked at Ingram with unconcealed antipathy. "Anything else?"

"Yes. There was your cancellation a few hours ago of this afternoon's intelligence board meeting." Ingram was the bookkeeper, ready for the audit. "I find that a dangerous decision, bordering on the irresponsible. Our intelligence indicates a possible military move against Premier Wang in China, and yet you block a responsible assessment. That violates elemental intelligence methods. It could have grave consequences."

"Ordinarily, it might," said Roudebush softly, "but in this case, we don't need a formal assessment. I already know of the military pressures on Wang. . . . You see, Arthur, I talked by phone this morning directly to Wang in Peking."

Ingram was stunned. He gazed blankly at the President for a moment, then lowered his eyes to his glasses. His fingers framed the spectacles in a precise half-rectangle. I, too, was overwhelmed. The President talking by phone to the Chinese Premier? Why?

"That surprises me, of course," said Ingram, recovering, "but it's of a piece with recent events. The director of central intelligence obviously is not in the confidence of the President. His value, therefore, is minimal. If you need a further reason for my resignation, you have just stated it."

Roudebush studied Ingram for a moment. His hands were

folded at his waist now as he tilted back in the chair. He had a pensive air.

"Arthur," he said, "I'm wondering. Do you have a promise from Governor Wolcott that you will be his CIA director in event of his election?"

It was a second shock for Ingram within minutes. He stiffened, was about to speak, hesitated. Then he said with words of apparent careful choice: "What Governor Wolcott may or may not intend is for him to say."

"I will take that as an affirmative answer . . . I thought so." Roudebush leaned forward so quickly that the springs of the chair squeaked. He placed his arms on the desk and glared at Ingram. "Arthur, I could spend an hour ticking off my reasons why your resignation should be accepted on the spot. It would, however, be a needless venting of the obvious. You already know them— from the Flycatcher operation, to a young lady named Butter Nygaard, to the sudden appearance of a CIA agent on the island of Tristan da Cunha. . . ."

I was watching Ingram. He sat immobile. My own mind went skittering after clues. What was this about the CIA and the island of Tristan?

"As I say," continued Roudebush, "I should accept your resignation at once. But I'm not going to. I am rejecting this . . ." He pointed to the letter on his desk. ". . . for the time being. Of course, it goes without saying that the subject will be reopened after the election."

"Whether or not you go through the formality of accepting it or rejecting it makes no difference," said Ingram. "I'm resigning."

The President whipped out his handkerchief and slowly polished the lenses of his glasses. It was his stalling ploy.

"Arthur," he said after a time, "we both know that your resignation at this time would be highly embarrassing to me politically. The campaign is entering its final phase." He glanced sharply at Ingram. "And your standing with Congress and the press is extremely high—whether deserved or not is beside the point. Image today often counts more than substance, and your image is a well-polished one."

"Sarcasm does not become you, Mr. President," said Ingram.

It might not become him, but it was certainly understandable. I could sense that Roudebush's anger was boiling beneath the surface.

Ingram stirred in his chair as if about to rise. "I think there's no point in continuing this discussion," he said. He had the appearance of a man in command.

"Oh yes there is," said Roudebush. "When you announce your resignation, you'll state your reasons of course. What you forget is that the President of the United States also has a forum. And, believe me, in this case, I'd use it. I don't think the American people would look favorably upon a man whom the President accuses of recruiting young scientists as spies . . . a man who plants a secret agent in a country club frequented by officers, both civilian and military, of his own government . . . or a man who goes to the incredible length of monitoring the private conversations of his President."

Roudebush, who had been speaking in a low, controlled voice, now raised the pitch as he pointed a finger at Ingram. "I think that in that kind of a contest, as ugly as it might get, there isn't much question about the victor—and it would not be Arthur Victor Ingram."

"Disclosing security information to gain political advantage happens to be the curse of our system," said Ingram, "but . . ."

"Political advantage!" retorted Roudebush. The anger blazed. "Will you please tell me who was seeking political advantage when your hired informer, Miss Nygaard, accompanied Senator Moffat to Louisville for a conference with Mr. Kulp? God knows what else you've cooked up on the basis of that girl's snooping."

The President hesitated briefly, then erupted again.

"Damn it, Ingram, do you realize what it means to place your own President under secret surveillance? Perhaps the real curse of our system is that you can't be hung for it."

"Of course," said Ingram coolly, "the system permits you to fire me." He grew icier as the President's temper flared. "But the record will show that I resigned."

This time Ingram did rise from his chair. He bowed, so slightly that it became a gesture of contempt.

"With your permission, sir," he said. "Further talk would be futile."

The President stood up, took several steps around the side of his desk. The two men faced each other in studied animosity.

"And when will you announce your resignation?" asked Roudebush.

"Tomorrow," said Ingram. He took a step toward the door.

"Just a minute," ordered Roudebush. "You may be finished, but I am not."

Ingram checked himself. He stood, a polite glacier, and stared at Roudebush.

"Arthur, if you announce your resignation tomorrow, you will make yourself a fool before the whole country." Roudebush enunciated slowly as if the pace of speech itself could contain his fury.

"We'll let the public draw its own conclusions about whether I'm a fool or not," said Ingram.

"A fool, Arthur," repeated Roudebush. "And the reason is that you've completely misjudged the nature of the Greer case. For that, you cannot be technically blamed. I emphasize the word 'technical' because I had intended to keep you fully informed. But I changed my mind when I learned about the young physicists. That underlined once more the gap in our thinking—and your lack of understanding of some basic concepts of this system of ours."

Ingram said nothing. He remained rooted in hostility.

"My judgment in withholding certain information from you was justified," continued Roudebush. "I learned last week that for more than two years you have surreptitiously monitored my private conversations via Miss Nygaard. In the light of that, I'm the one who would have been the fool if I'd taken you into my confidence on the Greer matter. Still, I did consider it—which doesn't say much, I suppose, for my judgment of men and character. . . ."

The President paused, tilted his head, and scrutinized Ingram anew.

"Even after that, however, I intended to honor your office, if not the occupant of it, by telling you about Steve this week. I thought this would be only fair so the Agency could prepare itself for the wind-up of the Greer case. And then, to my amazement, I learned that you had defied my specific orders by dispatching one of your agents to the island of Tristan. That was outrageous insubordination. It might have had disastrous effects too—if it weren't for the diplomatic skill of several men, Steve Greer and Secret Service Agent Don Sheehan among them."

My thoughts churned as I listened. The phrase "island of Tristan" evoked the scene of Larry Storm bent over a map of the South Atlantic . . . Greer, Lubin, and Kissich embarking from seaports . . . to Tristan island? . . . and the missing Don Sheehan . . . was he on the island too?

Ingram was a man transfixed. He moved not a muscle as he stood facing Roudebush. The President's arm swept the air.

"But that's all water over the dam now," he continued. "The fact is, Arthur, that you've been acting from a faulty premise. Just what that premise is, I don't know, but I suspect it's dead wrong. . . . Steve Greer has been operating with my consent and knowledge from the outset. His mission holds high promise for the United States and for the whole world. The results will be announced tomorrow."

He paused and folded his arms as he continued to survey Ingram. There was antagonism in his expression, but also, it seemed to me, a touch of pity, too. Roudebush was not a man who enjoyed the humiliation of another.

"And so, Arthur," he said, "I merely advise you that I think— although I cannot be positive about it—that you will be making a tragic personal mistake if you announce your resignation tomorrow."

"And I think you're wrong," said Ingram. "I believe that you will be making the mistake."

"Oh?"

"Yes, sir." Ingram, recovering, went to the attack again. "When the country learns that vital intelligence was denied us when you shut down the Flycatcher project . . . when the country learns that, with China on the verge of upheaval, you forbade your own intelligence managers to assess the meaning for the United States . . . When the country learns—"

"I assure you, Arthur," cut in Roudebush, "that you'll make yourself out a fool, if indeed you get much space in the press. . . . In light of what's coming, I rather doubt that you will."

"I intend to take that risk," said Ingram bitterly. "When the full facts are out, I think you'll find you've misjudged the temper of this country."

I was at a loss to know which man held the upper hand. The very intensity of their emotions hinted that neither was quite sure of himself. And my own intuition was swamped by the sudden flood of new impressions and half-facts.

Roudebush shrugged. "Perhaps I have, perhaps not. . . . For the sake of the project—and my own political hide right now—I'd prefer that the waters weren't muddied by the side issue of Arthur Ingram. But if you persist, then we'll just have to fight back, and when we're finished fighting, I don't think there'll be much left of you."

Ingram bowed. "May I leave now?"

"Of course."

Without a word of parting, Ingram turned and walked to the door. Just as he reached it, Roudebush said:

"It will be your worst mistake, Arthur."

Ingram looked back. "Or yours, Mr. President."

He squared his shoulders and left the room, closing the door decisively behind him.

Roudebush shook his head. "Well, thank God that's over with."

I started to leave, but Roudebush motioned me to stay. He walked behind his desk, shucked his coat, and hung it on the back of his chair. He sank into the chair with evident relief.

"I want that conversation recorded at once, Gene," he said. "Maybe you could hide out in an office upstairs for an hour until you finish it. Let Jill handle your shop."

"It's a madhouse," I said.

"It'll be worse tomorrow."

He flipped some pages on his desk calendar.

"Let's see, Gene," he said. "Our ten-day gentlemen's agreement —are we the last gentlemen left, by the way?—is up when?"

"October ninth. That's Saturday." I knew it without consulting a calendar.

"Then we're in no trouble," he said. "If all goes well, you'll learn everything tomorrow. . . . Gene, I want to apologize to you. You've been loyal and you've done a good job under tremendous handicaps. I wanted to level with you from the start, but I just couldn't. The nature of Steve's mission was too delicate. The smallest leak might have meant catastrophe."

"It hasn't been easy," I said.

"I realize that," he said, "but you're in good company. Most of the cabinet doesn't know. This has been the most tightly held secret since the Manhattan project, and with far fewer people cut in. We operated on a strict need-to-know basis. . . . I want to thank you for co-operating as well as you have. As I recall, we only had two disputes. You're a patient man, Gene."

"But I have to wait until tomorrow?"

"Yes." He glanced at his watch. "About another twenty hours or so. However, there are several things you should be thinking about. I want to present a group of people—including some foreigners—at a regular press conference in the State Department auditorium. Well, not exactly regular either. I want to present our story without any questions from the press. There'll be plenty of news without that. . . . It would be around noon, I should judge. We'll run better than an hour, and I want live television. . . . Now, that's the main question. Can we get all networks on short notice, say two or three hours?"

"You mean without mentioning Greer?"

"Oh no. By that time, you could inform the network people —and the press—that it would involve a major news break on the Greer case."

"No problem then," I said. "But I should have three hours minimum, so they can pre-empt the time of other shows and make mechanical arrangements."

"I'll get you the three hours," he said. "So, tentatively, let's shoot for noon as the time of the press conference."

"All right," I said. "In any case, I'll show up bright and early."

"If you make it early enough," he said, "you may see quite a show."

"Yes, sir." The way things were going, I would not be surprised if I were to witness a triple dawn. "Just a couple of other things, sir. My press conference is slated for four, but it's three-fifty now and you want me to bat out the memo."

"Put the press off until later," he said. "I imagine the troops won't be any more ferocious at five-thirty."

"And what can I say—about Greer?"

"Nothing," he said. "I don't want a hint of what's coming tomorrow. We can't afford a slip at this late date."

"All right, sir." I arose to leave, and already I could hear the infuriated pack snapping questions and insults at me. Then I remembered.

"By the way, we'll just get under the wire," I said. "Hillary Kulp's big explosion is slated for tomorrow night, all networks, paid time by the Wolcott committee. It's costing them more than $300,000."

Roudebush looked quickly troubled again. "I hope," he said slowly, "we'll be able to save the governor's people some money."

I rattled off the memorandum of the Roudebush-Ingram collision in just one hour. My memory was better than I had hoped, and the words flew out of the typewriter.

I was only an hour late with my press conference. When the pack stomped from the room at five forty-five, it left a mangled, dazed, and battered press secretary. But I did my duty, bloodied as I was. As far as the press could learn from me, we were no nearer a solution of the strange case of Stephen Greer than we were in those last frantic days of August.

Jill came to my place that evening and cooked our dinner. I was in a mood for half a dozen martinis, but anticipating what we were in for the next day, I called a halt after two each.

Of course, we failed to get to sleep until long after midnight. We spent hours trading our speculations. As it turned out, we were both wrong, but Jill came closer to the truth than I did, a fact that Jill, in that sweetly condescending manner that women have, has never let me forget.

20

Jill and I arrived at the press office at the ungodly hour of 6 A.M. Even after the second cup of coffee from the thermos jug Jill had brought, we were still in a mummified state and had not even bothered to remove our coats. The west wing had that air of weary vacuity which settles on even the most elegant hotel lobbies in early morning. In a distant office, we could hear the drone of a vacuum cleaner. It seemed odd to be in this office, for once solemnly quiet, with nothing to do but wait.

We were sitting on my desk, sipping our coffee, when my phone buzzed. It was Grace Lalley with the cryptic advice that we should go to the back lawn if we wished "to see something interesting."

Carrying our mugs of coffee, we went through the wing to the rear portico. Grace was standing in the rose garden, holding her coat collar closely against the morning chill. No other members of the White House staff were in evidence. We joined Grace on the lawn. The grass, stiff with frost, crunched under our feet. A thin layer of mist hung over the sloping lawn and the great trees were muffled in purples and grays. The sun had yet to appear above the Treasury Building to the east. We were alone, it seemed, in a still-sleeping city and the silence had a gentle, brooding quality.

Three Secret Service men appeared from the center of the house beneath the balcony. Then came the President, holding the arm of a woman who was chatting away at him. The President spotted us, and when both he and the woman waved, I saw that she was Susannah Greer. She was hatless, wore a trim, chic, blue trench coat, and seemed to be bubbling with good spirits.

"She's just had her hair done," whispered Jill. Had I been taking copious notes on this back lawn scene, that was one detail I would have missed.

Roudebush wore a snap brim hat and tan topcoat with upturned collar. He and Mrs. Greer stood waiting beside the Secret Service agents.

A few seconds later, we heard the clattering grind of a helicopter. It swung clumsily over the Ellipse and then headed toward the White House with its big rotary blades thrashing.

The chopper settled down, rattling and crackling like pots and pans in a suddenly disturbed kitchen, just a few yards from the President. The first man out the front hatch was Don Sheehan. He waved triumphantly at the President, then pointed behind himself. The second man was Stephen Greer. He jumped down, grinned, and held his hands up in a boxer's handclasp. Steve was dressed in a sport shirt, an old leather jacket, and khaki pants. Sue Greer ran out to meet him and they threw their arms around each other. Steve lifted his wife about a foot off the lawn as they kissed. Then Steve, with Sue clutching his arm, walked over to greet the President.

The third man, little to my surprise by this time, was Phil Lubin. He was smiling, diffidently, and he seemed uncertain as to just what to do. Then followed three men I recognized as members of the Army Signal Corps unit attached to the White House. The last two men to leave the helicopter proved as astonishing to Jill as to me. She plucked at my coat sleeve and asked: "Do you believe it?"

One was Larry Storm, wearing a windbreaker and denim trousers. The other was big Dave Paulick, who promptly began swinging his arms and doing rapid knee-bends the moment he touched the ground. Paulick, I noted, needed a shave.

The group walked over to and circled the President. While I could not see exactly what was happening, Greer appeared to be introducing the Signal Corps men. There was the hum of chatter, much shaking of hands, and a general aura of camaraderie. I did see Roudebush give Phil Lubin a bear hug and slap Greer on the back.

The helicopter lifted off the lawn and thrashed away. Almost at once another chopper lumbered toward us across the Ellipse. The crowd around the President lined up rather formally as if someone had reminded it of manners. The second 'copter disgorged six more men. One of them appeared to me to be an Asian and one was a burly fellow with long arms and a craggy, sunburned face. I had seen that face and that big, awkward body a hundred times. The man was Barney Loomis.

The new arrivals walked in single file toward the Roudebush welcoming party and, except for Barney, they looked about them with that mixture of anticipation and apprehension which mark the expressions of tourists deplaning in a strange land. Loomis pumped the President's hand, but the others were introduced formally to Roudebush by Steve Greer. There was a great deal of bowing and handshaking, and then the President led them all into the White House. The chopper took off, causing a furious rattle of leaves in the magnolia trees.

"Well, well," I said in one of my more trenchant spot observations.

"And just what was that all about?" asked Jill.

"Operation Alpha," said Grace Lalley. She smiled, a stately nursing of her secret, then walked back toward her office. She stamped her feet under the portico to shed the moisture from the lawn frost.

And that was all the enlightenment Jill and I got for some time. The President called me at about eight o'clock and instructed me to go ahead with the requests for network time. I could say there would be a group press conference, including the President, at noon at State with a major announcement on the Greer case. That was all the guidance he gave me, and I knew this was no time to badger him for more facts.

I spent an hour on the phone, including calls to New York and one to White Sulphur Springs where a CBS executive was vacationing. The arrangements took time, but there was no problem. The magic word "Greer" vaporized all network resistance. We could have had the entire afternoon if we had wanted it. Then, at 9:30 A.M., I made the announcement to the press.

The State Department auditorium began filling just a few minutes after the news hit the UPI and AP city news tickers. The UPI rang bells and triple-spaced the item for emphasis:

CORRESPONDENTS:

WHITE HOUSE PRESS SECRETARY EUGENE R. CULLIGAN SAYS THERE WILL BE A MAJOR NEWS BREAK ON THE STEPHEN GREER CASE AT NOON. PRESIDENT ROUDEBUSH AND "OTHERS" WILL APPEAR AT A PRESS CONFERENCE IN THE STATE DEPARTMENT AUDITORIUM. TO BE TELEVISED LIVE ALL NETWORKS.

10/7—RM0936AED

The trek of newsmen toward the State Department became a feverish migration when these ticker items appeared a few minutes later:

UPI-21
(Greer)
Washington—Two helicopters landed shortly after dawn this morning on the White House back lawn, it was learned from informed sources.

The White House was filled with rumors that alighting passengers included the long-missing Stephen B. Greer, close friend of President Roudebush, and Dr. Phillip J. Lubin of Johns Hopkins University, identified by some newspapers as the famous "Dr. X" first mentioned by Hillary Kulp, Kentucky state chairman of the Wolcott-for-president committee.

There was no immediate information available on the identity of other passengers.

10/7—RM0951AED

UPI-24
(Greer)
Rio de Janeiro—Air Force One, President Roudebush's personal plane, took off secretly for Washington last night from the Rio international airport, it was learned today.

Passengers were unidentified, but one U.S. source said they were thought to include Stephen B. Greer, the vanished Washington attorney who is a close friend of President Roudebush.

Air Force One passengers transferred from two U. S. Navy executive jet transports which flew to Rio from an unknown point.

10/7—RM1002AED

Correspondents:
The following advice to editors from the main UPI wire is being reprinted here for your information:

Editors—
Requests from p.m.s for a speculative wrap-up on Greer are being rejected. In the judgment of the UPI Washington Bureau chief, further speculation at this stage would be hazardous in view of the upcoming White House press conference. We are filing hard news only on Greer this morning.

10/7—RM1007AED

A little later one of the network vice-presidents called and, speaking for the industry, said there was such intense interest abroad that the television people would like to beam the press conference to the world via satellite. Did we have any objection? I got a quick presidential answer through Grace Lalley. He would be "delighted." So it was arranged. The conference would go worldwide.

I sent Jill over to the State auditorium and she reported back at eleven-thirty that the big hall already was jammed. Press gallery aides from Capitol Hill had placed folding chairs in the wide aisles and added two additional rows in front of the stage. Even so, there was not a vacant seat and reporters lined the back wall to the limit allowed by the fire ordinances. The aides closed the doors at eleven twenty-five, leaving a mob of frustrated newsmen milling about the lobby. A count showed a record attendance of newspaper, radio, television, magazine, and photographic people. The glass-paneled booths above the auditorium floor bulged with high-priced talent and the commentators began adlibbing a half hour before the start of the press conference.

I was summoned again to the back lawn of the White House at eleven forty-five. There were more than a dozen men standing

with the President, some of them strangers to me, and two
women. One of the women was Sue Greer, voluble and exuberant,
and a slight, elderly woman whom I did not know.

We piled into four limousines and drove to the State Department with a Secret Service car in the lead preceded by a platoon
of city motorcycle patrolmen. In the President's automobile, in
addition to Don Sheehan and another Secret Service agent, were
Steve Greer and Phil Lubin, one seated on each side of Roudebush. Another S.S. car followed the President's limousine. I rode
with the Secretaries of State and Defense and the chief of naval
operations, Admiral Freestone. The conversation was completely unedifying. They talked about the World Series and a
supergrade government pay-raise bill that the Senate had failed to
act upon before it adjourned.

In the wings of the State Department auditorium, the President himself lined us up as though he were the bustling master
of ceremonies arranging the parade of head table guests at a ban-
quet. He took delight in his improvised protocol. Ordinarily I
followed immediately behind the President when entering a press
conference. But today I was the caboose, separated from him by
a dozen people. Behind Roudebush walked Stephen Greer, the
two women, then a Chinese in a severe black business suit, a man
who turned out to be Russian, more strangers, Phil Lubin, Bernard Loomis, then the Secretary of State, the Secretary of Defense, and Admiral Freestone. Jill stood in the wings, a few feet
from my chair, with earphones on her head to monitor the TV
commentators. Don Sheehan took up a post behind the file of
marching people. I noted, as I walked out, that Larry Storm and
Dave Paulick were occupying aisle seats on the front row.

The buzz in the crowd of correspondents swelled to a rumble
when Steve Greer walked the length of the wide stage and took
his place before the first chair. The President remained standing
in a central position until we were all lined up. Then he motioned
to us to sit and stepped forward to the rostrum. It bristled with
microphones and was decorated with the huge, bright seal of the
President of the United States.

What follows is a verbatim transcript of the press conference together with my own reactions and impressions as it progressed.

The President: Ladies and gentlemen of the press, my fellow Americans, and those across the seas who are watching on television or listening by radio . . . I come before you today with a proud and happy heart. My good friend, Stephen B. Greer, has returned safely from a mission on behalf of his country and of the whole world. He comes home, not with a tidy conclusion, but with a beginning. It is a venture which has filled my dreams for many months, a beginning for you, for me, for all of mankind. But it is, I warn you, only a start. There is much work yet to be done, much patience, tolerance and forbearance to be exacted from each of us. But it is a beginning of great promise, and I exult in it.

A few words of digression here for my good friends of the various media before me. This will not be a normal press conference. That is, no questions will be entertained. The story to be told here today carries enough drama and portent. It deserves to stand by itself.

There is another reason too, which all of you competitive-minded people out front will, I hope, appreciate. One of your fraternity, Mr. David Paulick, editor of *D.P.'s Dossier*, recently came to my office. I learned that by dint of hard, unrelenting pursuit of the news, he had discovered a great deal about what, for many months, a number of us in the administration have called Operation Alpha. Since disclosure at that point might have wrecked our plans, I told Mr. Paulick the entire story and asked him to withhold publication for ten days or so. He promptly agreed. I think he acted as a patriot, but patriot or not, Mr. Paulick is a hard bargainer. He demanded his *quid pro quo*. After some discussion, I decided to fly Mr. Paulick to the scene of Operation Alpha so that he might get an accurate, firsthand picture. He was accompanied by Mr. Larry Storm, a special agent of the FBI, who has been commissioned to help gather material for an official history of the project. In short, in a special edition tomorrow, Mr. Paulick will reveal some of the colorful details of Operation Alpha. I think it was a fair bargain. I believe in rewarding enterprise.

Paulick beamed triumphantly, as heedless as ever of modesty's conventions, during this global commercial for his diligence. But most of the correspondents, who were now aware of Dave's presence on the front row, appeared less than happy at the paean to individual initiative. The press, I had learned, loves everything about competition save the winner of it.

The President: But that does not mean that we will refuse to answer questions about the matter. Next week, perhaps on Tuesday or Wednesday, I will hold another press conference and answer all inquiries I can. For Operation Alpha no longer has anything to hide. It seeks the light and, God willing, it may usher in a new era for mankind.

Several other short digressions before we get into the story. One man has suffered a good deal in the cause of Alpha. His corporation has been maligned, its stock driven down on the market, and his own integrity questioned. Yet, except for one understandable protest, he held his peace because he knew the enormous stakes involved. Research scientists of his company devised an intricate device which had an important bearing on the success of our project. Its nature will be described later, but I do want to introduce to you now a fine American, the president of Educational Micro, Inc., Mr. Bernard Loomis. Barney . . .

Loomis, who was more than a match for Paulick in self-confidence, arose and bowed. The newsmen, baffled, stared at him.

The President: Now I wish to pay tribute to a great and good man, a man who fled tyranny in his native Hungary in the days of Nazi occupation and who came to our shores to become one of us. He is a naturalized American citizen who has repaid us a thousandfold for whatever haven we provided him. He is a Nobel

Prize winner, an eminent research scientist at the plasma physics laboratory at Princeton, New Jersey, Dr. Felix Kissich.

Felix Kissich was a close friend of the late, great Leo Szilard, a fellow physicist from Hungary. You may recall that Szilard, after helping to develop the first atomic bomb, pleaded with his adopted government to refrain from dropping it on Japan without a prior demonstration of its terrifying power. His plea failed, but failure only rekindled the fire of peace in Leo Szilard. Some of the sparks from that talented and impassioned man struck a blaze in the breast of his friend, Felix Kissich. Dr. Kissich is also a man of vision who has seen further and more clearly than the statesmen and the politicians of the world. It is enough to say now that without Felix Kissich, there would never have been an Alpha.

Dr. Kissich is not here today. He is at this moment en route to Peking, China, where he will pursue his quest. But Kissich's wife, a brave and lovely lady, is with us today in her husband's stead . . . Mrs. Deborah Kissich.

The frail, little woman, whom I'd seen on the White House lawn, stood up, smiled shyly, and quickly sat down again. Several persons, probably science writers acquainted with her husband, applauded. The rest of the correspondents merely gawked at her.

The President: And beside her, another courageous woman and my very dear friend, Mrs. Susannah Greer.

Sue Greer radiated delight and pride as she stepped forward. This time there was a scattering of applause, but the chief sound in the auditorium was a rising murmur of conversation.

The President: You will hear more from me at the conclusion of this session. Now I think you should hear the story of Operation Alpha from some of the men who labored in it. And to start that story, I introduce to you my old and good friend, Mr. Stephen B. Greer.

Stephen B. Greer: My fellow Americans and listeners everywhere . . . As the President has indicated, this tale should be told by Felix Kissich, the prime mover of Alpha. I am grateful to be privileged to substitute for him.

But President Roudebush is being far too modest. If Paul Roudebush were a less bold and imaginative President, we wouldn't be here today. Alpha needed a man of world stature to succor it. It found him in Paul Roudebush.

I think you will better appreciate all this if I just tell what happened to me in conversational, narrative fashion.

For me, Alpha began one night three years ago in New York City at a meeting of the board of directors of the World Law Fund, of which I'm a member.

The Fund, as some of you may know, is dedicated to establishing a world of law to replace the violent, chauvinistic disorder which now marks the affairs of nations—and has for centuries. In today's world, nations still proclaim their sovereign right, indeed their duty, to use armed force in pursuit of their goals. In the new world, international law, not force, would arbitrate the disputes between peoples.

Visionaries have long sought to implant such a system overnight, an instant body of law and an instant global legislature, if you will.

But many of us have felt there is a much more practical approach: the slow accretion of law in area after area until eventually few, if any, international disputes or conflicts would remain outside the discipline of accepted statutes and codes. We have, of course, made significant progress. We have international law upon the high seas, on the fishing grounds, in the air and in outer space.

It would be unthinkable today, for instance, for a nation to resort to war to gain unlimited commercial air access to another country. Common sense tells us that each nation's self-interest is served by treaties which lay down rules for reciprocal landing rights for passenger and cargo planes. Likewise, countries within the great regional common markets would consider it insanity to war against one another for the type of trade imperialism which once propelled governments to conquest. Actually, international law and custom now rule virtually unchallenged in a dozen fields of human intercourse.

At our board meeting three years ago, we heard a number of speakers discuss the problem of expanding the rule of law into new areas. One of these men made an eloquent appeal on the banning of nuclear weapons. His theme was that the very existence of these monstrous killers—even if not used—sabotaged the goal of a world governed by law instead of force and violence. This was so, he argued, because the coupling of thermonuclear warheads to the fantastic ocean-spanning missiles means that whole cities and nations can be razed within hours. A psychotic or rash leader could wipe out half of civilization in an afternoon, law or no law. Even men of good will could unleash an inferno by accident, by miscalculation, or simply by massive retaliation to a single, stray bomb dropped by an enemy.

It was sheer folly, this man argued, to place nuclear weapons in the same category with conventional arms and then to contend that the H-bomb really had wrought no great change in the behavior of nations.

It is a favorite argument of some people, you know, that nations armed with atomic and hydrogen weapons aren't really much different from those armed with thousand-pound aerial bombs and sixteen-inch naval shells. The arms mean power in either event.

The crucial difference, it was pointed out, was that a huge stockpile of conventional arms does not threaten the very life of mankind on earth, while enormous reserves of thermonuclear warheads do precisely that. And that difference has provoked a deep, psychological change in man. For, if there is no real protection against the nuclear-armed, psychotic dictator or the nuclear-armed bellicose republic, why bother with law? Why, indeed bother with treaties, conferences, international courts, and security councils? They are all but fragile toys in the shadow of the hydrogen bomb.

So, it was contended this night three years ago, people and their laws cannot live in peaceful coexistence with the towering stockpiles of atomic and hydrogen weapons which could obliterate hundreds of millions of people—and their laws—in a single twilight.

The words were familiar and I realized that I had heard a similar theme in the cabin of Air Force One that sunlit Labor Day afternoon as we circled off the Maryland coast. That day the speaker was Paul Roudebush, and I recalled the deep impression he had made on me and Don Sheehan. I looked at Sheehan, who was standing behind our row of chairs. We smiled at each other. Then I glanced toward Jill in the wings. If Alpha involved some curb on the bomb, Jill had almost hit it right last night.

Greer: This man's name was Felix Kissich. I had heard this kind of reasoning many times over the years—and I hadn't bought it. But this night, his logic, combined with his fire and passion, made me review my own thinking. At the outset, I was by no means convinced that he was right—that the world's most urgent business was total nuclear disarmament, the destruction of all existing atomic and hydrogen weapons and the banning of the bomb. But I was intrigued and deeply moved. As a result, Dr. Kissich and I met a number of times that year in New York City. Some of our talks lasted far into the night. Gradually, he persuaded me. In short, I became convinced that the nuclear bomb must go.

Disciples are missionaries, of course, and one night toward the end of that first year, I had a long talk with President Roudebush at the White House on the subject. It was a pleasant surprise to learn that the President had been thinking along the same lines. He was already persuaded to our view, at least philosophically and morally, although he had never met Dr. Kissich. But our President is a practical man and, after our long discussion, he said in substance: "All right, Steve. But how? How do we go about it?"

There followed two night meetings at the White House of the President, Dr. Kissich, and myself. We came away with increasing awareness of our common belief that nuclear disarmament would never come in our lifetime, if ever, through ordinary diplomatic channels. Some progress, it is true, had been made: the test-ban treaty, the antiproliferation agreement, the pact to ban nuclear weapons in outer space. But all of these merely nibble at the edge of the matter and don't get to its heart. Also, even these fringe agreements have loopholes. Communist China and France, for instance, have yet to sign the test-ban treaty.

We concluded that the statesmen of the world were hobbled by an almost infinite number of pressures—national pride, the ancient tradition that every country has an inalienable right to arm itself to the teeth, fear of foreign treachery, the sorry record of disarmament conferences in this century, the conviction of many military officers today that an armed force without nuclear weapons is a sitting duck for any aggressor, and many, many more.

So we three arrived at what I could best call a dry-run plan. Briefly, it was this: Since national leaders were severely handicapped, psychologically and politically, from tackling the heart issue of banning the bomb, a new and unorthodox attempt should be made through the atomic scientists themselves—the physicists, the mathematicians, the chemists and engineers who build the bombs and whose theories result in the developing and refining of ever more sophisticated weapons. Perhaps if a group of the key scientists could evolve a nuclear disarmament plan, a practical plan on which the ranking scientists of all nuclear powers could agree, then the sheer prestige of such an informal international agreement might prod the statesmen to action. Just how this prestige would be applied, through the United Nations, via the marshaling of world public opinion or by more discreet appeals to the leaders, we were not sure. The important thing was to give it a try.

So Dr. Kissich set to work. He talked first with some of his fellow Nobel Prize laureates and then later with many men and women in wider circles of atomic science, always, of course, in strict confidence. Dr. Kissich at sixty-six is a formidably indefatigable man and one whose passion for a nuclear-free zone as wide as the world inspired his colleagues. It should be said, of course, that Kissich was plowing a fertile field, for since those few seconds at Hiroshima, many atomic scientists have been committed, both intellectually and emotionally, to abolition of the very weapons they work on. At any rate, Dr. Kissich traveled the world in search of allies. He went to many capitals, both in Communist and non-Communist countries, and he haunted the international conferences where scientists gathered.

I exchanged glances with Larry Storm, sitting in the first row. He shook his head apologetically. Larry, in our late talk at my apartment last week, had come close in his analysis of Kissich's views, but Larry's conclusion was dead wrong. He had missed a vital element—the physicist's understanding with President Roudebush. I began to glimpse the light now.

Greer: More than a year ago—the date was August 11—Dr. Kissich and I met again with the President at the White House. We had dinner there and then, in the President's oval sitting room on the second floor, we talked until four o'clock in the morning. Felix Kissich had succeeded far beyond his hopes. He had enlisted, under a bond of complete secrecy, 109 atomic scientists to his cause. These men and women, with few exceptions, were the outstanding theoreticians of the eleven nuclear nations, most of them from the five major powers, Communist China, France, Great Britain, Russia, and the United States. But Felix had gone much further. All of these men and women joined in a pact and pledged themselves to secrecy. The organization's name was Alpha—for "the beginning"—and it was dedicated to the abolition of all nuclear weapons.

May I make a slight detour here? Dr. Kissich, although he was a stellar member of the team which constructed the first atomic bomb at Los Alamos, New Mexico, had adamantly refused, for the past fifteen years, to do any work connected with nuclear arms. Instead, his research at the Princeton plasma physics laboratory has been dedicated solely to the task of converting the giant power of the H-bomb to peaceful purposes.

Dr. Kissich's position, which stems from a deep personal conviction, became one of the chief tenets of the Alpha Society. Alpha members have pledged themselves to abandon all further work on nuclear arms on and after a year from this coming January 1st. In other words, Alpha's members are giving the world's political leaders fifteen more months to reach agreement on destruction of existing nuclear weapons and prohibition of their further manufacture. If such agreement is not reached, the Alpha Society will stage a worldwide atomic strike.

Of course, while 109 key atomic scientists might cripple nuclear research, they could not by themselves stop production of weapons. But the original membership has grown. The list, as of last month, had expanded to 472 men and women in all, and these dedicated Alpha members believe that mere revelation of their existence and aims—which I am doing here today—will promptly swell their numbers by the hundreds and eventually thousands. And not just scientists, mind you, for the society welcomes the vast number of technicians, clerks, and administrative people who make nuclear production possible. With these new allies, the Alpha charter members have no doubt that warhead production will grind to a halt.

There was now the hurried scratch of pencils and pens all over the hall as the newsmen took notes on this major news break. I could imagine the bulletins on the press association wires right now—"Stephen Greer says Roudebush-sponsored scientists threaten worldwide strike to halt nuclear bomb production."

Greer: But I'm getting ahead of my story on this detour. When Felix Kissich disclosed the formation and goals of Alpha at that White House huddle fourteen months ago, President Roudebush quickly saw the significance for the future. I don't think I'm breaking a confidence if I quote the President. I recall that he looked at Kissich with a quizzical smile and said: "Felix, you're a blackmailer—for peace." This remarkable physicist accepted the phrase and said that it could well serve as a slogan for his new society.

With that as a starting point, we hammered out a method of

operation that night of August 11 a year ago. It was agreed that
Kissich would get Alpha members in each of the eleven nuclear
nations to nominate two of their number to serve on a drafting
committee. This required the most deft maneuvering by Kissich.
Every move had to be made in secret because the group had, of
course, no official status and could become a target of suspicion
for intelligence agencies in any country if word of its existence
leaked out. Also one slip by Kissich might galvanize the considerable pro-bomb forces and wreck the effort prematurely. After
months of probing, Dr. Kissich became convinced that an eleven-
nation body would be quite unwieldy and easily susceptible to
exposure. So he compressed his search to but five nations—ten
delegates, two from each of the big nuclear powers. Even this
was difficult, for these ten men had to be selected by their fellow
nationals of Alpha, had to possess an intimate knowledge of
atomic manufacture, and had to be fairly sophisticated politically,
so that the proposed agreement would reflect the practical and the
possible as opposed to the Utopian.

That's where I came in. We decided that I would attend the
meeting, not as a delegate, but as an unofficial representative of
the President of the United States, advising on both political and
legal angles.

From the outset, we realized that a major problem would be
Communist China—and for our world listeners, I mean nothing
invidious by that remark. But it was a fact, recognized by us, that
China, despite its entry into the United Nations, continued to be
alienated from the world community. There are historic and perhaps understandable reasons for this which I need not dwell on
here. Suffice it to say, such a condition existed. We did not know
what lay ahead, but we did feel that the President's representative should become thoroughly familiar with current Chinese
thought and mood.

Therefore we decided that, in addition to learning the rough
fundamentals of atomic physics and mathematics, I should begin
a tutored course in the Chinese language, customs, and policies.

That is the reason I met the famous Dr. X whom, I understand, so many of you have written and speculated about. I've

been largely out of touch recently with American newspapers and it was not until yesterday that I learned what a furore Dr. X and I have provoked. Here, quickly and parenthetically, let me say that the "X" is an "X" as in "heterosex."

A wave of laughter swept the hall, then another and another. Greer stood helplessly for a time, then turned and smiled at his wife and at Phil Lubin. My friend Phil appeared embarrassed by the sudden attention, although many newsmen were not sure whether or not Dr. Lubin was present. Greer finally raised his hands for silence.

Greer: Dr. X, as most of you know by now, is Dr. Phillip J. Lubin of Johns Hopkins University. He is one of the dozen ranking mathematicians of the world and has done a great deal of work in the atomic field. Dr. Lubin also has command of five languages, including a fluency in Chinese. More than that, he has kept abreast of current Chinese thought, culture, and policy—his avocation, if you like. Finally, Phil Lubin was one of the first American members of Alpha recruited by Dr. Kissich. It was Kissich who decided that Lubin would be an ideal tutor for me, since he could cover both China and the atom.

Dr. Lubin and I went to work more than a year ago, meeting weekly on Wednesday nights in a Washington apartment. Even my wife did not know where I went Wednesday nights. These were really hard-working sessions, for neither Phil Lubin nor I knew at what moment Kissich might complete plans for the conference. As weeks stretched into months, I became conversant with the basic problems of atomic research and manufacture. The Chinese was another matter—despite some long hours of clandestine homework in my study. I learned to understand what was said pretty well, but speaking is still difficult for me. So much for me, for the time being.

Felix Kissich finally wound up his preparations in April of this year. He had his ten men lined up, two atomic scientists of highest reputation from each of the five large nuclear powers. He and Dr. Lubin were to represent the U.S. members of the Alpha Society, with me as unofficial White House consultant.

Now it was up to President Roudebush to gain the sanction—or perhaps blessing is a better word—of the heads of government involved. This was vital in the case of the Soviet Union and the People's Republic of China, for scientists of both countries would have difficulty traveling abroad, especially on a secret mission, without top level consent.

This required intricate, patient, intense negotiating by the President. His quiet, personal diplomacy, extending over several months, might well fill a whole volume in the history of Alpha. There is not time to pinpoint details today, so I'll just touch the highlights. Felix Kissich paved the way for the understanding with Russia. He went to Moscow with a letter to Premier Kuznev from President Roudebush and spent two nights in head-to-head talks with the Premier. Following that, our President and Premier Kusnev had a number of telephone conversations via interpreters. At last, agreement was reached. In the case of Premier Wang of Communist China, President Roudebush had an introductory telephone talk with him. Then Dr. L. L. Cheng, a Chinese member of Alpha, conferred at length with his Premier, stressing, among other things, the sincerity of motive of the American President, whom Cheng had met. After that, the President and the Premier talked by phone four or five times via interpreters. Again approval resulted. Consent of the British prime minister was given after White House talks with the President at the time Prime Minister Bryce came to Washington this June.

I should stress that no government commitment to ban the bomb was sought at any time during this period. The basic theme of President Roudebush was this: We national leaders have all given lip-service to nuclear disarmament over the years. We have tried, but we have failed. Why not give the atomic scientists themselves a chance? If they come up with a practical method, then we can consult again. But let's at least give them the green light to meet and talk.

France, I regret to say, proved a difficult problem, perhaps one of our own making. Initial soundings by Kissich via French members of Alpha indicated that an overture by President Roudebush to French President Dubois might meet with an ambivalent response. Many discussions on methods of approach followed at the White House. In the end, the two French delegates decided they should attend the drafting conference as society members without government sanction. They felt it would be too risky, endangering the meeting's secret character, to contact the French President and get a neutral or negative reply.

President Roudebush always believed this did President Dubois an injustice and our President has worried a great deal about it. However, he yielded to the advice of the French scientists. Then last week, as agreement was being reached on Alpha, the President informed President Dubois fully of the developments by phone. Both the President and I believe that we owe the French nation an apology. At any rate, we trust that the French will give the same earnest consideration to the draft agreement as will the other powers. Needless to say, opposition by any large nation—whether or not a nuclear power such as France is—will make the road ahead exceedingly hazardous.

Jill removed the earphones on which she had been monitoring one of the networks, took a few steps from the stage wing to my chair and whispered to me. "NBC just cut in to say that Hillary Kulp has canceled his speech tonight."

I nodded. Also, I privately wagered that Arthur Ingram's resignation would not be announced today, as he threatened, nor on any of the days immediately ahead. If Kulp did not care to be cast as a monster about to decapitate the dove of peace, why would Ingram?

Greer: Frankly, we also had a domestic political problem. We raised this question: How could we carry out a secret venture of this global extent and importance in the midst of an American presidential campaign? There were many angles. For one thing, if the news of Alpha leaked out, would the undertaking founder in a political cross-fire, or would the President be accused of some flamboyant gesture for political advantage? If it remained secret until fruition, would the ultimate disclosure, such as that today, unfairly disadvantage the opposition candidate? And more simply, how could I, with my known relationship to the President, just drop out of sight without my disappearance becoming a political issue? To be completely candid about the background, I urged the President at a White House meeting in early July to postpone the entire project until after the election. Phil Lubin agreed with me. But Kissich argued that, viewed in political terms, there would never be a right time. If there weren't an American election, there would be one in Britain or there would be embarrassing internal pressures of one sort or another on the premiers of Russia and China. And if we postponed, contended Kissich, we might never again regain the considerable momentum we had achieved this summer.

The President agreed with Kissich, making the vote two to two. And, as you all know, in case of a tie, the President seldom loses. . . . And so, we decided to go ahead.

And now, since I've talked long enough, the story will be taken up here by my friend and tutor, Phil Lubin.

The President: Thank you, Steve. I'm now privileged to introduce one of the mainstays of the Alpha Society and of Operation Alpha, Dr. Phillip J. Lubin of Johns Hopkins University.

Phillip J. Lubin: I'm a poor speaker and I've never faced a crowd of this size, let alone a television audience, so please excuse me if I'm less than eloquent at times.

Perhaps you're wondering, why all the secrecy? Why not just go ahead and hold the meeting with a public announcement? Well, we . . . uh . . . all agreed that the inevitable debate and uproar might shatter our chances for success before we really got started. I don't know if I should mention this here—(he glanced toward the President)—but in this country, there were certain extremists to contend with. We knew that with their fanatic faith in the supposedly protective power of the bomb, they could launch a huge letter-writing campaign with the usual distortion, appeals to animal fears, and character assassination of the participants. They could accuse President Roudebush of scheming to disarm this country while other nations kept their atomic weapons, even though such unilateral disarmament was never, and is not now, contemplated by any of us.

And we feared there might be equally troublesome disputes in other countries. There was another important factor. Premiers of both Russia and Communist China made it plain that they could not publicly sponsor such a meeting. And we desperately needed government tolerance, at least, for the session.

Still another point. The foreign scientists, almost without exception, refused to attend unless they had positive assurances from President Roudebush that the Central Intelligence Agency would in no way be involved. The CIA, whether merited or not, has a very poor image abroad. Actually, the three government leaders, British, Chinese, and Russian, supported the stand of their scientists. So, President Roudebush gave his word of honor that the CIA would not be brought into the operation. In fact, he pledged that the intelligence machinery of this government would not be apprised of what was afoot. There was one exception for tactical reasons, Director Peter Deskowicz of the Federal Bureau of Investigation, and the President will discuss that later.

So, in the end, I believe that only a handful of persons in the U. S. Government knew of Operation Alpha: the Secretary of State; the Secretary of Defense; the Chief of Naval Operations, Admiral Freestone; the director of the FBI; the head of the White House Secret Service detail, Mr. Don Sheehan; the President's secretary, Miss Grace Lalley, and, of course, the President himself. . . . Am I right, Mr. President? Is that the list?

The President nodded. I noted that many of the newsmen, aware of the omission of my name from the list, looked at me with less hostility than I had become accustomed to in recent weeks. My emotions were mixed. While I had been exonerated of the charge of lying, I was also exposed as a press secretary who was not in the total confidence of his President. Dave Paulick's lordly smile did not help. Dave, who had shared that confidence, saw no reason to dilute his victory with humility.

Lubin: The President in return exacted a pledge from the other three heads of state that none of their intelligence agencies would place the conference or its auxiliary preparations under surveillance. This promise, we have every reason to believe, was kept. Dr. Kissich was visited once in a hotel room by a man known to be a local KGB agent. But when this fact was relayed to Premier Kusnev, he promptly investigated, and satisfied us that the Soviet agent had been acting under broad intelligence orders and that no one in authority at KGB knew of Operation Alpha. I might add that the Soviet Union was not the only country with an intelligence agent who brushed against Alpha. However, no penetration of Alpha was made and I'm confident the meeting was free of surveillance.

Instead, each government leader named a top civilian, unconnected either with the military or with intelligence, to act as his eyes and ears at the conference. Three such men were named as counterparts to Stephen Greer. Thus the sessions were attended by fourteen people, two delegates from France and two delegates and one observer from each of the other four nations.

In addition to these fourteen men, the personnel included two interpreters who were at home in the four languages, French, Russian, Chinese, and English. One of these interpreters was a British national, the other Russian.

Then came the problem of where to meet. We needed an isolated place, far removed from the normal haunts of you ladies and gentlemen of the press, a place where we would run little risk of being identified by the townsfolk or casual visitors. At the same time, the site must have good radio communications, so that the heads of government could be kept advised.

After much investigation, we finally settled on the island of Tristan da Cunha, deep in the South Atlantic. This is a small, remote, volcanic British island with about 250 inhabitants and a dependable radio facility. But better for our purposes, Tristan has no airfield and no harbor except a tiny one for small boats. Any ship aiming to land people or supplies on the island must anchor about a half mile offshore, then use small boats to reach Tristan. Normally, Tristan da Cunha's contact with the outside world is confined to a mail ship from South Africa which calls six or seven times a year. So, Tristan suited our purposes exactly, and it was agreed upon as the site.

In early July Prime Minister Bryce dispatched an envoy to Tristan via merchant ship from Cape Town. He was one of the British Alpha delegates. He had several long talks with Norman Green, the headman of the island. Green was told that a meeting was to take place which held portent for all civilization. Mr. Green, a philosopher in his own right, readily offered the island of Tristan for the Alpha conference, agreed to maintain tight security and to permit the landing of special equipment to beef up the power of Tristan's radio station. Later, as the conference progressed, Mr. Green was briefed more fully on its nature.

Since Americans had initiated the Alpha project and since Britain had supplied the site, it was agreed that the Russians and the Chinese would co-ordinate the travel plans. This was an intricate business, for fourteen well-known men from five nations, plus the two interpreters, had to make their way to Tristan in secret. It quickly became apparent that some U.S. official, vested with authority, would have to help the Americans with their travel arrangements. The President picked Donald Sheehan, chief of the White House Secret Service detail for this task. Some objections were raised by our friends abroad, who felt that Sheehan worked for an intelligence agency and thus breached the agreement against such participation. We finally cleared this hurdle by pointing out that Sheehan's only personal intelligence role was the collecting of information on persons or groups who might physically harm the President of the United States. In no sense was he connected with espionage in the standard definition of that word. So, as it worked out, the Soviets and the Chinese evolved the basic travel plans and Sheehan implemented them for the Americans, Greer, Kissich, and myself.

Sheehan made an early trip to the island. He came back to Washington, remaining here until after Labor Day, then returned to Tristan to become the general manager of our security.

The three Chinese delegates reached Tristan by flying to Buenos Aires, then chartering a motor vessel for the voyage to the

island. The Russians came to Tristan on a Soviet submarine which
made most of its South Atlantic trip submerged. The French and
British contingents were brought to the island on a British de-
stroyer. We Americans traveled by individual routes. As you know,
Mr. Greer left from the Burning Tree golf course under circumstances which many of you may feel now were needlessly spectacular. Actually, a less dramatic departure had been planned for
Steve, but it had to be abandoned at the last minute and a hasty
substitute devised. However, I think I'd best skip the details right
now, as well as the travels of Dr. Kissich and myself. They will
come out through Mr. Paulick or at next week's press conference
in any event. The main thing was, I suppose, that we all arrived
safely.

   I noted that Dave Paulick leaned over and whispered
   to Larry Storm. If Paulick failed to print elaborate itin-
   eraries of Greer and the other Americans in the *Dossier*,
   I had misjudged him.

Lubin: Preliminary talks got under way on Tristan September
8 without Kissich. We made some progress, but not until he arrived September 17 did the negotiating pick up speed. The reason,
I think, was that many of us were meeting one another for the
first time, whereas Felix was a good friend of every scientist in
the room. It was well known to everyone that Kissich had refused
for the last fifteen years to work on development of nuclear
weapons. Everyone trusted Felix implicitly and knew of his pas-
sionate conviction that the bomb must go. He was the catalyst
of Alpha.
   The main problem which dogged us was that of international
inspection of nuclear warhead dismantling. As you know, both
Russia and Communist China have balked at inspection on their
territory and have declined to alter their position appreciably over
the years. This time, while Russian and Chinese scientists agreed
to inspection, the personal representatives of the premiers fore-
saw major political obstacles. Had it not been for this old barrier,
the Alpha pact could have been forged in a week.

In the end, it was Mr. Bernard Loomis of the Educational Micro company who provided the breakthrough. For some years, working under an Atomic Energy Commission contract, Mr. Loomis's research division had been trying to develop a device which could detect the existence of nuclear weapons in stockpiles or in final process of assembly. In other words, no explosion would be necessary to activate a monitoring instrument many hundreds or even thousands of miles away.

As you know, today's art of nuclear detection depends on explosions. If there is no detonation, the existence of atomic weapons cannot be determined definitively—although aerial surveillance and on-the-spot intelligence may provide rough estimates.

But the new device, a quantum jump in the field of detection, was indeed perfected and tested last winter. The knowledge of its existence gave us great encouragement as we planned for Alpha. Last spring Felix Kissich got a thorough briefing on the new instrument's operation.

When Kissich described the invention at the Tristan conference, he encountered natural skepticism among his colleagues from other countries. They did not doubt his integrity, but they believed he might have been misled as to the capability of the device. So, late in September, Barney Loomis himself came to Tristan by orders of President Roudebush. He flew to Rio and crossed to the island in a chartered motor freighter, arriving, I believe, on September 29.

Mr. Loomis dispelled the skepticism. Not only did he buttress and amplify Dr. Kissich's technical explanation, but he read off a list pinpointing every atomic arms plant and stockpile in the world—as detected by the new discovery. This was a clincher, for the list tallied with the knowledge that each scientist had of his own country's atomic sites. Also, Loomis displayed graphs from the recording element of the instrument, lest some men might conclude that the list of atomic sites had been compiled from ground intelligence sources.

So Felix Kissich was able to argue persuasively that no inspecting team need set foot on a nation's soil. This was a dead issue.

Cheating now could be detected from afar and any nuclear disarmament pact could be policed from Geneva or, if you prefer,
from Greenland.

If skeptics remain in the scientific fraternity, the instrument is
open for examination by qualified experts from any country. President Roudebush has no desire to keep the technique secret at this
crucial stage of Alpha.

At the same time, I wish to make it perfectly plain that every
scientist who took part in those long discussions on Tristan island
supports, without qualification, traveling inspection teams as well
as use of Mr. Loomis's remarkable device.

> Most of the audience were now appraising the rugged,
> sunburned face of Barney Loomis. I was amazed to see
> that, for the first time since I had known him, Barney
> appeared embarrassed. I could only guess that while he
> cherished his role of the choleric, imperious business en-
> trepreneur, he was uncomfortable with his new halo of
> a peace apostle's helpmate.

Lubin: That roadblock behind us, we finished our work just
two days ago, on the evening of Tuesday, October 5. All ten
members of Alpha signed the agreement, Felix Kissich last at
6:50 P.M., Tristan time. None of the personal representatives af-
fixed signatures because each government, of course, reserves the
right to amend, change, or even reject the document.

I shall now, with the permission of President Roudebush, read
the agreement. Copies will be available at the rear of the auditorium as you leave.

We tried to keep it as simple and as brief as we could. Here
it is. I quote:

AGREEMENT OF TRISTAN DA CUNHA
1. The basic charter of the United Nations shall
be amended to forbid the production, possession or
use of nuclear weapons, of whatever type or size, by
any nation, group, or person.

2. All existing nuclear weapons anywhere in the world shall be destroyed on or before one year after the ratification of the substance of this agreement by the United Nations.

3. The general assembly of the United Nations shall elect a committee of fifteen members, including one national from each of the nuclear powers and no more than one member from any nation, which shall be empowered to carry out the provisions of Point Two (2) of this agreement by such methods, rules, and regulations as the committee may devise.

Unquote. That is all. Now it is apparent that Point Three gives no iron-clad assurance that Point Two, the abolition of all existing atomic and hydrogen weapons, will be implemented. Cynics may contend that Point Three renders the agreements just another piece of worthless paper. We of Alpha do not think so.

In the first place, it has the support, if not the signatures, of the four personal representatives of the national leaders of Britain, Russia, Communist China, and the United States.

Second, the head of the largest nuclear power, President Roudebush of the United States, has unequivocally endorsed the Tristan pact.

Third, we believe that today's disclosure will stimulate worldwide discussion and that world opinion will quickly rally behind the objective of Alpha. As of now, there is no reason to believe that the premiers of Britain, Russia, and Communist China will decline to embrace the agreement as official policy. Nor, for that matter, have we reason to believe that France will refuse to endorse it—nor any of the other nuclear nations. However, if any nation does reject it, we count on the pressure of world opinion to bring that nation into line. We believe that the peoples of the world will not tolerate a loss of this historic opportunity to erase the bloody shadow of the bomb from the earth.

Finally, even if the compact encounters heavy opposition and fails to be adopted at this time, we believe that the Alpha Society's drive to rid the globe of these lethal monsters will even-

tually succeed. For, do not forget that—as Steve Greer told you—
the Alpha members have sworn to boycott all nuclear weapons
development if the substance of Tristan fails to become international law within fifteen months. Our society now numbers
472 of the leading atomic and allied scientists of all nations. I
have no doubt that the number will quickly grow to several thousand men and women. Dr. Kissich believes that within a few
weeks our membership will include 95 per cent of the world's
atomic professionals.

A strike by the atomic scientists in all countries would effectively shut down research facilities. But when Alpha Society membership embraces the technicians and administrative people as
well, the nuclear production plants of the world would also cease
to operate. We believe this act would put tremendous pressures
on every nuclear nation.

Originally we planned to announce the Tristan agreement simultaneously in Washington, London, Moscow, and Peking. But
at the last minute, because of threatened premature disclosure
and some other factors, we decided to fly many of the participants
directly to Washington for this press conference. Of course, today's
satellite relay is giving us great impact around the world. However,
in a few days, new announcements will be made in the three other
capitals. Members of the Chinese delegation, plus Dr. Kissich and
one Russian, are today en route to Peking. Nationally mixed
groups are also en route to Moscow and London from Tristan.

Oh yes, in case you're wondering, members of the Alpha project
you see here on the stage left Tristan yesterday. We flew in helicopters to the carrier *Franklin D. Roosevelt*, which had reached
Tristan waters and anchored about a mile offshore. Aboard the
carrier we met Mr. Dave Paulick and the FBI agent Mr. Larry
Storm, who had just recently flown out to the carrier. Then two
jet transports took off from the *FDR* and flew all of us to Rio de
Janeiro. There we transferred to Air Force One for the flight to
Washington. Our last leg was aboard two Marine helicopters
which ferried us from Andrews Air Force base to the back lawn
of the White House. We arrived there this morning shortly after
dawn.

I think that's all. Most of us are sleepy and ready for bed. I'll just conclude by saying that my part in Operation Alpha has been the most satisfying experience in my life. I feel confident that the Agreement of Tristan will triumph. Thank you.

The President: Well done, Dr. Lubin. You underestimate your eloquence. . . . I would now like to introduce the other principals on the stage. You all know the Secretary of State, the Secretary of Defense, the Chief of Naval Operations and your favorite whipping boy, Gene Culligan. But we also have four distinguished guests who, I hope, will say a few words. First, a noted Chinese physicist, a member of the Alpha Society and a participant in the Tristan negotiations, Dr. L. L. Cheng.

Dr. Cheng (via interpreter): I am honored that my name appears first on the Agreement of Tristan. I believe today may herald the twilight of the dreaded nuclear weapons. I'm proud to belong to a society that is determined not to rest until the last nuclear bomb has been banished.

The President: Next, a renowned Soviet atomic theoretician, winner of many of his country's major scientific awards, Yuri Polyakov.

Dr. Polyakov (via interpreter): I salute my old friend, Felix Kissich, the man whose wisdom may well change the world in our time. I was the first non-American recruited into Alpha Society membership. I endorse the Agreement of Tristan. I am confident my government will support it and labor to see that it is implemented.

The President: Next, Great Britain's foremost nuclear physicist and one of her most gracious men, Sir Henry Marlow-Hyde.

Sir Henry: I too am convinced that Tristan can lead us to a new and more secure world. I take exception to only one thing said here today. (He turned toward the President.) We members of Alpha are not blackmailers, Mr. President. Rather, we adhere to the doctrine of civil disobedience so movingly expressed by your great American writer and philosopher Henry Thoreau. We refuse to co-operate any longer in building the bomb. We will not help ignite the fire-storm that consumes the earth. If that be treason, we are willing to hang for it—not as Frenchmen, Chinese, Russians, Americans, and Englishmen, but as citizens of the world.

The President: And, finally, a man who won the Nobel Prize for his pioneer work on isotopes and who was instrumental in developing France's first hydrogen bomb, Dr. Jacques Gilbert Martel.

Dr. Martel (via interpreter): I have signed many important papers in my life, but none which gave me such deep satisfaction as this one. I am sure my country will join in urging the United Nations to implement the Agreement of Tristan.

The President: On behalf of the American people, I thank you all.

And that is the basic story of Alpha.

I should like to add just a few things in conclusion. First, it should be stressed that none of the governments whose nationals appeared here today has yet endorsed or adopted the Tristan document. However, as President of the United States, I personally support the agreement. I realize that some alterations in the text will be inevitable, but for my part, I would like to see it written into international law without substantive changes.

Therefore, when the new Congress meets in January, I intend on the first day to send the Tristan text to the Senate and ask that body for a vote of confidence in the objectives of Alpha. . . . I will, as you realize, be President until January 20, regardless of the outcome of the election. . . . The Tristan understanding is not now a treaty among nations and thus requires no formal action by the Senate. But it does represent the policy of this administration, and I would like the world to know that the Senate of the United States approves that policy. I should add that this morning, via conference call, I talked with the congressional leaders of both parties and informed them of the facts as just outlined to you. The initial response was encouraging. It goes without saying that I would never have undertaken the long planning for Alpha if I had reason to doubt ultimate Senate approval.

Also, I wish to apologize to members of my official family who were not taken into our confidence on Operation Alpha. I decided quite early that secrecy could be preserved only by restricting information to a handful of people on a need-to-know basis. If any of my good friends and associates feel neglected, I should remind them that even the Vice President did not know what was afoot until this week, when I briefed him in full. Of course, had I become disabled, the Secretaries of State and Defense were prepared to inform the Vice President at once of the Alpha operation.

It is ironic, I suppose, that while hundreds of persons shared the secret of the atomic bomb's development in the 1940's, the Alpha effort to rid the world of that bomb was known to only a very few Americans.

One of these men was Peter Deskowicz, the respected director of the FBI. Mr. Deskowicz knew of Operation Alpha because it was apparent that once Stephen Greer disappeared, the FBI would be forced by public demand to investigate. At the same time, Peter and I realized the investigation would have to proceed like any other. To this extent the loyal and hard-working special agents of the FBI were pursuing a case that was—unknown to them—already solved. I hereby tender them my thanks and my apologies.

And now, for the future. In my mind, I can already hear the guns of opposition booming. There will be strong voices, many of them influential, raised on every continent. There will be those who will insist that national security—American, Chinese, Italian, Egyptian, depending on the nationality of the objector—will be shattered. To them I say: No. These grotesque arsenals of thermonuclear destruction provide no security—or the futile security of the man who protects his property by stacking dynamite in his basement.

There will be the cynics who claim that man is a killer animal and that no mere piece of paper will prevent him from employing the largest and most lethal weapons he can find to annihilate his enemies. To them I say: Perhaps. But man is also a rational animal with an instinct for survival. He cannot forever tolerate weapons that mean his own destruction along with his foes.

There will be other dissidents who will argue that a single nation, large or small, by its refusal to endorse the pact of Tristan can sabotage the whole undertaking. For them I reiterate Dr. Lubin's reminder. If governments fail to act to preserve the human species, the scientists themselves will stage the worldwide strike to halt further escalation of these instruments of insanity. Call these men blackmailers for peace, as I did in a light moment, or call them practitioners of civil disobedience, as Sir Henry does, the facts remain the same. The Alpha members are dedicated to the belief that mankind can no longer tolerate the "insupportable." They will not cease their efforts until the last nuclear warhead has been dismantled. I say thank God for men like Leo Szilard, thank God for the vision of Felix Kissich, and thank God for every scientist who had the wisdom and humility—and yes, the courage—to join the Alpha Society.

Ordinarily I would refuse to negotiate with a gun at my head, and it is evident that the Alpha scientists are leveling their sights right now at every political leader. But this Alpha weapon is a new kind, forged from the hearts, the souls, and the great good common sense of some of the wisest men on our planet.

And now an aside about American politics. You trained President-watchers before me know that an American president, for all his power, has very practical limits on the exercise of power. He has only so much political money in the bank and he cannot waste it like a spendthrift. He cannot, for instance, simultaneously overhaul the nation's railroads, stop the slaughter on the highways, raise living standards on every continent, check the alarming birth rate of human beings, abolish all tariffs, cleanse the air and water of pollution, eradicate poverty and send a space man to Jupiter. A President who tries to accomplish everything is a President seeking to level the Rock of Gibraltar with a peashooter. No, a president must husband his resources and his credit and channel them toward a very few possible goals. In my case, whether my remaining time in office be a few months or whether it be four years and a few months, I intend to have but one major aim—the goal of Tristan.

This brings us to the current political campaign in this country. It is an axiom that politics, like nature, abhors a vacuum. Thus, if I champion the Agreement of Tristan, it could be expected that Governor Stanley Wolcott, my opponent for the Presidency, would come out against it. I have always accepted this situation as a healthy one. It promotes a wide-ranging, intensive debate on the major issues facing a free society.

But this is a highly unusual situation. I believe that a clash on this issue between the two major party candidates for President —especially amid the heated pressures of the campaign's closing weeks—might rend the nation and ultimately destroy the hope which the Tristan agreement holds for us all.

Therefore, late last night, I called Governor Wolcott in Springfield and told him substantially what you have heard today. Of course, at that time, I did not have the wording of the agreement, but I did outline the objectives. The governor questioned me closely and I believe that my answers were candid. After more than an hour of discussion, Governor Wolcott said that he wished to give the matter further consideration. At seven-fifteen this morning, my secretary, Grace Lalley, dictated the text to the governor's secretary. The governor then came on the line and promised to let me know his thinking within hours.

He called me back at eleven-twenty. He said that while he could not commit other leaders of his party, he personally would support the spirit, if not the exact wording, of the Agreement of Tristan. He will make a full statement from Springfield later today.

I salute the governor as a great American and as a wise citizen of the world. His assent means that, whatever else happens to the Agreement of Tristan, it will not become a matter of bitter dispute between the two major party candidates for President. . . . The governor and I have plenty of other hard subjects to debate. . . . His assent also means that, regardless of who wins on November 2, the President of the United States will support the endeavor to make Alpha a reality.

And so, my friends, there you have Operation Alpha, a venture conceived in the brilliant mind of a Nobel laureate in physics, a saga which began at the fourth green at Burning Tree, a quest which I hope with all my heart will not falter until the last nuclear weapon has vanished from this earth.

I would ask every one of you listening and watching today, in whatever land, to search your minds, your hearts, and your souls, and then join the noblest of all crusades—the preservation of the human race.

Alpha is our beginning.

Epilogue

It was one of those fresh, bright days of June that seem as newly scrubbed as a schoolgirl in early morning. A breeze stirred the trees, a cardinal sang on a limb still damp from the night's cleansing rain, and the air felt cool and light to the skin.

Larry Storm, Dave Paulick, Miguel Loomis and I were about to have lunch in the Burning Tree Club's dining room, which overlooks the first fairway where Steve Greer began his extraordinary quest ten months before. We sat next to the open windows and watched the day dance about us.

We were in a buoyant mood. A round of drinks helped, but we had more solid stuff to celebrate. We had just defeated a team composed of the President, Stephen Greer, Barney Loomis and Jerome Freytag. We had bested the older group by eight strokes, and the losers had signed for our drinks before retiring to the White House for a consolation lunch.

Paul Roudebush had arranged the Saturday golf match as a triple salute: to the Tristan Agreement, to Jerry Freytag, and to Larry Storm.

The United Nations early that week had guaranteed the future of the Agreement of Tristan, endorsing it by an overwhelming vote. Machinery also was set in motion to amend the charter of the U.N., and a committee had been elected to devise rules and regulations for the dismantling of all nuclear weapons by October 5, the first anniversary of the signing of the Tristan pact.

Jerry Freytag had stunned the Congress and the country one week earlier by urging the abolition of his own job. The news was contained in a special message which President Roudebush sent to Congress, requesting legislation to disband the Central Intelligence Agency.

Freytag had been serving as director of the CIA since late November, when he replaced Arthur Ingram soon after Ingram's resignation.

In calling for dismemberment of the CIA, Roudebush proposed to delegate its military intelligence functions to the Defense Intelligence Agency, its diplomatic intelligence to the State Department, its paramilitary operations to the Defense Department, and its covert propaganda arm to openly subsidized programs of the U. S. Information Agency. Appended to the message was a letter from Freytag listing reasons why the Agency should be junked. The President adopted the core of Freytag's argument as his own: "A colossal secret agency, hermetically sealed from the people and unresponsive to the people, is not compatible with the institutions, traditions, and aspirations of an open society."

As for Larry Storm, he had been named an assistant to the director of the FBI, in effect becoming the third man in the command hierarchy of the Bureau.

I had a personal reason for enjoying this day, although the President had not included it among the causes for celebration. Storm, Paulick, and Miguel Loomis were all coming to the apartment tonight for Jill's twenty-fifth birthday party. Miguel was escorting Gretchen Greer, who had come down from New York for the week-end. All of them had attended our wedding on November 3, the day after the election, when Miguel served as my best man.

We all felt knitted together by our ties to what began as the "Greer case," then became Operation Alpha and the Tristan agreement. They were slender ties, perhaps, yet we felt as emotionally involved as those who had initiated the venture. It was as though we belonged to a special society, neither secret nor socially restricted, but exclusive nevertheless. For one thing, we were enormously proud of our connection with the endeavor that now, most certainly, would change the world. For another, we shared a great deal of knowledge about Alpha that remained unspoken outside the fraternity.

Paulick had revealed a fair amount in *D. P.'s Dossier* following the Alpha press conference. Paulick had an affinity for the lurid verb and the sensational phrase, but he got his facts straight. His most interesting sidelights were those involving Steve's bizarre manner of disappearance and the thorny problem of what to tell Mrs. Greer.

As recounted by Paulick, based on his talk with the President and a long interview with Greer on the flights from the carrier *FDR* to Rio and Washington, the facts were these:

Originally it had been planned that Steve would plead nervous exhaustion from overwork and would go to an isolated hunting lodge which Barney Loomis's company maintained in the Great Smokies a number of miles from Gatlinburg, Tennessee. Steve was to tell his wife, friends, and law partners that he needed a complete rest so that he might be fit to take a leading part in the final weeks of the presidential campaign. But once at the lodge, Steve was to leave the next day and make his way surreptitiously by motorcar and then chartered flights to Rio de Janeiro. From there, he was to sail secretly, as he did, aboard the *Casa Alegre*. Under this original plan, of course, there would have been no agony of uncertainty for Mrs. Greer. She would believe that her husband was recuperating in the fresh air of a mountain hideaway and that he would be home in four or five weeks. While the press naturally would print the news, it was assumed that newspapermen would make no attempt to disturb Steve at the lodge. Should an effort be made, however, the lodge caretaker, an old friend of Barney Loomis, was to keep newsmen and other curious persons off the grounds by one stratagem or another. The plan seemed quite foolproof.

Under the timetable, Steve was to tell his wife and friends on Friday and Saturday, August 27 and 28, tidy up his affairs at the office, then be driven down to the lodge in the Smokies on Sunday, August 29.

However, late Wednesday night Barney Loomis called from Los Angeles with bad news for the President. Barney said that fire had broken out in the lodge that day and that in attempting to fight the blaze with his lone assistant, the caretaker had been burned and was under treatment in a Gatlinburg hospital. The lodge was partially destroyed. This forced a quick change in plans. Greer and the President had a worried breakfast conference at the White House Thursday. It was recognized there was no time to concoct an elaborate substitute plan. The Russians, Chinese, and British were already moving toward Tristan.

Steve suggested the golf course route. Thursday evening was his regular day for golf. The course would have few players at that hour. The fourth green was not far from Burdette Road. Why not have a car meet him on Burdette? Since no better idea evolved, it was agreed. Hurried arrangements, switching the charter flights, were made.

Then arose a new problem: what to tell Mrs. Greer? The President contended that Sue Greer should be welcomed into the small inner circle of those who knew the facts about Alpha. To do otherwise, argued the President, would be to treat Sue in an unnecessarily cruel fashion. Indeed, she might crack under the strain. Steve said no, that if his wife were to be clued in, then it was only fair to include Deborah Kissich, too, since Mrs. Kissich was a much older woman and physically more delicate. But Steve contended that such extension of the small "need-to-know" group would be hazardous. None of the wives of the foreign delegates were being informed of Alpha.

Steve compared my situation as press secretary to that of the two women. The reason the President had decided to exclude me from Alpha, Steve reminded him, was that I might drop some hint inadvertently to the press. And certainly, I would be forced into a string of lies which could easily ensnarl me. Similarly, he said, if the women knew, they might give the game away by a nuance, an inflection, an attitude which newspapermen would pounce upon. Also, said Steve, the President failed to reckon with Gretchen Greer. Gretchen, he argued, would certainly be at her mother's side soon after Steve disappeared, and Gretchen was a strong, self-reliant woman whose composure and steadiness would prove a rock of comfort for Susannah. The President, unpersuaded, continued to insist that Sue Greer be told the truth. In the end, the two friends compromised when Steve hit upon the idea of the anonymous phone calls which were intended to be reassuring.

While Paulick had described these calls in the *Dossier*, he had not revealed who made them. We of the Alpha fraternity had learned that the calls were placed by Peter Deskowicz. In addition to disguising his voice, Pete was supposed to adopt a tone that would comfort Sue and allay any panic she might have. But Pete, more stolid than imaginative, was no actor. His performance was heavy-handed. Both times, he rang off abruptly. In the first instance, at least, this increased rather than alleviated Sue's alarms.

Many people who read Paulick's revelations revised their estimates of Steve Greer and began picturing him as a cold, insensitive man with slight regard for his wife's feelings. This, I think, was unfair to Steve. He was not happy to plunge Sue into emotional travail, but he did believe that the success of Alpha was paramount and that it should not be jeopardized by personal considerations. Also, he and the President were under intense pressure that Thursday morning, August 26. They had no room for maneuver, scant time to ponder alternatives. And, of course, Steve's distress over his wife and the sudden change of plans was reflected in his restlessness and impatience that Thursday noon when Miguel and I lunched with him in the law office.

Still, the incident did yield a clue to the characters of the two men, Paul Roudebush and Stephen Greer. The President was ready to take a chance on Sue Greer. Her husband was not. Sue said later in an interview that she was proud that Steve showed such confidence in her emotional balance and said she would not have forgiven him if he had been willing to place her in a favored position not enjoyed by Mrs. Kissich.

Beyond these human glimpses provided by Paulick, those of us in the inner group of Alpha shared many insights still denied the general public. Few people knew, for instance, that one of the reasons the President accepted Arthur Ingram's resignation without the customary "Dear Arthur" letter of regret was Ingram's employment of Butter Nygaard to spy on the presidential office. There were other undivulged but significant items . . . Operation Flycatcher, now a memory . . . Roudebush's October telephone talk with the Chinese premier, which sped the dénouement of Alpha and helped crack the military pressure in Peking . . . the fact that the Labor Day H-bomb test explosion in China, which so upset President Roudebush, had taken place over Premier Wang's objections . . . Senator Moffat's hidden alliance with Ingram . . . the late-hour appearance on the island of Tristan of Bill Hughes, better known in the top echelons of the CIA as "John" . . . how Don Sheehan, who was "Joe" to Bill Hughes and also the "Angel" of the Tristan dispatches, dealt with Hughes on Tristan da Cunha without revealing his own identity . . . or even the real reason why Maury Rimmel resigned from the club where we were lunching this Saturday in June.

Our thoughts probably turned to Rimmel because Joe Hopkinson, the broker who helped Rimmel search for Greer that August night, was eating at a nearby table this noon.

"I can't help feeling sorry for Maury," said Paulick in a low voice. "There's no malice in him. He's just a guy who picks up a buck where he can."

"You're mellowing, Dave," I said. "Since when did you start shedding tears over the downfall of lobbyists?"

"I agree with Dave," said Loomis. "I don't think the SEC could ever make those stock-rigging charges stick."

"Your dad's convinced they're true, Mike," said Storm. "There's not much doubt that Rimmel and Brady Manship tried to drive down the price of Educational Micro by rumor."

"But that's not why Maury quit the club, and you know it," said Paulick. "He resigned because he was sure that the President knew he was on Ingram's payroll—which meant Maury would be exposed as a locker room informer."

"Roudebush would never have said a word to the Burning Tree board," I said. "Actually, he was kind of fond of Rimmel."

"I suppose Maury had an attack of conscience," said Paulick. "It happens now and then."

"Not often enough," said Storm. "How about Silkworth and Kulp?"

The two names were storm flags to Alpha's inner circle. They evoked memories of the final, hectic weeks of the presidential campaign. Governor Wolcott had kept his promise. He supported the Tristan agreement right through election night, not with Roudebush's fervor, of course, but without equivocation.

Matty Silkworth and Hillary Kulp were another story. Behind Wolcott's back, they connived with leaders of the pro-bomb forces, which began organizing within hours of the famous Tristan press conference. On the surface, Wolcott headquarters was committed to the governor's support of Alpha. But word quickly spread from Springfield that if Wolcott were elected the Tristan pact would die on the vine. Thus Wolcott gained the backing of two antagonistic groups—loyal members of his own party who approved his public stand for a nuclear-free world and those members of both parties who opposed the Tristan agreement and who believed the real Wolcott was reflected in the whispers from Springfield.

We had evidence from our source inside Wolcott headquarters that Silkworth and Kulp abetted the underground campaign to neutralize Wolcott's position. The two men met secretly with pro-bomb leaders and funneled some Wolcott committee funds into the drive against Alpha. Whether Wolcott suspected Silkworth and Kulp personally we did not know, but we did learn that he once called his strategy staff together and warned it against undermining his public commitment.

Events proved the accuracy of Roudebush's comment at the Tristan press conference that politics "abhors a vacuum." Many Americans had sincere misgivings about Alpha, fearing that elimination of nuclear weapons would shift the world balance of power to Communist China with its vast land armies and inexhaustible manpower. Undoubtedly these people would have gravitated to Wolcott anyway on the "lesser of two evils" theory. Perhaps what Silkworth and Kulp really accomplished was to sustain, encourage, and widen that trend.

It became apparent in the last days of the campaign that substantial voter opposition to the Tristan agreement existed. Roudebush took to the stump in a series of one-night stands to defend himself and his goal. Many candidates for Congress and state office denounced the President as a visionary, a dupe or a "soft-boiled idealist" who would unwittingly sell out his country in a nuclear Yalta. Some leaders of Roudebush's own party deserted him on the issue. And Wolcott, as uneasy as he may have been over the whole episode, fell heir to hundreds of thousands of votes cast by the enemies of Alpha.

While Roudebush won re-election, he gained only 53 per cent of the vote, hardly a landslide that could be heralded as a mighty mandate to ban the bomb.

As a result, after the election, Paul threw himself into a new campaign to sell Alpha to the American people. Other men mounted a similar drive abroad. Alpha members labored in almost every country and many government leaders and elder statesmen enlisted in the cause. Yet the world sensed that the United States was the critical battleground, for if the nation which conceived the bomb now refused to bury it, success in other lands would yield a barren harvest.

The President's evangelism, covering thousands of miles and tons of newsprint, became the focus of contemporary history . . . His flight to Rome and conference at the Vatican, followed by the fervent papal appeal for demolition of atomic weapons . . . Roudebush marching down Fifth Avenue at the head of the giant Alpha parade . . . His stirring inaugural address, invoking the "spirit of Tristan" . . . His hour-long TV speech, a brilliant and slashing performance, when he refuted, point by point, the arguments of right-wing organizations which were flooding Congress with fifty thousand letters a day and decrying the "folly of Tristan" as a Communist-line saboteur of American defenses.

The United Nations vote was a testament to many persons, but especially to the zeal and stamina of Paul Roudebush. Yet victory arrived just in time. We were all beginning to fear for the health of the President. He had driven himself relentlessly. I became haunted by nightmares of another Woodrow Wilson in the White House, an exhausted, crumpled, and palsied victim of a futile battle for an ideal.

Now all that was behind us. Roudebush slept twelve hours the night after the U.N. vote and he awakened an elated and invigorated man. His recuperative powers were remarkable. He brimmed with vitality and enthusiasm. His zest infused us all. It was good to be alive.

We shifted to small talk, ordered a second round of drinks, and began rehashing the golf match. We had played in two foursomes. In one, Greer and Jerry Freytag were paired against Larry Storm and Miguel Loomis. Greer had scored low gross and, for the first time in his life, he birdied the tough fourth hole.

"Steve told me something this morning that I hadn't realized before," said Miguel. "I don't know why, but that fourth green got him talking about Arthur Ingram."

The barman arrived with the tray of drinks and Miguel waited until we were served.

"Steve was saying that he admired many of Ingram's qualities," Miguel continued. "He thought Ingram's dedication and singleness of purpose would have made him a great man if it were not for his blind spots."

"Ingram had enough of those," said Paulick caustically. "Did Steve have any particular one in mind?"

"Yes," said Miguel, "and it provides a kind of ironic footnote to Alpha. You remember that afternoon, two days before the big press conference, when there was a flap at DIA and in Ingram's office over the Navy's seascope? The area around Tristan island?"

"Tuesday, October 5," I said. "Same day the agreement was signed."

"Right." Miguel looked through the open window toward the long, green fairway. "Well, Steve says Ingram made a small, but for him characteristic, mistake that day. When General Palfrey called him about a Russian cruiser and a Chinese merchant ship heading toward Tristan, Ingram could have saved himself some embarrassment by checking one little point."

"What was that?" asked Paulick.

"Ingram neglected," said Miguel, "to check out the meaning of the Chinese freighter's name."

"The *Ho P'ing Hao*," said Storm.

"Yes," said Miguel.

We looked at one another with mutual comprehension. The

whole world now knew the meaning of *Ho P'ing Hao*—"the peace ship."

"Interesting—but characteristic?" asked Paulick. "No, I think Ingram's fundamental mistake was a kind of slavish devotion to intelligence as an end in itself. He saw the Agency and himself as the guardians of an America imperiled by the interminable cold war—at a time when the cold war was already melting away. He was basically a watchman, not a planner or innovator. For instance, I can't imagine Arthur Ingram ever taking the leadership in an adventure like Alpha."

This unusual psychological theorizing by the hard-nosed Paulick surprised us. He was the nuts and bolts man.

"I wonder," said Miguel. He stared at his drink for a moment. "Are Roudebush and Ingram so different, after all?"

"What do you mean?" asked Larry.

"Well, Dave is implying that Ingram believed that the ends— as he saw them—justified the means," said Miguel. "But how about Roudebush? Instead of going straight to the people with an open plea to ban the bomb, he rigged up a secret mission. He encouraged Kissich to blackmail—it's his word—him and the rest of the world into destroying atomic arms. The whole deal was under cover with a lot of secret finagling. . . . Why do you think he did it that way, Gene?"

"I'm not sure," I said. "I know Paul, and then again I don't know him. He's the forthright crusader and he's the maneuvering politician. I suppose he's learned the hard way that people and their leaders seldom respond to reasoning or moral supplications. What really moves them is pressure and plenty of it. In this case, it was the heavy pressure of the Alpha scientists."

"So the President is another Ingram, isn't he?" asked Miguel. We looked at one another for a moment. I wondered whether our mutual esteem for Roudebush foreclosed an objective answer.

"Be more exact, Mike," said Storm. "In what way?"

Miguel replied with another question. "The ends justify the means?"

"Not unless you approve of the ends," said Paulick quickly.

"Very cynical, Dave," said Storm.

"Well, anyway, Ingram will give us his version," said Paulick. "I hear he's writing a book."

"And who's going to write the real inside story of Alpha?" asked Miguel.

"Dave's the writing man," I said. Paulick looked pleased. I paused. "But I've got the material . . . Roudebush's talks with Ingram in my presence . . . a promise from Admiral Freestone that I can have his orders to the FDR . . . Jerry Freytag's diary."

"Not to mention a seven-hour talk with me one night," said Storm. He grinned.

I looked at Paulick. "You lose, Dave—for the first time."

"With my kind of friends," asked Paulick, "who needs enemies?"

I began writing the first chapter of Vanished the next night and finished exactly one year later.

Nothing material to the story of Alpha has been suppressed to spare the feelings of anyone. No facts have been altered to favor the President or any other friend of mine, no scenes changed, no conversations tampered with. My aim has been to tell the truth without sacrificing the narrative of Stephen Greer's disappearance. In the writing, I had but one loyalty—to history. As for Miguel's question about Paul Roudebush, I found no answer.

Eugene R. Culligan
Washington, D.C.
June 20